T0369518

That's Peggy O'Neal

Love and War at the Same Time

A. Russell Bailey

WestBow Press books may be ordered through booksellers or by contacting:

WestBow Press
A Division of Thomas Nelson
1663 Liberty Drive
Bloomington, IN 47403
www.westbowpress.com
1-(866) 928-1240

ISBN: 978-1-4497-1705-6 (sc)
ISBN: 978-1-4497-1706-3 (hc)
ISBN: 978-1-4497-1703-2 (e)

Library of Congress Control Number: 2011928531

Printed in the United States of America

/WestBow Press rev. date: 06/20/2011

Prologue

Seventy-eight men lined up alongside the dock in New Orleans, staring at their home for the next few days. The ship was a beauty. It was designed as a freight hauler, with two levels of cabins above. It had been painted with bright, fresh colors. The first level was open for freight, which would be mostly cotton bales. The boat was a new side wheeler with an enclosed wheel on the right side of the ship. It was one hundred eighty-nine feet long, with a twenty-six foot beam and was listed at four hundred ninety-one tons. And it was new, just bought by the government from the builder for the river traffic. The owner named it "GREAT EXPECTATION."

The seventy-eight were sailors and Marines, officers and enlisted men, who had been told to report to this ship for a trip up the Mississippi River to a destination yet unknown. The mission was a secret, but it had something to do with a new weapon just invented by a doctor, and given to the ship's captain to transport northward. He had been carefully chosen, the Marine detachment was highly recommended and the ship's crew, under the direction of the officers and Boatswain Reeder would make the trip with minimal difficulty.

The ship's officers, Captain Thomas, Master-at-Arms Jim Roeder and Boatswain Artemis Reeder, walked down the line of men, starting with the Marines. The captain asked the Marine Lieutenant, Phineas O'Rourke, about his force and the officer replied, "We have twenty-three men, including two Master Sergeants, two sergeants and eighteen men, split nine for each group. We will split the watches into two men for four hour periods. We'll have two men on guard at all times."

Captain Thomas looked up at the three masts and asked, "Can they climb the rigging if necessary?"

"Yes, Sir, indeed Sir."

The captain nodded and said "Join us," to the Marine. They walked on until he came to the shortest man, or boy, in the group. He asked, "How tall are you son?"

"Four foot, eight and a half, Sir."

"You sure of that? How old are you?"

"Fifteen, Sir."

"Do you have your papers with you?" The small recruit handed the captain some folded papers, which the captain, George Thomas, opened and read. "You had your physical?" The boy nodded. "And you have your parent's permission?" Again the boy nodded. "Do you realize how hard this will be on you?"

"Sir, I've wanted to be a sailor all my life. I'll be a good one, you'll see."

"Son, you will be called a 'Powder Monkey' or variations of that. You will be doing a dangerous job, carrying powder to the guns, but a necessary one. Don't let the old timers get to you."

After completing his inspection, Captain Thomas moved his group back to the middle of the line of ship's men and called, "Jake Prosser, step forward."

Jake Prosser, twenty-two, six feet one inch tall and muscular, with straight blond hair tied into a knot behind his head, stepped out of the rank and saluted. "Here, Sir."

"Mr. Prosser, have you seen your assignment?"

"Yes, Sir."

"Have you been given instruction on it?"

"Yes, Sir."

"And what is your assessment?"

"I'd put it right there, in front of the stack, on the starboard side."

"And why there?"

"It's on the more populous side, I mean after we leave here, we'll have Natchez, Vicksburg, Greenville and Memphis. There isn't any major town on the west side. So, building a stand and surrounding it with some kind of protection, it's best set up there."

Captain Thomas followed Jakes pointing and slowly nodded. "Good idea, Mr. Prosser. Well done. You may return." Jake saluted and stepped back into his place along the line.

Marine Lt. O'Rourke stood with a frown on his face and when Jake was back in position, he asked the captain, "Sir, is this something we should be involved in?"

"No, Lieutenant, we have it covered. With the talk of secession and the possibility of trouble along the way, you'll have your responsibilities enough to keep you busy."

"But, Sir, he's a sailor," spoken with as much disdain as he could.

"Yes, Lieutenant, and so am I." O'Rourke closed his eyes and bowed his head, realizing he may have just made the ship's captain angry. He could not let that happen.

Five years earlier at a dock in Cincinnati, a high-school Junior, Jake Prosser, came aboard a ship, whose captain was George Thomas, as part of a high school information tour. After exploring the ship, the visitors were given a "Naval Aptitude" test. It was supposed to be a light episode set up by the captain, but Jake did so well that George Thomas decided to keep in touch with the student. Now, his protégé was on his ship, giving the captain a moment of memory.

As the officers gathered for a moment to discuss options, they concluded all was ready to board the ship. Captain Thomas, with the other officers at his side, smiled as he shouted, "All ship's company, find your home."

At that moment before anyone had a chance to move, a carriage exploded onto the scene and halted in front of the group of officers. A coachman jumped down from his high seat and hurried to the carriage door. He swung it open for a young woman, dressed in the latest fashion for a party, not for traveling. The doorman helped the lady down the step to the dock and she stood there while two huge suit cases were dropped to the ground. She was dressed in a light green taffeta dress that protruded from her body by a hoop skirt and whose bottom ten inches of skirt were little frills sewn into the fabric. She had a light colored handkerchief around her head and she carried a small green parasol.

"What's this?" Thomas almost shouted, angry at the disturbance. "Who are you?"

Without a word, the lady handed him a letter, which the captain opened. In moments, his face grew a deep red and he turned to keep from showing his unhappiness to the new guest. With three or four deep breathes, Captain George Thomas turned back to face the young woman. "Are you the bride to be?"

Timidly, she spoke, "Yes, Sir."

"Travelling without escort or companion?"

"My father had faith in you as an honorable man."

Agitated, he asked, "Did he not realize there are seventy-seven additional men here with me? All right, this says you are going to St. Louis, where your wedding will take place, is that right?"

"Yes, Sir."

The captain barked, "Mr. Prosser, see to the lady's luggage."

Jake looked at the two bags, both could weigh seventy-five pounds or more and he stepped out of the line and said, "Captain, Sir. . ."

Thomas looked at him and said, "Washington, step out and help him." A big black man, taller than Jake and much stronger appearing, followed him to grab one of the bags.

Thomas barked another order, "Second cabin, port side."

Jake paused, "That's. . ." He paused and continued with the luggage. He spoke to the woman, "Ma'am, if you will follow us, we have to climb that long ladder to the top of the boat. Your cabin is up there."

The hoops in her skirt made the climb difficult until, with great embarrassment, she reached down and held one side of the hoop in her hand, so the other could get by the ladder rails. It showed the ankle of the side she held. After her first step, she heard the command, "Eyes front!"

Chapter One

It was a lovely day for a boat ride in April, 1861. The weather was perfect, the food was great and there was a special passenger, one who was to be the bride of a general's brother. And not just any general. This was General Courtney Clay Patterson, second in command of the Army of the Potomac, Western Command, headquartered in Cincinnati, Ohio. The groom was his brother. And he was wealthy. Jake Prosser had a special vantage point of this special passenger, and every time she escaped the close confines of her room, he saw her. He saw her and couldn't approach her to even ask her about her day.

Oh, how he wanted to. She was fabulously beautiful, tall and stately, dressed to perfection. Of course you would expect the eighteen-year-old daughter of a prominent surgeon to never wear anything less than the current styles. Most of her clothes emphasized her face and her smile, set off by the matching jeweled ear rings she wore.

Her name was Margaret O'Neal, and her dark hair was curly, even when held in the bun. There were times when she "let her hair down," and the sight was enthralling. When those times occurred, he remembered his assignment was to protect her from any assault. That required discipline, for he fanaticized about ways to meet her. If only! Every time she came from her room there was a Marine somewhere, watching.

His dedication to orders had gotten him that assignment. He was a sailor from Ohio, who had grown up in a lower income family in Cincinnati, watching different kinds of boats ply the river. It was his childhood desire to become a member of the US Navy and sail those same waters while in uniform. It was only a hope that one day might be realized. And then it happened. One day while cutting wood on his uncle's farm, an ax head slipped its restraint and hit his right leg just above his ankle, causing a serious gash and loss of blood, requiring a stay in the hospital.

Depression hit, first, at having the injury and second, at missing a chance to join the navy. It brought him in contact with a psychiatrist and the doctor's nurse. They thought his despair was so great as to create thoughts of suicide, and they put a special watch over him. Slowly he healed, and just as slowly, the doctor's nurse, Rebecca Shiley, and her patient, grew closer together, until she proposed marriage. He was walking around, getting strengthened by directed exercise and her care, and he agreed.

It was a simple wedding. He had nothing to offer her and she had the only employment. They lived with an uncle, Henry and Emma Prosser, while Jake hunted work. He avoided his parents. His parents came from Germany and believed in strict authority in the family. As such, Jake was never able to please his father. His mother spoke little English and while Jake was growing up trying to learn English, he constantly asked her to repeat herself

Each time he told a potential employer about his accident with the ax, the prospective employer would change the topic and eventually, Jake would be dismissed. It went that way for two years, with their romance slipping away, and on his twenty-first birthday, Jake was able to join the navy. Rebecca moved back to her own parent's home and the marriage seemed to end. Jake left Cincinnati for his life on the high seas, or on the Ohio and Mississippi Rivers.

Now, aboard ship, he was constantly aware of the visitor. He had heard her laugh with other sailors as she stood along the railing. He had seen how she wrinkled her small nose when she laughed and he had to force himself to look away from her when she stood there. He knew she was special. Occasionally she would look up at him and smile, in fact, he never saw when she wasn't smiling. This trip was to carry arms to the soldiers fighting the Indians in Iowa and Minnesota. But, she was the prize of the brother of a general, second in command in the northern tier of states. The rumors floating around said her father wanted to run for Congress and she was the bribe.

Jake's reverie was interrupted as he sat in his fortified space when someone called his name. "Hey, Prosser, Captain's Station on the double." He climbed out of his enclosure and down the ladder to the deck, leading to the Captain's station. They were on a side-wheeler, passenger ship, heading north from New Orleans to St. Louis. It was a ship that earlier had hauled nine hundred people, mostly Mormons, going to Fort Benton in Montana Territory, for the rest of their trip on foot to Utah. A sailor on the ship told Jake that all cabins were full with no room for another person. The first deck was basically open for hauling produce, especially cotton bales, and it was packed with people.

But with tensions in Washington D.C. and the Southern states, most of the sailors agreed, the ammunitions were bound for use against potential internal enemies. With Jake's suggestion when they first received the weapons, the ship's captain had taken the liberty of installing a turret on the top of his ship, beside the ship's smoke stacks, housing a Gatling gun. Jake Prosser was the guard and operator. They had taken three days for that work and now were travelling north again. It was the tenth of April and they were making an astonishing ten miles an hour against the current.

He reached the captain's deck and reported, saluted and froze at attention. Their special guest stood next to the captain, smiling, looking at him. He stammered, "Reporting, sir."

Captain Thomas looked at him over half glasses and said, "Prosser, Miss O'Neal wants to walk around the ship and has asked for you to escort her."

"Me, sir, But. . .me? Yes, sir." He had seen her smile as he looked over the metal sides of his turret, but had never gotten as close as he was then. He was always looking down on her and could not really see how pretty she was. Oh, he knew she beat anyone he had had ever seen, but now, he looked at that oval face, with her green eyes shining, and he stammered, "Yes, sir. Where does the lady want to go?"

The captain snorted, "We're on a boat, Prosser. We're in the river, surrounded by water. Where do you think she would like to walk?" She giggled and Jake felt two inches tall. He tried to talk but could only squeak.

The captain solved the problem by ordering an aide to open the door and usher Jake out followed by the gorgeous Peggy O'Neal. Her first action was to clasp his arm above the elbow and start walking. Jake tried to keep his mind on the job at hand, but, at just over six feet tall, could only see the top of her head and couldn't think of anything to say. Her grip on his arm was just below his upper muscle and she commented on how strong he was. He told her he was a "coal heaver," working in the boiler room. They walked several paces without any further conversation and she said, "Tell me about yourself, Mr. Prosser. That's a German name, isn't it?"

He had run across some Irish sailors during his time in the navy, but they didn't have the lilt, that almost-laugh in their speech. He managed a "Yes, Ma'am," through a tightened throat that made his voice almost come out as a squeak. He walked stiffly, as if walking while at attention. She stopped, pulling his arm so that he turned around to face her.

He stood there, rigid, all six feet of him. She snickered, "Mr. Prosser is there something wrong with you? You walk so. . .I don't know, so tight, like a tense spring. Am I the cause of that?"

"Oh, no, Ma'am, uh, yes, Ma'am." His normal German ruddiness took on a deeper hue, "You see, we don't often have pretty women on the ship, an' I, well, I'm not used to walking with pretty ladies. That's usually done by the officers and the Marines, when we have pretty ladies on board, Ma'am."

She tilted her head slightly to the right and coyly asked, "Are you uncomfortable with pretty ladies, Mr. Prosser?"

"Yes, Ma'am. I mean, like I said, we don't have many women on board and my job is usually in the furnace area."

She looked up at him. "What do you do there? Are you a boss there?"

He snorted. "No, Ma'am, I'm a coal chucker. We burn a ton of coal or eight cords of wood a day while underway."

She was quiet a moment before saying, "A ton I understand, but how much is a cord of wood?"

"Wood in a stack eight feet long, four feet high and four feet wide."

She reached for his arm and they started walking again. There was no talking as they rounded the fantail of the ship and she stopped again. "Are you uncomfortable, Mr. Prosser? Would you rather go back to that enclosure?"

"Oh, no Ma'am. To be blunt, Ma'am, I prefer being out here walking with you." After he said that, his face grew red again and she looked up at him to respond, but saw he was embarrassed.

They walked on and she asked, "Mr. Prosser, do you have a lady friend?"

"No, Ma'am. Well, I did but we kinda separated. We got married, but it didn't stick. I couldn't find a job after I was injured an' then I had this chance to get into the navy, an' she just kinda left me. Well, I guess I kinda left her too."

"How were you injured?"

"Chopping wood. The ax head broke off the handle and cut my leg."

She stopped, "That must have hurt terribly."

"Yes, Ma'am. It took two years to really heal. Ever' once in a while I still get pain from it."

They finished their trip around the deck and climbed down the ladder to the next level. It was a longer walk, and there was less talking. After a trip around the ship on that level, she climbed the ladder to her room and as they stood at her door, she asked, "Mr. Prosser, would you be willing to make this a daily event? Perhaps twice a day. That room is so confining and, as they won't let me walk alone, would you be willing to share your time with me?"

His heart jumped and he almost shouted "Yes," but restrained himself. "If you wish it and if I can get approval from the captain, Ma'am. Yes, I would like that."

"I will talk to him. Oh, how long do you think this trip will take?"

"We're going at eleven or twelve miles an hour. I've been told the river is over six hundred fifty miles from New Orleans to St. Louis. Plus, there's the stopping for fuel. One of the men told me on one trip they had to spend three days chopping wood in Arkansas. It could take ten days or more."

"Then, Mr. Prosser, I'm thankful for your willingness to walk with me around the deck. Thank you." She opened the door to her quarters and disappeared inside. He stood there, dreaming of the next time.

The first hiccup in their plan came the next day, the eleventh, when they faced the waters from flooded streams across the north central part of the country, requiring more fuel against the rushing tide. Tree trunks and other debris floated against them. With the buffeting of the ship, Peggy O'Neal wasn't allowed to leave her room and the boat had to stop along the shore of Arkansas to cut more wood. Twelve men with saws and axes took a skiff to the shore as the ship was anchored in a cove, away from the rushing waters. Load after load of the fuel was brought to the boat until the captain thought there was enough. As he stood there, it was getting dark, the captain didn't want to take chances against the flooding current, especially since they had a calm loop in the river's flow to harbor in for the night.

Jake's relief was slow in getting there so he had to continue his watch. In previous watches, Jake had been concerned about their limited ability to warn the ship's personnel of a problem. A rope had been lowered from a steam valve to be used as a warning. Jake tried to stay awake, but his thoughts were on a pretty Irish lass and several times he had to shake his head to bring himself back to his surroundings. Suddenly, he was fully awake, as he heard a twig snap and what might have been a warning by someone.

He gripped the rope from the alarm and listened more intently. There was no light, as the northern storm was having its affect in the peripheral jet stream, but he was aware of someone on the bank, just less than thirty feet from the boat. He grabbed the rope to the whistle and pulled. The whistle screeched, someone on the bank swore and fired a shot in the direction of the boat. Jake swung the six barrels of the weapon he controlled to where he heard the sounds and turned the crank to fire it.

A Gatling gun had six barrels that rotated as a crank was turned. As the crank is turned, bullets drop from an attached supply tube into the chamber of the barrel then in position and a hammer fires the bullet. The tube held fifty cartridges, but if the operator wasn't careful, he could run through fifty bullets in a few seconds. The barrels rotated so that one barrel doesn't get too hot and melt. As fast as the bullets were fired and as hot as the gasses are from that firing, if there was only one barrel, it would melt.

When the whistle sounded and the gun fired, those sneaking up on the bank swore and ran away. On the ship, he heard a woman's scream, which he was sure came from Peggy O'Neal's room, and men shouting and swearing. The captain rushed to Jake's spot, barefoot, pulling his suspenders over his shoulders, "What's all that racket, Prosser?"

"I heard someone out there on the bank. I listened and heard another sound, so I pulled the whistle and fired five or six rounds."

"You're sure you heard something?"

"I heard men swearing after I fired the gun, Sir."

Captain Thomas looked from Jake into the darkness of the land and held that pose for several seconds. "You did well, Prosser." He turned to go and stopped. "Where is your relief?"

"I don't know, sir, he should have been here a couple hours ago."

There was some noise inland, of people moving around. "Fire a burst, Seaman."

"Yes sir," and Jake turned the crank to fire his weapon. He swung the barrels slowly from left to right as he cranked. After a span of twenty or so shots, he stopped and waited.

Both he and Captain Thomas saw the light flicker through the foliage for an instant and Thompson shouted, "Give it a burst there!"

As Jake started his procedure, the door to the cabin below where he and the captain stood burst open and Margaret O'Neal charged out onto the deck. "What in the world is going on?" she screamed, hardly capable of being heard above the clatter of the gun.

The firing stopped and both Jake and Captain Thomas exclaimed, "Miss, O'Neal." The captain continued, "Please, go back into your cabin and get down on the floor. We may have some shooting coming this way. Quickly!"

She looked up at them and then out into the darkness in time to hear a rifle explode and hear the bullet hit the side of the ship. She screamed and ran back to the safety, such as it was, of her room and Jake fired another burst in the direction of that rifle shot. He changed the cartridge feeder tube and waited for further orders. After several seconds, there was another flickering of light and Jake fired in that direction, resulting in a loud explosion. After that, silence.

Thomas ordered, "Bo's'n, pipe general quarters." The man with stripes on his arm lifted a small whistle and blew a three toned sound, resulting in men appearing from every corner of the ship. Thomas said, "Prosser, go see how Miss O'Neal is doing. If she is able, have her step outside and listen"

Jake left and climbed down the ladder to the lower deck and knocked on her door. "Miss O'Neal, are you all right? Can you talk to me for a minute?"

A three second delay followed before her door opened and she burst out, throwing her arms around Jake's neck, crying with fear, almost in panic. Jake spoke calmly, patting her on her back, trying to assure her the problem was past. She clutched him as though her life depended on it for two or three minutes and gradually gained control of her emotions. With tears on her face, she released her hold on him and backed away.

"I'm sorry, Mr. Prosser. I've had a terrible experience with a gun in the past."

"I understand, it's frightening even to me sometimes. The captain wants to speak to us."

They found the captain overseeing the landing of the men. "Miss O'Neal," the captain started, "are you all right? I know it's rather alarming to be awakened by that sound. I think we have things under control, now." To the men, he explained, "It appears these are Bushwackers, a group of slave sympathizers who want to create havoc along the river. They've been operating along the river for five or six years, now, killing anyone who disagrees with them. Since this is a Federal ship, it just became the subject of their anger. Bo's'n, break out the armaments. We will protect our own if necessary. Take your stations. Prosser, see to Miss O'Neal."

What did he mean by that? What am I supposed to do? I can't go into her cabin with her. He said, "Come, let's go to the other side of the ship away from the shooting." He took her arm and led her away from the land side, to the river side. He tested the door to a cabin on that side and found it unlocked. Inside, he found a chair, which he brought out for her to use. He looked at her and their eyes met, she still showing concern. He knelt before her and tried to make her feel comfortable.

Rifle fire from land was answered by a barrage from the ship. Someone had opened the arms cabinet and every member of the ship's company had a weapon. Jake heard firing from higher up and saw Marines up in the masts, secured by the ropes and hidden by the masts, firing at something on land. Someone had taken Jake's place at the Gatling gun and it created the loudest background for the rest of the noise. At the initial sound, she screamed and threw her arms around Jake's neck again. She clung tightly, crying, shaking with fear, as if her life was in danger.

Chapter Two

The barrage lasted about three minutes, and when Captain Thomas gave the order to cease fire, after the echo ceased, there was total quiet. Then, "Assault team, to the boats!"

There was shouting and three loud splashes as the small boats dropped into the water. The ship rocked as men clambered down ropes to the boats and rowed toward shore. Fifteen men, all Marines, sloshed ashore, pulling the boats up on land to keep them available. Ten long minutes the people on the ship waited for information and it finally came.

The Marine sergeant shouted through cupped hands, "They're gone. Ain't nobody here. We saw signs of blood, but they're all gone."

Lieutenant O'Rourke shouted in reply, "Thank you Sergeant. Come back home."

After the fight, while the men were going back across the narrow gap of water to the ship and everybody waited for their report, Peggy O'Neal had removed her arms from Jake's neck and sat with him holding her hands. She looked at the deck and said, "I'm sorry, Mr. Prosser. Guns bother me. I had an older brother who went hunting with some friends and came home dead. I'm sorry. You must think me very forward to throw my arms about you as I did. I apologize."

He released her hands and reached out his right hand for her chin. Lifting it slightly, he raised her head to look at him. "Guns in the wrong hands frighten me too." He smiled, "And any time you feel like hugging me, I'm available." The early sunrise created just enough light for him to see her blush and he quickly added, "I'm sorry, Miss O'Neal, That was uncalled for. I will be more careful about what I say if I have the opportunity to talk to you again."

Softly she said, "I do hope you'll walk with me again. I enjoy talking to you."

"Now I'm the one blushing." The sound of heavy shoes interrupted them as a Marine appeared, saying, "Captain Thomas wants you right now. I'll see the miss home."

Jake looked at her and then at the sailor he didn't know and muttered, "I guess I'd better go. If you. . .I'll see what the captain wants and meet you at your room."

Jake rounded from the stern and met a very irate captain, whose first words were, "Up to the wheelhouse!"

Jake went ahead of him and opened the door, holding it open for his captain. Inside, Captain Thomas stuck his balled fists on his hips, leaned from the waist until his face was just inches from Jake's and shouted, "What do you think you're doing, Prosser, hugging that woman who is going to be someone's bride in a few days?"

"Sir. . ." Jake stammered, "I. . .she. . .Sir, the shooting scared her. She lost a brother recently and the shooting frightened her."

"She what, lost a brother?"

"Yes, Sir, and she's afraid of guns, and when the shooting started she jumped and grabbed me, I guess for support, 'cause it scared her, Sir." He waited for the captain to say something, and when nothing came, continued, "She shook like a leaf in a windstorm, Sir. She was really scared."

"Then it wasn't you and her. . ."

"Oh, no sir, Sir, I would never. . .Sir, she's too good a woman to do that. She was scared out of her skin."

Thomas stepped back and straightened up, dropping his hands to his sides. "Oh," he said, and again, "Oh."

"May I go now, Sir?"

"Yes, but watch yourself. She's promised to the brother of a general and we don't want to cause any problems, now do we, Prosser?"

"No sir, Sir. Thank you Sir for the reminder."

Jake left the wheelhouse and turned toward Peggy's cabin and stopped. I shouldn't go see her, but I told her I would. If I knock and see if she's all right and then leave, I'll do that. Jake tapped on Peggy's door and she opened it immediately.

She whispered, "You came. I didn't think you would."

He returned in the same voice, "I told you I would, but I can't see you any more. The Captain thinks we. . .that I. . .you're promised to another. I gotta go," and he turned around and left her with the door half opened. She stood there, holding the edge of the door, following him with her eyes, her mouth open.

Jake climbed up into his nest and checked the count of the cartridge tubes for the gun and found only two. He left it and found Bo's'n Reeder to get some more. Reeder found the Coxswain, an old sailor named Carter, and told him to help Jake. They carried eight tubes of ammunition to the gun's nest and, as Jake stacked the ammunition for easy access, Carter asked about the weapon. Jake explained what he had been told, that the gun was a test weapon, given to the government for testing in the northern states, by the inventor, Doctor Richard Gatling. It was something new and basically untested. There were three units and they came to this ship because the designated recipient was a friend of the inventor. Carter had heard it fired, but hadn't been told anything about it until that moment.

The ship carried the flag of the United States and as they passed a town nestled in the hills along the river, Jake heard the whine of a ricocheting bullet before he heard the sound of the shot. He scrambled around the smoke stacks looking for the source of the shot and saw the puff of smoke indicating another incoming bullet. He saw the source and, again, heard the sound as it hit and thudded into a wooden plank.

Captain Thomas heard the same sounds and ordered a return shot by a marksman. There were hundreds of the new Springfield

'61 rifles in the ship's hold and Cox'n Carter quickly found one that had been used in the last confrontation for the sharp shooter. As the ship chugged past the town, two more puffs of powder were seen coming from the hills around the town. The rifleman picked one target and fired his weapon, approximately five hundred yards across the water.

To accommodate that distance, a two-step slotted sight had been installed over the barrel of the weapon above the chamber. It was a single shot weapon and took several seconds to load for the next attempt.

Thomas had the ship steered along the opposite shore, farther away from the attacker and there he ordered more sharpshooters to be employed in defense of the ship and the people on it. He also found out there were two more Gatling guns on board and ordered them brought up from below. He also ordered Jake Prosser to set them up for their use.

Jake's training consisted of a thirty-minute session. The person describing the weapon to him figured Jake would be the one to tell the tester at the end of the run how it was to be used, never anticipating its use before then. Captain Thomas knew his course and knew that in the northern states, there was still some Indian activity, so he ordered one set up. Then he built a metal nest for the gunner to hide in. The two being set up now would be without that protection, and were being mounted, one, across the top deck from the first one and the other on an open space at the fan tail of the ship. The guns were set on a tripod which allowed them to swing from side to side, covering almost a one-hundred eighty-degree span.

When the rifleman returned fire from the ship, Margaret burst from her cabin and looked up at Jake. "Mr. Prosser, what's happening?"

"We're under attack from the shore. Someone in the hills over there is firing at us."

"Do you know why?"

"No, Ma'am. Unless he just wants to be a pest and a bother. He did come close with his first shot."

"Will you be all right up there? You're exposed to attack from either shore. Are you afraid of getting shot?"

"I guess it goes with the territory. We're in the Navy and sometimes people shoot at us."

"Mr. Prosser, are we at war? Why would someone shoot at this boat? Who would be shooting at us? What can we do?"

"Miss O'Neal, I would suggest you get back in your cabin and stay there until someone knocks on your door to tell you it's safe to come out. Right now, the shooter or shooters are on the other shore, so you're safe, but we have no idea what's ahead."

She stood with her hands clasped at her chin. Jake could see she was nervous but had no idea what to do under the circumstances. He wanted to hug her and tell her everything would be all right, but he didn't know that. He could only hope. He came down to her deck level and stood there several seconds, frustrated in his own mind, not knowing what to say or to do, until she reached out toward him. He took her hands and said, in his best bravado voice, "You'll be all right. We'll protect you." He released her hand and said, "Now, best you get into your cabin until we find out what's going on."

They were still south of Natchez after five days. They had taken time to cut wood and find some coal, albeit, a limited amount. The attack the previous night had cost them time and now, this unknown, shooting from the river banks, had forced the captain to change course to some degree. It was getting dark when they stopped last night, fearing the trash coming their way might damage the paddle wheel. It stuck out five feet from the right (starboard) side. Even though the captain had sailed the river, he never faced gunfire or this kind of storm trash before.

They sailed past Natchez, Mississippi and were amazed at the lights and activity so late in the evening. Captain Thomas called the leaders, the Second Mate Peters, Bo's'n Reeder and Cox'n Carter. "I don't know what happened today, but I don't like it. We've brought up the extra weapons and I want you, Mr. Reeder, to select ten men from various duties, arm them and position them along both sides, fore and aft. Find two men to operate the Gatlings guns and have Prosser instruct them. Report back in ten minutes. Dismissed."

Reeder, Carter and Peters conferred for a minute and split, each hurrying to different parts of the ship. In that ten minute time, they gathered again, followed by twelve men, whom they lined up outside the wheelhouse. The captain appeared and shouted across the top of the ship to Jake, "Mr. Prosser, would you join us please?" Jake made his way to the wheelhouse and Thomas continued, "Mr. Prosser, take two men and instruct them on the weapon you are overseeing and tell them how to operate the thing."

Jake pointed to the two men closest to him and they followed him to their assignment. He explained about the feeder tube and showed how it fit on the weapon. He attached one, aimed the barrels into the river and turned the crank to fire the weapon. He emphasized the importance of how fast they turned the crank, for too fast and the gun would jam. He also emphasized that these were in a test condition and no one knew too much about them. As in a normal introduction to a new weapon, riflemen would take it apart and assemble it again. Jake had done that under Reeder's supervision at the start of their trip. Now, he was instructing the two men assigned to care for these pieces of the army.

As the ship steered past Natchez, running with lights dimmed, the watchman on the prow called, "Boats approaching from starboard side."

The captain ordered general quarters and Bo's'n Reeder piped that order. Men scurried about to their positions and waited. The boats, six in number, were coming across from an island. In one boat, two men carried a long board. A man stood in the center boat with a megaphone and hollered, "We are members of the River Defense for the Confederate States of America. You are flying an enemy flag. We order you to stop so we can board you and see if you are carrying war material. If you do not stop the paddles, they will be jammed and broken. Give me a short toot to signify you understood the order."

Captain Thomas in the wheelhouse pulled the cord for a short blast of the whistle, but did not decrease the speed. Instead he shouted back, "Sir, what do you mean an enemy flag? This is the flag of the United States of America."

"Then you haven't heard. A state of war exists between your flag and the Confederate States of America as of noon today, the twelfth of April, 1861. We will come aboard your ship, Captain, and decide if you are to be our first war prize."

"Sir," Thomas shouted back, "we are armed and the ones holding that plank will be the first to die if, in ten seconds, they do not move from our path. Do it! Now!" and he started counting.

The two men holding the plank stood as if to cast it into the path of the paddlewheel, and as they did so, both were shot by men on the ship, the plank falling out to the side. However, the empty boat bounced over to the path of the ship and wound up right under where Captain Thomas stood. The other boats in front of the ship scurried to get out of the way and as Thomas passed the defense spokesman, he cried through his megaphone, "You will never get past Vicksburg. They'll sink you!"

As his ship passed that situation, Captain Thomas called for his Bo's'n to pipe general quarters. It was done and the men gathered. "Men," he started, "we are at war. It seems there is a Civil War between the North and the South and we are in Southern waters. We will pass Vicksburg in six or seven hours. My recollection is that it is about sixty or seventy miles north of here. When that last bunch gets back to the cable, there will be a reception committee waiting for us. What happens then, I don't know, but break out the life preserves and fit everyone. They'll keep one afloat for a bit." He turned to Jake, "Mr. Prosser, can you swim?"

"Yes Sir."

"See to the woman," and he turned and went back into the wheelhouse. A somberness gripped the ship's personnel. What were the chances of going against a frigate or a ram ship? The captain said 'six or seven hours,' so that meant he was going to run through the night, putting them in Vicksburg around six o'clock in the morning. An attitude of defeat settled over the men and Jake, in his duty to 'see to the woman,' didn't know how to tell her they were probably going to be sunk. Uncertain, almost timidly, he held the life preserver behind him as he knocked on her door.

She opened the door and when she saw him she smiled. "Mr. Prosser," she sang, "I was hoping you'd stop by so we could take our walk. I heard shooting a while ago and I was concerned you might not make it." He hung his head for an instant and when he looked up, she showed a look of concern. "What's wrong? Your look tells me something is not right, what is it?"

"Miss O'Neal, we got problems. It seems the North and the South are at war. The shots you heard earlier were from a bunch of row boats that tried to take us captive. The captain ignored them, but the last thing one said, was that when we get to Vicksburg, we'll be sunk." Her eyes opened wide and her hand flew to her mouth. He continued, "Miss O'Neal, can you swim?"

"Why no. It is considered below a refined lady's dignity to go to a public beach dressed in. . .in. . .no, I do not know how to swim."

"Miss O'Neal, Ma'am, I'm gonna have to put my arms around you to get this preserver tied. I know, it ain't what a refined lady allows, but, I gotta do it." He brought it out from behind his back and held it up for her to see. "Now, your arms go in these two openings, and it lies against your. . .front and I tie these around your back. It isn't too difficult, an' I promise I won't touch you—"

Just then a good sized log, floating with the current, crashed into the port front of the ship, jarring the vessel and anyone who was standing. Peggy fell back into Jake's arms and he caught her. He quickly helped her to stand upright and said, "I mean I won't touch you unless you're falling."

She turned and faced him. "Thank you, Mr. Prosser." She paused a couple seconds before asking, "Mr. Prosser, would you think ill of me if I asked you to put your arms around me and hold me for a little. I'm frightened, Mr. Prosser and you are the only one I know, if only a little. And right now, I need my father. You'll have to do."

She stepped forward giving Jake little choice. He opened his arms and wrapped her close to him and there, on that moonless night, in the middle of the Mississippi River, with an unknown future, Jake Prosser's dream came true. She nestled against him with her head on his shoulder, her breath against his neck. He closed his eyes but tried not to think of the repercussions if anyone saw them, but only of the girl he held. After about thirty seconds, she whispered, "Thank you, Mr. Prosser. I feel better now."

Chapter Three

Dawn broke under a blue sky seen through shifting, puffy white clouds, in a sea of tree branches and dirty water. A small city, hiding upon two-hundred foot cliffs above the river, almost midway between New Orleans and Memphis, had become a shipping center for farm products, especially cotton. Railroads that came from across the state brought in people, making Vicksburg one of the largest cities in the South, and certainly, one of the most important

Captain Thomas held his ship a hundred yards south of the docks, waiting to determine the logic of approaching their docks. He saw one ship, low down in the water, with three canon ports facing his vessel. Thomas called his Bo's'n, "Mr. Reeder, pipe all hands on deck." Reeder put his whistle in his mouth and piped a three-tone call, bringing all personnel to the top deck, except two men who stayed in the boiler room. The one female guest was another exception. In a minute, the Marines scrambled up the mast poles to positions above the deck.

Margaret O'Neal did not appear, so Captain Thomas told Jake to see about the woman. He went down the ladder to her deck and knocked on her door. It opened to the most beautiful image Jake had ever seen—a woman in perfect display from her dark hair to the white kid mid-calf shoes. She must not have slept during the night for her hair arrangement must have taken hours to prepare. She had taken off the life preserver.

Wide, thick rolls of her hair, started at the crown of her head, went around to the rear, where the hair dropped in tight curls down her back. Each roll was decorated with gold stars. She had a tiara of gold, holding shiny diamonds, perched above her forehead. A necklace of green amethysts, with gold washers between the amethyst balls hung just above her cleavage.

Her dress was light green, a bell shaped skirt from her very thin waist down with layers of frills, shaped by a bustle. The blouse was fitted, with puff sleeves, tapering down to the wrists. She had a dark paisley shawl, folded in a triangle, around her shoulder.

Jake stood there with his mouth open, unable to speak. This visualization was beyond anything he could imagine. She moved, rather glided past him out onto the deck and took his arm. She looked up at him, apparently expecting him to start walking, but he was frozen to the deck. "Mr. Prosser, is something wrong?"

He woke up to her question and grunted an answer, but started walking toward the prow. They stopped short of the end of the cabins and waited. Men looked at her and she whispered to Jake, "I felt that if I was going to meet my maker, I'd go dressed in my best." He grunted another answer and she looked up at him again. "Mr. Prosser, do you ever pray?"

He answered back, "Pray, you mean like to God?"

"Yes, Mr. Prosser, pray to God."

"I did when I was a kid, but not since."

She said, "I think it is time to pray now, wouldn't you agree?" Without his answer, she started, "Almighty God, thou who holdest the world in your hands, wouldst thou control this situation? We, Your people, are calling on You for help. Hold this ship and the people here in Your mighty hand. We give thanks for the safe trip thus far and trust You for the future."

She still held his arm at the elbow and looked neither to the left nor the right. Jake didn't know what to say or do. He had never had someone pray for him, certainly no one who looked like the woman standing there.

The gun ship facing them had the three front ports open with the nose of a canon at each window. The tall stacks puffed black smoke and a flag, with a red background, having a black "X" from corner to corner showing thirteen white stars. Was this to be the first battle of the day-old war?

Captain Thomas stood at the prow with a megaphone and said, "State your intentions."

"We will board your ship to see if you carry any contraband for the enemy. Stand to. Our men will start their—"

Before he could finish, one of the men standing with the captain, using binoculars, spotted Peggy O'Neal and shouted, "Whoo-eee, would you look at that!"

He handed his glasses to the captain, who directed his gaze where the other told him. As he looked and the men aboard that ship took turns looking at Peggy, Jake slipped away from the woman's grasp and nodded at one of the men whom he had taught about the special weapon. The other man disappeared around the other side of the ship, coming to where his gun placement was at the fan tail. Jake got out of sight and climbed into his nest and brought his weapon around to bear on the other ship.

The gunship's captain shouted, "We will come aboard to see your personnel!"

Thomas replied, "You are not welcome here and we will defend these people to the death."

"If that is your wish, we can grant it."

At that point, Jake stood up and shouted at his captain, "Captain Thomas." He pointed the six barrels out toward the middle of the river and turned the crank, spraying a dozen bullets out into the river. He stopped and brought the weapon back to bear on the other ship.

"Captain, I had always heard that the Southern male is, above all things, a gentleman. We were enroute when this affair started, and haven't had time to reach our destination. We need coal and wood to get there, and will pay for the product."

Ignoring the statement about needing fuel for their furnace, the captain asked, "What kind of weapon is that?"

"That's called a Gatling gun and will fire fifty 45/70 cartridges through six barrels in ten to fifteen seconds. You seem to have the overall power advantage, so we would have to be selective in our targets. I don't mean to leave a threat, but I can predict, with some certainty, you would be our primary target."

"I can understand that. All right, you can load coal and wood north of there, just before the sharp cutback of the river. And Captain, if you come back this way, you'll stay."

"I understand, and I thank you, but may I ask you a question?"

The gunboat captain answered, "That depends. What is it?"

"Since this so called war is only a day old, how is it the South has an active River Navy?"

"That's a fair question. Since we were stationed here, when Fort Sumter happened, we took control of the boat and let those sympathetic to the North leave."

Thomas chuckled, "A peaceful mutiny, is it? Well, thank you Sir. Good luck."

Thomas drove his ship along the beach to the spot north of where they were, just before a place where the river almost doubled back on itself. He found piles of wood and coal and a loading crane. It took hours to finish the loading and was almost noon before they were able to continue their trip. They had two hundred twenty miles to Memphis and, at ten or eleven miles per hour, would be on the water for twenty-two hours, or until almost noon the next day.

Through that whole time—the confrontation, the loading of fuel and payment for it, Peggy stood with her arm on Jake's elbow. It wasn't until the ship started to move on its northward course that Jake looked at her and asked, "Can I ask you a question?"

"Of course."

"Why did you dress up like that? I mean, you are the most beautiful woman I have ever seen and out here, with a bunch of sailors, and the possibility of them sinking us? Why?"

She was silent for several seconds before she answered, "Mr. Prosser, I bought this dress, or rather my father bought this dress just before I left New Orleans. It was to be my wedding dress. I didn't want to die without dressing up in it."

"You must have taken the whole night to fix your hair. How did you get all this little doo-dads in there where they belong?"

She laughed. "Those little doo-dads, as you call them, are worth a lot of money. But again, if we were going to be sunk, I wanted to dress up nice for when I meet the Lord."

"You're serious about that religious stuff, aren't you?"

"It isn't 'religious stuff,' Mr. Prosser. It is my life." He didn't answer right away and she said, "Come, walk with me."

They turned towards the tail end of the ship and she took his left arm again at the elbow. The swish of her dress was the only sound for several steps. She stopped and looked up at him. "Mr. Prosser, I have the feeling that I am making you uncomfortable. I don't mean to. If you would rather forego these walks, I would understand."

He took her hand off his elbow and held it with both his. "Miss O'Neal, when you asked me to hold you last night that was a dream come true. I'm sayin' this because I know you're pledged to someone else and I don't want to give you trouble, but right now, as pretty as you are, I want to hold you again. I think about you and that possibility every moment of the day. So, if you want someone else to walk with you, <u>I'll</u> be the one to understand."

Shocked, she looked up at him. After a few moments, she managed, "Mr. Prosser, I. . .don't know what to say. I only imagined a friendly walk to get out of the stifling room, and. . .I. . .Mr. Prosser, it's probably best if I go in now."

Jake walked with her back to her cabin and stood in anguish internally at the prospect of not seeing Peggy O'Neal again. He stood, head bowed, as she turned one last time before she closed the door and shut him out. After a minute of distress, he straightened up, and marched to the wheelhouse to see the captain. "Sir," he started, "might I go back to the boiler room?"

"You had an argument? Good. It's just as well. She's going to leave us in St. Louis for a new life, while you are mine, it looks like now, until this war situation is over."

"Yes, Sir." Jake made his way to the boiler room to resume his old jobs. While in a cabin on the upper deck, one young woman cried deep sobs at the thought of what she was getting into. She would try one more time to see him and explain. At supper that evening she asked Captain Thomas for permission to speak to Jake one more time.

His answer was slow in coming, for he saw how much anguish Jake had and thought there would be no benefit to anyone to permit the meeting. She persisted and he finally granted her wish, against his better judgment.

After Jake bathed, he came to her cabin and knocked on the door. She opened it immediately and stepped outside. As before, she took his arm and they walked toward the fantail, for this one last meeting. Once there, she turned to face him, grasped his hands and said, "Mr. Prosser, I wanted to explain my situation. Please don't interrupt me, for this is going to be difficult enough as it is. I have been brought up in a motherless home. My mother left when I was four because, she told me, she expected her husband to be more than someone behind a newspaper or taking her to parties or being that other person in her bed.

"She lied to me. They had a terrible fight. She broke his jaw. As I grew older, I found most of my friends homes were like that, single parent families. There was one friend who was not like that. She and her family were Christians. To compensate, my father gave me everything I ever wanted, the best schools, clothes, everything. All I had to do was say something and it was mine. That was fine until last year." She paused to take a couple deep breathes and continued.

"My father has always been interested in politics. He argued with me about every decision the government made. As a result, to keep the argument from being one-sided, I developed an interest in politics. I learned how to argue effectively and it was there I found my situation. We are from Pennsylvania, originally, with my father having a six month residence in New Orleans. Before we left Philadelphia, my father met a man, a general, who had a brother. His wife had recently passed away and he was looking for another woman to share his parties with, and he was rich beyond our wildest imaginations. So, I became the pawn, my father agreed to my being the man's wife for his financial support in running for congress."

Almost imperceptibly, Jake asked, "Is that what you want?"

"Mr. Prosser, I have been spoiled to think money could buy happiness. If a person is not happy with a lot of money, there must be something wrong with their appreciative mechanism. I told myself I could be happy living in a large house with servants and, of course, the eventual children. I mentioned my friend who was a Christian. She has presented me with one problem. You have presented me with one as large, if not larger.

"Her difficulty is, how do I, as a Christian, break my word to my father when I have found I truly don't want to pursue this agreement. The second is, how do I go into this loveless marriage when I know there is one who would love me, and may already love me. I never dreamed of that possibility, but it is here waiting for me."

He looked down at their clasped hands, and then into her face. "I don't know anything about the Christian thing. I made a promise too, one when I joined the navy, and the events of the past week tell me I won't be free for some time. As far as loving you, there is no question about it. As far as when we might be together, I have no idea."

"Could we not get married and set up a home where I could, say, teach school and you come home with permission from your commander?"

"And if I get killed? I wouldn't do that to you."

"Others do, and manage to have some happiness."

"I can't, my darling Peggy, I just can't. There is too much uncertainty now, and what if you were with child and I got killed? There will be enough of that as it is."

She looked up at him, tears forming in the corner of her eyes. "There are clouds up there and only a quarter of the moon. The next time clouds cover the moon, will you take me in your arms and kiss me, kiss me as if you loved me? It may be something I will have to remember for a long time."

That wish came true in the next minute as a darker cloud covered the moon and seemed to hold in its pattern longer than the rest. In that time, Jake took Peggy into his arms and drew her close, kissing her with the stored-up passion he had reserved just for her. As the cloud cleared and they separated, it seemed that the man in the moon looked over the crescent and smiled.

They separated still holding hands. Through her tears she said, "Mr. Prosser," and started to laugh. "It seems rather silly for us to not use our given names after we kissed like that. Is your name Jacob?"

"No, just Jake. Dad said if they named me Jacob, everyone would call me Jake, so that's what they named me."

"May I call you Jacob? It will be just between us and it will be special."

"Sure. Now, I have a question for you. This Christian thing, how did you find out about it?"

"As I said, my friend's family is Christian, and after I saw how they lived, I asked her about it and she took her Bible and showed me some Scripture. Do you have a Bible, Jacob? I have one and we can read from it the few days left of our trip."

"I don't know if the captain will give me permission. When I asked to go back to the boiler room he said it was best, that you belonged to somebody else and I was his. I don't think he'll let me see you that much."

"I think I'll see the captain tomorrow. Until then, remember that kiss, Jacob, and trust there will be more like that in the near future."

Chapter Four

In a carriage at the Army Camp Dennison, outside of Cincinnati, a husband and wife argued. He had just been given a leave and further duty after that leave. She talked louder than was necessary for he was right there beside her, but she wanted him to understand, "I will not let that innocent eighteen year old girl marry your brother. I will not let that happen!"

His response was to laugh. "In the first place, a girl of eighteen in these days probably isn't as innocent as you might think. Secondly, the arrangements have already been made. They are to be married in St. Louis in five days. Orville has asked me to stand with him. At that time he will write a check to her father for two hundred thousand dollars as payment for his bride. That will allow the greedy old scoundrel to run for the United States House of Representatives. God help us if he might happen to get elected. But, as for us interfering in that wedding, it won't happen. I won't let it happen, do you understand?" He looked intently at her, waiting for her response.

There was a pause in their conversation as his wife digested that. "Who is she?"

"Just some girl, Peggy O'Neal, whose father is a doctor, you know, a country physician who challenges the wintry storms to bring healing to the downtrodden."

"You shouldn't make fun of him. He might be a good man."

"Good man or not, if he's willing to sell his daughter to get money to run for congress, he, in my book, is a scoundrel."

"Courtney Clay Patterson, you called that girl's father a scoundrel, what do you call your brother? He chases every woman who allows it. This is his fifth marriage. He drinks to excess at least every week, and you are willing to bring that young woman into that arrangement? If that is your attitude, then I will find some way to get to St. Louis to prevent that from happening." She changed her vocal entreaty to a plea. "Courtney, please don't let that happen. He ran his poor wife to death, one party after another. If he wants a wife, let him get some. . .some woman who agrees to that lifestyle. But, please don't let this thing happen to this girl."

"Evelyn you're getting worked up over something that isn't any of our business. Now, calm down and let Orville marry whom he will. We don't have to be involved."

"You say the wedding is in five days? When are you leaving?"

"I have a ticket for tomorrow. I leave at nine in the morning."

"I better pack for you. Will you wear your uniform on the ship?"

"Yes, under the current situation, I'd be out of uniform if I didn't. Oh, better plan for two weeks away. I have to go north from there. The army's getting some new weapons and I have to see about instruction and field training. In fact, this is an unknown. I may be away from home longer."

"What about your laundry if you are away longer?"

"I'll manage somehow. Maybe I can find a private to do it."

"Did you check with General Hilderbrand? He's the one in charge here isn't he?"

Courtney laughed, "He'd be a good commander if they could get him away from his writing fantasy. Oh, he's all right. At least he's a solid moral man. That's more than we can say for some of his staff. He and Colonel Wallace make quite a pair."

"Like your brother," and she turned away before he could respond.

Courtney Clay Patterson had been a good soldier, willing to do the appointed tasks without complaining. He was the son of a minister, but felt that life too restricting. He was not a troublemaker, but entered the army at age seventeen, much to his father's displeasure. His brother, who was to be the groom in the upcoming marriage, was two years younger and when Courtney entered the military, Orville ran away from home. The decision to enlist was prompted by the election of Andrew Jackson in 1828, a general who made it big. Clay was a sergeant in 1836 when the Alamo fell and he wanted to go help Sam Houston. It was then he met and married the daughter of his commander in Virginia, Evelyn Cooper, daughter of Colonel Adam Cooper.

He was a young lieutenant in 1839 when he was sent to Florida to help quell the Seminole Indian uprising led by Osceola. The Indians, joined by some blacks, massacred over a hundred troops, and even members of a negotiating committee. As a result, the army spent seven years contesting with those members before moving them west of the Mississippi. In 1847, he was selected to learn Morse code when the first telegraph came out. After John C. Freemont invaded California and set up a state Government there, Captain Courtney Patterson was in the contingent that went to California to set up communication facilities within the state.

Now, in 1861, with the help of a military wife and father in law, he sat as second in command of the northwest region of the United States, having to deal with a sot of a brother and an angry wife. He was up early, expecting a breakfast that would keep him until noon on the ship, when he would get a sandwich. His suit cases were waiting at the door, but Evelyn was nowhere to be found. He looked for a note of some kind, but could find none. He had a schedule to keep, so he grabbed a piece of bread, dipped it in honey and headed for the door.

The ship was a new steamer with screw propulsion. Gone were the side or rear paddle wheels. With screw power, the ship would turn fifteen miles per hour. Going down the Ohio, with the current flow, they might make twenty mph. Considering the time spent stopping at Louisville, Kentucky, Evansville, Indiana, and Cairo, Illinois, the trip would take almost two days. Without those stops, the trip might be made in twenty hours.

The ship already had about a hundred passengers, who came from Pittsburg and other stops, when it arrived at Cincinnati, There were nearly another fifty people getting on at Cincinnati, a military presence being most prominent. Because of the war conditions that existed, all military personnel were given a first place in line. The last one to board was an elderly, stooped woman, who moved slowly up the ramp and onto a bench at the aft portion of the ship. She carried simple paper bags with handles on them, from which she pulled a banana and a sandwich.

Other passengers looked with disdain at the poor woman. She was unable to walk steadily as the ship got underway. A woman stood and assisted the poor lady into the ladies room for her convenience and waited until she was done. She then assisted the elderly woman back to her seat at the end of the bench. The trip was to take almost two days and various people stopped by to help grandmother, as they started calling her. She graciously thanked everyone for their concern and consideration.

All day people brought the elderly woman drinks and food as the ship sailed down the Ohio. It was a smooth trip, riding the flow of the river as well as the propulsion of the new screws. The stops at the various cities were longer than scheduled because of the quickness of the trip and arriving before the anticipated time. The speed changed slightly as they arrived at Cairo Illinois and turned north up the Mississippi, going against the current. St. Louis was just ahead.

Her destination was unknown. She had no specific place to stay, but had read of a refuge called YWCA, founded in 1858 in New York City and was spreading to some cities across the country. If St. Louis didn't have a home like that, then she didn't know what she was going to do.

Captain Thomas held his ship to the middle of the river until they were a few miles south of Memphis. He slowed his ship to barely making forward motion looking for a place to stop and cut wood. There were so many switchbacks in the course of the river it was not hard to find a quiet eddy to rest in while the men went ashore to cut wood. Jake was assigned his place in his gun nest to watch over the fifteen men. That put him directly above the cabin of the young woman.

Jake was given a spy glass to scan the horizon and see if there were any problems. As he looked, with one eye in the glass and one eye closed, he heard a snicker and looked down to see Peggy O'Neal laughing at him. "I talked to your captain," she said with a wider grin.

"What did he say?"

"I told him I wanted to have you walk with me after supper tonight and he agreed. I mean, what else could he say when the sister-in-law of the second in command at the Cincinnati headquarters asks a favor?"

Jake smiled, "You sneak." He smiled down at her and added, "I'll see you then, but right now I have to watch for anyone interfering with our wood cutters. Go back inside so I won't be distracted by your smile." She smiled again and disappeared into her cabin.

The job of cutting and hauling wood took hours, for the captain wanted enough to get to St. Louis without stopping anymore. Wood was stored in several of the empty cabins along the lower deck and some on the top deck where Peggy's room was located. Thomas' orders were to fill enough rooms and they would run all night. They were done just before suppertime, so he delayed departure until after that meal.

Jake met Peggy after the boat got back out into the river channel and they walked back toward the aft of the ship. He said, "Miss O'Neal, I have composed a poem for you." She raised her eyebrows and tipped her head a little. Jake started:

"Who's that smiling all the while, that's Peggy O'Neal,
With her hair done up in style, that's Peggy O'Neal
If she talks with a cute Irish brogue
And she acts like a sweet little rogue
Sweet personality, full of rascality, that's Peggy O'Neal."

"Mr. Prosser, that's sweet, that's really sweet. Did you think that up yourself?"

"I did. My mind has that picture of you from the other day down at Natchez."

She paused while looking at him. "I see you are here. The captain talked to you?"

"Captain Thomas was not happy when he told me. He insists this is a poor decision and can't lead to anything good."

She didn't speak for a few seconds and when she did, it was muted. "I know. Jacob, we'll just have to make sure it doesn't turn out that way."

"Gonna be hard. We got another three days on the water. And that's without trouble."

Another quiet response. "Jacob, do you want to forget meeting me tonight?"

Without hesitation he answered, "Would a thirsty man forget a drink of water? Of course I want to meet you, as often and as long as possible."

"I wish you had said yes. Jacob, you're making it very hard for me. I'm falling in love with you and yet I'm on my way to my wedding with another man."

"You make the call."

There was a long pause and Peggy finally answered, more quietly than she had spoken before, "Come when you can and Jacob, I want to hear that poem again."

"Bring your Bible with you. Maybe we can talk about that Christian thing."

When the ship was underway at night, there were two torches on each side, top and bottom decks, to light the ship and to be a signal for other ships on the water. Jake took a chair from two empty cabins for him and Peggy to use while she explained "this Christian stuff." He thought it best to think about something other than that beautiful woman sitting next to him, for if his mind was occupied, his emotions could be better controlled.

She started by praying for guidance in explaining salvation, for that's what the Christian stuff boiled down to. He couldn't remember when he was in church the last time, only that it had been a very long time. She opened the Bible to the Gospel of John and turned to the third chapter and started reading. She read the first eighteen verses and stopped. "Jacob, do you understand born again?"

"Not really. I could think of some dumb questions to ask you but you probably hadn't thought of them. You tell me what those verses said."

"Well, the man Nicodemus wanted to find out if Jesus was real and he was a member of the powerful religious group, so he had to come at night. You understand that?" He nodded and she kept on, "Jesus said, 'except a man be born again he cannot see the kingdom of God.' I imagine that's where the problem starts. Right?"

"Like I said, I could ask some dumb questions, but why don't you try to explain what you think it means?"

Peggy tried to remember the path her friend led her through in introducing salvation into her life. She remembered the verse in Romans that said "All have sinned and come short of the Glory of God." Next, after reading the verses in John about being born again, she turned to I John, and read the first chapter. She then told how Jesus Christ, the Son of God, died on the cross to give us freedom from sin. She added, "Now, I don't know how it happens, I only know that when I prayed and asked Him to forgive my sins, I felt different."

They talked longer with her Bible open on her lap. Bo's'n Mate Reeder walked past "on his rounds," and reported to Captain Thomas that they were reading the Bible. Thomas said, "The Bible? Have you been drinking?"

Assured he had not been drinking, Reeder led his captain to a place where they could see the pair below doing what the Bo's'n said. "And she still has two more days before we get rid of her." They looked to the right and saw the lights of the city of Memphis and the captain steered his ship to the left, along the Arkansas side. "Go douse the torches," he ordered.

"With them still out there?"

"We'll have to take the chance. You'll be around. Nothing's gonna happen."

Bo's'n Mate Reeder went along the port side of the ship, capping the torches and hanging them back in place. He passed the couple and said, "Better go in, Miss. And you," to Jake as he walked past, "get up to your nest just in case."

The two stood and as Reeder walked around the tail section of the ship, Jake and Peggy embraced and whispered goodnight. She lifted her face to him and he took that as a signal. Their kiss was long and hungry, separating only after she whispered, "No, Jacob, we can't."

Chapter Five

The boat from Cincinnati arrived in St. Louis in late afternoon the second day and docked. Passengers exploded down the ramp, as did General Patterson. His brother met him the last step and drew him off to the side. "Clay, am I happy to see you? I was beginning to wonder if you were going to stand me up. Come, let's get a drink. The hotel bar serves a Pineapple Julep that will knock your sox off. You do have sox on, don't you?"

"Listen, Orville, we need to talk first. Where are you staying?"

"I'm in the Planter's House. It's a fabulous place—four floors with the private suites on the roof. I thought about buying it, but that would restrict my movements, so, that's out. What's wrong?"

"I've been thinking about this girl you intend to marry. How old is she?"

"I'm told she is just short of eighteen."

"Have you met her?"

"No. That's the excitement of it all. We have never met, nor have I seen a recent picture of her. Her father showed me a picture of her at age ten, and what a beauty she was then. I know the dress she'll be wearing. She knows to come to this hotel and register and, from that point on, everything is automatic."

"You only know what dress she'll be wearing? Isn't that living dangerously?"

"Clay, I live for excitement, for the unknown. The anticipation of this girl, this young woman is enough to make me quiver. You ought to try it sometime."

"I've got enough excitement with Evelyn, trying to figure what she's going to do. She insisted I try to stop this wedding. I know she's up to something. She was gone when I got up the other morning. I don't trust her. She's up to something."

"Forget her for tonight. Come on, let's get a drink. They have a cider, they call it Applejack, which is powerful. A glass of that will make you sleep for a week."

"Cider? Come on, now."

"I mean it. They take several vats of cider, the hardest they can find, and set them outside to freeze in the winter. When they have a crust of ice on them, they skim off the ice as best they can and do it again. Eventually, they get rid of the water and what is left is, wow! Somehow they preserve and store it for future use. They give you a shot glass to sip. Two is the limit. Come on."

The grandmother had watched people leave the boat and she struggled with her possessions, which consisted of two paper bags with handles. People saw she had food in one, for she took fruit and an occasional sandwich from one bag. The other must have been clothes. She sat on a bench at the stern of the ship the whole trip, rising to walk from time to time, but never getting too far from her possessions. Other passengers offered her food, and she accepted some, but was very selective in that. A younger person was willing to bring her coffee, but the grandmother insisted on paying for whatever she drank.

Now, she followed the people off the boat, being the last to leave. Everyone seemed to be rushing to a new large hotel that took up half a city block. She saw the sign, Planter's House, and figured most of the passengers would be able to fit in there. There were other hotels along the street and she walked toward one of them. There were two across the street from the luxury building, three story wooden frame buildings, which must have been there a long time, and she went inside. She wanted a room on the second floor that faced the front, and she got it.

The room was nothing like what she would have fixed if she ran the place, but it was to be home for at least three days. The furnishings were bleak—a single bed, a small dresser a wash basin on a rickety stand and a wooden chair. She pulled the chair next to the window and sat. She stayed in the chair for a few seconds, got up and walked to the wash stand. She dumped what was in the second of her bags on the bed and straightened them out, laying them flat. Then she disrobed, putting the clothes she had worn for three days on the bed, rolling them up and putting them in the bag. When she finished washing, she lay down on the bed, for it had been a long, restless trip.

Praying was not something Evelyn Patterson did, but thirty years of marriage hung in the balance. How could her oldest son, now a First Lieutenant, understand her going against "orders" as she was doing? Her three daughters might support her, especially the youngest, Grace, but the one that was important was the general, and he had specifically forbidden his wife's involvement. She was taking a chance. She had to think. It could end in disaster.

She needed a single, young woman, a pretty one, who was free of family obligations. She had to be available immediately, with no restrictions. But where would someone like that be found? She couldn't go to a church and find her, because she would have to lie. She would have to say she was someone she was not. The street? She could go out on the street that evening and perhaps satisfy her quest. That would be different. She just hoped there was one she could find without too much effort.

Darkness came on the street at eight o'clock and the street became alive with people, dressed in every type of covering from tuxedos and evening gowns to hard labor clothes. And of course, the street girls had their own type of dress. This was a different effort for Evelyn. She had always looked down on the person she wanted to hire. But, today was different—she needed that person to protect an innocent young lady from a lecherous brother-in-law.

This was a new experience for Evelyn, and she wasn't sure how to proceed. Walk the street for the first hour and see what happened, then, if the opportunity presents itself, make her pitch. At the door, before venturing into a new world, she entered another world never seen before—she sat on that wooden chair and prayed. "God, I don't know how to do this, talk to you, but I understand you hear when we try to talk to you. I'm lost. I want to protect a young woman from a scoundrel and I don't know what to do and I don't know her. I want to get a substitute, a girl from the street, who would be willing to lie for a thousand dollars. Once this other girl, this Peggy, is safely out of town, then the girl I get tonight can reveal who she really is, too late for Orville to do anything about it. So, would you help me, please? I'm desperate."

Evelyn wandered the streets for an hour, looking in store windows, looking at people. By ten o'clock the families had gone home and what was left were the party people. She tried to pick out the working girls, those who were in the prostitution business and read their facial expression. She said hello to a couple to see their response. One looked at her, a middle aged woman, and laughed. The other one just raised her eyebrows and kept walking.

She found a bench in front of a boarding house and sat. She talked to herself, hoping God, if He wasn't too busy, might listen in. "I don't know what I'm doing. And I'm out here at this time of night with these people and they think I'm looking for business too. What can I do?"

While she was contemplating, a horse drawn carriage raced past down the street about a block, where the body of a young lady came hurling out. The coach then sped on into the night. Evelyn got up from her bench and hurried as fast as old grandmother legs would carry her, and found the girl bruised, scraped by the bricks she landed on, with blood oozing from under her hair in back.

Evelyn reached the girl and exclaimed, "Oh my dear, let me help you," and she squatted next to the girl on the ground, trying to comfort her. "Come with me to my room. I'll wash your hurts and see if anything's broken."

The girl was crying and moaning too, making it more difficult for Evelyn to talk to her. Slowly, she responded to Evelyn's offering and her tears stopped. The girl's dress, such as it was, was torn, but Evelyn would have to wait until morning, the fourth day, to get her another one. Evelyn asked, "What is your name, Dear? I'll take you to my room and wash your hurts."

"No, there's no need. I'll be alright."

"Why, you're hurt. The way you came out of that carriage and landed on these cobblestones, you have to hurt somewhere. And you're bleeding. You bumped your head. Come, let me care for you."

"Why. Who are you and what am I to you?"

"I'm Evelyn Patterson. I'm here in search of a special young woman whom I will pay a thousand dollars to. But, for right now, let's get you upstairs so I can clean you up."

"Why me? You say you want to give someone a thousand dollars? Who does she have to murder? What does she have to do?"

"She has to stand in for another young lady in a wedding. That girl will be coming on a boat from the south. As far as I know, she and her intended have never met, but I'm taking a risk in doing this because the man is my husband's brother. He's rich beyond your wildest dreams, but he's a drunk and a womanizer. The young woman I want has to stand in for the girl I'm trying to protect and then, at the wedding night, she will go to their closet to prepare for bed, but come out fully clothed and announce who she really is. By that time, this other girl will be out of town."

The visitor looked at Evelyn and said, "You're doing this for a girl you've never met? Why? What's she to you?"

"I just feel like I have to make some effort."

"It's a God-thing, huh?"

"You might call it that. Look—"

"Rose."

'What's your last name?"

"Petal. It's French, pronounced Pe-tall."

"Rose Pe-tall? That's a pretty name. Look, Rose, I'm not a praying person. I don't remember praying for anything before in my life, but

I prayed about finding you." Evelyn lifted the back of the girl's long red hair and said, "The oozing has stopped, but we still have to get you washed up and into some better clothes."

"What's wrong with these clothes? It's who I am."

"No Dear, it isn't who you are. It's who you are trying to become, for some reason. It can't be the adventure of that life, for you might have been killed. Is it the money? I venture to say you are from a large family that has had some terrible financial need, and you have been unable to learn any trade perhaps because circumstance did not permit you going to school past, say fourth or fifth grade. How am I doing?"

Rose bowed her head and tears fell onto hr lap. A slight nod was Evelyn's answer. Between sobs, Rose revealed, "I'm the oldest of eleven children. My sisters all have flower names—Iris, Dahlia, Daisy, Lilly and Holly. Mother has been sick a lot and now she can't get out of bed. Daddy farms eighty acres south of here in clay and it won't grow anything."

"But kids," Evelyn whispered to herself.

"So I came to the city to get a job, but every man I talked to wanted—"

"And you thought to join the corps. You couldn't, and the man threw you out." Rose nodded again. "Rose, I will give you the thousand dollars for your family whether or not you decide to help me. If that is the case, I'll have to try a different approach. But, let's get you up to my room so we can clean you up a little. Then we'll plan."

Chapter Six

On day three, Jake had been given a break from his duties and was soon at Peggy's door. He explained he wanted her to explain those Bible verses to him, the ones about being born again, so that he could understand what they meant. She tried, with her limited understanding, and then she prayed with him. Late in the afternoon, the ship GREAT EXPECTATION plowed through the dirty waters of the Mississippi River south of St. Louis during a wild rainstorm. Thunder and lightning accentuated a rocket-like wind that forced everyone but those whose outside presence was imperative, to stay in their cabins. Peggy spent this time praying, asking for a safe ending to their journey as well as God's intervention in this potentially disastrous wedding situation.

Captain Thomas was at the helm. Having made this trip before, in better weather conditions, he knew the twists and turns of the corkscrew course this river took and, because of those twists and turns, while navigating a course he could barely see, he had to slow his speed. The wind was from the northwest and while the ship was heading into the wind, he had control of his boat. But when the wind was broadside to the ship, Thomas fought the wheel to keep the middle of the river, away from the shallows along the river's edge. That duty in these conditions would be nearly impossible for a novice.

This was a first for Jake, too. He had been sent to the boiler room to fill his duty there, away from that beautiful young woman. He pondered the Bible verses she read to him and spent half of his time in pause mode, thinking, instead of shoveling fuel into the fire. Time after time the chief had to holler at him to keep the fire stoked and time after time, Jake paused after his immediate response.

The chief criticized him, swore at him and, for a time, Jake responded, but it was always short-lived. Finally, the chief cursed him and told him to get out of his sight that Jake was as worthless as any man he ever had to deal with. Jake tried to protest, that he had no where to go, but the chief promised this would go on his record and the captain would have to deal with the problem when they got to St. Louis.

Jake left the room, thoroughly chastised and condemned. Their area had a closed off "foyer like" room between his work station and the outside, and he stood there several seconds, watching the rain to see which way it blew. At that moment, his outside door was on the lee side of the storm and he opened the door to leave, but the river changed its course. That brought the ship heading into the storm, putting Jake with a small ledge overhead to protect him from the rain.

The river took another turn, this time leaving Jake again on the lee side of the storm. Knowing that was only temporary and knowing that soon he would be on the storm side, he thought of only one place to go. It would be against the wishes of the captain, but at least it would be out of the rain, and the captain was busy at the moment.

Jake dashed for the ladder that led to the upper cabin area and arrived, breathless, at Peggy's door. He knocked rather impatiently and when she opened the door, he brushed past her and pushed the door closed.

"My Heavens Mr. Prosser," she exclaimed, "what in the world are you doing here?"

"I'm sorry, Miss O'Neal, but I was in the boiler room, and wasn't doing very well and the chief told me to get out, he didn't want to see me again, and I. . .well, I wanted to see you and. . .well, I remembered the Bible verses you read and—"

She laughed a happy kind of giggle. "Mr. Prosser, are you telling me you faced this storm to see me and hear more of the Bible, or did you just want to see me?"

"Well, yes. I mean, I was thinking about that kiss, and, well, I liked it." He stopped and looked down at the floor. "Miss O'Neal, I gotta go see the captain. I should never have come, but I wanted to see you. We aren't making as good time as yesterday and might be tomorrow before we get into St. Louis." He turned, opened the door and disappeared into the storm.

Jake went to the wheelhouse to report to the captain and was greeted with swearing and accusations of incompetence and stupidity. Jake stood there during the captain's tirade and when it was finished, Jake said, "The chief down there told me to get out. I wasn't keeping my mind on my work, Sir, and. . .well, I'd like to get back down there with the promise of doing better and carrying my load."

Thomas told Bo's'n Reeder to take the wheel and he turned and looked at Jake several seconds without speaking. Finally, he asked, "You been with her?"

"Yes, Sir, I stopped to tell her the storm has slowed our speed."

"That's all?"

"Yes, Sir. Sure I wanted to see her, but, I knew it was wrong and I wanted to get back downstairs."

Captain Thomas told Reeder, "Take him back downstairs and keep 'im there. We'll work out the rest of it when we get to St. Louis."

Reeder turned and motioned for Jake to follow him and they went back to the boiler room. Reeder walked to the chief and said, "Captain said to keep 'im here. He'll deal with 'im when we stop in Louie."

In her cabin, Peggy was fighting mixed emotions. "Why did Jake come and burst in here like he did? Just when I had put him in his proper place in my life, this happens and I have to go through it all over again." She picked up her Bible and sat in her only chair and flipped the Book open. She stuck her forefinger on a verse which read, "Commit thy way unto the Lord; trust also in Him: and He shall bring it to pass." (Psalm 37:5KJV).

She closed her eyes and prayed, "Lord, I don't know what to say. I know this is not the right way to make a decision, but I don't know what else to do. What if I had found the verse that said 'Judas went out and hanged himself?' I couldn't have done that.

I will leave my future in Thy hands. I have come to realize that this agreement my father made is totally wrong. Your Word tells us not to be unequally yoked together and, the little I know about my intended is that he's middle aged. I will have no life at all. But, if that is Your will for my life, I submit."

Meanwhile, Evelyn took Rose shopping for some modest day clothes. They left in the morning when the sun was shining, even though there were clouds moving across the sky. They arrived at the first store when the rain started. The wind had not started to blow but was showing signs of increasing by the minute. Rose selected some garments and Evelyn paid for them, and stood back to admire. She was looking at a very pretty young woman, a red haired, somewhat freckled face with a cute nose and green eyes. The girl smiled easily, after getting to know this friend, and the two shared some happy moments as they finished their shopping.

Then, the wind started blowing and the drizzle that was in progress turned into a real downpour. The blast rattled store windows and shook the building. The two ladies were not prepared for that event, and asked the store manager if they might stay until the storm ended. In the hope that they ladies might purchase more items, the request was granted.

Rose expressed concern for the amount of money Evelyn spent. "My dear young friend," Evelyn stated, "my husband is a general in the army of the United States. I have had an allowance for years and what money I am spending now, is but a small portion of what has been accumulated. Don't bother your curly head."

They sat and talked. They watched the rain and listened to the wind, expressing concern that the windows might break. No one was on the street, not even the police as the storm left no question as to who was in control. After about an hour of the heavy blast, it diminished and eventually stopped. They took their packages, thanked the manager and left for their hotel room where they could talk and plan.

In Evelyn's room, she sat on the edge of the bed and Rose sat in the chair. The older woman said, "I feel so strongly about this, but you are the one who's going to be at the mouth of the lion, so to speak. How do you feel? I don't want to force you into something you fear."

Rose pondered and hesitated several seconds before answering. "I feel obligated to you—"

"No, no, no! I don't want you to go into this because of the money. And if you are afraid of what might happen on the wedding night, I won't ask you to go on. I'll try to think of something else."

Rose was silent for some time before responding. "You almost have a passion for this. You don't even know the girl."

"That's right, I don't know the girl, but I do know the man. He's a scoundrel, a man with wealth who feels he can buy anything or anyone he wants. I don't know the whole agreement, but my husband said the girl is the price of Orville's contributing to her father's venture into politics. He wants to run for Congress and he basically has sold his daughter into slavery to accomplish that."

There was another pause as Rose thought. "You make it sound so bad, and yet you want me to get involved with the man. I don't know. . ."

"Rose, I know this sounds bad. I didn't want to sugar coat it, but Orville isn't mean, just someone who thinks his money can get anything he wants. I don't even know how he found the girl or her father. All I know is, no matter her standards now, in six months she'll be a drunk because of his practices."

Rose stood and said, "I have to think about it. If I come back, I'll do it," and she walked out the door.

Evelyn bowed her head, closed her eyes and wept.

Evelyn skipped her evening meal because of near depression. She was at wit's end. There was no hope now for that innocent girl. She would be destroyed and then dumped. That's the way Orville did things. He would force her to go to Bacchanalian orgies and in time, no matter her standards now, she would eventually submit. If she didn't, she would be ridiculed, laughed at, scorned and ignored. Eventually, she would be the butt of every joke anyone could imagine. Now, there seemed to be no hope.

Evelyn interrupted her thought process with the thought about prayer—was it an accident that Rose appeared in what seemed to be an answer to prayer? "Why would God pay any attention to a woman like me, who has never been to church in my life?" She sat in her chair and pressed her fingers against her forehead. "God, You know this little girl, this young woman who is coming on that boat. Is there any way to stop this marriage from happening? What do I do to keep it from taking place?"

She sat, her thoughts running without control, from one situation to another. She was interrupted by a light knock on the door and she burst from her chair to open the door to find Rose Pe-tall. Both ladies stood, without talking for a couple seconds, until Evelyn asked, "Does this mean. . ."

"I couldn't get away from your description of the man. You said he isn't violent. On that basis, I'll help you, her. Now, tell me how you plan to contact her."

"I basically have no plan. Wait, let me finish. From what my husband has said, she's coming on a river boat later tonight or tomorrow. My husband will probably be there so I'll have to go in some disguise. She will be the only girl, woman on this boat, so that won't be a problem. The problem, as I see it, will be to stop her and convince her of our story."

Chapter Seven

The previous day, Evelyn had paid a dock worker to keep an eye out for the ship with one pretty female passenger, and to come notify her as soon as the ship was in. She asked the hotel for another blanket and she and Rose traded time on the bed and the blanket on the floor for their sleep time. Anticipating the arrival, but not knowing the time, Evelyn dressed in her disguise clothes, in case she saw her husband.

The call came early in the morning of day four. She and Rose caught a carriage and hurried to the river in time to see her husband talking to a man in a Naval Officer's uniform. She saw three other men in uniforms off to the left, one, an officer who would be her husband's aide, and two enlisted men, standing next to three bags of luggage. "He must be talking to the boat captain," she muttered. She looked at Rose and said, "That man over there in the army uniform is my husband and he's talking to the captain of the ship. Do you think he'll recognize me?"

"If he studies you, he might, but not if he just glances at you."

As they waited, one very pretty young woman walked down the gang plank to the street level, leading two men with heavy luggage. Evelyn heard her husband say, "Miss O'Neal, I hope you have had a very pleasant journey."

The young lady nodded, but didn't smile, but just kept walking until she was away from the ship. Two of the ship's personnel carried her luggage set the bags down and one turned and went back up the ramp. The other stood for a moment, looking at the young woman. She reached out her hand to him, touching him on his arm and quietly said, "Jacob, I pray you will find understanding in what we've read and I thank you for helping me see what love might be. I will always remember your poem, and pray that some day we might meet again."

He only nodded and strode toward the ramp. As he drew even with the captain and the general, Captain Thomas halted him. "Seaman Prosser, this is General Patterson. He would like to talk to you about the guns. Do you have that one still set up?"

"Yes Sir, Sirs."

Thomas ordered, "Take the general and show him how it works, but for Heaven's sake, don't fire it. He has asked for you to come with him and instruct the men who will be using it."

Jake smiled a little and answered, "Yes, Sir, come this way." The three walked up the ramp onto the ship, leaving the girl by herself.

Evelyn ordered, "Come," and she moved quickly toward Peggy, still waiting, looking for some guidance. "Miss O'Neal," Evelyn started, "may we talk to you for a moment about your wedding?"

Thinking these two people had come to take her to her hotel, she smiled and answered, "Of course. Are you going to help me get ready for the wedding?"

Evelyn answered, "That's what we want to talk to you about. Oh, first, I'm Evelyn and this is Rose."

Peggy turned to Rose, presented her hand, and said, "You're very pretty."

Rose took the hand and curtseyed her best American farmer curtsey while holding Peggy's hand. "Thank you, Ma'am."

Evelyn said, "Miss O'Neal, this is very delicate, and I'm afraid I'm going to encroach where I have no right, but this is for your good." Peggy frowned at the words and started to respond, but the older woman said, "Wait until I have finished. What do you know about your intended?"

Offended, Peggy asked, "What is this all about? Who are you that you have an interest in my future husband?"

"Miss O'Neal, I'm his current sister-in-law. The general you talked to is his brother, my husband. All I ask you to do is ask Court. . .the general this one question, 'what will my life be like married to my intended?'"

Peggy frowned deeper. With wrinkled brow, she asked, "What do you think my like will be like married to your brother-in-law?"

"Miss O'Neal, are—"

"Call me Peggy. You have my interest now."

"Yes, Miss. Are you open to life in the ways of the world? I mean, do you partake of the fermented—"

"No! Of course not! I'm a Christian! What kind of question. . ." She stopped and looked at the woman. Calmer and quieter, Peggy asked, "Is that what my life will be? That kind of gathering? With—"

"I'm afraid so, Peggy. Courtney and I have been married thirty years, which may come to an end as soon as we get back to Cincinnati. Orville has had four wives, you are, were to be the fifth. All others were hopeless drunks after the first six or nine months. He never had any children, but seemed more content in ruining their lives, especially if they had a moral background, if they had made a habit attending church." Evelyn paused and Peggy, as if startled, stood with her mouth open. Evelyn said, "Courtney and Orville are from a minister's home and every time Orville talks about home, it's with anger."

She glanced up and saw her husband talking to the captain and that other sailor, walking their way on the top deck. "I have to get away. But make sure you ask him that question. What will my life be like if I go through with this wedding?"

"Wait," Peggy implored, "and what will I do if I don't go through with the wedding? What will I tell my father?"

"Tell him the truth. And come back with me to Cincinnati." She handed Peggy a piece of paper, "This is where I'm staying. There are all kinds of teaching positions open now with the war threatening. I'll find you a place to stay and Courtney will never know about it."

Surprised, Peggy argued, "Cincinnati? I don't know anything about Cincinnati."

"But you came all the way from New Orleans without knowing anything about your intended. The general's coming, I have to go so he won't see me," and she hurried away, followed by Rose. At that point, the general was at the top of the ramp leading to the dock. He stood with his back to the street, talking to the captain and that sailor.

Peggy walked toward the end of the ramp and stood there. General Patterson looked up at her and she said, "General, how did you know my name when you greeted me?"

"Hello Miss. How did I know your name? You're to get married to my brother. I had intended to be there, but I just received my orders to go further north on this ship, and the captain is getting ready to leave."

"General, I have to ask you a question. Since he is your brother, what will my life be like after my marriage to him?"

Stunned, the general faltered in his response. "Why Miss, I, uh, why would you expect me to know something as private as that?"

"You're his brother, are you not? If he is approximately your age, you know if he has been married before. I'm only asking what you saw in his relationship with his other wife, or wives."

"Miss, that's not a fair question. Look, I have to get on that ship to go further north. I really can't take time now to get involved in your queries." He told his aides, "Get my stuff on the boat and take it to my cabin. Captain Thomas will tell you which one." He turned back to Peggy, "I'm sorry I can't answer your questions."

He turned to go back up the ramp and Peggy spoke more loudly, "Evelyn didn't think you would answer my question."

That stopped him in mid-step. "Evelyn?" Louder, "Evelyn?" He screamed, "Evelyn, you wait until I get home. We'll settle this then. I ordered you to stay out of it."

Evelyn took off some of her disguise to show who she was and stepped into his view. "Evelyn, I'll deal with you when I get home."

She said nothing. Rose put her arm around the older woman and said, "I'm sorry." Evelyn fought tears that came to her eyes, but looked at Peggy.

"Come," she said, "Let's talk to Miss O'Neal."

They walked to where Peggy stood, who said, "You risked your marriage to protect me? Why?"

"Miss, Peggy, I heard you were young, I decided I couldn't let what happened to his last wife happen to you. Virginia was a sweet girl, a little older than you are now, but Orville ruined her, made her drink, ridiculed her when she said no, and in a few months, she was a sot. I argued with Courtney, who told me to stay out of it, but I couldn't let that happen. We've had thirty good years with four children. I hope he'll think before he gets home." She took a deep breath and added, "Now, we have to complete plans for the wedding. Rose is going to stand in for you."

Evelyn called for a couple men waiting beside a building and said, "I'll pay you to carry these bags to the hotel."

On the way, they discussed how Rose was to fill in for Peggy and at the hotel, Rose signed in as Peggy O'Neal, which resulted in the ladies being led to an elaborate room, on the roof. Elisha Otis had shown how to carry people and supplies up from one floor to another in what he called a "lift" as early as 1853 and had some hotels involved as test buildings. The ladies had never been on a thing like that before and as the operator closed the door for them, they showed some concern. Slowly, it lifted them to the very roof, where they saw the most glorious and ornate room any of the three had ever seen, set up for the young bride.

There was a note pinned to a pillow and Peggy read it:

> "My beautiful young bride, I didn't greet you because I want this to be a complete surprise. It may be strange to you but I live on the edge of surprises and challenges. If I see a challenge I don't like, I try to change it. I live by the excitement of the challenge. You, my young bride, will be my next challenge. I look forward to the excitement."

Peggy stood there with her mouth open, "I'm a challenge? He looks on me as a challenge?" She turned to Evelyn, "It is beginning to look like you may have rescued me from a life of degradation. My life, my beliefs are a challenge? I think not!"

Evelyn turned to Rose. "Having heard the note, how do you feel about this game? I don't want to take a chance on you getting hurt."

Quietly, she admitted, "I am a bit apprehensive. You said he isn't violent. Or at least, hasn't been in the past. I'll take that chance. I agreed to it."

"You may have agreed to it, but that was before the note and before he regarded his next bride as a challenge."

Rose looked down at the floor several seconds and when she lifted her gaze, had tears in the corners of her eyes. "You gave me a thousand dollars to pull off this, this. . ."

"Charade," Peggy volunteered.

Rose looked at Peggy as if she didn't understand the word. She turned to Evelyn and said, "I'm doing this for you. You showed you cared for me when you helped to get me off the street. I'll not forget that. You said you prayed and I was the answer to your prayer. When I get home, I'm going to look up a pastor who believes that way. I want my family to understand what prayer is."

Peggy showed delighted surprise. "You believe in prayer? How wonderful. I was afraid I'd be here all by myself."

Evelyn held up her hand to stop the praise. "Peggy, I prayed in desperation. I did not pray because I believed it, but I prayed because I had no idea what else to do. I've never been in a church in my life. My husband and I were married by a judge in a courthouse in Virginia. But, that's going to change. I'm going to pray about my marriage and ask you to help me. If I lose my husband over this, it was well worth it to keep you from the clutches of his brother."

They discussed what agreement Peggy had made between her father and Orville and found out the only thing he would look for was a young woman in that frilly dress Peggy wore on the boat, during the confrontation at Natchez. Peggy unpacked it and Rose stood with her hands clasped at her neck, saying, "O-o-o-oh it's beautiful. I've never seen anything like that."

Rose tried it on and it fit perfectly. Now, all Rose had to do was stay out of Orville's sight until ten o'clock in the morning and meet him in the ballroom off the lobby. And to remember to say her name was Peggy O'Neal.

Quietly, Evelyn confided to Peggy that she was concerned about the wedding time. That usually meant Orville had a big party planned. "Would you be uncomfortable if we stayed until after the wedding? I don't want to leave Rose hanging out there by herself."

Peggy agreed, adding, "I think I'll write to my father and tell him what he almost got me into." Her emotions came out, almost in anger, "He couldn't have investigated the man at all to have made this agreement." She paused and frowned, "Could his passion, his fantasy, about being a Congressman have been so strong as to jeopardize my life like this? Did he not care what happened to me? I wonder if the hotel provides paper and pen."

Evelyn commented, quietly, that the North and South were at war and that if her father was still in New Orleans, he would never get the letter.

Chapter Eight

Nearly thirty years had elapsed since the end of the "Black Hawk" wars that saw the end of Indian raids in Illinois and Wisconsin. There were incidents of fighting, but not the organized attacks by the Sauks, Fox, Sioux and a mixture of other tribes. That so-called war began at a time when there was still British involvement in the internal affairs of the United States. It was at a time of expansion westward down the Ohio River and across Kentucky and Tennessee, and, eventually, to the Mississippi.

Settlers were moving into Indian lands north of the Ohio River, into the territories of Indiana and Illinois, and claiming them for their own. After an absence of several months, Black Hawk came to his home in Saukenuk, Illinois, upriver from St. Louis, to find a white family living there. He tried to get them evicted, claiming the current treaty signed in Washington, but could not. His intent then, after having been driven west across the Mississippi, was to return to Northern Illinois and Southern Wisconsin and drive out the whites. His actions created fear among the citizens as far away as the village of Chicago

Now, with war against the South becoming a reality, a grandson of Neapope, the chief lieutenant of Black Hawk, had gathered a collection of like minded warriors, mostly young, mostly adventuresome, and mostly dissatisfied with their lives as subjects of a government they have learned to hate. Black Hawk and his followers, fought for a purpose—their lands and the way treaties with the Government were broken. But this man, (he called himself George Washington Neapope), had one purpose—that of repaying the whites for their aggression against his ancestors. He was a born leader and because playmates listened to him, he found it easy to expect men to listen, also. He found willing listeners among the Sauks, the Sioux, the Winnebago and a smattering of other peoples in Northern Illinois and Southern Wisconsin.

Raised in a Mission school sponsored by Methodist Missionaries, he was always a little ahead of the others in his thinking and in his challenges during Indian games. His anger against the white encroachment came when he was thirteen and learned from an old Sac Indian of the Bad Ax Creek battle, where over three hundred of Black Hawk's band, including women and children, were killed. Their effort to escape the Army's attack brought them to three hundred foot cliffs in high grass and fallen timbers and they had nowhere to go. Another seventy women and children were taken to a camp, where sickness broke out and many of those people died.

At seventeen, he managed to get to the Bad Ax Creek area and saw where the battle took place. When he saw the cliffs that his ancestors had to slide down to get into the Mississippi, without boats, he vowed to make it right. From that point on, G W Neapope started his planning against the government. He called himself George Washington because he considered himself a leader of people against a foreign ruler. He was determined to lead an army against this government in a second battle of Bad Ax Creek, with a different outcome. He was determined.

He became an evangelist, using methods learned from the Methodist preachers, carrying his message throughout the Indian Territories of Minnesota, the Dakotas and as far away as Montana. He was smart. He spoke of the glory of yesterday and mentioned names familiar to his listeners. He vowed to return the glories of the past.

His approach was to condemn the US Government for breaking all the treaties and then he got specific, talking about selected battles. He always chose those battles where a great number of women and children died at the hands of the army. One by one he picked up followers. Slowly, with careful consideration, he chose very carefully, young men who agreed with him, who could lead in case of his demise. At a great rally in upper Minnesota, he gathered the leaders and outlined his plan. The first attack would be at Fort Hadley Brown, upriver from Prairie du Chein, Wisconsin, to capture arms. The fort was named for a hero of the battle of Fallen Timber, that battle that took the life of the great Indian leader, Tecumseh.

Most of G W Neapope's activities were in the outer regions of the US control and into Canada. Because of the lack of communication from those areas, when he attacked Fort Hadley Brown with nearly a thousand followers, they were totally unprepared. When the fort fell, the attackers, tasting the blood of their white enemy, reverted to the brutality of other Indian victories, as at Fort Pitt and others where the captured and wounded were scalped and mutilated. The attackers took as many of the weapons from the fort's stockpile as they could carry, and broke the stocks of the other rifles. Their take included three, three pound cannons and one five pounder.

When a survivor made his way to Fort Two Rivers at Prairie du Chein a week later, it was the first indication of trouble, and men and ammunition had to be rushed to the town of Prairie du Chein and Fort Two Rivers. The GREAT EXPECTATIONS, already underway from New Orleans, was carrying a shipment of new weapons to replace outdated pieces, and the timeliness of their arrival became clear. General Hildebrand had sent a cable to General Patterson in St. Louis, telling him of the urgency, telling him more men and supplies were on their way. Until other help came, GREAT EXPECTATIONS paddled northward, with a detachment of Marines, a general, an army captain, a sergeant and a non-commissioned enlisted men aboard.

They listened as Seaman Prosser tried to describe the Gatling gun and how it worked. As carefully as he could, with the ship sometimes rolling with the force of the river flow, Jake disassembled the weapon on a table in one of the cabins. Thereby, if one of the small parts of the gun would roll off the table, it would not be lost.

Twice Jake broke down the gun as the others, including Captain Thomas, watched. The sergeant, who came with the general and the Marine Sergeants, had, as part of their duties, taken apart all the weapons in the army arsenal. Sergeant Hanratty controlled the conversation, trying to keep Jake from being distracted. When Jake finished the disassembly the second time, he offered Sergeant Hanratty a chance to put it back together. He insisted Jake guide him, and the two of them worked to return the gun to its firing capability. Then Jake insisted the sergeant show what he learned by doing it himself. He did the job with only a couple suggestions from Jake.

This brought some contention from the other Marine sergeant and the Army sergeant. Hanratty was the choice of Lt. O'Rourke because of his service length, but the other men saw this gun as the key to advancement and wanted to learn as much as possible about it.

Jake's involvement was another issue. Because of his education, where he could read, write and do numbers, he was given an initial promotion to Ordinary Seaman. Usually, all enlisted men came in as Landsmen, and it took three years experience before they "knew the ropes," a term developed from duties aboard sailing ships, and were promoted to Ordinary Seamen. And Jake's being the one who knew the new weapon angered the Marines. <u>They</u> were the weapon's specialists. <u>They</u> were the ones who were given the job of instructing and showing how things worked. <u>Not this Ordinary Seaman</u>.

There was a conference in the General's stateroom late into the night with Captain Thomas, the general's aide, the sergeant and the Marine leaders discussing the news, anticipating new orders and worrying about the start of another bloody Indian war while engaged with the South. Dawn of the fifth day found Jake in front of twenty-nine soldiers at Fort Two Rivers, with the three Gatling guns from the ship. As he made one move towards dismantling the weapon, the army sergeant and Sergeant Hanratty followed the same action. The twenty-nine men were split into three groups, carefully making notes as to what was done. When they finished, the three instructors assembled the weapon for it to be torn down again.

General Patterson stood apart from the activity and watched. If he saw someone not paying enough attention, he reminded them one time of why they were there. A second time brought dismissal. That happened only one time. After that, all men kept their attention glued to the process with the guns.

As the general and Captain Thomas stood together, watching the activity, Patterson commented, "Your man seems to know that gun pretty well."

"That he does," the captain replied, "but I almost had to throw him in the brig on the way up here."

Surprised, the general turned his head to the captain. "O-o-o-h? He doesn't seem to be a trouble maker."

"It wasn't trouble from him, it was that woman we carried from New Orleans. She got tired of sitting in her cabin and wanted an escort for walking around the ship. She saw him in his gun nest and asked if he could be her escort. Then she asked for him twice a day and it grew from there. I had to send him to the boiler room to shovel wood for the fire."

The general was definitely interested, since that woman was to be his brother's wife. "Did you notice anything. . .untoward? I mean, did they—?"

"Oh, no." He paused, as if remembering, and added, "One time, when we had a confrontation on the way, they were seen hugging. It seems she lost a brother in a hunting accident and the shooting frightened her." The captain quickly continued, "It's just that they spent a lot of time together reading the Bible."

"They what? Reading the Bible?" incredulously the general responded. "You have to be fooling me, Captain. Reading the Bible?"

"Not fooling, General. In addition, my bo's'n saw them holding hands once. So, I'm glad we got rid of her. She was too much of a distraction." The captain wanted to tell General Patterson that he knew she was on board only because of somebody pulling some strings somewhere "up the ladder" from him. He waited for the general's next comment, which surprised him.

It came as a whisper. "I wonder how Evelyn found out."

The instruction process lasted three days. The general and the commander at Fort Two Rivers had to be sure of the troop's ability with the weapon for there were to be more coming from the factory. These twenty plus men would be split up and be sent to different army units as new guns came from the manufacturer. The general even asked for the loan of Seaman Jake Prosser for a six month period. Captain Thomas said he would have to follow channels to get an answer. There was a cable office at the fort, which was quite busy during those three days.

Wires were sent between General Patterson at Fort Two Rivers, General William Hildebrand at Cincinnati and Commander Montgomery, commander of the Union Northern River Fleet. General Patterson wanted, needed, the ship GREAT EXPECTATIONS, to ferry men to Fort Hadley Brown to see the extent of destruction there. There were also, according to the report of the one who got away, bodies that had to be buried. Captain Thomas wanted to get back to his own duties, but was at the mercy of the War Department in Washington, DC. Finally, the decision was made that the ship, the captain and all personnel would be under the direction of General Patterson as needed, not to exceed sixty days.

The army started loading equipment—guns, tents, horses—onto the boat in preparation for leaving. The bottom freight area was adjusted with rope fences to contain the horses. A contingent of Winnebago Indians, those who had once fought the whites for their land, agreed to come along as scouts, hoping to prove their allegiance to their new leaders. A force of nearly two hundred fifty men, with the three Gatling guns and thirty Indians were loaded and planned to sail north as soon as light appeared the next morning. And by that time, thought one seaman, she will be married.

Hundreds of new people moved through the lobby of the elite hotel all morning of this, the fifth day, looking for the ballroom. There were people in evening dress, anticipating a party that would last well into the night, or perhaps even into the next day. Diamond tiaras were as common as a broach on a lady's shoulder. Multistrand diamond and pearl necklaces hung around the necks of ladies wearing jeweled evening gowns. The French dialect was almost as common as English, both the British and the American versions. Everybody was laughing, drinking and apparently having a good time. Everybody but two young ladies.

Evelyn had kept them separated from the crowd. She had even taken them to her room at the old hotel to be sequestered until she returned. This was one meeting she meant to have with the expecting groom, which he was not going to like. During their few minutes together in her old room, she asked Peggy about prayer, and how it was supposed to be done. Peggy explained it was just talking to God, telling Him what you felt and what you hoped for. Then they prayed. For her, it was a simple prayer, asking God to control the events at what was supposed to be a wedding party. With that done, she returned to become a grandmother again, and to crash her brother-in-law's party.

When Peggy's father arranged for the wedding, he told Orville the kind of dress she would be wearing. It was going to be exciting, a woman he never knew, had never seen, being identified by only the dress she wore at his wedding. He was charged so that the liquor he drank didn't seem to affect him.

At two minutes to ten, the morning of the fifth day, the minister was in place, guests were lined up, the groom was there, waiting for his bride. The door to the lobby opened, just slightly, and the skirt of that dress that he was expecting to be worn by his bride, was seen. He yelled, "YEA!" and swung his arm in a wide circle, and the noise stopped.

As Grandma stepped through the door, she held that dress, the symbol of young womanhood, in front of her. After thirty years of military life, bearing four children and being a part of army festivities, there was no way she could get the dress on. There were people standing across from the door and it took a second for their response, but, as soon as they saw this stooped old woman, with grey wig and sun bonnet, dressed in a house dress, the roar of laughter could have been heard out on the street.

"What is the meaning of this?" Orville shouted as he walked toward her, "Who are you and what have you done with my bride?"

"Your bride won't be here today. If you had left the ceremony for the evening, she might have attended, but where you are getting married in the morning, so you can spend the rest of your day drinking, she won't be here."

Laughter still swept across the room uninhibited. Coarse shouts from the men about the evening were heard, making Orville glare with unrestrained anger. He cursed the woman as granny took off her wig and became Evelyn. That really promoted a screaming session. Most had no idea who this woman was. They could only tell she was about Orville's age and that he knew her.

Finally, he stopped screaming and explained, "Folks, this is my brother's wife. She has the unmitigated gall to interrupt my wedding with this foolishness, hiding my bride, because she feels I'm an unfit husband or something."

"You said it, I didn't." Evelyn shouted loud enough to be heard, "I have not been a participant in three of his other four weddings but the fourth I saw how he destroyed the woman. Virginia was a sweet girl, and you turned her into a drunken sot. I was not going to let that happen this time."

"So you've turned noble all at once. You have been such a mouse. Where did you get your courage to face me, and ultimately your husband? When Clay hears about this, there will be fireworks. I will be there when that happens." He laughed, loudly, to cover up his frustration and some embarrassment. He came close to her, with a couple inches separating their faces, "All right, you've had your fun. It was good for a laugh, but it's time you scoot on out of here so we can begin the festivities. As you leave, send what's-her-name in so we can do the marriage thing."

"You didn't listen to me. Unless you pick someone from this crowd, there will be no marriage. I won't let you ruin the life of that young woman. We will leave for Cincinnati when I leave here. Courtney's up north somewhere with the army, looking into an Indian attack, so it will be a month before he gets home. By that time, I'll have my things in order so that if he wants a divorce, I'll give it to him."

Still shouting louder than needed, Orville said, "So, that's the way it is. You ruin my life, your life and Clay's life all because you have some noble bone somewhere in your body that tells you to not allow this. And what do you think Clay will say when I tell him about your interference?"

"If he's as honest as I think he is, he'll congratulate me and tell me I did the right thing."

"Woman, I could kill you for this!"

"No you couldn't Orville. You aren't a violent man, just a tool of the devil."

He screamed, "Did you hear that? She called me a tool of the devil! She, who's never been to church in her life called me a tool of Satan. How do you like that?"

"You're right, I have never been to church, but that's going to change as soon as I get home. I prayed, Orville, I prayed and asked God's help in confronting you and He did it. Now, I am done. I have given you my message so now I will leave. Go on with your party. You don't need the pretense of a wedding to get drunk."

As Evelyn turned toward the door, Orville grabbed her and screamed, "No you don't. You said I turned Virginia into a sot. Well, I'll show you how it started. She said she wouldn't drink." He turned to the crowd, "Somebody bring me a bottle." It was done, and the person opened it. Orville put his arm around Evelyn's neck and lifted the bottle toward her mouth. She squirmed, but could not break his hold. She cried for him to stop, but he would not.

Aroused by the noise in the ballroom, a head appeared and a voice came from the doorway. "Hotel security. Let the woman go or be arrested for assault."

Chapter Nine

There was a tearful goodbye when the ladies separated at the railroad station. While Evelyn was confronting Orville, Peggy and Rose were getting acquainted, and they each found a friend. As their conversation progressed, Rose asked Peggy for explanation of prayer and her faith. Peggy did her best to explain prayer, saying it is only talking to God, but believing that what you are asking will be done. Rose had never heard it explained that way. Her family lived away from any town, on land that was mostly clay, being worked by a tired man and a pair of sick mules. Her younger brothers, the third and fourth children in her family, worked under their father, but they still had only one team. For the most part, it was her father's pride that kept them from church, being too poor to buy decent Sunday clothes for the family.

Evelyn was tempted to go with Rose to her home, but that would have put Peggy as an extra, out of place and uncomfortable. So, instead, Evelyn gave Rose an extra thousand dollars to help the desperate family buy another pair of work animals and help her sick mother. And perhaps, there would be enough to buy clothes for all the children. When Rose told the family her story, she was sure even her brothers would agree to come to church with her.

As Evelyn and Peggy watched Rose depart, there were some uncomfortable seconds as neither one spoke. Finally, Peggy turned to the older woman and asked, "Why did you do this? Please understand I'm grateful, but, you didn't need to put your marriage in jeopardy."

"I saw what he did to Virginia, his last wife, and how he changed her. I knew nothing of you but what my husband told me, and he knew only what Orville had said. Knowing Orville's background, and his hatred for anything decent, I couldn't take the chance of him doing the same to you." Peggy didn't respond immediately, so Evelyn continued, "You know, it is strange, the difference between the two men. They grew up in a parsonage—"

Peggy interrupted with a heavy sigh and "Oh, no. What happened?"

"From the little bit Courtney has told me, he refuses to talk about his childhood, but let slip once that the people were intolerant of children. In fact, there were no children in the church except the pastor's two, and everything they did was criticized. When Courtney joined the army, Orville ran away. He's maybe two or three years younger than my husband, and was pretty bad, morally. He got lucky in cards, poker, and won some money. Then, he would buy drinks for older men, get them drunk and take their money when they couldn't see the cards. He bragged about his technique to Courtney and me. Now, he's wealthy beyond imagination. It couldn't have come fairly."

A pause in their conversation prompted Evelyn to suggest they get to the docks at the river and get tickets for the boat ride to Cincinnati. They had to wait a couple hours for the southbound boat to Cairo, Illinois, and guessed they would have to wait there for their ride up the Ohio. As they waited, and as they talked, the two developed a fondness for each other. Peggy explained her education, and Evelyn promised she would use her influence to get the young girl a teaching assignment.

On the boat, they sat for a while and grew tired and restless, so they walked around the main deck. Peggy explained this boat was basically like the GREAT EXPECTATIONS, and told Evelyn of the sailor she met and of their time together. Evelyn said, "Your wistfulness indicated to me a serious desire to see him again."

Embarrassed that she was so open, she blushed and turned her eyes down. After a short pause, she said, "Yes, I would like very much to see Jacob again. But with the war coming, I wonder how long it will last. More, I wonder, even if it lasts a month or two, I wonder if we shall ever meet again."

Softly, Evelyn said, "You just talked to me about prayer and believing in what you pray for. Does it not work for you too?"

"I'm sorry. Yes, of course it does, if it's in God's will."

Evelyn looked at her in a quizzical way, her brow furrowed, and asked, "Am I missing something here? You never spoke of God's will before. How do we know what to pray for? How do we know if what we're asking is in God's will?"

"I'm sorry. There is so much to know, so much to learn, and I'm such a poor teacher. I've only been a Christian a few months, and am still learning. My problem was that I had to learn most of it by myself by reading the Scriptures. I'm sorry if you feel I mislead you."

Evelyn studied the younger woman several seconds before saying, "I'm beginning to think there is more to this being a Christian than going to church and saying a prayer once in a while."

At Cairo, they bought tickets for an eight o'clock AM departure for their destination and found a hotel near the river junction with the Ohio. After supper, Peggy explained her understanding of Jesus' statement about being born again. She opened her Bible and traced scripture through Romans and Ephesians. As they got ready for sleep, Peggy prayed with Evelyn, who accepted God's plan for her life and marriage. Then, almost apologetically, Peggy mentioned the verse in I John, chapter one, that says, "If we confess our sins, He is faithful and just to forgive us our sins and cleanse us from all unrighteousness." She admitted she didn't know all that meant, but was probably a personal thing. She also admitted that God had shown her things in her own life that needed change. On that note they went to sleep.

After breakfast in the morning, they boarded a ship for Cincinnati. With the storm behind them they would make good time. The question Peggy faced was what to do. Evelyn had mentioned teaching. Peggy had never considered teaching, even though she had

had a full and thorough pre- college training. For Evelyn, the future was completely unknown, for the last thing she heard from her husband was that he would deal with her when he got home. With her interference in Orville's wedding plans, she could only envision one outcome—divorce, disruption of her family, denunciation of her as a person.

They walked the decks of the boat going east and happened to see two soldiers, sitting on the aft portion, looking over the water as it bubbled from the fans. As they walked by, they heard one soldier mention something about that Gatling gun, and Peggy reached for Evelyn's arm, pulling her to a stop. .

Peggy said, "Please forgive me for inserting ourselves into your conversation, but I heard you talk about the Gatling gun and I was wondering if you saw a sailor who might have been teaching that thing?"

One answered, surprised she would know Jake, and "You mean Jake? Now there's a prize young man. We were up at Fort Two Rivers waiting to come south and talked to the soldier who came up with him. They used a cabin on the ship to avoid losing parts. Once, he was blindfolded and still beat that lunk of a sergeant. General Patterson even tried to get him assigned to the army, but that was a no go."

Tears filled Peggy's eyes and she turned her head, Evelyn informed the pair that "He is her friend." The two nodded as Peggy wiped her eyes.

The one who talked, added, "Well, Miss, he's one fine man, and he's quick on that gun. He told us he had to use it once down at Natchez. Were you there then?"

"That wasn't at Natchez, that was Vicksburg. There was a gunboat, one of those low things, which stopped us and told us he was going to board us. Jacob fired that thing and the captain said their captain would be our target. He let us go."

The soldier smiled. "Yes, Ma'am. That's what he said. I told you that to test you. Sometimes, people hear things and claim they were involved. He also said something about a pretty dress."

She blushed slightly, smiled and nodded her head.

As the ladies continued their walk, Evelyn turned her head to face Peggy. "What was that about a dress?"

"The dress you carried into the ballroom was to be my wedding dress. It was the prettiest I had. When that gunboat threatened to sink us, I put it on. I wanted to be in my best clothes if I was going to meet my maker."

Evelyn frowned for a second and asked, "Would that matter? I mean, what we wear, will we still wear it if we see God?"

"No. I was being foolish. Perhaps it distracted them for a minute. They didn't sink us."

The Patterson's home started out originally as a five room bungalow, but add-ons, due to his rank as a general with meeting requirements and social obligations, had almost turned the house into a mansion. Half of the building was living quarters. The other half, the added part, was one big room he used for his meetings, as large as some smaller hotel's ballroom, with smaller side rooms.

Peggy had grown up in the lap of luxury and had seen large houses, but when she saw this one, she stammered, "Your house is. . .nice. It's so. . .different."

Evelyn laughed. "It is that. When we bought it, Courtney was a colonel, and most of his social activities were either on the base or in his commander's house. Then he was promoted and things changed. Come, let's go inside and I can show you the rest of what we lovingly call home."

Chapter Ten

General Patterson

I got pretty well acquainted with that sailor on the way up here. I found he was being punished for something and was kept in the boiler room until we asked for him to come and instruct some of us on that gun. That night, I couldn't sleep and as I walked the deck, I found him walking too. Jake was trying to force himself to forget that pretty dark haired girl with the green eyes who had invaded his heart, the one Orville was supposed to marry.

The boat had taken on a full supply of coal from the Fort Two Rivers and, with all the men now trained on the weapon, he wasn't needed. The captain had talked to the chief in charge of the boiler room and had gotten a reprieve for Jake from his previous offenses. Now, under the watchful eye of his chief, Jake shoveled coal.

The plan was for the ship to go as far north as it could, to some fort the French had built a hundred or more years earlier. It had been abandoned because of Indian attacks. A French Catholic, Father Pierre Mondurat, had sailed up the Mississippi River with Frs. Pierre Marquette and Luis Joliet. He saw in the Indian tribes of the Mississippi River Valley his field of endeavor, while Marquette and Joliet moved on to the Great Lakes.

Fr. Mondurat had some success in his working among the Winnebagos, the Menominee and the Fox and Sauk tribes. However, the Dakota Sioux and the Hurons from Canada made war against the local tribes, causing his efforts to be frustrated. He gave up after a few years and went to join his brother missionaries, but the walls of the old fort still stood. Most of the buildings had been torn down by the Natives and used for their own buildings at other sites. But the grounds were there.

As the commanders of the field troops, I inspected the grounds and found a metal case with papers inside. I knew no French and all writings inside were in that language, so I called for someone in the forces who knew French and found one, a former high school teacher who read it for me. It was a record of an effort by the missionary to translate the New Testament into the Winnebago language. He had only the first three chapters of Matthew completed. Out of curiosity, I had my subordinates check to see if one of the Indian guides knew that language, and found one. That brought back a lot of memories, growing up in a parsonage. When I was a kid, I knew the Bible pretty well, and asked the person to read it, to check on the Frenchman's ability. It had been many years, but what I heard did resemble the English version of the Gospel of Matthew that I remembered.

It was time to get down to business. I called the staff and had the men assemble and orders were given. Supplies for five days had been established and handed out. "Go under a white flag," I ordered, the Marines didn't agree, "and <u>do not abuse it</u>. <u>Do not fire your weapons unless fired upon</u>. Find out where this Neapope is located and see if you can get him to parlay. He has to be tried for the murder of the people at Fort Hadley Brown, but don't tell him. Choose a gathering place, invite all tribes, whether they agree with him or not, and when they are assembled, we'll show them the gun. If it is as frightening to them as it was to me the first time I saw it, there'll be mass defections from his group. You have your orders. May God go with you."

I just stood there. In the thirty-five years since I joined the army that was the first time I used that name. That verse, "Train up a child. . ." came to my mind and started a whole chain of memories. I had thought very infrequently about home, wondering if our parents were still alive. Strange, the way I felt then. I looked at the ground at my feet and remembered a lot of things. The movement of the men as they dispersed had no affect on my thoughts right then. Thoughts of the church members, and what they did to my parents made me angry and I woke from the trip down memory lane. I stood by myself in the middle of the field. The troops and their commanders had gone and I looked around, somewhat embarrassed. I turned and went toward the command tent, still thinking about what happened out there.

It was a rough command post, with an army cot, a chair and a field table. I sat on the field chair in the tent and thought about Evelyn. She had done the right thing to protect that young woman from Orville, but why. What was her motivation? She had seen very little of Orville the past four years. She refused to have anything to do with him, even to converse about him if she could help it. So, why did she insert herself into his affair? The promise to deal with her/it when I got home brought up more questions—what was I going to do now when I agreed she did the right thing? But that had to wait. We had a killer to find and apprehend.

We waited three days for word, when a rider galloped into camp at full speed, shouting the enemy was running northwest toward the Canadian border. The three groups had joined and the officers were trying to decide what to do. I told the courier it was up to them since they were in the field and I was somewhat distant from them. He said they were going to try a pinchers, with one group doing a forced march straight west and another northwest, hoping to get Neapope between them. The third group was to follow the tracks, even though the wily cusses had been smart and left few of them.

No one had thought about the mosquitoes in June along the river. They were brutal. I almost ordered to keep moving rather than making camp since we had no netting to hide under. Someone mentioned a smoke fire, burning green wood. They had tried it and it seemed to work. Well, anything, even if it only kept some of them away, would be better than not. But that meant we'd have to have someone feed the fire and smell green wood burning night and day. Which is worse?

I was the ranking officer in the group of ten, with four enlisted men to do the grunt work. The Marines had been split into the three groups with O'Rourke here with me. After the breakfast of hard tack, black coffee and bacon and eggs, we crossed the river to the west side hoping to keep moving while the others searched.

Then it happened. Neapope had been found, rather stopped by several chiefs along his way. They didn't want any trouble with the big father in Washington. Members of several tribes insisted he and his sub-chiefs meet with the general. It was to take place four days journey from our present camp. The trooper stated that chiefs of several villages indicated they would be there. I was concerned about the facilities for a gathering that large.

We would have to go in a carriage. We carried the gun in the box behind the seat, in its broken-down condition. I thought it would have more of an impact when they saw someone taking a short time putting the thing together before firing it.

We, I and my subordinates, prepared for the trip and left the camp amid questions about our safety. It would have been so easy for them to lie to the troopers that he wanted to parlay, and get us out there for an ambush. One of our group expressed that fear. I said "We are on a mission of good. We will go in. . ." I paused, hesitating to mention God. That would have been twice in the same day. I was going to say we go in the protection of God. Why now? After thirty years of forgetting the people called Christians, why has it come back to me this way? I wonder if Orville is having the same difficulty.

We arrived a little later than scheduled and found the field full of various Indian tribes. I'm from the headquarters in Cincinnati and had no idea there were so many tribes in this area. Each tribe was represented by a series of flags, and there were a bunch. I knew about the Sauks for that was the tribe Neapope was from. But, there were flags surrounding a small space in the center, which must have represented a thousand people. Whoever picked the site chose a place in a small valley, so the people could stand on the sides of the hills and see everything that took place.

A group sat in a circle with no identification. I had no idea if Neapope was there or these were designated chiefs to see how we would react. I stood with my people behind me, waiting for some direction. Three chiefs in full headdress met us. One held out a long willow stick with a knob on one end. He said, "Come, we smoke pipe."

I followed him to a circle apart from another group. I didn't understand what was going on, but after a few silent minutes of passing that stick, with the others sticking it in their mouths and sucking smoke, I got the idea. It wasn't something I was happy about, but I wasn't going to offend these men, especially where there were a thousand of them and forty of us. So I sucked, and coughed, and they laughed.

We talked. I understood most of their words, as they spoke in broken English, and I got the idea they stopped Neapope because they didn't want any trouble with the army. They made it sure that I knew the treaties that were broken, but right then, they were peaceful. Well, all but one. This chief let me know he was angry. He started his rant with pretty good English he picked up in the missionary school. His village was a straggler from the Shawnee tribe and he reminded me of the way some man he called Bahd-ler and others had invaded their Ohio lands, had destroyed their Kaintuck hunting grounds, and driven them west. I asked the sergeant who he meant by Bahd-ler and he said the person was probably Simon Kenton. He led a group of adventurers west from the Pittsburgh area, and because of him, thousands of Revolutionary War veterans moved west to the new lands. Being from Cincinnati I had heard of Simon Kenton, who at one time was called Butler. Now, his people were small. The chief ranted several minutes and finally stopped.

I did not apologize, but in an awkward way, tried to say we were out there to stop trouble between their peoples and the father in Washington. I'm afraid I did a poor job, but in a little while, after they looked at each other and got a nod from the three sitting there, they pointed to another group, and I got up and walked to the other group. I stood before the other group. They didn't move.

This was to be a game, with him as the winner. When we get the gun together, we'll see how he reacts to that. Still standing, I said, "I have come to find out the reason for your attack on the fort and the murder of those men there."

One of hose sitting, whether it was the leader or not, I had no way of knowing, said in good English, "You represent a corrupt government that breaks treaties and kills Indian women and children. That's the reason I called myself George Washington. Treaty after treaty have been broken by you, all the way from the Ohio land and Kaintuck to here. In the battle of Bad Ax Creek, (he stood up waving his arms), you killed three hundred women and children when you made the Winnebago move the canoe. They had nowhere to go but to slide down the face of the cliff into the river. They all drowned," he screamed, "they drowned, women and children. That's what you did!"

We stood there during his rant and when he finished, I asked, "May we sit down?"

Angrily, he answered, "Why should I let you. We should just finish you off here and now."

I glanced back over my shoulder and saw that the sergeant and private who were working on the gun had finished, and had it set up on its tripod. I turned back to the man who was talking, and said, "I have something to show you. Come with me." He didn't move. I smiled and said, "Have it your way." I turned to an officer standing near me and said, "Get the eye glasses."

He left for the wagon we came in and brought a bag, which contained four long-range, single tube magnifying glasses. I took one and scanned the horizon and out about six hundred yards I saw a small tree, with a trunk I guessed to be about six inches in diameter. I gave my glass to the sergeant and told him the direction to scan. He did and saw the tree. I said, "That's the target. Strip it."

He knelt behind the gun with the glass focused along the barrels and turned the crank for one shot. He watched it hit the tree and waited. I handed three glasses to three obvious chiefs and told them where to look. As they focused on something out there, I said, "Go." The sergeant turned the crank, slowly so as to not affect the direction he was firing until the feeder tube was empty.

I turned to look at the men with the spy glass and they stood open-mouth, eyes wide. A thousand Indians were chattering in some Indian dialect. They dropped the glass and almost as one, a thousand

Indians left the scene. The only ones who remained were the eight men who sat in a circle on the ground ahead of me. They didn't, or couldn't, move.

I ordered the sergeant to put a new tube in the gun and told those sitting to stand up, they were under arrest for murder. Slowly they got up, looking at the gun aimed in their direction. Only one had a smirk on his face and I took that to be G W Neapope. I walked over to him and said, "You are under arrest for murder of a hundred twenty seven good men. Walk over to the buggy. Now." He spit at me.

I looked at his friends and said, "You tie him up, or you're going in too."

Neapope pulled a twelve-inch knife from his belt and reached for one of his former friends. The sergeant, still with the gun, cranked out two shots into the ground in Neapope's direction and he dropped the knife and stood still.

I spoke to the others. "This is powerful medicine. Don't fight against it again. If some other comes to you and wants to rebel against the father in Washington, saying that we are a foreign government, don't believe them. We do not want to fight you, but we will if you attack any more of our forts. The white man is coming. There is a place called Europe and they are coming from there to find greener pastures and better land. I just wish there was a better way."

We bound Neapope and loaded him into the carriage, broke the gun down again and it and the sergeant rode in the box behind the seats. I rode his horse. For four days the sergeant had to listen to Neapope rant about justice and unfairness of the white man. We made it back to the rough camp by evening of the fourth day and loaded aboard the ship. I wanted to get to Two Rivers as soon as possible. I hadn't bathed in over a week.

I filed my report from Two Rivers and waited for orders. G W Neapope was turned over to the guards and was destined for the lockup at Jefferson Barracks near St. Louis. I would have the enjoyment of listening to him rant another day or so. I guess he has a right to squawk. We haven't honored the treaties with the Natives very well. I hope they tell me to come home, but, since fighting had started with the Confederate States, I might go anywhere. The cable told of fighting in Virginia, probably at some of the places Evelyn and I visited early in our marriage. When I get to St. Louis I'll have to buy her something.

It has been three weeks since that incident in St. Louis when I told her I'd deal with her when I get home. I wonder what I will find. She's been so compliant over the years, it's hard for me to imagine any difficulty, but, I'll find out within the hour. I guess I'll go report in to see if my status has changed, and then go home. What will I find? What will she say? Will she apologize for interfering in Orville's wedding, or is that something that will be a bone of contention with us? Does it have to be? She has been a good wife, a good friend and mother to our four. I have to think about my future—what do I want to have as a home after this meeting?

Chapter Eleven

Evelyn Patterson

Once home, we ladies enjoyed a cup of hot tea and talked for a few minutes. We were exhausted from the trip and from the emotion of the wedding involvement. After tea it was time for bed, with the agreement no one was to move before nine o'clock the next morning. I showed our guest to her room and closed the door, without latching it, hoping for a night time breeze to counter the stifling humidity that occurs along the river during late spring and summer.

With Peggy tucked in and the lamps turned down low, I went to the kitchen, which opened to a screened patio and sat. "What do I do now? After thirty years of marriage, will it all end when Courtney gets home? What I did was right. How do I convince him of that?"

I looked out across their yard. We couldn't see the Ohio River, but could hear the chug of the engines and the whistles as boats moved east and west along that body of water. It had been a pleasant home, high on a bluff with smaller hills blocking our view of the river. The back yard with its flower gardens, the shade trees that block both the early morning and late evening sun, were our combined ideas. It is our home, our decorating ideas. Not that we hadn't seen some interesting places and taken ideas from those visited, but it was our interpretation, after talking about what we saw, of those things.

No need to dwell on that. If it happens, it will happen. If we can get past this, I'll once again be the compliant wife.

When the general was assigned to this camp, he said it would be his last move, that we had been across the country serving the needs of the government long enough. My mind went back over the years—Florida, Texas and eventually Mexico with General Scott, the west, roughing it with the Indian patrols to California to work with John C Fremont. It had been interesting if not exciting. And now, another "engagement," another challenge. This one seems serious, with the salvation of the State at stake. Why would they start it? They can't possibly win, and a lot of men will die.

What will Courtney's situation be? He's second in command here. He has a lot of experience, as have all other generals at his level, but he's never commanded a field operation. He's been called an "idea man," someone who can think and create. But that's a thought for another time. Right now, I have a problem. What will happen when he gets home? I guess I'll have to start getting my things in order starting tomorrow. I'll pack my things as many as I can and get ready to go. And I'll have to do it without Peggy knowing about it. Perhaps, if he sees the suit cases at the door when he comes in, maybe that will cause him to think. I'll keep them in my room until then. One problem—when will he get home?

There's another fly in the ointment. I encouraged Peggy to come home with me to get a job as a teacher. I know some people, but I don't know what influence they might have in teacher selection. I'll have to bring some together at a party, and let them see her. That will be a start. To some men, if they see her, as pretty as she is, she wouldn't have to do more than spell her name and they'd hire her.

I wish I could have helped Rose a little more. Such a sweet girl and such miserable circumstances. With her mother so sick, she'll probably become the mom if anything happens. Living where she does, what chance does she have for a happy life? She'll marry soon and become just like her mother. That's one thing I can't solve.

Peggy talks a lot about praying, about casting your every care upon the Lord. I wish I knew how to do that. She said just talk to Him, He'll understand. She prayed with me and said my sins are gone. I wish I could understand that, how by simply praying your sins are gone. Without doing anything as payback.? I've been a good woman, never cheating on my husband or even gossiping with the other wives, so I don't know what sins I might have. But she quoted something about all having sinned, so I guess I'm in that group. But to simply ask God and it's done? It seems so simple. There must be more to it than that. Perhaps if I start going to church I'll learn more of what this is all about.

Peggy O'Neal

The trip from St. Louis was both delightful and depressing. I am not Mrs. Orville Patterson. I'm still Peggy O'Neal, Miss Peggy O'Neal. The more I hear of what happened while Rose and I were in Evelyn's room makes me wonder what would have happened to me if I had refused to drink his liquor. It's frightening. And, according to what Evelyn said, and she has known him for thirty years, he delights in destroying a girl, or woman who has some strong convictions. Evelyn told me a little about their childhood. His actions must be in response to the way they were treated.

Evelyn is a wonderful person, but I can tell her life is changing, has changed. Perhaps she responded to the little God-window we all have. If we listen to it, it becomes stronger. You know, when she prayed for someone to help her and You sent Rose, that was the beginning of a new life for her. Now, will her husband follow? And Orville, how could he be what he has become, coming from the same home as the general?

When I heard about Jacob and how You used him to teach others, that was delightful, and even if it was something to kill other men, I was excited. I could feel a quickness in my heart. Isn't it strange that someone I met and knew for only four days would have such an impact on my feelings? Oh, that I might see him again, I miss him so. Would You make it possible? And now that he will be fighting in a war against people I know, how will I handle that? Oh, if it were not so.

Now that I am here, what do I do? Evelyn. . .I know I'm supposed to honor my elders and call her Mrs. Patterson, but that seems so formal for someone who is so down to earth. As I said, Evelyn has introduced me to several of their friends, all military, and all seemingly using the party to ingratiate themselves to the general's wife. I watched to see how she handled all the buttering, and she smiled, being gracious on the outside. I wonder how she felt on the inside.

She did get me connected to two schools and I met with the school board of each institution. Each group had a man as the chairman, and each group promised full support in the school. Each school board had one older man who watched me with eyes that made me feel nervous. Most of the schools in the area now are one-room schools and have classes of thirty-five to fifty. The salary in the one of thirty-five children is two hundred twenty-five dollars. Add another fifty dollars to the salary of the one with fifty students. The school year in each school is one hundred eighty days. Any days off because of weather will have to be made up at the end of the year. The problem will be setting up classes for all the grades, one through eight, for the whole year. Fortunately, I'd have two months to get organized.

I like Evelyn. She came with me to each of the meetings and, having lived in Cincinnati for some time, knew what questions to ask when a statement was made about living conditions. In one school, I would have to pay rent, which would take a good part of my salary. Evelyn came up with an answer—I move in with them after she and her husband settle any difficulty about her meddling in Orville's life. Moving in with them would create another problem—how to get there. That's easy, she said. We have a barn, a horse and a buggy. It's two miles to one school and a little more than that to the other. Of course, that would mean I would have to learn to harness the animal and I've never done that in my life. Oh, my, do I want to do this?

She apparently read my concern for she said, she would help me learn the way if I felt I had to. They have an outside man who does all that and more. The question I asked her was "How soon will that be? Soon, very soon. You'll be with us, or I'll be with you."

I didn't like the sound of that, but said nothing. But it worried me. Was she willing to give up her marriage without a battle because of me? Perhaps I need to go back to my home in Pennsylvania. Maybe Daddy will be there if he can get away from New Orleans. Certainly they won't hold him because he's a northerner. He's a doctor and they might consider him an enemy civilian. One thing that worries me, they might not let him go and make him minister to the wounded from the battles. Evelyn told me of the Rebel's prison camp at Andersonville, Georgia. That's a terrible place. They might send him there.

I pray for him as I pray for Jacob, and my faith needs a boost sometimes. How can a war solve anything? How can killing people be a solution to any kind of question? Well, perhaps there are some instances, but not that many.

I dread the day the general gets home for that will be the day I find out my fate. I can't imagine that he'll be pleased to see me, especially since I heard him basically threaten Evelyn as he went up that ramp. I don't want to be the cause of their marriage ending. I guess that's not my fault, but it is in a way. If Evelyn hadn't been so absolute about me and keeping me from marrying Orville, I'd be married, and we'd be having our first fight, but she'd be home safe.

I've had a good education, the best, but I've never dealt with other people very much, especially children. And how do I deal with those two men, should it come to that. I'll have to set some specific rules that. . .Jacob! I can tell them my intended is in the navy and we'll be married when he is free from his obligation. Lord, that's only a little lie. Is that so bad? I intend to marry him, if. . .Oh, Lord, please make it possible. Oh, my, how can I be so distressed, confused about a situation? Oh, I want to see him.

Jake Prosser

Another day in the pit shoveling coal. At least that's better than fighting the different sizes of wood chinks. The dried stuff burns so fast it hardly seems worthwhile using it. But coal is hard to find, except at army bases or ports along the river. And dirty! I smile every time I think of how Miss O'Neal looked when I showed up at her door that last time aboard the ship. She must have known it was me.

No one else would have shown up at her door, especially with the captain the way he was.

We've been up the river for a week now, as the general and the army chase that guy, what's his name, George Washington Neapope? They'll find him and when they assemble the gun and show it off, that should change some minds. I can't imagine any Indian, no matter how much he hates this country, going against that gun. It's just. . .it's just. . .devastating. Whoever thought of putting six barrels together that rotate to keep one from getting too hot, is a pure genius. And to have a tube feed cartridges to time it with the turning of the barrels, man, he is sure smart. And then to have the crank trigger the firing, it's almost beyond my ability to imagine. But, I'm one of a few who can take it down and put it back together, and do it blindfolded.

I wish I knew what my future held. I hope I don't spend the rest of my four years in the boiler room shoveling coal. I'd have to spend most of my money for clothes. And never get away from the smell. What woman would want to meet a man with that kind of stench hanging over him? Naw, I suppose for four years I'll be without any chance to meet a woman or, for that matter, anyone. But I'm here. Hmmm, come to think of it, that Miss O'Neal didn't seem to mind my being near her. I wonder where she is now. I guess she's married and they probably are off someplace on a honeymoon. I wonder if I'll ever meet another woman like her. No, not like her. Not even close.

I heard someone talking to Captain Thomas about me. He was holding a piece of paper and said that some of the rams are getting the gun and they want me to train them. I saw a ram, once. It's barely two feet out of the water, like the Monitor and the Merrimac back east. It has two or three guns in front, I think about a twenty pounder, and it rams other ships. The other ships can't shoot at it because it's so low in the water. What would a Gatling gun do on a ram vessel? I don't know, unless it would be to rake the deck of the other ship to keep sailors from shooting down on us.

If I was transferred to one of those warships, at least I'd get away from the chief and his anger at me. If he had met someone like

Miss O'Neal, he'd spend time thinking about her too. I think I've done pretty well in living in the reality that I'll never see her again. I mean, how can that possibly happen? She's married to some guy in St. Louis, and I'm in the navy, heading for some fight. I have to hope there might be another Peggy O'Neal with a different name, somewhere waiting for me.

What did she say to me there on the dock in St. Louis, that I've shown her what love might be like? I could show her a whole lot more given the opportunity, but that will never happen. Well, what's the use of thinking about her? We said goodbye, and that probably is the last I'll see of her.

Now, to think of what I heard and what it means. It probably means I'll be put on some warship and get into some fight somewhere. Guess I can only wait until it's announced.

There's the general and the rest of the army with an Indian. I guess I'll find out pretty soon what's going to happen, good or bad.

Chapter Twelve

Jake stood before Captain Thomas, and Captain James Montgomery, commander of the U S Northern River fleet, and listened to the commander read from a piece of notebook paper. Jake, wore his dress Shelljacket and white pants, stood before the captain, who was dressed in his Senior Commander's Frock coat, with brass buttons and shoulder boards and epaulets.

"Jake Prosser, because of your tireless devotion to extra duty as gunnery instructor, which was most effectively done, in addition to your regular duties of a coal heaver, I issue you this day a temporary promotion to Gunnery Mate, with a salary of twenty-seven dollars a month, and a transfer to the USS Quonset as general Gatling gun instructor. I say temporary, because there are some qualifications that must be fulfilled to make it permanent. Those qualifications are listed in this booklet," and he handed Jake a booklet of four pages, with the title "*QUALIFICATIONS NECESSARY TO RENDER MEN ELIGIBLE AS SEAMEN GUNNERS.*"

The commander continued, "Tell me, Jake, are you a hunter?"

Jake hesitated, "Well, I've hunted some, but all we had was an old musket, and it was too much bother."

"And how were you as a student? Did you complete your preparatory classes?"

"Yes, Sir, I knew I was going to join the Navy and so I studied hard."

"Good. Now, Jake, there are standards for this position. Those standards are identified in item number four of your paper. Within a period of four weeks, you will be tested for your ability with small arms, in addition to your knowledge of standard and Decimal Fractions and the use of Logarithms. Do you think you can handle those things?"

"It's been three years since school, but, yes, I believe I can."

"Your new duties will include, but not be restricted to, teaching specified sailors within the command, first, how to use the weapon effectively and safely, and second, how to set up the gunnery command post on each vessel in the command. Congratulations, Gunnery Mate Prosser, and welcome to your new home."

Jake stood there, afraid to say anything, because he was completely surprised at the announcement. He had been told at breakfast that he was to dress in his best uniform. It was a uniform he had never worn, since he spent most of his time, until the special assignment, in the boiler room, "heaving" coal. Before that, as an Ordinary Seaman, he spent a lot of time swabbing the deck of his ship. The commander waited for a few seconds, and finally asked, "Mr. Prosser, have you nothing to say?"

"Excuse me, Sir," Jake apologized, "I'm so surprised I couldn't think for a minute. But, thank you, Sir, thank you very much." Jake saluted as the commander held out his hand, then recovered and accepted the hand shake.

"Isn't there something else you would like to say?"

Jake stood, now getting uncomfortable with the questions, and stammered, "I. . .I'm not sure, Sir."

The commander smiled, "Can you use the extra money?"

Jake heaved a sigh of relief, not being sure what the commander was getting at. "Oh yes Sir, oh indeed. I'm saving my money for a farm outside of Cincinnati. Before my time is over, I should have enough for the farm and some animals."

"That's good thinking, Sailor. Of course, we never can predict what might happen, but here on the rivers one should be pretty safe."

"Yes, Sir."

Captain Montgomery handed Jake an envelope and said, "These are your orders. Report to the Quonset by oh-eight-hundred-hours tomorrow. Until then, you're free."

"Yes Sir. Thank you Sir." Jake saluted and the two captains turned to go, leaving Jake standing by himself. He didn't drink, and he had money, so what could he do? His first thought was to buy a present for his. . .but he didn't have a girl friend. He decided to send his mother a present and a letter. With that decision, he found a jewelry store and bought his mother a nice pin and sent it, with a note, to his home. As he mailed it, he realized this was his first letter home since he enlisted. Perhaps his parents would look on it as a sort of peace offering.

A second stop was at a book store. He wanted to get a Bible. Peggy was so positive about having one that made him want one too. He had never owned one, and, except as a child one year in some Sunday school, had not seen one until the one Peggy O'Neal showed him. What was that Scripture she read him? John, something. That night before he went to his old bed, Jake found the John something he was looking for and read it again and again. He went to sleep thinking "(3:16) For God so loved the world that He gave His only begotten Son, that whosoever believeth in Him should not perish but have everlasting life. (17) For God sent not His Son into the world to condemn the world, but that the world through Him might be saved."

The next morning, Jake stood alongside the USS Quonset and looked at his new home. It was two hundred-twenty-eight tons, one-hundred-ninety feet long, double side-wheeler, capable of fourteen miles an hour on the Mississippi. Going downstream, the speed was higher, depending on the river flow. He looked at it with admiration. It was shorter than his first ship—GREAT EXPECTATIONS—but so much more powerful. The G E, as the sailors preferred to call it, was a transport conversion, with an open area below and two decks of cabins above. It had one small gun at the front and one aft, but they weren't for overpowering an enemy, but for defense.

The Quonset was a "Ram." The nose of the ship was heavy plated steel. It's mode of attack was to ram the side of a wooden vessel, or even a thin-plated ironsides, and, with that contact, blow the side open with its cannon, two twenty-pounders at the front of the ship. For broadside attacks, the ship had four thirty pounder cannons on each side. The Navy used two basic guns—a thirty pounder and a twenty pounder. The thirty pound cannon could fire a twenty-nine pound shell sixty-seven hundred yards, or almost four miles. Up close it would be devastating. The twenty pounder fires a nineteen pound shell about two and one half miles. The "Captain's Deck" was atop the structure, between the two massive side wheels. As he studied the ship, he could envision two places for mounting the Gatling gun—aft, between the smoke stacks or in front of the wheelhouse.

Jake waited for the flag to be raised before climbing the ramp. He stopped at the top of the ramp, saluted the flag and then the ensign receiving him. He walked onto the ship with his most exciting challenge—teaching the most powerful hand weapon the Navy was getting, to men, some who were as old as his father. He had the class roster and glanced down the list. Everyman on the list was a Chief Gunner, a Gunner's Mate or a Quarter Gunner, all with more than ten years in the Navy. Jake closed his eyes and slowly shook his head.

"How am I going to teach these men? I know the gun, but they won't believe anything I say."

He found his quarters. Crew quarters were small, the largest was the captain's, followed by his staff. Enlisted men's rooms were ten feet square with a double bunk against one wall and dressers along two other walls. The bottom bunk in his room had clothes on it, so he concluded the top bunk was his. Crew quarters were in the middle of the ship, below the wheelhouse. The mess hall was there too. His room had one small window, or port, and two small, three-drawer dressers. The small amount of clothes he had would fit in one dresser drawer with space left over. He placed his Bible on top. Then, with a bound, he landed on the upper bunk.

His thoughts flashed from one thing to another, with much of the time having Peggy as the focal point. Try as he might, he could not get her out of his thoughts, and, try as he might, he saw no way of ever seeing her again. It haunted him, the idea that she, a married woman, took up so much of his thoughts.

He heard a bo's'n pipe and knew it was time for lights out. Supper had been a meal of beef gravy on bread, a serving of green beans and coffee. He had eaten by himself, watching the men come in together, laughing and having fun—until they got to the food line. With the comments Jake heard from the others, he gathered this was a regular offering. It was edible and it was food. He ate it.

He was asleep quickly and was awakened sometime during the night when two drunken sailors banged on his door and stumbled, laughing and cursing, into his room. One flopped onto the bottom bunk as the other tried to climb up to the upper bunk, but was unable because of his inebriation. Jake lit a match, which brought another round of shouts and swearing. The man on the bottom bunk swore and asked, "Who are you?"

"My name is Jake Prosser. I'm here to teach the use of the Gatling gun."

"Why are you here? We don't need you. Git out so we can get to sleep."

"I was assigned to this room. Since the bottom bunk seemed to be occupied, I took the top bunk, but this is my room, I was appointed here, so I stay."

That brought on louder cursing. With the door still open, the noise attracted the attention of the night watch, who stopped by. The smell of liquor, the cursing that was taking place and the rowdiness of the two, made him blow a whistle, bringing the captain of the watch. Jake proved who he was and who told him about the room. The two were led away, still cursing at the invader of the room.

The only room large enough for the class of twenty-two people was the mess hall, and that is where Jake's class was to be held. When breakfast was over and the tables cleared, the weapon was brought in and tables moved to present an idea of classroom. A board had been brought aboard from land and used as a backing for note paper. A tablet had been made by nailing butcher paper to the board and Jake was given a box of crayons to write with.

Jake came in while the "students" were milling around and when they saw him, froze, every eye on the new person. Jake saw twenty men, most as old as his father, with ten or more years in the Navy. He looked at his class roster and called the class to order.

"Please take a chair so we can get started." Only a few moved to find a chair. Jake bit his lip and said, "This class is for the purpose of teaching you about the new gun. It is a multi-bullet weapon, with a stack to feed the firing mechanism. You—"

Someone interrupted him. "You're the one that put Stump and Bobby in the brig."

Jake was taken back with the charge and quickly became defensive. "No, I didn't! They came into the room drunk, cussing and shouting. One was so drunk he couldn't climb up to the top bunk. They left the door open and their noise brought the night watch. I didn't say a word. What they did and where they are is totally their fault." He paused and looked at the roster, "I see two, no three Roberts. What's that one's last name?"

No one spoke, so Jake leaned against a table and said, "Look, I had nothing to do with those two men being in the brig now. I was given that room to bunk in. The bottom bunk had clothes on it, the upper was bare, so I threw my stuff in the drawers and took it. Now, you guys have been selected to teach your people about this new weapon. It's a terror, more fearful than anything you ever saw. It will cut down a six inch tree at a thousand yards. But, you have to have instruction on it. That's why I'm here. I did not set up this class. Captain Montgomery is responsible for that. If you object to my being here, contact him, or Captain Laughlin, the captain of this ship. Now, I am going to take roll. If you do not answer, or if you use some other name than your own, I will take that to the captain and let him deal with it. You won't see me again, but you will miss out on learning the most dangerous weapon in our arsenal."

Someone laughed. "We hear that about every weapon we have. What makes this one so special?

Jake looked at the man who questioned and around the room at the other who had various degrees of smiles. "You'll learn the capabilities through the instruction, but let me tell of an incident as we were coming north. The war started after we were underway. As we approached Vicksburg, a Rebel Ram met us, threatening to board us. The captain said no. I got to the gun placement and cranked off half a dozen rounds into the river. Their captain stopped and, when Captain Thomas threatened him as the first target, he let us go. It's devastating, it is so powerful. Now sit down so we can get started."

He started reading the list of names for the class, pausing after each name to get a mental image of the one who answered. The men started moving toward chairs, objecting to what was taking place, but accepting that there was nothing they could do about it.

A gun had been set up by the ship's crew, who were told to wait in the back ground for any further instructions. Jake stood in front of the weapon and described it, as best he could, without using technical terms. "It fires a 45/70, 350 grain cartridge. Shells are gravity fed into each breech through a hopper, or stack feed, on top of the gun. The current hopper holds fifty cartridges, although there is a double-stack feed being tested which will enable the weapon handler to fire continuously, up to twelve hundred rounds per minute." He heard several men gasp at that.

"Of course, you will have to have two men reload the empty stack as you continue to fire. Now, are there any questions before I go on?" He moved around the gun as it sat on the tripod, which had one long leg of heavy steel pointed ahead and two of the same material spread behind as support. He pointed to the six barrels.

"The kind of heat generated by fifty cartridges like that would melt one barrel, so six barrels are used." He held the crank and said, "I won't go in to the gearing mechanism of the weapon except to say it works. Turning the crank rotates the shaft, changing barrels. Cartridges drop individually into the groove of the feed for each barrel. The firing mechanism is then sealed to contain the gasses for propulsion. It is instantaneous. Each barrel contains the firing mechanism to explode the charge and drop the spent cartridge on the ground."

The men sat staring at the gun, some with their mouths open, unable to believe what Jake had told them. "Tomorrow, we'll take it apart so you can see how it works."

Chapter Thirteen

General Courtney Clay Patterson, home from the wars in the north, faced another in his home. He had battled these thoughts for two days. First, she needs to be taught a lesson, countered with the thought that she did the right thing. But he, as a general, couldn't allow his wife to cause dissention among people close to him—his brother or other military. Of course, the unknown was, at least to him, how she would react to his decision.

He mounted the steps to his front door, opened it and stepped inside. Their home had a short hallway leading to a parlor on the right and a larger living room on the left. The hallway then extended back to the dining room and kitchen. Staring at him as he stood just inside the door, were five traveling bags, three he recognized and two he did not. His wife stood at the corner of the living room, dressed in traveling clothes, with a light coat draped over her arm. She wore clothes he had seen many times before—a chocolate skirt and outing jacket. She said nothing, waiting for his reaction.

After several seconds, he realized what was taking place and said, "These are yours?"

"Mine and Miss O'Neal's."

"Can't we talk about this?"

"The last thing I heard you say was you would deal with it when you got home. I assumed you were so angry you meant to have me either apologize to Orville or you would take drastic action. I <u>will</u>

not apologize. What he was planning, what he has done in the past, is wrong. I refused to let an innocent girl get torn up because of the greed of her father or the lust of the man she was sold to. If it happens again, I will have the same response the next time."

He looked at her and saw the determination in her face. He drew his lips tight and looked at the floor. Raising his head to face her and nodding towards the extra suit cases, he said, "Those hers?"

Peggy stepped out from the corner of the living room on the right and stood in the middle of the hallway. Dressed much as Evelyn, Peggy wore a traveling suit of burgundy, with a lace-edged blouse. She greeted him, "Hello, General Patterson."

He had a rush of thoughts, from her having no business being here to how pretty she was. He paused while he sorted out his thoughts and finally said, "Good day, Miss O'Neal. I trust you are well today."

"Yes, thank you, General."

Evelyn broke in with "Miss O'Neal has been staying with me while you've been gone. She has a job teaching school at Fillmore, and will start in three weeks. We went shopping for a horse and carriage for her yesterday and found one, at what I consider a good price. Dependent. . .no, I won't say any more. The decision is yours."

"What does this luggage mean? Are you leaving me?"

"You said you would deal with me when you got home. You were unhappy, almost angry. I didn't know if you were going to send me off or what you intended to do."

"Send you off? Woman, why would I do that?" He spoke loudly and paused to use a different approach. "That was an emotional time for me. You were adamant about helping her, and I was just as determined that you didn't get involved. With a war threatening and my involvement there, I let my emotions get carried away. As far as sending you away, I would be a fool to destroy thirty years of life because of some perceived slight to my brother." He smiled slightly, "How would I bake for the next staff meeting?"

"Is that all I am, a cook and bottle washer, who prepares the house for your staff meetings and gives you some comfort when you need a person to talk to?"

Courtney sighed, deeply. "That was a mistake. I was trying to ease the tension. Look, can't we sit down?"

The parlor was a small room, fifteen by fifteen feet, with one curtained window and a tied drape across the opening. It had a picture of Mr. and Mrs. Courtney Patterson on their wedding day, she sitting and he standing, holding his officer's hat across his chest. There was a small table, three chairs, and an upholstered love seat. Peggy waited to move to a chair until she was invited, and then took one away from the other two.

The general said, "Let's start over. I came into the house and see five bags, indicating someone was going somewhere. I had been bothered for two days with the thoughts about what you did, thoughts that told me you shouldn't have involved yourself in Orville's affairs, but that you did the right thing. Now, I seem to have made it worse by my stupid comment."

He shifted his position to face her directly, leaning his elbows on his knees. "Evelyn, we have thirty years of marriage behind us, thirty good years, with four lovely children. The thought of you leaving me over something like this is beyond. . .I can't imagine that happening. It can't happen. I love you, have loved you since before we were married, and the thought of living without you would be. . .I would give up my military life to save our marriage."

Shocked, Evelyn's hand flew to her mouth and she exclaimed, "You would do that. . .retire and give up your rank to save our marriage? Courtney, I have never asked that. All I wanted was for you to accept that I have thoughts and opinions too. My thought, my opinion was that Orville didn't deserve a chance to ruin another life after what he did to Virginia. I had to try to stop it."

He nodded deeply, silently. After a short pause, he said, "And you did." He looked at the woman whose life he had shared for thirty years and said, "You know, I'm glad you did. I mean, apparently I have taken you for granted for a long time. My being a general and giving orders has carried to my nest, your nest, and it wasn't supposed to. It won't any more." He looked at Peggy, and back at his wife. "What have you decided with our guest?"

"She has been staying in the guest room while you've been gone. That might be inconvenient with her teaching. I thought we could set up one of the side rooms off the main hall for her. There's a kitchen there and she would be away from us if she needed to have guests. We have our yard man, who helps me with harnessing when you are gone and I would imagine Simon would be willing to help her."

His head bobbed three or four times. "You know, during the winter we don't heat that big hall except when there's a meeting. What will she do for heat in her corner of the world?"

"We went to the hardware store and ordered a stove for her." His open mouth was clue for further explanation. "Now, wait until I have explained a little more. She needs her own space. There will be times she will have to rest. It's going to be rather exhausting the first few weeks, so I thought that during the winter months, I could have her room heated and prepared for a tired body. And, when you are gone, she would be someone I could talk to."

He smiled. "You have it well thought out." He nodded and raised his eyebrows, "What with the war we seem to be in, my orders may change too, so I guess your thoughts are good. When is the stove coming? Have you considered stove pipe?"

"The stove is coming tomorrow, and seal for the opening in the roof." Before he could ask the next question, she added, "Simon says he knows someone who can put the stove pipe through the roof."

"And seal it?"

"He says so."

"Could it be tied into the one that's up there, in the attic instead of cutting a new hole?"

"I didn't think to ask him that."

"All right. Miss O'Neal is going to stay with us, in a room off the main hall. How far is the school you'll be teaching at?"

"Two miles." Peggy paused then quickly added, "Is that a problem?"

"No, I was just wondering what neighborhoods she would be going through. There will be conscription for the war, and that might mean some policemen will be called up."

Evelyn glanced at Peggy then back at her husband. "We've been through this before. Do you think it's going to be bad?"

"On July sixteen, at a place called Manassas. We sent a force against one of their better generals, Joe Johnston. He's a smart tactician. I met him once at a conference, when we were in Texas. We were doing all right until they brought in reserves from somewhere. Then they routed us. We had over three thousand casualties. I don't know what they had."

Evelyn clasped her hands against her chest. "Oh, my. Then you don't think this will be over in a few weeks like Mexico."

"Pro'bly not."

The three were silent for some time, each with his own thoughts. Evelyn broke the silence with "Dear, do you think—"

"I don't know. I'm a general in an army that has just lost a battle. There will be a shake-up. President Lincoln can't let this go without some response. There have been skirmishes in Missouri and naval battles off the coast of Virginia, but Manassas, or Bull Run, as they call it, is the only major land operation. There will be more. Many more. As enthused as the rebels are with this victory, we may be on the defensive for a while."

Evelyn looked at Peggy and back at her husband, "As uncertain as your future seems, I'm glad Peggy, Miss O'Neal has agreed to stay here."

"Yes," he agreed, "it will give you someone to talk to. I have to go out to the base and see what my orders are, see if I'll stay here or go somewhere else."

He stood and said, "Now, will you put these cases away. I don't want to have to worry about the possibility of losing you, especially at this time."

"Yes dear." She had a slight smile as she continued, "I prayed this would turn out all right."

That stopped him. He had turned toward the door and now, slowly, he turned back to face her. "You prayed? You know how I feel about that."

"Yes, dear, I do. I prayed in St. Louis for someone to help and found Rose. I'll tell you about the whole process when you come back. And I prayed during these days waiting for you. And with the war situation, I am going to pray more. In fact, Miss O'Neal has suggested we have a Bible study in one of those side rooms."

He looked from Evelyn to Peggy and back again. His first reaction appeared to be anger as he thought of all those years in the parsonage, where the church members were so unkind, both to his parents and to the two boys. There was nothing but criticism and hateful suggestions about how the father should preach and how he should raise the two boys. Several seconds passed before he spoke. "Do what you will." With that, he left.

Tears came to Evelyn's eyes and she reached into an apron pocket for a handkerchief. Peggy stood and touched his wife's arm. "Perhaps it would be better for me to go somewhere else. My being here has brought nothing but unhappiness to you. I don't want any more of that, so I'll just leave. I can find another place to stay, perhaps in the home of one of the children's parents."

"No! You will not leave. If Courtney has to go somewhere else, I won't be able to follow him this time. I'll have to stay and I want you to stay with me. We might have to have that Bible study on nights when he is at the base, but we are going to have it." She paused for a second, "If you still want to do it."

"Oh, I do. But I don't want to cause you any more trouble."

Evelyn smiled, "You haven't caused me any trouble, dear girl, you have been the bright spot in my recent days. If I may, I would like to look at you as my fifth child. Oh, I'm not going to dote on you or try to run your life, but I want you in my home. I just feel that right now, especially, we need to think about prayer and God."

Hesitantly, Peggy asked, "Would you like to pray now?"

"Especially now."

Peggy looked at the room. "I try to kneel when I pray. It's just some idea that I had when I was converted, and it's only for me. If you don't want to kneel, we can sit in the chairs." Evelyn nodded and they drew two chairs close to each other so the ladies could pray and hold hands. Peggy fervently prayed for the general and for whatever area he might go to. Then, she prayed for Evelyn, that God would give her strength and wisdom to be a leader among the people. Then she prayed for herself, that God would guide and help her in her teaching assignments.

When she said "Amen," there were tears in both their eyes. Evelyn reached out and pulled Peggy close to her and whispered, "Thank you." After a moment of tenderness, she added, "Now, let's go get your room ready."

They stood in the doorway of a room, perhaps thirty feet square, but bare of furniture, except for a table and two dozen chairs. There were two small windows, high up in the wall on the long side of the room and a small broom closet in one corner. They walked through that room to a smaller room behind it. This room was smaller, fifteen by fifteen feet, with more windows high up on the wall. This would be the room Peggy would live in.

Peggy had never had to make decisions about furnishings before as that was done by her father and his servants, or the people he hired to do the job. She clasped her hands at her chin and looked at Evelyn. "Oh, my, I have no idea where to start or how to decorate."

Evelyn's head bobbed, "Fortunately, this isn't my first one. Our first apartment was this empty when we got ready to move in and this will be a challenge much like that." She put her hand to her chin. "Curtains and drapes. We'll need a bed and a dresser, and a room divider. I suppose we can use that table, you'll have to have one for your school work. And an armoire. Can you think of anything else? There are three of these rooms around the large room. What would you think of making a doorway between this room and the next one? Then you could sleep in one and live in the other."

"No, but could we take it a little slower? You're so far ahead of me my mind is throbbing trying to keep up with your suggestions." She giggled a little nervous laugh. "Could we just take the room apart and talk about each corner and what you suggest? And what would the general say to knocking a hole in the wall between these two rooms. You better talk to him first."

Evelyn agreed and the two of them took each corner of the room and methodically established what was to go where. Then they looked at the room next to it, with the prospect of using that one too.

It took an hour, but both were satisfied when they were done. Now, came the hard part—spending the money for what they decided.

Chapter Fourteen

Jake finished the class he was teaching and, by that time, all the older men in the class respected him for his knowledge of the weapon. He set up the gun on the fantail of the Quonset and let each of the men fire five bullets into the river, just to get a feeling of turning the crank and making it work. They were tied up at St. Louis and the Quonset Captain had alerted the police as to what might happen. As expected, there were reports of some kind of war along the river front.

Missouri had become a battlefield as Pro-slave and Anti-slave armies battled for their beliefs. Across the state, from St. Louis to Kansas City and south to Arkansas, these groups fought. Only the Missouri River was deep enough to handle the Quonset-type ships, and Jake was in no position to know anything about battle plans for that area. He was on a mission, an assignment, to teach sailors about the Gatling gun. Soon, some of the ships along the rivers patrolled by the North would be getting that weapon and their sailors needed to understand how it worked.

The war in the east had paused after the battle of Bull Run. Federal forces were in such disarray that higher officers decided more training was required, and got President Lincoln's approval. Naval activity consisted of shelling Rebel bases along the coast line around Virginia and New Orleans.

Jake finished his class in a week. For the most part, the men realized they had an incredible new weapon, one that could change the outcome of a war. One member of his class, Otto Schnell, refused to go near it. When he saw the fire power that Jake demonstrated on the river that day, he announced to his officers he would not touch it, that his Quaker faith forbade killing someone. They gave him a Captain's Mast Court Martial, stripped him of his previous rank of Gunner's Mate, Second Class for refusing to obey an order, and made him an Ordinary Seaman, at sixteen dollars a month. He said if that was God's Will, he would abide by the decision, but he would not use that gun.

The question came up in the court martial trial as to how he got into the Navy as a Gunner's Mate when he refused to use a weapon to kill an enemy. His answer, "We haff always guns. We were not at war. I hit targets easy, so they make me gunner. Now we are in war with real enemy. I cannot shoot another man."

Jake was given a week to fulfill his arms obligations for his new rank. He had to shoot one hundred twenty rounds from a rifle at targets from two hundred to eight hundred yards distant. It was outside his area of knowledge, but he also had to fire twenty rounds from a six pounder at targets, some of which were moving. The men who were in his class spent time coaching him on how to use the gun and helped Jake understand its use. At the test, his officers said his performance was acceptable and they passed him.

Anchored in St. Louis, they had an opportunity for week-end leave they would not have later while aboard the Quonset. He wore his dress uniform, a white duck jacket, trousers and vest made up the summer uniform. Jake didn't drink, and he was saving his money, so he looked for free activities to go to. After eating a light lunch, walking past a church, he found a book lecture on Longfellow's poems. "Discussion today centers around Evangeline, The Village Smithy and The Wreck of the Hesperus." He had read Evangeline and the Smithy, whose "muscles on his brawny arms were as strong as iron bands."

Reading poetry was not his idea of a fun outing, but he went and was pleasantly surprised. A young woman with a pronounced

British accent was doing the reading, perhaps not as pretty as Peggy O'Neal, but better to look at than the sailors he spent the week with. The attendees were mostly women, with four men, all older than his father, and himself. He found a back seat as the reader was quoting from Evangeline—"This is the forest primeval. The murmuring pines and the hemlocks."

She interrupted herself to announce a new visitor, a member of the US Navy, and greet him. Everyone else in the room turned to smile at Jake and nod or wave at him. The reader announced to Jake, "My name is Elisabeth Wilshire, Betty to my friends. We just got started and if you haven't picked up a brochure, there is one on the table by the door." Jake looked around and saw the papers. He got up to retrieve one for himself and returned to his seat. Betty continued.

She went over the background of the story, when the French people were moved from their Grand Pre home in Arcadia to a foreign land of New Orleans. She explained that a hundred years earlier, the French and British were engaged in battle for the control of Canada. Some Native born sided with the French, and some, mainly the Iroquois nation, agreed with the British. The British didn't trust the French residents of the Isles and therefore decided to move them.

Jake had read the poem before and the only thing he could remember was the Acadians building snowman guards outside their village to protect them, while they went to a party. He didn't remember Evangeline's boy friend but knew there must have been one. Betty droned on but Jake didn't mind. He thought her dialect was interesting and he began trying to imitate her sound, quietly of course. Soon, she was finished and he was disappointed. She had given him two hours of respite from the noise aboard ship and the language of the crew. He stood to leave.

"Oh, please, remain with us for a tea," Betty implored. "We have a delightful entré for you, assuming you eat our crumpets and drink tea." She paused for only a second before continuing. She looked at Jake, "Of course, you are an American. You drink coffee. Well, we have that too. Everyone, just follow that young lady and she will lead you to your buffet."

Jake walked close to Betty as she stood at the lectern, organizing her notes for the next portion of the talk. She greeted him, "Sir, I find it interesting that a man, so young, should appear at our reading. Are you a literary student?"

"Not really. I had a couple days leave and saw your sign. I remember reading it in high school, and thought I'd check it out. You presented it very well."

"Well," she said, slightly offended, "I should hope so. I've been doing this for ten years now. I should know what I'm talking about."

"You must have started when you were ten," he said, and quickly shut his mouth. She laughed—a clear, happy laugh that made others stop in their tracks and look her way.

"Oh, Sir, you truly know how to turn a ladies head. But to be honest, I wasn't much older than that. Come now!" and she reached for his arm, "let us join the others in our celebration of God's wonderful gift to us."

"You mean the food?"

"Oh, no, well, that too. I was thinking about the gift of literature, the gift of the mind that would permit someone like a Henry Wadsworth Longfellow to write such beautiful poetry for the masses to indulge themselves with. This story is the best example of faithfulness and the intensity of women. Of course, there are stories about men, too, but nothing like the story of Evangeline. Longfellow must have had some knowledge of a love destroyed, to write so brilliantly for us."

"When you put it that way, you make me want to sit through another session."

Betty turned a little pink and derided his statement with a wave of her hand. "My dear friend, you keep talking like that and Ill make sure you sit through another session," and she laughed again. After realizing what she said, turned a brighter pink. Jake laughed. He stood there with a crumpet in one hand and coffee in the other and looked at her. She was probably his age, since she was slightly more than ten when she started her readings. Her face was longer than Peggy's, and narrower. Peggy's hair was dark, Betty's hair was, as his mother called that color, dishwater blond, but perfectly coiffed. She was slightly shorter than Peggy, but better filled out. Betty's eyes were large and added to her express ability. But Peggy had kissed him, twice. And that memory would be hard to dislodge, unless. . .

As he was leaving the literary club, she met him at the door, as she did all the guests, and they talked for a minute. She invited him back the following week when she would be reading the Englishman, Samuel Taylor Coleridge, and his poetry, emphasizing "Rime of the Ancient Mariner," and "Kubla Khan." As for that one, Coleridge admitted it was the result of an opium-induced dream. Jake said that if he could, he would be at the reading the following week if he was still in the area. She frowned, as if asking what he meant. "I'm in the Navy. We are at war. I have no say over what I do or where I go."

Jake walked the streets of St. Louis after the readings were done. He had no direction and was not on any time constraints. In his mind he held two pictures—the one of Peggy in her wedding dress, with her hair done just so, and the other, of Betty, standing before him doing the readings. Occasionally, her eyes would stray in Jake's direction and their eyes would meet, and her forehead would resolve into a shade of pink. His life was tied to a Navy Ram boat and, with his country at war, he had no idea where he would be a week from that day, or even the next day. And he had no idea where Peggy was at that moment, so, no matter how they compared, in his mind, Peggy was nowhere to be seen. Betty was here in St. Louis.

Saturday night, he stayed at a small hotel a short distance from the river Five thirty was his usual time for rising, and when he got dressed, he walked out to an empty street. There was neither place to get breakfast nor a church to go to for another four hours. He went back up to his room and lay back down on his bed. Where would he be the following Saturday? He was scheduled to have another class to teach starting Monday. The first class took four and a half days. With some cutting, he could get done in under four. Did he want to do that? When he got back to the ship, he'd have to go over the schedule and see what might change.

Jake was greeted at the top of the ramp by the Bo's'n, Jock Grimes. Jake saluted the flag and stepped off the ramp. Grimes looked at him and said, with a sneer, "You're early. Wassamatter, You cou'n't find any women or no one to drink with?"

"I don't drink and I just came from church."

The bo's'n howled. "You what! You come from church? You don't drink an' you go to church, you mean you're one of those saintly goody-two-shoes?"

"No, I didn't say that at all. I said I don't drink and I just came from church. I am a person who believes that there is a God and that He sent His Son to us, which we celebrate at Christmas. I believe that Son, whom we call Jesus Christ died on a cross for our sins, and I have accepted that as true for my own life. Do you have a problem with that?"

Angrily, Jock answered, "The problem I have with you is that you sucked up to some general or captain and got a plum that a good man was cheated from. That's the problem I have with you." Jock suddenly grew angry and shouted at Jake. "How long you been in the Navy? I know, you been in three years. In three years you got two grade jumps. Some of these men were Landsman for three years and an Ordinary Seaman for six before they got to where you got in three. How did you do that? Who'd you butter up to?"

On sudden inspiration, Jake smiled and said, "What would you think if I told you I spent five days and was kissed twice by the most beautiful woman I ever saw?"

Grimes let loose with a string of oaths that Jake had ever heard. He swore until he ran out of breath, and when he stopped to take another breath, Jake asked him, "How does it make you feel to know you are swearing in the presence of God?"

Jock spit and fumed some more and while he was trying to think of something to say, Jake walked past him to his cabin. Once inside, he leaned against the door and closed his eyes. "Now what?" Again he smiled. "I wonder what he would have thought if I told him about the literary meeting yesterday?"

Heaving a long sigh, Jake remembered the reason he came in early and got his notes for the class he taught. They were a mess, as he hadn't taken time to organize them, so his task was harder than it might have been. He hadn't taken time to write a daily class procedure, but, as he looked at the papers he had, he started to organize a plan in his mind. Slowly, the teaching assignment came to mind and he wrote as he thought. After an hour, he had his class lesson done and felt he was ready for the next class.

There were nine ships in the squadron the Quonset was in, so that meant it was possible, if all the Chief Boatswains, Boatswain's and Boatswain's mates were to have training on the gun, he might have to have almost thirty men in this class. He closed his eyes and muttered, "Oh, no." Jock Grimes would be one of the students.

Chapter Fifteen

As Jake entered the classroom Monday morning he was greeted with twenty-two angry men, some angry, others curious. Some stood with arms crossed at their chests, glaring at him, as Jock Grimes told everyone of Jake's Naval experience. "Three years," Jock screamed, "three years, and he's a Gunner second. Three years!"

Trying to reduce tension, Jake spoke with a slight smile on his face. "What did you want me to do, volunteer to go back? Tell the captain that I really haven't served long enough to merit this class? Then who would teach you men the new weapon?"

A chorus of names went up from the assembled men, none of whom had ever seen the Gatling gun, a fact which Jake mentioned. They scoffed at the idea that none of these men could figure out the character of that gun, and they told him so. "Well, we seem to have a stand off. What do you suggest?"

Jock Grimes screamed, "You gotta earn your way up to that stand," and he let go with a howlish laugh. "You gotta walk through all of us to get there, Seaman. When we get done with you, you're gonna wish you'd never heard Navy," and he laughed again.

All pretenses for civility gone, Jock had just challenged him. Now, it became serious. Jake looked over the men, still maintaining a calm appearance. Inwardly, he was in turmoil. These men, all old Navy, had probably been in more fights than he ever heard of. The one advantage he might have would be in his condition—he was in great shape from chucking coal chunks. His arm muscles were tight and his hands were tough. He could probably outlast any one of them in a fight. But the fight itself, that was the problem.

He was no fighter. He had seen the write up in the newspaper about John Heenan of the US and Tom Sayers of Britain and their challenge for a bare knuckle fight. One was being proposed in England, and the Cincinnati papers had the story with pictures of the latest fighting styles. Jake read the story and saw the pictures, but that was as close as he ever came to being involved in a fight. Obviously, the time had come. This would be the test. He asked, "What are the rules?"

That was greeted by another loud laughter. "Rules?" Jock mocked, "he wants rules in a fight," and they laughed harder.

"Just so I know," he said, "biting, kicking, fingers in the eyes, these are okay?"

Somebody in the room asked, "You sure you don't drink? That sounds like a lot of bar fights I've been in," and another round of laughter resulted.

"One more thing," Jake said, in quiet contemplation, "one at a time or all at once?"

They exploded with another round of laughter. Jake noticed that two or three in the back of the class were quietly observing what went on. He didn't know their names, but figured they would be the ones to oversee the class when the fight was done. Someone hollered, "He wants all at once. Let's give it to him."

Jake saw the man sitting closest to him was enjoying the sport, but had not participated in the shouting. He sat there smiling and Jake told him, "Better move, Mack, or you'll get hurt." Mack got up and scurried to a far corner. Jake took off his jersey top, walked to a corner of the room and pushed the desk almost into it, leaving a narrow aisle for him to maneuver. He took the pose he remembered from the newspaper and flexed his muscles. The muscles in his upper arms bulged. He challenged, "Come and get it, or are you all talk."

Those who went along with Jock Grimes in the challenge saw that Jake was serious. It had reached a place where it was either put up or shut up, and he was in a position where it would be difficult to reach him. To say it better, behind the desk and protected by his back by the wall, he was in a place where only one man at a time could get to him. They would either have to move the desk or crawl over it. The one aisle open was room enough for one man to face him. It was decision time, and the other men waited for Jock to make his decision.

The other men started calling Jock to make his move. Jock saw, as did everyone else, the muscles on Jake's upper arms and his chest. Jake stood there flexing his muscles, waiting for some movement on the part of the others. After several minutes of waiting and challenging calls, someone in the back of the room stood and walked to the front. He was from another ship in the squadron and introduced himself, "I'm sure most of you know me, although Jake probably doesn't. I'm Chase Willingham, Master-at-Arms on the Exeter. I think we've seen enough." He looked at Grimes. "You complain about Jake's time in the fleet, you said he has to walk through us to get to that lectern. All right, what do you say now? It's yours to either fish or cut bait. We're waiting."

Pure hatred showed on Grimes' face as he glared at Jake, but he said nothing, nor did he move. Willingham said, "That's enough. No more talk about our instructor. He's put himself ready for a challenge, but none has come, so let that be the end of it. We've wasted an hour of class time and I want to hear about that gun. So let's get on with it," and he returned to his seat in the back of the class.

Jake pushed the desk back where it had been and put on his jersey. The gun had been set up by the ship's maintenance crew and an empty tube was there, along with one that was full. Jake started with the explanation of how the weapon worked, how the crank rotated the barrels and forced a cartridge into a chamber on the barrel. All eyes, except those for Rod Grimes, were glued to the weapon. His were fixed on the instructor. This strange piece of death-dealing mechanism had their interest beyond what the first group showed last week. It surprised Jake, for only an instant, that there was so much more interest by this class than the first. He continued talking with a new intensity.

At the end of the day, Willingham came to him and said, "I'm sure there is a story there, but how did you happen to be there when the need for an instructor opened?"

Jake's mind raced over the events of the past month and he looked away from the questioner. "It's a long story, you sure you want to hear it?" After Willingham nodded, Jake started at his high school contact with Captain Thomas and went on to explain the assignment, ignoring the presence of the Marines on board. He spent three days working with the gun before they left New Orleans and was given the opportunity to ride with it as they traveled north. He told about the confrontation at Vicksburg and chasing G W Neapope in the northland.

Willingham tilted his head slightly and a smile spread slowly across his face. "I can't believe your captain gave you the assignment instead of the Marines. Did he recognize you from before? I wonder what the reason was."

Jake had been in the Navy long enough to realize that Master-at-Arms was the rank of a leading Petty Officer, so he hesitated a moment before answering. "Sir, do you believe in God?"

There was a pause of several seconds before Willingham answered. "I've been in situations where I could see the result of a higher power being imposed on our lives. It's kind of hard, because of the ridicule of the masses, to admit to that belief, but I'd have to say yes, I do believe in a higher power. You call it God. I'll accept that, but maybe hesitate to full admission. I can see how there might be some control over events the way things have turned out. If things go bad, I'll have to remind myself what I just said," and Jake smiled.

Jake approached the classroom the second day with a mild sense of anticipation. He didn't want to confront Jock Grimes again, but didn't want to appear unable to handle a negative influence in the classroom. As he approached the door to the room, he found two class members waiting outside. "It's locked," one said, "we sent for a maintenance man to get the key."

Minutes passed, a key was brought to the room, but when it was tried, it would only go into the keyhole a short quarter of the length. After several attempts, it was determined the hole had been blocked. The chief maintenance man was called and options discussed as men gathered for the class. Suddenly, at the appointed class start time, the door was ripped open and a Seaman scurried away from the room. Jake stepped inside and saw why the door had been locked. Inside, Jock Grimes stood behind the Gatling gun with the fresh ammo stick protruding from the top. The desk had been moved across the room and the gun's tripod placed on the floor behind it. A nearly empty bottle of liquor sat at one corner of the desk. All six barrels were aimed at the door. A man, irrational and drunk, stood behind the gun.

Chase Willingham, the highest ranking member of the class, stepped to the open door and, before he could utter a word, Grimes screamed, "He taught us well, didn't he Master Willingham? Now, he's going to feel the effect of his instruction. He's gonna die here today. Embarrass me, will he? Now, watch him crawl and beg not to die."

Willingham, still standing in the open doorway, said, "Come on, Grimes, you've just ruined your years in the Navy, and for what reason, because you think someone got a break. Give it up, man."

"You!" Grimes screeched, "You! You're supposed to be a leader of men, someone for others to follow into battle. You're supposed to be fair, but you took his side yesterday, you took his side and mocked me. I've been in this Navy fourteen years. I earned every step, every stripe. He comes along an' takes the job I should have had, or you. You should have had it. But, no, he got it." Grimes' vocal volume rose higher until he screamed, "No, after only three years, he gets this plumb and," Grimes was crying now, "a grade that I worked eight years to get. It ain't right." Grimes' head bobbed with each word, to emphasize his feelings.

Both Jake and Willingham stood uneasily in the open door as Grimes ranted and cried some more. He told of all the distasteful jobs he had done because of some order from a higher-up. He told of all the times he had given up his time to do the time of someone else, be it a watch or an errand. He ranted for several minutes without stopping, until his emotions drained from him and he stood, head bent, crying like a child over lost candy. He still had his hand on the crank so the two men were hesitant to do anything.

There was movement outside the door and the ship's captain, Homer White, filled the doorway. He was a big man, tall and heavy, and his presence commanded attention wherever he was. He spoke with authority, "Bo's'n's Mate Grimes, step away from that weapon and come out of the room. Now!"

That order seemed to waken Grimes from his lethargic state and woke him to his original demand—that of the unfairness of Jake's award. Now, fully rational, and in charge of his emotions, all traces of the liquor gone, he answered in a clear voice, "No, Sir, begging your pardon Sir, but I've ruined my life and there's only one more thing I have to do before I die, an' that's to take out that phony, that fraud, who got this plumb and cheated someone else out of it."

He swung the barrels of the gun at Jake. "Now, you who don't drink and who goes to church on Sunday, call on your God and beg for your life." Jake didn't move. Grimes screamed, "I said, call on your God to save you now." To the others, they saw Grimes getting back into the same emotional pit he was in before and they exchanged looks, without saying anything. He saw and quickly snapped back in control with a smile. "No, we ain't goin' down that road.

Captain White spoke again. "Mr. Grimes, come now and talk to me. We'll discuss this situation and, if you've been unfairly treated, we'll rectify it, but step away from the weapon now."

"I'm sorry, Sir, and meanin' no disrespect, but I gotta see this through. I gotta make my point so that he doesn't steal another poor slob's rank and job." He turned directly to Jake. "Now, you Holy Fraud, it's your turn to die. You're going to be listed as a casualty of the war."

In split seconds, Jake's peripheral vision caught movement behind Willingham, outside the door. Jake saw a marine with a rifle hiding behind Willingham, gun up to his shoulder. Jake shouted "No!" at the same instant Willingham raised his right arm to stop

Jock from firing. With Willingham's arm raised, giving clear a view to the Marine, he fired, the bullet going under Willingham's arm, between him and the captain, striking Grimes just eight inches below his chin, driving him back away from the crank on the gun.

Men shouted, swore and screamed. The tenseness of the confrontation caused big men to sink to the floor. Jake rushed to Jock's side, looking for a pulse, but there was none, and it was his turn to fall on his knees, next to the body of Jock Grimes, as the man's blood stained his shirt and poured out on the floor.

Captain White came and viewed the scene, with life's blood flowing from the wound, he said, "Someone take him to Medical. Mr. Prosser, I want to see you on the deck immediately."

Jake answered, "Yes, Sir." He hesitated a moment before asking, "Could Mr. Willingham come too?"

"I'll get to him. I want to talk to you first. Move, now!"

Jake lifted himself from his kneeling position, took one last look at Grimes as men came to carry him to the medical unit, and walked out the door behind his captain.

In the captain's office, Jake stood at attention, arms rigidly at his side, head and eyes fixed on Captain White. The captain ordered, "At ease," and Jake clasped his hands behind his back and separated his feet about eighteen inches. Still tense, he appeared more relaxed.

"Now," the captain stated, "what was that all about. I just lost a good man. You didn't pull the trigger, but how did that Marine know to be here? Did you order him in?"

"No Sir. Not at all Sir."

"Then who is he? Do you know him?"

"Sir, may I speak freely?" A nod from White was his approval. "I came north from New Orleans on the GREAT EXPECTATIONS, with a load of arms and three Gatling guns for the army up north. They were test weapons, given to use against an opponent and not just on the target range. I was given the care of the guns on the way and the instructions concerning them. There were about twenty Marines on board, under a Lieutenant O'Rourke and a Sergeant Hanratty and I think this man was one of Hanratty's group."

"And you didn't order them in here?"

"No, Sir!" The high pitch of his denial indicated the tension of the moment. "I left the Great Expectations when Neapope was brought to St. Louis for Jefferson Barracks. I had the week end and when I came aboard Sunday, the Bo's'n met me and laughed at me for coming from church. Somehow, he found that I have only had three years in the Navy and still was awarded with a grade. Yesterday he tried to get everyone to fight me and—"

"Fight you? How did he do that?"

"He said I didn't deserve to have the grade, that anyone could have taught the glass. Then he said I had to 'walk through everyone there' to get to the lectern. Mr. Willingham was there and got the class back together. Then this today. I don't know what happened, or how the Marine was brought in."

"How many challenged to fight you?"

"No one. I got my back in the corner and pushed the desk in front of me."

Captain White stood for several seconds alternately looking at Jake and various spots within the room. He asked, "Who gave you the grade, Mr. Prosser?"

"Captain Montgomery, Sir."

Homer White's eyebrows went up and his lips pooched out. "Captain Montgomery? When did you meet him?"

"After the thing with Neapope, Sir. He said there were a lot of men who needed to be instructed on this weapon, Sir, and as I had done it with the Marines on the G E and the army up north, I guess he figured I could do it for the Navy."

A quick nod and "You may go, send in Mr. Willingham, please."

Jake found the Master in the classroom and told him the captain wanted to talk to him. The spot of blood was still on the floor and the other members of the class stayed out of the room. Jake went in and sat down. He looked at the blood and thought of the events of the two days. "What next?" he asked himself over and over again.

Master-at-Arms Willingham was in with the captain for an hour. At the end of that time, both men stood at the door, tight-lipped.

They saluted and Willingham walked away, the captain following him with his eyes until he disappeared down a ladder.

Chapter Sixteen

Jake knew something was up, for Captain White had dissolved the class and sent the men back to their own ships. Jake was given leave for the rest of the week, and was told to report back at oh-eight-hundred the following Monday. This left Jake with the ultimate problem—a sailor with leave, in a strange town, with limited moneys, knowing no one. Oh, he did know someone. He knew that English gal who wasn't as pretty as Peggy, but who was here, while Peggy was in another world.

He had his duffel bag packed with clothes for the week and found a carriage to take him to the same hotel he stayed in before. After registering, he walked the street, troubled about this sudden leave and the way it transpired. The Master-at-Arms on the Quonset, Jeremy Blake, knocked on his door at supper time and handed him papers for a five day leave—Wednesday through Sunday. No questions were allowed, and no information given. Very mysterious and very troubling.

His wandering eventually led him to the church where Betty Wilshire had her literary group. Wednesday morning? Did he expect someone to be there on Wednesday morning? But, he tried the side door that he had entered that Saturday and found it unlocked. Inside, he heard voices and followed the hallway to an office, where four people were talking, one who was Elisabeth. Jake stood in the doorway and a man of fifty, spotted him and jumped up to greet him.

He was much shorter than Jake, maybe five foot six or seven. His dark stringy hair followed a completely barren path from his eyebrows to the back of his head. He walked in a hurry as he approached Jake, speaking fast to welcome Jake to their presence. When Betty saw Jake, she smiled and said, with her cute British accent, "Father, he's the one I told you about."

The man introduced himself. "I'm Henry Wilshire, pastor of this English Covenant Fellowship. Elisabeth told us about your attendance at her reading last week and, if I may be blunt, I am surprised that one your age, and a sailor, would be interested in Literature."

Flustered at the statement, Jake stammered, "Well. . .I. . .uh, I'm not exactly interested in all Literature, just some of it. I read both Evangeline and the Village Smithy in high school and I thought it might be interesting to hear another thought about it. I don't know anything about her subject this week, and, honestly, I hadn't planned on coming, but was given an emergency leave until next Monday with no where to go, so here I am."

Immediately, Betty had a solution. "Father, why not invite him for supper tonight and the prayer service afterwards. Perhaps, he's free Sunday for church and dinner then, too."

Jake started to protest and opened his mouth to speak. He father looked at her and frowned. "Perhaps we could check with your mother first before making any invitations she doesn't know about. But, I think it's fairly safe to invite. . .uh, I'm sorry, either Elisabeth didn't remember your name, or I have forgotten it."

"Jake. Jake Prosser, sir. I'm from Cincinnati originally. We're docked here for a short time. I'm sure orders will come through for us to move shortly."

"Well, Mr. Prosser, why don't we invite you for dinner Sunday after our Bible study and worship services? Oh, what time would you have to leave to get back to your ship?"

"We're docked down here where Mr. Eads is talking about building his bridge. I guess he's going to be busy as long as the war lasts building gun ships for the Federal Government. If I get there by six thirty, I'll be in before the evening flag."

Betty piped up, "And you'll be sure to be at the reading this Saturday."

"I'll be there."

She was silent for a moment before addressing her father. "Daddy, Ralph Waldo Emerson will be here for a lecture Friday evening at the Broadway Hotel. What would you think of my taking Ja. . .Mr. Prosser to the lecture for something to do that evening?"

"Ralph Waldo Emerson? Do you think that's wise? You know his stand about our beliefs. Transcendentalism is not in our manual."

"I know, Daddy, but he was a minister at one time."

"Í heard that, but he isn't now."

"But wouldn't it be interesting to hear from a mind like his?"

"The Bible is our guide, and it warns us that Satan, our adversary, comes in many forms seeking whom he may devour."

"But—"

"We'll talk about it."

That was the end of the conversation. Jake felt a little discomfort in the ensuing minute and shifted his stance. "Well, I guess I'll be going. What time is your service tonight?"

Henry answered quickly, "Seven o'clock. You might get here a few minutes early and meet some of the members. We're a close group, and are interested in what's going on with the war situation."

Jake apologized, "I, uh, don't really know much about the war. I've been in my own little world with a little job, and don't know anything about what's going on elsewhere."

"Oh? Well, perhaps you can tell us a little about what your job is, what you have been doing."

"No, Sir, I'm sorry, it's a secret job. I, uh, well, I guess I should be going. I'll be at the reading Saturday," and he turned to retrace his steps back down the hallway.

Almost to the door, he heard the little female voice calling him. "Mr. Prosser, Mr. Prosser, wait, please."

He stopped and waited for her to catch him. "Mr. Prosser, please don't think poorly of father. He has the burden of the church and doesn't want to let advanced thought cause members any problems."

"What is that trans. . .what did he call it?"

"Transcendentalism. It's exercising the mind. Developing thought processes."

"I'm sorry, Betty, but if your father is afraid of it, then you should be too. I don't have the mind to keep up with someone that advanced, so I'd not be interested anyhow. My interest is in sailing and being the best sailor I can be. And being the best man I can be through Christ. Now, we are at war and that dictates my interest." He turned and left, with her standing there with her mouth open.

Jake left the church and walked. And walked, eventually winding up at the wharf where the GREAT EXPECTATIONS was tied up. He watched as the crew scurried around at various jobs from painting to scrubbing the three decks. He stood there several minutes until one of the crew recognized him and called him to come aboard. Jake walked up the gang plank and stood at the top and asked permission to come aboard. Bo's'n Reeder met him and gave permission.

Reeder led Jake to Captain Thomas who greeted him with a hearty hello. Jake saluted and said, "I've been given a few days for some reason and I have no place to go, so I just wandered in to see how the crew's doing."

"Gettin' ready to ship out, Jake. Goin' to the war. We're going to Cincinnati to pick up troopers for the eventual fighting down the river." He paused, then, with concern in his voice, said, "Tell me, what happened over there yesterday?"

Jake bowed his head and was silent for a few seconds. "I don't know how it got out of hand so quickly. Bo's'n Grimes somehow found out I only have three years in the Navy and I'm the same grade as he after fifteen or so years. He and some of the others challenged me to a fight, said I had to walk through them to get to the lectern, but when I got my back in a corner they didn't want any part of me. Then, yesterday, after I had explained how the gun fired, he found the full stack of cartridges for the weapon and had it pointed at the door—he was going to shoot me. Master-at-Arms Willingham from the Exeter was there and he tried to get Grimes to back off. Then Captain White came in and somehow in the distraction, a Marine, one of Hanratty's men, shot Grimes. How he found out about the situation is the question. They think I somehow called him over there."

Waiting for effect, Thomas said, "Grimes was here Monday evening talking to Hanratty's men. They must have told him about your time in service, and he—"

"He was drunk. There was an almost empty bottle of liquor on the desk."

Thomas looked away from Jake, across the dock and up the street ahead of them. Without looking back at Jake, the captain said, "Hanratty's a good man. No nonsense. Grimes must have made a threat about killing you that the sergeant got wind of and sent his man to check it out."

"What's happened to the one who did the shooting?"

"Hanratty hasn't released his name. Oh, I know it, but he's asked to keep it quiet. There'll be a hearing Monday after—"

"They dismissed the class Tuesday and sent all the others to their ships. I stayed in the classroom until maintenance came to clean up the blood. Then, last night the Master at Arms handed me papers and said I have leave until Monday. Do you know what's up?"

Thomas shook his head and walked down the outside deck and leaned against the railing. He looked down at the floor and then, without raising his head, looked at Jake out of the top of his eyes. "They're setting you up for a Captain's Mast, a Court Martial. They let you go so they can gather the information and set up the judges and counsel. Friday, they'll probably call you in and introduce you to your lawyer."

"Why! What did I do?"

"Captain Montgomery did you no favor in raising your grade and setting you on a ship with all those old salts. You did a good job teaching that gun, and when they caught the rebel up north, he may have let his good intentions override wisdom. Eventually, you were going to say or do something that offended one of them and, voila, troubles. You see, it's unwritten, but a fact, that a recruit serves three years as a Landsman. Then, he can be promoted to Ordinary Seaman and serve there six years before eligible for the rank of Gunner's Mate, second. It takes another three to six years for the first step, where he can get to be In Charge, and beyond that, Chief Boatswain's Mate. Had you stayed here after the promotion, there would have been no problem, except perhaps with the Marines, and that's because of the job they had you do. They think they're the only ones who know how to shoot a gun."

"I don't understand," Jake said, puzzled at the different standard between the two ships.

"First, the main duty of the Gunner's Mate is responsibility for a gun. He has to make sure it's firing well, the ammunition is available, and, they occasionally hit their target. There's a lot involved. You had two classes for the Gatling gun, and, I imagine, two more scheduled. After that, you would have been given a crew and would have had to train them in the operation. That's what the old timers were complaining about. You didn't have the background to do the job your rank requires. You understood the only gun we had, so the upgrade was no problem, here."

After a silence of a couple minutes, Jake asked, "What do I do? What's gonna happen?"

"They'll bust you back to a coal chucker, take the grade away. If the judges want to placate the angry old timers, they might bust you back to Landsman and make you start over." Without smiling, he added, "Three more years in the coal bin."

Jake wiped the corner of his eye with the back of his hand. "Captain Thomas, Sir, I've dreamed of being a sailor on these rivers since I was big enough to dream. What can I do?"

With a kindness in his voice, Thomas asked, "Would you be interested in coming back here?"

"Would I! Can I, could I, may I?"

Thomas laughed, "You could and you may. To be honest, Jake, I wondered about the possibility as soon as I heard about the situation. Bad news travels faster than good news."

"What do I, you have to do to make it happen?"

"First, I have to send a message to Captain Montgomery. Captain White has contacted him and told him, I'm sure, what they plan to do. We should wait until tomorrow and then send my cable." He waited a few seconds before asking, "Where will you spend the night?"

"I'm at the hotel across from the big one."

"Why don't you check out and come here? Your bunk is still empty."

"You mean it? Really?"

Smiling, he answered, "I'll talk to the chief in the boiler room and Mr. Reeder. They'll be happy to see you again."

Jake was given his leave and he hurried to the hotel to cancel his reservation, grabbed his gear and then rushed back to the ship. As he climbed aboard again, he thought, <u>Cincinnati! I wonder if I might get a couple days to see my parents again</u>. A second thought came, <u>I wonder do I want to. I suppose Mom got that mail by now.</u>

Chapter Seventeen

Peggy O'Neal

Oh, what in the world have I gotten myself into? I had no idea that teaching would require so many meetings, so much money for supplies and a constant need for more money for personal things. And clothes! Everything I had might just as well have been discarded, or at least set aside in some closet. I could hardly teach in a new bride's wardrobe. And the other clothes, beside that bride's dress, are clothes for a rich man's wife, party dresses, even the under clothing. I had no idea of the cost of a whole wardrobe, even buying conservative "working-girl's" dresses. If Cincinnati hadn't been on the river where shipping is easy, I don't know where I would have gotten my things. Philadelphia? Not likely, not after. . .

And Evelyn, bless her heart, if it hadn't been for her, I'd have to teach the first day in that wedding dress. That would have been a shocker. But, Evelyn must have had thousands of dollars saved for some occasion, the way she has funded my needs. First, were the school supplies. Amazing what they didn't have, but this is a new school, named after a former president. Maybe I was spoiled by the school I went to in Philadelphia, for they had a teacher for each classroom, and no teacher had to teach two subjects. Say hello to the real world. But, that was a city school and I agreed to this arrangement.

It was interesting when we went shopping. The store had fliers from Paris! Evelyn said they come up the river from New Orleans to the various cities along the way. Bringing stuff overland from New York or Philadelphia is not reasonable. They had some fliers from London, which will be hard to find since New Orleans is now in enemy territory. The store had a good quantity of dresses on hand so they shouldn't run out too soon.

This last month I have met with the school board at least once a week, turned down two marriage proposals, learned the way from Evelyn's home to the school in my buggy and learned that I have to straighten the classroom when the day is done. They even want the shades pulled to a certain point on the window. Thanks a lot. Perhaps I can teach the children to do it. The chairman of the board said that since we are at war, the men might be called up for military service and I'd have to train a new man as janitor, so I might as well do it from the start. At least I don't have to build the fire in the morning. Yet.

And the children! Their level of education is next to nothing. Grammar? Their English grammar is atrocious! How am I going to combat the "ain't" and "nuttin'" they use? How am I going to correct the grammar of children who are in the sixth grade, who have had a life of poor teaching? History? They know about Simon Kenton and Daniel Boone, but little else. How am I going to train youngsters who refuse to try to learn. "Gramps never had no schoolin' an' he done aw-rite." What am I going to do? If I had only paid more attention to the teachers in those classes. I did my lessons and the teachers? They were just there. Now I'd like to talk to one of them for a while.

I found out there will be a picnic the first day of school, a kind of giant pot-luck, where everybody brings for their own family and then stuff gets thrown together. A kind of get-acquainted time for children, parents and teacher. And the school board. Just can't forget the school board.

I have to tell you about Evelyn. She's a jewel. Her husband has been dispatched to someplace south so she has all the time and nothing to do. Well, she's finding something to do. Rolling bandages, visiting the wounded, (they're using some of the barracks at the army base here for hospital rooms), being a mother to young mothers whose husbands are fighting. And escorting me all over. And she wants me to start a Bible study some evening. She said she'd pay for a nanny if some of the young women have babies. But, with the hall there and empty, she thought it would be a great idea. She says there's a Methodist College just across the river in Kentucky and I think I could go there and get some material. I haven't told Evelyn yet, and maybe there'll be another way. I don't know anyone in Philadelphia who would send me the kind of material I'd like for a Bible study. The churches we went to were High Church.

Evelyn suggested, rather demanded, I get some very conservative clothes for the first week in school, get a pair of glasses, the non-prescription kind, and wear my hair in a severe bun, pulled tight so that it changes my looks. She said that if I don't, I'll have trouble with the older boys flirting and even fighting over me. It wouldn't hurt to have a cheap ring to wear as if I was married. If asked, I could say my man's in the Navy, which he is. At least the man I want is in the Navy.

Let me tell you about school, the building. There is one door in or out, with a large window on either side of the room for an emergency exit. It's one large room with different sized chairs and some long tables. The chairs are for the children when they are reading. If they are doing some kind of work, like arithmetic or writing, they take their chair to a long table in the back of the room and work there. When they leave the school, they neatly place all their books and papers on the chair. That is their property for the school year.

I dread the first day. I've organized everything that can be organized and found out there'll be forty-one kids in the school. I guess I should stop calling them 'kids.' Some of the sixth graders are almost as old as I am. I've got a sand box for the little ones for their recess time, with a fifth or sixth grade girl to sit with them that part of the day. I'll have to start them on the alphabet and their numbers. That should be interesting. Second grade will do some reading, but I have no idea how that will go. I can see it will be like pulling teeth without any deadening. From third to sixth grades will be a mix of numbers, grammar and reading. I don't know about geography, the country has changed so much in the last few years. Less than a hundred years ago this area was under the control of Indian tribes. I also need to get some Civics classes in for the older ones to teach them about the Constitution and the government. They must know how it was founded. And then prepare for the Bible study class for Evelyn. Why can't I say 'No?'

I apologized to Evelyn for taking up so much of her valuable time. She has her own schedule and doesn't need me to hang on her skirts but I'm desperate. Perhaps it won't be as bad as I think right now, perhaps the school board will realize the pay for teaching forty-one kids, children, is miserly at best. But I agreed to it.

Tomorrow is the "all-school" picnic and Evelyn has agreed to go with me. She knows some of those people, through community activity I guess. She's been linked to the army for thirty years with her own family interests, so I don't know how she might have had time for any outside activity. She's an amazing woman. We're taking hot dogs, potato salad and a few vegetables for two. The way these things usually go there'll be enough food left over to feed the Navy, so we won't worry about leaving hungry.

Evelyn came up with an idea about name tags for everyone. We'll have forty some children and, possibly, sixty or more adults. My mind just can't handle remembering all those people. So, we'll need paper and pins, and a promise by the parents not to trade name tags after my first greeting. I mean, it could get impossible if, after I see someone with the right tag on, then he goes and trades with someone else before the next time I see him. Certainly no one would do that, would they? Ha!

I was talking to Evelyn the other day and she asked what I would have done if I hadn't come to Cincinnati with her. It took me by surprise, because I hadn't thought about it. I couldn't go home, because without Daddy, I have no home. I couldn't go to Philadelphia. I have no friends in that city. When Mother left Daddy, she spread such malicious gossip that I couldn't believe. But she did it for a reason. She wanted his friends, I guess I should have said that in quotes, his friends to shun him and ostracize him to get me back in her control. Fortunately, it didn't work.

You have to understand my mother and who she was. A Swedish teen ager, her father managed to find some money and bought a ship building company that built fishing vessels. Nothing gave her more pleasure than going out on one of those vessels and directing the operation. At sixteen, she had her own boat. At twenty-one, she was a millionaire.

Daddy grew up working on the streets of Philadelphia, doing any odd job he could to get some money. I mean he earned a penny any way he could. He saw what an education meant to people and he was determined to go to college. When he was eighteen, their paths crossed as he was working on the wharfs where her ship came in. At that time he was working for a market, managing their fish department. His job was to get the fish to market early, and mother was always there early. A week of early meetings, a date or two, and she agreed to fund his college, if he promised to marry her after graduation.

They got married and a brother and I were born. Mother didn't want any more children, Daddy wanted to practice his new found talent and raise a family. They argued and she hit him. Now, she was strong as a man and it put Daddy in the hospital. She broke his jaw. My brother was six, I was four and saw what happened and swore I'd never speak to her again. Since then, especially after my brother Bradley was killed, Daddy and I have been one for all and all for one, so to speak.

Evelyn has become the mother I never had. I don't know if she is uncomfortable with it, but she at least endures my presence. Without her, I don't know what I would be doing, perhaps trying to find another man. Or trying to get Jacob to quit the Navy, and there is little chance of that. So, I look forward to this teaching year, with the help of my "mother Evelyn," as what I can do. . .no, what I have to do to be productive. When I ask myself what have I gotten myself into, it's because I am totally unprepared to handle little children, or big children for that matter. But, it is an honorable profession and I can earn my keep.

The carriage Evelyn recommended is a bit dressy for my first one. It will carry four people, has four doors with a three foot, they call it a boot, in back. It's covered, with isinglass curtains that can roll right down in case there's a change in the weather. These curtains have buttons along each side to keep them from blowing in. It's black with red wheels and is really pretty. It's set up for one horse, where the horse is hooked between two things that look like forks.

How I will ever pay Evelyn back all the money she has spent on me, I'll never know, but I'll start a fund for that with my first paycheck. I will not be a leech on someone else's pocket book.

Chapter Eighteen

Peggy O'Neal had never been so upset, well, not since she was four and saw her mother put her father in the hospital. This was different. This was nerves, emotional upset, forced on herself by the demand on herself to do a good job. She had never been this upset, not even when she was going to marry a man she had never met. Then, she had made an agreement and was paying back her father for all the things he had done for her. This was different. She was on her own. Evelyn had gone out on a limb and spent hundreds of dollars for her needs and now, it was Margaret O'Neal's time to prove it was not wasted.

This was Monday, technically, the first day of school, but it was a day for fun. Simon, the yard man, had hitched the horse to the buggy and stood waiting for the ladies to emerge from the house. He had loaded several medium-sized boxes into the back of the carriage and stood holding the horse's reins. The ladies came out carrying a picnic basket with their food and, with Simon's help, climbed into the carriage.

The terrain along the river at the area of the Patterson home was low hills. The banks along the river were steep and tree filled, with more hills inland. The Patterson's home was back from the edge of the first hill so that the river was not visible from the house, but it was from the edge of their property. Many of the houses along the river were along that same ridge, heading east from their property.

The new schools was east of Evelyn's house, set back from the edge of the hill for safety's sake, but close enough, perhaps two hundred yards distant, at the top of a gradual slope, to see the ships plying the river. The school building faced south, so that the students would face north inside, and not be distracted by the beauty of the scenes toward the river.

The picnic area was at the south end of the school property and the tables had been set up as a sort of fence to keep the children from falling down the hill. There were almost two acres of open ground between the tables and the building so there was plenty of room for the children to play. When Peggy and Evelyn were preparing for the year, they found a magazine containing current games and Evelyn agreed to fund the purchase of some. Those were the boxes in the back of the carriage.

As they neared the school, Evelyn watched Peggy sitting next to her, wringing her hands. "Peggy, calm down. It can't be as bad as you have anticipated."

"Me? I haven't. . .you're right. I'm sorry. I am a poor example of one who trusts the Lord. His word tells me He'll go with me everywhere and help me and here I am tied in a knot. Can we stop and pray?" Evelyn agreed and halted the horse and Margaret voiced her concern in prayer for help and strength. As she finished, she smiled and nodded.

It seemed that all the students and their parents were already at the school. Someone appointed by the school board was directing parking of the buggies and getting the food to the serving tables. As the ladies walked toward the gathering of the people, Evelyn heard, "The Lord is my Shepherd, I shall not want. He leadeth me in the paths of righteousness for His name's sake. Yea tho' I walk through the valley. . ."

Children rushed at her to get a look at the new teacher. Various comments "You're pretty," or "My name is. . ." or a multitude of other greetings so that it almost overwhelmed Peggy. She was rescued by members of the school board as they came to greet her. A man, dressed in suit and white shirt, came and stuck out his hand. She remembered his name and took the proffered hand, greeting him with "Good morning, Mr. Schaffer. This is my landlord, the wife of a Union General. This is quite a gathering," and she smiled.

"We're happy you came, Miss O'Neal. Yes, the children have been waiting to meet you. Shall we go meet the parents?"

The place was near bedlam with children racing back and forth between the incoming teacher and the kid's parents, describing her, excited about how pretty the new teacher was. A few shouted instructions to the crowd and order was slowly restored. Albert Schaffer held up his hand and called, "All right now, folks, let's get the children calmed down so we can introduce our new teacher." He waited a few seconds before announcing, "Folks, this is our new teacher, Miss Margaret O'Neal. She has a few things to say before we eat dinner, so, Miss O'Neal, it's all yours."

She stammered a greeting. "Good morning, I. . .this. . .you can tell I'm a little nervous, so let me start over." She bowed her head and prayed a quick prayer for guidance and help and started again. "Good morning. My name is Margaret O'Neal, but I prefer to be called Peggy. Is that all right? Of course, the children will call me Miss O'Neal, won't you children?" A variety of responses came back agreeing to that order. She continued, "I understand that some of you have never been in school before. If this is your first year going to school, will you raise your hand?"

All the littlest responded along with a few who were older, possibly as old as eight or nine. She said, "Now, please don't think I'm picking on you, but you older ones, do you know you're A-B-C's? I'm asking that to get some idea about how to setup the classes." There were four, three boys and one girl, who identified as not having gone to school before. Of those four, the girl knew her alphabet, the boys did not indicate so.

"Now, we're going to do a lot of reading and numbers. It's called Mathematics, or arithmetic. It's what the captains of these ships take to know how to read charts and sail the rivers. In the older grades, we will learn sentence structure so you can learn to communicate—"

A man, presumably a father, shouted, "We don't need none o' that stuff. The idée o' school is nonsense." Peggy was so completely surprised, she lost her train of thought and the man continued, "You come here with yore high falutin' jabber. It ain't never sowed a seed nor shucked a ear o' corn." He called a boy, "C'mon Sam, we got work ta do."

A boy, one of the four who indicated they had never been in school, started weeping and cried, "Aw, Daddy, cain't I please stay?"

Schaffer walked over to the man and said, "Ephraim, why don't you let him stay and come to school? Try it for a while. If it isn't to your liking, then pull him out, but let him come and be with the other kids for a while."

Ephraim looked bothered as his eyes moved from Schaffer to the teacher and back again. "Don't see no sense in it. He ain't gonna be nothin' but a farmer an' I got me a spread what's doin' pretty good." He thought a minute and finally agreed, "Well, awright, he kin stay. But the minute he ain't doin' his work, he comes out."

Albert Schaffer agreed and looked at the teacher, who also agreed. With that, Schaffer nodded toward Peggy and said, "All right, now, Miss Peggy, go on with your talk."

"Some of our reading in the upper grades will be in the Bible. Some of the words are too difficult for the younger children, so we'll probably hold off until maybe the third or fourth grades, and then the reading won't include any difficult names or places. It's just to give the student a better cross-section of material. I understand this is a new, school and supplies are somewhat limited. So we'll do the best with what we have." She pointed to the man who directed the parking of the buggies, "Could you please bring my carriage here? I have some boxes in the back that I need now."

The man ran off toward the assembly of buggies and came back leading the horse. When it got there, Peggy walked to the back and opened one box. She pulled out a ball, four inches in diameter, and a pine stick, skinned free of bark and straight, about two feet in length. "These are Knurr and Spell. I think it originated in Germany and came to this country when the Dutch came to New Amsterdam. Has anyone seen these before?" There was no response, so she continued.

She pulled a ball from the box that was made of canvas, a little larger than the last one. It had a canvas cover which was sewn with a hard string. Inside was a small rubber ball wound with string. "This ball can be used with the last stick as an object to hit. It can be used either by ones self or with other people in teams."

She reached for another object in the box and before it was shown, a man hollered, "Wait a minute, what's all the game stuff? I thought kids were going to school to learn, not to play."

Peggy hesitated for an instant, and spoke to that man. "Sir, this is the month of August. I understand the fall days are rainy and cloudy and there will be times when the students will not be able to get outside. Some of these toys are for days like that. The ball and stick are for a recess time when the children will get outside to play. They <u>need</u> a time to play, even though they are here to learn. You must have <u>both</u>, a time of study and a time to relax and play. Are you satisfied with that explanation?"

The answer was "Ya, I guess."

Schaffer interrupted Peggy with, "Look, folks, she's doing a good job explaining what's going to happen, but we came here to eat as well as listen. Now, why don't we break for a little to eat our dinner and then listen to the teacher again." That met with approval and people separated into family units, with close friends, to share their meal and discussed what they had heard. Mr. Schaffer came to Peggy and asked, "Miss O'Neal, some of the parents are asking how you are going to implement your plan for teaching."

"The little ones will have A-B-C's and a time of play in a sandbox. If they are used to taking a nap, we'll have to have a large towel or small blanket for them to lie on. Grade two will start with arithmetic and penmanship as well as their letters. Third grade will have arithmetic as well as spelling and the beginning classes of English and Grammar. And fourth through sixth grades will be taught their classes. I might have to combine the fifth and sixth grade lessons, having one lesson the first year and emphasizing the other class the next year. Second graders going to third in the years that we taught fourth grade material wouldn't be ready mentally to handle that change."

A mother, sitting in the front row, holding her five or six-year-old daughter, said, "Can you do all that? Won't you need some help?"

Peggy shook her head. "It's a contract I agreed to, so I'll have to make it work. But thanks for asking."

"But," she persisted, "won't the children be deprived of good teaching if you can't do what you've planned?"

"I think I can handle it. I might have some trouble at the start, but when I get organized, it'll go smoothly."

Almost under her breath, the woman asked, "And what if it doesn't? Is my daughter getting the education she deserves?"

People busied themselves with eating and talking, evaluating the new teacher and her plan. There were some shaking heads, not seeing how she was going to do all she planned. As the people finished eating, and were cleaning up afterward. Peggy got their attention by saying, "Folks, I have other items in this box that will be used when the children are kept inside because of the weather. We'll have hopscotch, inside table bowling, a game where six people can play on a board with holes in it, using marbles, which was used by the Chinese centuries ago, and a game called the Bilbo Catcher. This is a game with a cup on a stick, whose object is to catch a ball tossed by a team mate. We have two of those for two games. These are all inside games.

The woman who spoke to Peggy came to her and asked, "Miss, my name is Becky Schaub and I would like to ask you a question, if I may." Receiving permission, Mrs. Schaub said, "I don't see how you're going to be able to teach and do all the things you intend to do. I don't mean to push myself where I'm not wanted, but would you object to someone helping you, volunteering to do some of the things you have scheduled? It seems to me you've set up a killer schedule and you'll burn out before the year's half over at this rate."

Peggy's mind raced through a series of thoughts. Was this woman sent by the school board so they wouldn't have to pay her as much? What would the board say if she agreed to let this woman come and help her? I wonder what Evelyn would think of this if I said yes? She looked at the mother and studied her a few seconds before saying, "It's a schedule I agreed to. I think I'll be able to handle the load."

Not satisfied with the answer, Mrs. Schaub continued, "But, Miss, are you sure you can do this? You've set a high standard for yourself and, if I read the signs right, this is your first assignment. How are you going to handle a recess where the children are out playing and someone gets hurt? You won't be able to leave the children to get help. What will you do?"

Peggy thought for a second and asked, "What do you have in mind?"

"I thought perhaps I could take the little ones and keep them busy while you control the older activities." She didn't say anything for a moment, but it looked to Peggy that she wanted to say more. Becky blurted out, "Miss, I have a child, a five year old boy who doesn't speak. I thought if I could have him in school, he might be inspired to start speaking."

Hesitatingly, Peggy spoke, slowly, uncertain of saying the right thing. "I don't know. Where would you sit him? What would he do while you're with the other children?"

"I. . .uh, just thought he'd fit in with the other small ones. I. . .Miss O'Neal, I don't mean to impose myself on you, so forget I asked anything."

"Wait, Mrs. Schaub, I don't know if I should."

Evelyn had been talking to a friend whose husband was in the army and saw the serious conversation Peggy was having and walked her way. She stopped short of the two to listen to the topic of discussion before involving herself in their conversation. She waited until she was certain of what was being said and joined the two as Becky said she was still worried about Peggy's ability to handle everything. She needed a helper.

At that moment a ship's horn let the world know they were there and getting ready to dock. Everyone at the picnic turned to see the cause of the noise and Peggy recognized the ship. "Evelyn," she screamed, "it's his boat. That's Jacob's boat, but it isn't. His boat was yellow and red and white, this one's dull gray." She looked at the top of the structure and saw the same crow's nest where Jake had spent his time on their trip north and saw him behind the gun. "Evelyn, that's him. That's Jacob in that nest on top. Jacob," she screamed at the top of her lungs, "Jacob, it's me. Oh, Evelyn, how do I get down there?"

Albert Schaffer looked at Peggy in disbelief. How could a mature young woman who is going to teach our children act so irrationally? He looked at other members of the school board and some of the parents. Whom have we hired to teach our children? Can this emotional person be trusted to be a positive influence in our children's lives?

Evelyn saw the looks going around and quickly walked to where Shaffer was standing. She said, "Her fiancé is on that ship and she hasn't heard from him for a couple months. With your permission, she'd like to go down and try to see him."

Schaffer took a quick survey of the others nearby and gave his permission for Peggy to leave the picnic. Evelyn went to the young woman and told her. They gathered their belongings and shoved them into the back of the carriage, climbed aboard and headed down a street that Evelyn knew would take them to the waterfront. Peggy sat with her eyes closed and her hands clasped tightly, as if she was uncertain as to Jake's response when they met. She only hoped he remembered.

Captain Thomas stood holding the spy glass while still watching what was happening on the hill two hundred yards away. His Chief Boatswain stood next to him. "Mr. Reeder, pipe all hands. Who's duty section today?"

"Alpha section."

"Tell the others they are free until flag time tomorrow. And tell Mr. Prosser he's going to have a visitor shortly."

Chapter Nineteen

Jake stood at the top of the boat ramp waiting for this "visitor." The message Bo's'n Reeder gave him was that Captain Thomas said there would be a visitor coming to see him soon. There was no identification only that one would be there. He waited. A one-horse carriage, one he didn't recognize, turned off a side street onto the street past the ship. It stopped at the end of the loading ramp with the driver's side toward the ship. A passenger emerged for the other side of the carriage wearing a wide-brimmed sun bonnet, holding her hand up to her face. She waited for the carriage to move out of the way before she took off the sun bonnet and lowered her hand.

"Peggy?" he whispered, then shouted, "Peggy, you're here!" He ran down the ramp to the street and stopped in front of her. "I thought you were getting married. What happened? You didn't get married, did you? What are you doing here?"

She held up her hand. "One question at a time. Now, no, I didn't get married. It's a long story I'll tell you some time, but I'm not married. What am I doing here? I teach school, or I will teach school, up there on the hill. We're having a picnic and when your boat docked and blew the horn, I saw you and came down. The woman I'm with is the wife of the general, whose brother I was supposed to—"

"You mean General Patterson? I met him when we took him north to fight some rebel Indians. So what. . .oh, you're teaching school. Here in Cincinnati. Well. . .I, uh, look, I have the rest of the day until five tomorrow morning. Could we go somewhere and get a sandwich or something?"

"We can go out to Evelyn's and have a meal, and spend the rest of the day talking and planning. But, before that, would you do me one huge favor?"

"Of course."

"Jacob, will you hold me? Will you put your arms around me and hold me? I have missed you so terribly and I desperately need your arms around me." Surprised and a little indecisive, Jake opened his arms to her and she came immediately and snuggled against his chest. He remembered she asked the same thing earlier on their trip north, saying she missed her father. "Oh, Jacob, I have missed you so much. You're being here today is God's gift to a desperately needy woman, who wanted to hear you tell me one more time that you love me."

Still locked in the embrace, he rubbed his whiskered face against her cheek and whispered, "Peggy O'Neal, I have thought about you often, but every time, the thought of your marriage ended my memory of you. Now that you aren't married, will you permit me to think of someday our getting married?"

"Oh, yes!" she squealed, "Oh, yes," and she turned her face to him and kissed him full on the lips. "Oh, Jacob, I long for that day." He held her at arm's length to look at her and she said, "Come, I want to introduce you to Evelyn. She's the general's wife and wants to meet you."

They walked hand in hand to the carriage where Peggy introduced Jake to her friend who said, "Why don't we go home and get off the street? I'm sure some of the people question the display of affection here on the street. Come. You two get in the back. I imagine you'll want to sit together."

Jake helped Peggy into the back seat of the carriage, then walked around to get in the other side. She snuggled up to him, hugging his arm, to the place where he began to feel uncomfortable. Margaret O'Neal had found her true love and Jake, though he would favor getting married some day, was not ready for it now. She kept a steady stream of marriage talk while they rode and, as they neared Evelyn's home, said, "Jacob, you have hardly said a word. Is there something wrong? Do you feel differently than you did on the ship going north?"

"No, of course not." He took a deep breath. "Peggy, I'm in the Navy and we are at war. Maybe it will never come to the rivers, maybe it will. Maybe I'll get through without an injury, but maybe I won't. I don't want to leave you with an invalid in case something goes wrong. Can't you understand that?"

"Not really. The time to get married is when you're in love."

"Are you saying that if we wait a while, you may not love me as much then?"

She let go of his arm and buried her face in her hands. "Oh, no, that was the wrong thing to say. No, Jacob, what I'm trying to say is that I love you, and I assume you love me, based on your actions. I don't want anything to dampen that feeling." She took a breath and before Jake could respond, she continued, "I did it again. I guess I should just revel in your presence."

Fortunately, for the conversational needs, they arrived at the Patterson home. Jake stepped out of the carriage and looked at the house. "Wow. This is great. How long have you lived here?"

Evelyn looked at Jake, not really sure how to answer him. "Do you mean when did we come to Cincinnati, or when did we move into this house?"

Peggy answered for Mrs. Patterson. "They came to town about four years ago and added on to this house when her husband got his promotion. They use the side rooms for staff meetings and other official parties. And I live in one room of that added area."

Jake hesitated in his response and Evelyn said, "Come, let's get something to eat and we can talk." Evelyn led them into the kitchen and pointed to a chair for Jake while the ladies started cutting bread for sandwiches. Evelyn told Jake, "Through that door and to the right there's a crank above our cooler. The crank is attached to a lined tin container that is our cooler. Go and bring up the container. It has ham and cheese in it."

Jake did as directed and brought up the tin. It was about twelve inches in diameter and perhaps fourteen inches deep. The lid was clamped on with four levered clamps. Inside, Jake found a chunk of ham and a small roll of cheese and a container of tea, which he took into the kitchen. Evelyn explained, "That was the idea of the man who did the work on the house. We told him we needed to have some way of keeping some foods cool and he dug that well for us. It's bricked up all the way and is wonderfully cool, even in the summer. It keeps meat and even milk cool enough so we don't have to throw it out after one use. At our last house, if we didn't use all the item within one day, we pretty much had to throw it out, especially during the summer."

They sat down to a meal of ham sandwiches and cool tea. Peggy said, "Evelyn, Jacob made up a poem on our way up the river. I think it's cute. Jacob, tell her your poem."

After refusing and seeing Peggy disappointed, Jake finally agreed:

"Who's that smiling all the while, that's Peggy O'Neal.
With her hair done up in style, that's Peggy O'Neal.
If she talks with a cute Irish brogue.
If she acts like a sweet little rogue.
Sweet personality, full of rascality, that's Peggy O'Neal."

After a period of laughter and comments, Evelyn suggested they eat. Evelyn asked Peggy to ask the blessing, which she did, and they started eating. Evelyn was curious about what Jake had done since he left Peggy in St. Louis so Jake explained about the training on the gun. When he got the describing the weapon, Evelyn interrupted him, "Jake, how long have you known me?"

Surprised, he said, "Huh?"

"How long have you known me?"

"An hour, pro'bly."

"You know me as the wife of a Union General. What if I was a spy? What if I didn't believe in the stand my husband was fighting for, that I preferred the position the South has taken and was sneaking confidential information, like army intentions and plans to someone in Southern authority?" Peggy and Jake both sat there, open mouth, eyes wide open. Evelyn saw she was confusing the two and stopped her story.

"Now, I said that to emphasize the part that if you don't know who you are talking to and even if you think you know them, you might not. You might be giving confidential information to a spy. There are such things, Jake, and they live among us. So, be careful who you talk to and describe what you are doing. You might be giving secret plans to an enemy."

Jake still sat with his mouth open, mind whirring. What did he say? Who had he talked to and said anything about the weapon? Did she say she was a spy, or that she might be? What was she getting at?

She spoke. "Jake, I can see that I have confused you. I didn't mean to. All I meant to say was that when you are talking about something as important as that gun, you have to be careful not to divulge classified information. That's all. Just be careful whom you talk to. Now, let's change the subject, shall we? I understand you are from Cincinnati. Where did you live? Perhaps we could go see your parents this afternoon if it isn't too far."

Jake bowed his head. "I don't know. We lived in a poorer section of town, down along the river. Dreaming of being a sailor on the river was all I had to do when I was a kid. You wouldn't. . .I mean our house isn't anything like this. You wouldn't like it."

Peggy frowned slightly as she looked at him. She said nothing for several seconds before asking, "Don't you want me to meet your folks?"

Jake looked down, his eyes glued to the floor and slowly shook his head. "I'm sorry." He looked at Peggy with tears in his eyes. "I never knew a fine woman till I met you. I got no right to ask, or even think, you could accept where I come from. I'm from the dregs, the scrapin's. If they hadn't took me in the Navy, I'd pro'bly be in jail now."

Surprised, Peggy looked at Evelyn and put her hand p to her mouth. "Why would you say something like that? You're a fine man, Jacob, why would you think you'd be in jail if the Navy hadn't accepted you?"

He nervously fiddled with his hands before answering. "Most of the guys I grew up with are either dead or in jail. That's why I said that. I grew up where there was no hope. The men became thieves and the women became. . .They. . ." Neither woman spoke for a while and Jake continued, "The only reason I went on through high school was because of my dream of the Navy. Without that, I had no hope."

Peggy expressed her thought, "But now you have hope in God. You did read the Bible didn't you?"

"Yeh, I read it and understand some of it, but can't believe that God would care whether I lived or died. I mean, who am I that He should care?"

Quickly, Peggy answered, "You're a soul whom Jesus died for. He gave His life for you to be free of sin."

"I've read the first three chapters of John a dozen times, and I come up with the same question—He had everything, why did He do it? I mean, a God, being born of a woman here on earth is beyond belief, and living among the people, and then permitting Himself to be hung on a cross. Why did He do it? If God is all powerful as some say, couldn't He have just said something and made it happen?"

Peggy answered, "That's the questions a minister asked and he preached on them before I got on that boat. I'll try to remember what he said, but it's like, a thing called Divine Love. We can't understand it because we're human, but God's love, and this is someplace later in the New Testament, said, that while we were yet sinners, Christ died for us. I can't explain it. You'd have to get a minister to answer your questions, but, God loved us because He wanted fellowship with us. I know it's crazy, but that's the best I can do."

While Jake thought about that, Peggy asked, Evelyn, "May I ask you a very personal question?"

Surprised, Evelyn hesitated slightly, "Well. . ."

Quickly, Peggy corrected her approach, "That was the wrong way to ask. Let me try this. You and your husband have been married a long time. I think you said thirty years. Now, I would like to marry to Jake, as soon as possible. He doesn't want to leave me with a child in case something happens to him, or he doesn't want to leave me with an invalid. What have you seen in your time associated with the military and newly wedded soldiers?"

"Oh, my. You want the hardest first." She wrung her hands a few seconds before asking, "I presume you are talking about the two of you." Both Jake and Peggy opened their mouth to answer but Evelyn continued. "I have seen terrible disappointment in the lives of a young bride when her new husband was killed. It is devastating, terribly disturbing, when a couple has plans for a life together and something happens to one of them. And things happen in life outside of the battles of war. My dear, I don't know how to answer you. I can see your point and I can see Jacob's side. I think he is being honorable in this stand, avoiding the pleasure of marriage for a few days, knowing he may be sent into a serious battle where terrible things might happen." She shook her head. "I'm sorry if I disappoint you, but I agree in this case with Jacob."

Peggy looked away for a moment and tried to smile when she looked back. She reached for Jake's hands and had to release one to wipe a tear. Jake spoke as tenderly as he could, "I'm sorry, Peggy. I wish I didn't feel so strongly this way, but I do. I'd almost agree to go ahead with the marriage to keep you from feeling so bad, but I think it would be wrong."

Still holding his hand, she brought a smile through teary cheeks and said, "Will you agree to marry me the minute this thing is over?"

He smiled and leaned over to seal his promise with a kiss. The kiss was interrupted by banging on the front door. "What on earth?" Evelyn said as she got up to answer the door. She opened the door to four members of the school board, with Albert Schaffer leading them. "Hello Mr. Schaffer, your hammering on the door sounded urgent. Come in and tell us what is so important."

"That woman!" he growled, "and her amorous display on the street! Mind you, in front of God and everybody. She either will marry that man right here or will be banned from teaching in our schools."

Incensed, Evelyn said, "And who do you think you are that you can make that decision for them? They have talked about marriage, but Jacob is concerned about being wounded and giving her an invalid to care for. That is a noble decision, and one that he made and she accepted. Now, what is this poppycock about her not teaching in our schools?"

"I will not have that woman, with her public amorous exhibition, having an influence on our children. She is no better than a. . .a—"

Jake jumped up and in two quick strides was at the speaker's side with his fist cocked, muscles tensed. He grabbed Schaffer's shirt front and threatened, "If you say the word at the end of your tongue, you will speak your next words with a broken jaw from a toothless mouth."

The other people were shocked and the ladies moved one or both hands to their face, while the male members of the group offered a variety of expressions. Schaffer tried to push Jake's hand away from his shirt and twisted his body away from a direct blow. Fearfully, he exclaimed, "Unhand me you ruffian! Let go of my shirt."

"That woman will one day be my wife. Not now, but when the war is over. That is a promise I have made to her. She is as fine a Christian as you can find, and I resent your attitude. Now, if that is all you have to say, you can leave."

Schaffer managed to get himself gathered together and stood, "That is not all I have to say, and I'll thank you to keep your grubby hands off me, you dolt. I could have you arrested for assault. These witnesses would verify my charge. I am not some weak, helpless individual. I know the law and have friends. So, you can expect a visit from the gendarmes within the hour." He stood, "And as far as your lady is concerned, I'll see that she never teaches in any of our schools. Good day to you." To the other, "Come,"

As soon as the door closed behind them, Evelyn stood and issued an order, "Jacob, go tell Simon to ready the carriage. Peggy, do you have the contract with you?" She dug in her purse for the legal paper which said she was hired to teach in the new school. "All right, we are going to see Mayor Hatch. Just because that man has money, he thinks he can rule the city. He ran and was defeated, so now he throws his weight around trying to rule those of us who aren't as filthy rich."

Jake asked, "What does he do?"

"He is the dean of men at Cincinnati University. He is also owner of a farm equipment manufacturing business." They were aware of Simon's presence at the door and they made their way to the carriage. After a short ride to the center of town, the group arrived at the city building and was led to a waiting room.

The mayor came in and greeted Evelyn, who explained that his son is one of her husband's staff members. There was a short explanation as to the school problem and a quick promise that "This lovely young lady will certainly be able to teach in our school system. What time do you be getting to school in the morning?" She told him. He smiled. "What if I meet you on the way? I'd like to see Schaffer's face when we get there."

Chapter Twenty

The presence of Cincinnati Mayor Hatch accompanying new Teacher O'Neal was a blow to Shaffer and the score of parents he had gathered to protest her employment. Some came because of the way the board president described the kiss between Jake and Peggy. Some came because they had heard she was a beauty, and wanted to see for themselves. Mayor Hatch greeted the people as he rode up on his horse and said, in a voice loud enough to be heard throughout the crowd, "Will all you parents come into the school for a quick meeting. I want to clear up any misconception about Miss O'Neal before this gets out of hand."

The building was as long as it was wide, perhaps fifty feet square, facing south, with one door in front as the entrance, and a window on each side to be used as an emergency escape. The mayor stood on a concrete step in front of the door and waited for the people to get the invitation fixed in their minds, that he wanted them to come inside. Slowly, so very slowly, the parents started moving in that direction, with Albert Schaffer bringing up the rear. Knowing most of the people, Hatch greeted each person by name as that individual approached the main door and told them to just stand alongside the walls, for it would be a very short meeting.

Inside, he picked out two or three women and asked why they were there, and the story they told was somewhat different than what Schaffer saw. He wanted them to think the worst of the new teacher.

Hatch explained the young couple were sweethearts, but hadn't seen each other for two months, and couldn't write because Jake was in the navy and the young woman was traveling. As such, they didn't have the other's address. Then Hatch blistered Schaffer and told him to leave the young woman alone, that her education from a school in Philadelphia qualifies her to teach. If, at the semester evaluation, she is found wanting, they will make an adjustment at that time, but until then leave her alone.

The crowd dispersed and Mayor Hatch left. However, two of the women returned and just stared at Peggy. There was no conversation, just a silent stare. Twice, Peggy tried to get the ladies involved in an explanation as to why they were there, but there was no response, just the silent stare. She tried to ignore their presence and started assigning seating for those students in the room. She had no problem with the little ones, but the older students began to present difficulties, for there were some, boys mostly, but some girls too, who were older but had not gone past the fourth grade, and she had to carefully place them.

It seemed strange to her, coming from a Philadelphia background, where it was assumed that children in her neighborhood would follow the usual procedure and get an education. But, in the new areas of the west, those areas like Ohio and Indiana, that had only been settled within the last fifty years, education was not that clear nor usual. The memories of Simon Kenton and Daniel Boone and their battles with the Shawnee for possession of the land were more prominent.

A knock on the door changed the attention as Peggy opened the door to Becky Schaub, the lady who had volunteered to help at the picnic. She came in and saw the two women and spoke to Peggy, but in a voice loud enough for the others to hear, "I decided to pray for you this morning. If you felt uncomfortable with my offer to help, at least I could pray. As I prayed, I felt a strong urgency to come here and see if I could help. Now I know why." She turned to the two visitors and said, "I know you. You two ladies are from the same social level as Mr. Schaffer. I'm not, and I would imagine that Miss O'Neal is not either. I think if you are not going to help, it might be a good time for you to see if there is something you need to do at home."

A "Harumph" was their only response, as the gathered their long skirts and headed for the door.

Peggy stood with her hands clasped at her throat and when the door closed, she said, "Thank you, thank you. I didn't know what to do. They didn't talk, they just stared and I was getting frantic. Thank you." She reached out for Becky's hand.

Becky smiled, "Thank our God, for it was He who impressed me to come." She clasped her hands in front of her waist and looked down at the floor. When she looked up he eyes were moist and she struggled with a smile. "Miss O'Neal, I had a selfish reason for coming this morning. Oh, I felt it was the thing I was supposed to do, but, there's another reason. I told you, I have a five year old son who is slow in maturing. The doctors say there is nothing they can do, but I know that somewhere, somehow, God has something better for him than a life of being laughed at and scorned. I believe that you are the key to his. . .I hesitate to use the word healing, but, I will say it. You are the key to his healing."

Peggy's hands flew to her mouth and she cried, "Oh, no! Me? Oh, Mrs. Schaub, I'm just a new Christian myself. I know nothing of healing or even how to pray for it." The students in the room listened to the conversation. Some, the older ones, began to understand and those out of immediate sight of the teacher began to whisper and snicker. Peggy caught the sound and turned with anger at those students who were participating in the disrespectful attitude, and she scolded them.

"Students! There are nine words I want to impress on your minds. Whenever you see or hear of someone who may not be like you, I want you to think of these words—'There but for the grace of God go I.' No one has a guarantee of anything in this life, certainly, not health or wealth. You get an education in order to help in those areas of your life, where an education might give you the knowledge of a better life. Sometimes, it doesn't happen. Sometimes, it's out of our hands. But we pray and leave our lives in the hand of a loving God."

She paused and more quietly said, "Now, Mrs. Schaub said she felt impressed to come here this morning. And now I have the same feeling regarding Mrs. Schaub's son." She turned to Becky and asked, "What is the boy's name?"

"Jaimie."

Peggy's eyebrows raised and she said, "Isn't that an unusual name for a German child?"

"I'm Irish," and in a soft whisper, "I wasn't married. I just took the name of his father."

Peggy knelt on the school floor as every student watched. She said, "Jaimie, would you come here and let me hold your hand?" He hid behind his mother's leg, holding her skirt, sucking his thumb, and didn't move until his mother reached down and led him to the teacher. "Jaimie, don't be afraid. I'm going to pray for you and I want you to understand what I'm doing. You've heard your mother pray, haven't you?" A slight nod was his response.

"All right, now, Jaimie, don't be afraid. I'm going to pray for you. Can I hold your hand?" A slight movement that Peggy took as a "no," gave her the idea he didn't want to be there, as he cuddled more closely to his mother. Peggy nodded and began praying. "Father, your Word says that we can ask and it will be given to us, if we seek we will find and if we knock, it will be opened to us. We bring this child, Your child, dedicated to you at his birth, who has a problem. At one time when a blind man was brought to You, Your disciples asked if he sinned or his parents that caused him to be born blind and You said, it was for the Glory of God that he was born blind, and you healed him. Now, I, we ask you to show God's Glory, and His Mercy, and heal this boy of his problem. And we'll say thank you. Amen."

No one moved. Hardly anyone breathed as they looked at Jaimie, expecting something to happen. But there was no change. Jaimie's mother began to weep and Peggy rose from her kneeling position and grasped the mother's hand. "Wait. Don't give up just yet. Perhaps He is testing our faith. Wait until tomorrow."

The rest of the day was suppressed. During recess breaks, there was little exuberance on the part of the children, but the older children gathered in small groups, looking at their teacher. The younger children, especially those who did not come from Christian homes, talked about the different type of school that day. Those with Christian backgrounds, shrugged their shoulders and waited, for it was something they had seen their parents do.

At the end of the day, the children rushed to their conveyance to explain what happened at school that day. Those to whom prayer was a part of their lives, it was interesting that their children had a teacher who believed in prayer. To others, such as Albert Schaffer, who was angered that his plan to rid the school of that teacher was met with interference by that busybody mayor, something had to be done. Tomorrow! Waiting for things to smooth out was out of the question. His sixth-grade son, who witnessed the activity today, would be like Paul Revere and tell all their friends the radical religionists were coming. Meet tomorrow for a final confrontation.

An exhausted young teacher reached her home and sat in her carriage several minutes. Evelyn watched from her window, concerned that something had gone terribly wrong. After several minutes of sitting, Peggy got out of the carriage and moved toward the house. Evelyn greeted her at the door with, "Bad day?"

Peggy nodded, short quick shakes, but said nothing. She walked through the parlor and down the hallway to the kitchen and sat at the table with her elbows on the table and her hands cupped against her forehead. "Today was exceptional. Tomorrow will be plain terror." She went on to explain all about the visit by the mother and her child, and praying for him during class time. "Some of the children, I assume those whose parents are Christian, accepted what went on as if it was the usual thing to do. Others couldn't stop whispering. I imagine there will be quite a crowd waiting for me when I get to school."

"Do you want me to come along? Perhaps I should send Simon with a message for the mayor. If Schaffer is going to be there, Mayor Hatch should know about it."

Peggy crossed her arms at her waist, leaned back in the master chair against the top of the arched back. "It's too much to ask you, but would it be possible for you to escort me past that mob in the morning? I know it isn't your fight, but I'm afraid of what might happen, and more afraid of what I might say." Peggy went on to tell about the two women who came into the classroom and just stared at her, never saying a word.

With that, Evelyn called Simon and asked him to take a message to the mayor that he really needed to be at school in the morning.

It was late when Simon got back home, but he had a promise from the mayor that he would meet the ladies on their way to school.

Peggy spent a restless night, praying and walking, with very little sleep. In her mind, tomorrow might be the end of her teaching career—only one day. Some resume.

After muster of ship's personnel Tuesday morning, as the men were lined up on the prow of the ship, they felt a tug, a jerk and the ship moved gently away from the dock, into the swift-flowing Ohio River. They moved west down the river, past the ship building operation going on there. The boat slips that once held passenger ships like the G E, now had Union gunships on those skids. Jake saw six in various stages of completion, all with paddle-wheels on both sides, ships that one day would sail these rivers looking for Confederate ships to battle. One, almost finished, was being painted, while the next one to it was being armed with thirty and twenty pounders canons. They would soon be staffed with sailors like him. Heavy fire power for war on the rivers.

Walter Thomas, captain of the GREAT EXPECTATIONS, or G E as the men called her, called Jake to the wheelhouse and told him, "We are going to Jefferson Barracks to pick up troops for some guy named Grant. We have to transport them to Cairo, Illinois where Grant is fighting rebs. This tells you how bad off our troops are when some guy, a store clerk in Galena Illinois, is given a command. But, forget that. We have a bit of a problem with you. You are a Gunner's Mate second, and, as of right now, you don't deserve that grade. So, here's what we're gonna do. Mr. Reeder is going to teach you everything you need to know to hold that grade. We're going to be on the water four days, so in that four days, you will be an accomplished Gunner two."

"Yes sir," was all Jake could think to say.

"You will learn organizational structure, you will learn duties and command procedure. It will be intense, but Mr. Reeder has agreed to do it. So, get to it. He'll meet you in your old room. One word of warning. Mr. Reeder takes pride in his job and in his knowledge of the US Navy. If you have a question, don't let him go on thinking you understand, but don't ask stupid questions. Your school grades show you have the ability to think. Use it."

Jake left the captain and found what Reeder had prepared for him, a room full of pictures, diagrams and charts, attached to the walls of the room. Without asking how much Jake knew or had told him, Reeder started off with the command structure on a ship, his ship, and identified the ranking Petty Officer as Herman Gunther, Yoeman. The Master-at-Arms was Wilhelm Roeder. "Now, don't get us confused. He was a fighter and served in the German Navy. He's responsible for order and conduct aboard the ship. As an old school German, he's very strict."

Reeder continued, branching to the duties of a gunner and of his mate. Jake was told of his responsibilities while engaged in combat. One duty was to assist in fighting fires that might result from enemy attack. That was the first charge after his normal attack function. As a Gunner's Mate, second, he would be assisting with guns at the rear quarter of the ship, on both sides. He would be in a crew of seven men, plus the possibility of having a "Powder Monkey," a boy under eighteen years of age, who carried powder cartridges from a passing cart to the next gun.

If Jake hadn't wanted to be a sailor all his life, the concentrated, forceful way the information was given him, might have discouraged him. But, he knew his promotion was a gift from a grateful captain for his teaching of the Gatling gun, and he knew he had a lot of learning to do to get up to his grade level. So, as he had done in school, he made one-line notes regarding certain elements of the information given him to go over it again when Reeder left him.

The ship was about halfway to the Mississippi at meal time and Jake wondered how Peggy's day had been. He thought of her and prayed for the Lord to bless her and help her.

Chapter Twenty-One

Wednesday morning, Evelyn insisted Peggy eat breakfast, if only toast and coffee. A friend had made the most delicious apple butter and Evelyn set that jar on the table. After they ate, Evelyn suggested they spend some time in prayer and Peggy agreed, but insisted Evelyn pray first. Peggy's mind was confused—if she was supposed to teach, why was she having so much trouble getting started? Not familiar with prayer techniques, Evelyn just talked to God, explaining her desires for Peggy that day. That was done and Peggy gathered her equipment for school. Simon had harnessed the horse and hooked it up to the carriage and notified the ladies. They were ready to go, and Peggy wondered what would happen.

The answer came a block from school when men and women, supposedly parents, met her and Evelyn with signs and verbal abuse. "KEEP GOD IN CHURCH," or "WE DON'T NEED YOUR TYPE OF RELIGION." There were other signs and much verbal cruelty, calling Peggy names she could never have thought possible. To cap the annoyance, they saw Albert Schaffer standing on the step, while they were a block away from the school.

While the ladies concentrated on the mob ahead of them, they heard a voice next to them and saw Mayor Hatch astride his horse. He appeared magically and glared at the people who formed a pathway to the front door. Albert Schaffer stood on the step, a crumpled hat in one hand, with the other, as a fist, stuffed against his hip. He pointed with the hat-held fist and shouted that a school board meeting that morning had rescinded her job, and that she was not welcome at the school from that moment on.

Peggy sat beside Evelyn, weeping with her fists held against her face. Suddenly, while they were still thirty feet from the step, Becky Schaub, carrying her son, burst through the line of people. She was crying, and called, "He spoke to me, Miss O'Neal, he asked if he could go to school this morning. He has never said more than yes or no, but he asked if he could come to school."

Peggy's shoulders slumped forward and her body shook as she cried. Evelyn put her arm around Peggy's shoulders and pulled her close. Then there was another sound, one of support for Peggy and what she did, coming from a smaller group off to the left of the front step. They thanked God for Peggy's faith and her confidence in God. They called for Schaffer to accept her as an outstanding young woman and a good teacher.

Mayor Hatch dismounted and walked up to Schaffer. "Get your board members inside. I want to hear your complaint." He looked out over the crowd to find Becky Schaub and called her. "Ma'am, will you come in for a minute? I want to hear from your lips what happened in there."

Schaffer called five people from the crowd who came to the door and followed him inside. Hatch moved his hand to encourage Becky Schaub to enter, but she was still holding her son. The mayor nodded to tell her it was all right, and she entered. Then the mayor closed the door behind him.

There was no sound from the inside of the building for the fifteen minutes, until the door opened and Becky made her way to the carriage where Peggy and Evelyn sat. People tried to intercept her and ask her what was going on inside, but she shook off all their grasps and managed to climb into the back seat. "Oh, Miss O'Neal," she exclaimed to the two ladies, "there was almost a fight. Mr. Schaffer is so. . .so demanding, and Mr. Hatch refused to let him say anything.

Peggy asked, "What did they have you do?"

"I told them what I told you, that while I was praying for you yesterday, I felt very strongly that I was supposed to come here with Jaimie and have you pray for him."

Peggy asked, "I wonder what's going to happen now."

"Mr. Hatch is going to call you in there to talk to them." Evelyn, still sitting with her arm around Peggy's shoulder, gave her a squeeze.

Nervously, Peggy wrung her hands. "What can I say? They will want me to resign, I'm sure. What do I do if I can't teach?"

Evelyn hugged her closer and said, "Don't ask for problems that aren't there. If that is the choice, we'll think of something. But don't anticipate problems. Let's just wait for the questions, then you give them answers."

They sat a few minutes until people started filing out of the school. After five or six left the building, the mayor stood in the doorway and motioned for Peggy to come. She didn't see Schaffer, so he must still be inside. She gripped Evelyn's hand and begged, "Pray for me, please. Pray I'll say the right thing and not get upset at whatever happens." She got out of the carriage and walked to the door.

Mayor Hatch greeted her, "Thank you for waiting. There were some things we had to clear up first before talking to you. Please come in and go over to the higher grade's reading area."

As stated, the school was a square building facing the south. Inside, the teacher's desk was against the north wall and the desks and chairs were fanned out in a half-circle with small chairs of first graders to the left and the sixth grader's chairs to the right. Albert Schaffer sat in one of the larger chairs, waiting, glaring. Mayor Hatch walked with the young woman around the outside of the circle until they came to the front and each took a chair. The mayor spoke. "We are going to be civil. I will ask a question and the person I ask will answer. Do not interrupt, and keep your tone courteous. Now, Miss O'Neal, would you tell me what happened in the classroom yesterday?"

"Miss Schaub had talked to me at the picnic Monday, volunteering to help at recess with the little ones while I had the older students with their games. I told her I didn't know if that would be permitted—"

Albert Schaffer opened his mouth the interrupt, but the mayor raised his hand and said, "I said there would be no interruptions. Go ahead Miss O'Neal."

"Anyway, she came and told me that when she was praying for me, she felt impressed to bring her son to school to have me pray for him. I prayed and nothing happened, so we went on with the school plan."

"That's it? You didn't say anything about prayer for healing?"

Thoughtfully, and slowly, she answered, "I don't think so. Well, I did pray for his healing, but that was all. I remember asking Jaimie, Miss Schaub's son, if I could pray for him, but I didn't say anything more. I asked if he would let me hold his hand and he said, I mean, he shook his head no, so I prayed and his mother put him with the first graders."

Mr. Hatch paused a moment before asking, "That's it? And what did you do then?"

"I continued with the lessons. We had beginning reading for the second graders where I introduced their material. Some of the older children were weak in arithmetic, and I had to go over some basic things. All in all, I thought we had a good day."

Hatch turned to Albert Schaffer and asked, "And what is your complaint about what she did?"

Angrily, he shouted, "Religious stuff needs to be kept in church. Period! She came in here to teach and yet she flaunted her religion in front of my kid and every other kid in school. They didn't need to see her call on an imaginary. . .some supposed Celestial Authority to heal a kid from what, because he couldn't talk? If he'd been raised right, that would have been a natural result of his upbringing."

Shocked, Peggy responded, "Mr. Schaffer," she exclaimed, "how—"

Mayor Hatch held up his hand. "Remember, no interruption. Now, Miss O'Neal, is this idea of prayer going to be a regular item in your school?"

"Mr. Hatch, I didn't come here intending to cause problems, or to convert anyone to believe as I do. But a woman had a child who was physically impaired, and asked me to pray for him. I could do no less." She took a breath, "But, as I said, I did not, nor will I come to school intending to cause problems. But I am a Christian. I can do no less than be ready to help if the need is presented. I don't know what to say other than that."

Schaffer shouted, "See! She said we can expect the same thing again and again. I insist you dismiss her so we can hire an older woman who will be more stable for our classroom."

Mayor Hatch, sitting on the corner of the teacher's desk, looked down at the floor. He was silent for several seconds. He looked up from Peggy to Schaffer and said, "I'll have to think about it. Now, I want your promise, both of you, that if I rule against your wishes, you'll accept it with grace."

Schaffer glared at Peggy without saying anything. Peggy nodded. The two were dismissed but the mayor stayed there, walking around the room with his hands clasped behind him, muttering, "The joys of being a mayor."

The two groups waited outside the school, those in support moved down to be near the carriage to encourage Peggy, while Schaffer and his people moved closer to the door. Some of them left the area because of other duties, but there were still a few more of them than those near the carriage. Children from both groups mingled between the two.

Several minutes elapsed before Mayor stood on the step and called the pupils to his side. He told them, "I want to talk to the third graders and those older, but I want to talk to you one at a time, and I want you to promise when you come out, not to tell what we talked about. Will you do that?" He turned toward the door, paused, and spoke to the children and parents again. "On second thought, I'll keep the children I talk to inside. That way they won't be under any pressure to keep from speaking to their parents or friends."

He called the first child, a third grader, and they entered the building. In two minutes, he was at the door again, calling another student. It went like that until he had called fifteen or so children and then the door opened and the little ones rushed out to their parents. Mayor Hatch motioned for Peggy and Schaffer to come back inside, which they did.

They stood just inside the door and he said, "I talked to the children and not one of them said anything about being offended by Miss O'Neal praying. Most said their parents prayed, and thought that's what their teacher should do when there was a problem. No one, well, only one said anything negative about her teaching ability. They all thought she did a good job. And all the boys said they wanted her to come back because she is so pretty, to quote them. So, Miss O'Neal, the job is yours, with this provision. Keep your praying at a minimum. Some agree with Mr. Schaffer that it is unnecessary in school."

Albert Schaffer stomped out of the building, down the step to the dirt and kicked a stone out of his way. He growled all the way to his carriage and jerked the rope loose from the hitching rail and climbed into the buggy. Once loose from the other horses and buggies, he whipped his animal into an immediate gallop, disappearing around a corner in three seconds.

Peggy stood with her hands clasped at her waist with her head bowed. She said nothing for several seconds until the mayor called her name. She looked up, her eyes damp, and said, "I didn't want to cause a problem, but when Miss Schaub told me about Jaimie, I felt I had to do something. I'm sorry to cause you this trouble. But what do I do if another mother asks me to pray for her child?"

Hatch pursed his lips and tilted his head to one side. After a short pause, he asked, "What is it the Bible says about being wise as serpents and harmless as doves? I guess my advice would be to use your better judgment." Then, as he turned to the door, he asked, "Do you think you can make anything of the day that's left?"

"I think I can. I think it's important for the children to come to school now. I think they'll be all right." When the mayor opened the door and called the children, they rushed inside to their chairs. He nodded and smiled, turned and walked to his horse. Peggy stood on the front step and waved at Evelyn, who waved back and turned her horse around for home. She would have to come back for Peggy when school was done, but this trip was a learning experience for someone trying to find her way as a new Christian.

Chapter Twenty-Two

Things got a little better for Margaret O'Neal as the week wore on. The uncertainty of each day diminished and the classroom process smoothed out as students accepted their new teacher, even though some called her a "religious nut." In fact, the only fight of the week came as a result of that epithet. The participants were a student whose parents prayed often and, as no surprise, Albert Schaffer's son, Wilfred. Miss O'Neal talked to both boys, keeping them facing into a back corner of the room for a while.

When she released them back into their class, she talked to all the students. "I am a Christian. I have certain beliefs that I will keep to myself, unless one of you wants to talk to me about them after school. We will not talk about our beliefs during class time. That would only create turmoil. Now, we will continue with our class time and from tomorrow on throughout the semester, we will stick with our schedule. Understood?" A unified nodding of their heads gave agreement.

She moved ahead with alphabet study for first graders, reading for the classes and arithmetic for grades two through six. She combined some classes for consecutive grades, but in some cases, there was too large a span between what the students knew and what the combined material taught. As the week progressed classes were easier. Each day ended with some student telling the teacher how much that person enjoyed the work. On Friday, many of the students gathered around the teacher's desk, expressing their appreciation for her teaching.

As Peggy gathered her personal items for her trip home, Becky Schaub came into the room with another woman, slightly older than she. She began, "Miss O'Neal, this is Carolyn Murray, my neighbor, and she wants to talk to you about your beliefs." Becky hesitated a moment before continuing, "I've tried to tell her, but she has questions I can't answer. Would you talk to her, please?"

Peggy looked at both visitors a couple seconds before saying, "Oh, dear, now? I'm sorry. My time is planned and I have to get home soon." She saw the letdown on Becky's face, and hastily continued, "I'm sorry, Becky, but would tomorrow be all right? That would give us more time to talk, if it's all right by you."

Becky looked at her friend, who agreed, and they set a time of ten o'clock in the morning for the meeting. As they agreed, Peggy said, "Can you give me some clue as to what the discussion will be?"

Carolyn answered, "I just started reading the Bible. My brother just became a Christian and he wanted me to read the Bible to see where he is coming from when he talks to me. But, I can't get past Genesis. Who did the men marry? If God created Adam and Eve, where did the women come from that their sons married?"

The question surprised the teacher and she sat with her mouth open, eyes darting around the room while she thought. It only took three or four seconds, and when she focused on the questioner again, she said, "I'll try to find the answer for you. Can we delay the meeting until eleven? I'm sure my hostess will have some goodies for us then."

Peggy entered the Patterson house carrying an armful of books and papers. She went directly to her room, set the books down and flopped onto her bed. She stayed unmoved for two minutes, hardly breathing, before she inhaled deeply, and asked herself, "Will I always be this tired or will it get easier as the year passes?" She stirred, rolling to her side so she could see the work awaiting her and then remembered her promise to Becky and Carolyn about their meeting the next day. She sighed, falling back prone.

Peggy heard the light finger-nail rap on the door but didn't respond immediately. Instead, she heaved another sigh and rolled to the edge of the bed, where she dropped her legs over the side and pushed herself into a sitting position. Then, she said, "Yes, come in."

The look of concern on Evelyn's face as she opened the door made Peggy smile. "I'm all right," she offered, "just worn out from the week. I had no idea it would be so strenuous, trying to organize and teach children. But, I'm into it now, and after the effort of the mayor and you to get me the job, and to keep it, I could hardly back out."

"When I saw you come in and you didn't come to the kitchen as you have done, I wondered if there was a problem."

"No. . .Well, yes. The problem is that I have never done this before and for a while I felt I was in over my head. I'm sure things will smooth out as the days pass and the pressure will ease." She looked up at an anxious host and added, "No, it will be all right, and thank you for your concern." She paused a moment before standing, "There is one other problem, well, not necessarily, but potentially. You remember the woman at school who brought her child to be prayed for?" Evelyn nodded.

"Well, she has a neighbor whose brother recently became a Christian and is encouraging his sister to understand what it means. She started reading the book of Genesis, which describes creation and the development of the Nation of God's people and read where Adam and Eve's sons married, took wives, and had children. She wants to know, if Adam and Eve were the first two people, where did their sons get their wives. And, that's a question I have never studied."

Evelyn's hand went to her mouth and she muttered, "Oh, my. What are you going to tell her?"

"I don't know. As I said, I've never studied it. In fact, I don't remember having it asked before. I don't know what to do. I can't just brush her off. That would hurt Becky's faith and perhaps this other woman might give up. No, I have to find the answer, somehow."

Evelyn sat in a chair and the two pondered answers, with each one failing to give a satisfactory answer. There couldn't have been other people on the earth if Adam and Eve were the "first" male and female. Where did they come from? She had to go outside their circle to find an answer.

After a quiet time of several seconds, Evelyn offered, "There's a huge church in the center of the city. It's the largest in town and the pastor is in the news often. His name is Josiah Baker. He might give you some time and give you an answer."

"How do I see him? I'll have to go to his church and hope he'll give me a few minutes."

After another pause in their conversation, Evelyn added, "There's a Catholic University, St. Xavier College that only takes students from this city. It's small, and it's on the west side of town, but perhaps they could give you the information you want."

"I wouldn't know how to find it. Do you think Simon would go with me?"

Evelyn smiled, "I'll guarantee it."

Both Evelyn and Simon accompanied Peggy on her search early Saturday morning. Simon drove the buggy and the ladies sat in the back seat. Simon had been born in the city and had seen its growth. The college they sought was about three miles from their home and they were there by nine o'clock. The school taught Jesuit policy and the studies were for young men dedicated to that ministry.

The trio arrived at the school and, because they had no idea of whom to ask for, hailed the first official looking person walking across the campus. He smiled as they explained their need and, as they finished, went with the ladies to the administration building, where they found Father Justin Herman, head of the Religious Instruction. They were led to his study and given chairs. They sat and explained the reason for their search.

He smiled and said, "That is the problem of the Bible, leaving out so much that we have to make some assumptions. First, and, if we believe the Bible, this is the least possible theory. The story of Adam and Eve is a myth, that there were other people on the earth as far back as ten million years ago, and the sons happen to find one of the available women from that culture. As I said, if you believe the Bible, that is automatically excluded.

"Second, the creation story in the Bible is incomplete. True, Adam and Eve were created by God as the beginning of His people, the Jewish Nation, but He created others to fill the earth. There is no record of them because the Bible is the story of the Jewish people, who came from Adam and Eve. Those who argue that idea, point to the 'orders' God gave Moses and Joshua to kill, execute all residents in their path as they came from Egypt. They say that those who were under this order were believers in another god, or gods, as the case may be.

"The third one creates another problem, for it means God permitted incest. That the sons of Adam and Eve married their sisters." Both Peggy and Evelyn looked at each other and back to the speaker. He smiled and continued. "If we accept this as God's plan for populating the earth, we have to justify what we cannot accept now as a way of life. We can by believing that the creation of God was perfect, that the blood was untainted, and that until the Law from Sinai, it was not unusual for this to happen. Of course, Adam lived nine hundred thirty years and when he died, there were some millions of people on the earth so that practice was not needed"

The ladies were silent, so the priest continued. "This presents us with a conundrum. We, in our living, have come to accept the standards of a Holy God, and see this answer as it goes against every criterion we have for decency. But that's today. In the beginning, as God was building His nation, He permitted this. . .this seeming variance, knowing the blood was pure and that it was only temporary. I have spent considerable time in prayer and in discussions with other men, and this is my answer. I have to accept this to believe that Adam and Eve were the first couple, and that there were no other peoples populating the earth. Are you all right with that explanation?"

It took several seconds for both Evelyn and Peggy to accept his story, and after a time, they both nodded.

Their ride home was quiet, neither one willing to express an opinion about what they heard. As the carriage pulled into their drive and Simon halted before their porch, Peggy asked, "What do I tell them when they get here? Will they be willing to accept his account?"

"Tell them what he said, and tell them where it came from. Tell them that he spent much time in prayer and study, and this is his conclusion. They may not be Catholic, and they may even have some hesitation about his version, but there is, as far as I can tell, no better answer."

The other ladies weren't due for an hour, so Evelyn decided to make some cookies and have them with coffee after the meeting. The oven was heated and the batter shaped and placed on a cookie sheet. As they waited, Peggy asked, "Would you mind terribly if I prayed for this meeting? I have an uneasy feeling for some reason and I think it best to leave it in the Lord's hands." Not waiting for approval, Peggy bowed her head and prayed. It was short, but fervent, that both Becky and Carolyn would understand God's working in the answer and in the discussion and that both ladies would be enlightened by this visit. Then she thought of Evelyn, who was in the same boat as the other ladies, and prayed that she understand and gain from the discussion.

A table was set as the doorbell rang. Evelyn went to answer and saw through the window in the door, there were six women, and two buggies tied out front. With a loud whisper, she called Peggy. When Peggy got there, she frantically threw her hands up to her face and cried, "Who are they? There was supposed to be only two women. But, open the door and we'll do the best we can."

Evelyn opened the door and greeted the ladies. Four women, starchy and hostile, marched past the hostess and into the parlor. Without an invitation to be seated, they lined up across the outside wall and plopped themselves down in the two love seats. One who appeared to be the leader, drew her glasses from her traveling bag, pinched the nose piece to fit her wide-based proboscis, and tilted her head in a haughty air, asking, "By what authority do you plan to fill the mind of our young friend with this nonsense about a fantasy god? Certainly you can't believe those stories about god who can make a world out of nothing in a seven day period."

"Correction," interrupted Peggy, "it was six days. On the seventh, He rested."

"You look to be intelligent women. How can you possibly accept that stuff as fact?"

Before Peggy could answer, Evelyn placed her hand on the young woman's shoulder and stepped forward to face the inquisitors. As calmly as she could, Evelyn asked, "And who might you ladies be?"

The speaker answered, "I am Helen Montague. That young woman came showing her ignorance of the facts of life, willing to not offend a friend. But she has another friend, one whom she invited to this. . .this, uh, gathering, who told us. We came to protect young Carolyn from the likes of you."

Still maintaining control, Evelyn said, "Will you four please leave?"

"What?" Helen shrieked, "You are asking us to leave so you can fill that poor girl's mind with garbage about this fantasy you call god?"

"I asked you to leave. What are you going to do?"

"If we go, she," pointing at Carolyn, "goes too."

Evelyn looked at Carolyn and asked, "Do you want to stay?"

Both Becky and Carolyn were crying, embarrassed about the scene and she nodded her head as she wiped her eyes.

Helen Montague angrily said, louder than necessary, "You are basically throwing us out of your home? Where is that so-called Christian kindness you are to show to others? Where—"

Evelyn stormed, "I will try to maintain my composure, but that will be difficult. You seem to know our beliefs and have shown us that you are the kind of person to take advantage of certain circumstances. Who are you that you can come into a home uninvited and insult the resident? Who are you and what gives you the right to insult the residents of that home and their guest, even though you might know that person too? Who are you to come in here and—" she stopped, emotionally at a point of rage.

Evelyn reached over to the under shelf on the table where she found two bells, one small, the other much like a cow bell. She picked up the larger one, thinking Simon might be in the barn with the horses and, gripping it with all her strength, shook if as if she was shaking some part of Helen Montague. In a minute, Simon appeared, breathless and asked, "Ma'am is something wrong?"

Still maintaining her control, Evelyn said, "Simon, open the door for the ladies. If they do not follow you out that door, go find Officer Bryan and bring him here, telling him we have had four women invade our home, and I want them out. Go! Now!"

Simon didn't wait to see if the ladies got up, but raced out the door, off the porch and down the street. The other ladies with the Montague woman looked at her and stirred uncomfortably in their seats, but did not stand. Helen laid her hand on the leg of the woman next to her to calm her.

There were five minutes of a tense stand-off as the four visitors sat unwilling to leave without Carolyn. Simon appeared, huffing and puffing, followed by Officer Bryan. The policeman was a big man, over six feet in height and strong from following the work-out rules the city required. He came in and recognized Helen Montague and sighed, "Oh, hello Mrs. Montague. Why am I not surprised to find you here?"

Surprised and annoyed, Evelyn exploded, "Do you know this woman? <u>How</u> do you know her? What has she done that it doesn't surprise you to find her here?"

Officer Bryan answered, "Her husband, Henry Montague, is on the city council. Mrs. Montague has, what's the right word, a penchant for. . .well, being an unwelcome visitor. . .are you folks religious?" The look on Evelyn's face answered his question. "Come along, Ma'am. Leave these good people alone before they charge you."

That was an idea Evelyn hadn't thought of but welcomed. "Yes! Officer Bryan, I want to charge her with home invasion. Of causing my emotions to be terribly upset, so that I may have to lie down. I might even have to go to my doctor for medication. Yes, sir. Tell me how do I proceed with this charge."

Bryan looked at Evelyn a couple seconds before answering, "You're sure you want to do this?"

"I am indeed. I'll give you ten seconds to convince her, but after that. . ."

Officer Bryan walked over in front of Helen, grabbed her hands and pulled her, in spite of screaming protests, to a standing position. He bent his knees and lowered his shoulder, catching Helen at her waist, pulling her onto his shoulder. He straightened up, knocking the woman's wide-brimmed hat from her head. The woman sitting next to Helen grabbed it and the other three headed for the door, followed by the officer and his load. Outside, Bryan set Mrs. Montague on the ground next to her carriage, turned and tipped his hat at the home owner. He turned back to the offender and said, "Ma'am, it is best you go home. You upset that woman and may find yourself in front of a judge."

Inside, the ladies stood in stunned silence at all that transpired, and when the officer saluted them, all four broke out in uproarious laughter. Two managed to flop onto the love seats, one found a chair and the other just leaned against the wall, shaking, crying, laughing, with the emotional release they felt. After several minutes, the laughing stopped but an occasional snicker was still heard.

Peggy said, "I don't know if we can answer your question about Adam's sons' wives, but, Evelyn has prepared some cookies and coffee. Perhaps, with a little refreshment, we can bring our minds back to the real issue." Evelyn motioned for their guests to follow her and they went to the kitchen for some plain sugar cookies and coffee. They took their places and, after the blessing, ate, commented and laughed about what had happened shortly before.

Slowly, the conversation shifted to the purpose of the visit and Peggy started to explain, as she could remember, what Father Herman told them. When she mentioned that God seemed to permit incest, both visitors gasped, and Peggy hastily explained the options. With Becky and Carolyn accepting the explanation, Peggy offered this suggestion, "Read the New Testament. Start with the Gospel of John, then the others three at the start of the New Book. The Old Testament is instructions and history of the Jewish Nation. If you continue in that section of the Bible, soon you will be in Leviticus and Numbers and will be completely discouraged.

The New Testament is the story of Jesus. That's what affects our lives today."

Chapter Twenty-Three

Peggy was emotionally spent Saturday afternoon and in spite of having papers to go over, she needed a change. She asked Evelyn if they could look for a church for Sunday. Again, Simon was called upon to harness their carriage horse and drive them around to churches within a few blocks of their residence.

Because of Evelyn's past, where she had never been in a church service, and Peggy being from out of town, the ladies toured their community without any basic knowledge of the churches there. They passed a few, some small and two or three whose building covered most of a city block, but were not drawn to any based on what they saw. Somewhat discouraged, Evelyn had Simon drive back through a neighborhood close to their own home just in time to see a man place a sandwich-board sign alongside the road, advertising church the next day. The sign read "Community Fellowship, Faith Based Worship," and the time and day of the service.

They stopped the carriage and talked to the man, who explained he was a "Lay Pastor," who had started the church in his home because the churches didn't satisfy his questions about the Bible and life. The ladies talked to him and found there were eighteen people who came the previous week and thought there might be more this week. Both ladies looked at the house and had the same thought—twenty people in that house would push out the walls.

The man explained his name was Gary Carpenter. He felt the need for a basic conservative church, whose beliefs mirrored his own. He had a wife and two children and decided to start a group and let the Lord direct from that point. He worked as a framer building ships and, since they were getting busy with gunships for the Navy, his study time was severely limited, but he would go until he could go no more. When asked about his preaching material, he said, "There is a new seminary, Evangel Seminary, about a mile from here and I have gotten some books and material from them. But study time is really a problem."

They drove the two blocks to the Patterson home with the thought percolating in Peggy's mind—what about using the big room? They would go to church the next day and find out about their beliefs before committing their house to an unknown group and beliefs.

Peggy found new spirit and attacked the paperwork with vigor when they got home. Evelyn commented on the change of attitude from the tired person Peggy had been to the excited person she had become, and all because of going to church. Peggy said, "When you are a part of a group of friends, like I was in New Orleans, who support you and help you, and then have none of that for months, I really feel dry inside, spiritually. Hopefully, tomorrow will have an answer."

Sunday morning they went to church. Evelyn asked Peggy what she should wear and, after seeing the clothes in Evelyn's closet, Peggy recommended the attire. Simon readied the carriage and waited for the ladies to appear. As soon as Peggy alighted from their carriage she was recognized by two excited, screaming girls—Amanda and Sarah Carpenter, the minister's daughters. The girls came running to the carriage, exclaiming about how good it was to see their teacher in church. They literally bounced with joy in their greeting. Their exclamation brought the minister and the girl's mother to their sides and both ladies were greeted and made welcome by those nearby.

One other student, a sixth grade boy, was there from the school, and he stood with his parents, pointing at Peggy. They came to meet their son's teacher and express their thanks that she was a Christian.

Inside, when everybody was seated, it was partially-controlled bedlam. The little children sat on their parents' laps, and with the passing minutes, their interest in the group waned and their bodies needed a change of position, so they started to squirm. As Peggy watched, her teacher's instincts told her she needed to volunteer to help. Her human instinct told her to wait, this was her first service. The others might think she was trying to take over.

Her teaching won, and she interrupted the minister in his speaking to take the little ones to another room and tell them Bible stories. Seven children, up through grade four, were herded into the kitchen, where they sat on the floor in a corner of the room and listened as Peggy told of the battle of Jericho, with vivid descriptions of crossing the Jordan and marching around the walled city seven times. At the appointed time, she had all the children clap their hands and shout, to indicate the walls falling down. The interruption came at an inappropriate time in the sermon and ruined the closing.

Peggy was the object of some mild criticism when church was over, as people, especially older women, commented on the noise from the children as the pastor was finishing his talk. After the congregation had gone, Mr. Carpenter found Peggy and Evelyn talking to his wife. He let them finish their topic before speaking. When the opening came, he said, "Thank you for thinking of the service by taking the children. They were getting restless and I was having trouble concentrating on the message. We had twenty-two here today. I don't know how we're going to get any more inside." He looked at the sky, "I suppose there might be some Sundays we could meet outside, but this is the middle of September and weather here will be rather uncertain for the next several months."

Peggy looked at the ground. She didn't want Evelyn to feel pressed into making some commitment about opening her home to the church gathering, so she kept quiet. She heard Evelyn call her name and, without looking up, Peggy said, "It's your home. Actually, it's the general's home, so it's up to you how you use it."

The Carpenters looked at each other, then back at the ladies with frowning and questions in their looks. Still not looking at Evelyn, Peggy explained, "Mrs. Patterson is the wife of a general, fighting somewhere south of here. She, or they, have a large house with a huge room that has been used for staff meetings and parties. Right now, with him gone, it isn't used at all. They have four smaller rooms off the main room, one of which I'm staying in, but. . ." She hesitated, watching Evelyn. "I can't say anymore."

Evelyn turned and walked toward the buggy. Peggy excused herself and followed. She caught up with Evelyn and asked, "Did I say something wrong?"

"Not really. But as you were talking, I had the thought 'What would Clay say if he knew I was considering opening our home up for a church. He has had nothing good to say about church and church people since we married, and if he could come home with a service in progress, it might get ugly."

"Oh, my, I would hope not." She said no more for several seconds, all the time looking at Evelyn. Finally, Peggy said, "I hope I didn't offend you by talking about the room. It's so big and would be perfect for what they want to do."

"Peggy, dear, this is no new to me. Remember, I've never been in a church service until today. You brought me into a whole new world and I don't quite know what I'm supposed to do. I know we have the room and I know the preacher would appreciate it, but what would my responsibility be? Do I bake cookies, provide drinks, what would I do?"

"Oh, no! No, you wouldn't want to get that started, not unless the pastor comes to you on some specific occasion and asks you for those things. But only once, even with that request. No, people are to eat at home and come to worship." She paused to look around the room. "We would need chairs. Perhaps he has some place where they can be obtained."

Evelyn interrupted her friend, "We have had as many as seventy people here for dinner and a dance. Clay has chairs somewhere, here on the property. I never inquired, but they were always there. I was busy with the food. We have a storage shed out back. Perhaps they are in there."

Peggy excitedly clapped her hands. "Oh, that would be wonderful." She looked around the room. "We don't have a piano, but a good song leader can sing without an instrument. Perhaps someone has a squeeze box. That might work."

Evelyn laughed, "You mean one of those things you squeeze that's about a foot square? I saw one at a carnival once. Would they use that in a church?"

"If they had no other means of music. The bigger question is how would you handle having a bunch of people coming into your house every week, looking over your things, commenting about your house?"

That made Evelyn pause again for several seconds. "There is a separate entrance to the big room. Could we talk to the pastor and make sure everyone uses that door?"

Peggy put the fingertips of her left hand on her lips and thought. She nodded her head and said, pensively, "That could be done. But there's one other thing. Toilet facilities. As the congregation grows, there will be more children who need to use the toilet. How can we handle that?"

"We have three. Remember, we have had military parties here where there has been drinking and some long night parties. Clay thought of that when he had this built. We have our own out the back door and two for men and women out that door," pointing to a door at the opposite side of the large room.

After further discussion, they agreed to invite the pastor's family for supper that Monday and talk to him about using the house, along with who would set up the room and who would clean it. To Peggy, there was an air of excitement about having a church in the house where she was staying. Evelyn was not so sure, but was open for discussion.

Monday morning Peggy woke up singing, which should have been a warning. She sang a hello to Evelyn at breakfast and hummed as she washed and dressed. She primped at a mirror as she picked up her papers and she got ready to leave. Simon had the carriage ready for her and, with the thoughts of talking to the pastor about church, her mind was dreaming of wonderful things to come in worshipping her Lord.

The first change to her attitude came as she approached school and saw a luxury carriage, with two sleek horses, waiting for her at the door. A short, rotund man of fifty stood outside the buggy, smoking and fuming. He scuffed his boots as he waited for her to stop and exit her buggy, and could hardly hold back from cursing at her. Children scattered when Peggy got out and the man started shouting.

"You insufferable Christians, it's too bad the Romans didn't finish you back then. At least we'd not have to put up with you now!"

Angrily, she asked, "Would you please do me the decency of introducing yourself before you attack me? How dare you come here and show your intolerably bad manners as you make a fool of yourself before these children. Who are you and what is your purpose. State it and be gone!"

"You attacked my wife. I'm Claude Montague and you ordered that brute of a policeman to attack her and cart her out of your house like so much flour or beans. She was—"

Peggy rose to her full height and towered over the little man. She stuck her finger in front of his face and declared, "You tell me which you and your wife would prefer, an embarrassing moment or a law suit for home invasion. She and her three friends entered my friend's home unannounced and uninvited. They plopped themselves down on her furniture and called her names. When they refused to leave as ordered, we sent for the local policeman who took her out, yes, like a sack of flour. She was asked to leave, and then she was told to leave, but she refused. My friend did the only thing a home owner could do under the circumstances. Now, what were you saying about us insufferable Christians? I might call you an unbearable Atheist. Now, if that is all you have to say, kindly get into your carriage and leave these premises."

"How dare you! You can't order me around like—"

"You are on school property and I am the teacher. I am the only authority here right now. I can and I do order you to leave the property. If you want to carry your rant out on the street, do that, but get your horses and wagon off the school property! Right this minute!"

She returned to her buggy, picked up her books and papers and started toward the school. The children, hearing every word, clapped and shouted approval for their teacher. Claude Montague led his horses back to the street where he stood, hands on plenteous hips, glaring at the scene. As the students and teacher ignored him, he climbed back into his buggy and drove away.

The students were excited that she would have enough courage to better an older man in an argument. She herded them into the building and once the door was closed, she leaned against the wall for support. There would be a new topic of conversation around student's supper tables that evening.

Chapter Twenty-Four

Jake Prosser was frustrated. He and the rest of the crew of the Hannibal, a sister ship to the Cairo, waited as the ship was being outfitted at the Mound City Shipyard, across the river from St. Louis. This is another ship named for major cities along the Mississippi River. Two hundred fifty-one men reported every day to the commanding officer's quarters at Jefferson Barracks and every day they were told the same story—"There have been some unexpected hold-ups in the process. The ship should be ready within a week." These were "Pook's Turtles," iron-clad river gunboats, designed by Samuel Pook and built by James B. Eads in his Mound City shipyard.

The "unexpected hold-ups" involved the forty-two pound rifles, a smooth bore weapon that had a tendency to explode. The military was trying to correct that problem by rifling, milling grooves into the inside of the barrel. At this point they were having minimal success because of the time it was taking.

Jake didn't mind the wait for it gave him more time to become proficient in his duties. He talked to the older gunners and their mates, packing every bit of knowledge he could into his head and onto notes he kept with him. This floating fort carried thirteen cannons of various strengths—three protruding from the prow, the others layered along each side. Jake's duty was second in command of a forty-two pound rifle, in the aft position of the ship. Each crew was responsible for the matching weapon on both sides of the ship.

There were twelve men in the crew plus a "powder monkey," a male under eighteen years of age, whose job it was to bring ammunition to the weapon. In a fight he had the most dangerous job aboard the ship as he was carrying bags of powder to the different guns in his responsibility.

The ship and those of its class were the talk of the military. Each was 175 feet long with a fifty-one foot beam at mid ship. They weighed 512 tons and had a draft of seven feet. Her steam engine was powered by five coal-powered boilers with a 22 inch cylinder with a stroke of 6 feet producing 140 lb/per square inch. A paddle-wheel was the poorer choice than propellers for propulsion and in some ships like the Cairo the wheels were moved inboard, directly behind the stacks, for protection. Even though she did not use a propeller, she was the fastest of the class.

Health issues were a major concern with the coal smoke and, in battle, the smoke from gun powder. Ventilators circulated fresh air through the ship, and draft systems pulled new air into the furnace. When this system worked, the crew was not affected. To accomplish this, a system of machine-driven fans and blowers was used, forcing fresh air into the ship. To aid the air circulation, small wind sails were placed over open deck portholes catching fresh air and improving ventilation below decks. With two hundred fifty men in a ship only 175 feet long, with the power supply, and all the materials, gun powder and shells and coal for power, sleeping quarters were cramped. Six men slept in a room on three stacked bunk beds, with their personal items locked in a two by three by three foot cabinet.

While the men waited for their ship to be readied, Jake found time to go to the church for more literary readings. Betty Wilshire couldn't compete with Peggy O'Neal in head to head comparison of looks, but Jake was in St. Louis and Peggy was in Cincinnati. Try as he might, he couldn't stop thinking of Betty, so after his first visit to the reading, he took another sailor with him. The next time he went, he took that man and another sailor. Keeping them quiet about their orders turned out to be difficult. Pretty Betty and her quaint English dialect inspired one of the men to divulge more than Jake wanted them to. Jake had to interrupt the man twice.

Even though the Gatling gun was still installed on some ships, as it would be on the Hannibal, it was a thing of the past, at least for Jake. He was reminded of it when he happened to see Captain Thomas on a street in St. Louis one evening. The G E was docked, waiting for orders to move south past Cairo. That was all the captain could tell Jake, but that meant there were war plans made. A new field commander, General U S Grant, or Unconditional Surrender Grant, to the men who served under him, had been appointed. He had a reputation for throwing force into a battle, thinking that force alone could turn the tide. In all his battles, the body counts were unusually high. But he had President Lincoln's approval. The stories of his drinking were legends, but the president made some comment that if that was the key to victory, he'd buy all his generals liquor.

It was late Saturday evening when the men got their report—they would be leaving for maneuvers and testing their new ship at dawn Monday. They were given Sunday free time, but had to be on board at oh-four-hundred Monday morning. Jake decided to go to church. He had talked to Betty's father and was satisfied as to his doctrinal position, so Jake rose early Sunday morning and headed for church.

He waited until the service had started before he went inside and found a seat in the back row. The minister talked about prayer, citing the need for faith as well as works. Faith was something of limited experience in Jake's Christian life. Peggy had read Jake the Gospel of John and John's letters, and he was aware of the Savior's love, but had not had much instruction in having faith or how to use it. He would read more about it. As the congregation stood for the dismissal prayer, Jake snuck out the sanctuary door to the vestibule. Betty had seen him and was there waiting for him.

"Were you going to leave without speaking to me?" she asked.

"I. . .uh, I'm leaving tomorrow, and I didn't. . .I have to get back to the ship."

"But without speaking to me? Without saying anything to me?"

"I'm sorry Betty, but I'm promised to someone else. You are—"

"A diversion? Don't tell me how pretty I am, or how much you enjoyed the readings." She became angrier, "Don't tell me that you're glad we met, that the readings were interesting or anything else. You led me on, thinking you cared enough to spend your time off with me, even though it was in a group. I thought that was your way of getting to know my father so you could. . .Go! Get out of here and don't come back."

Jake muttered an apology and as he turned, he bumped into the people who had come out of the sanctuary. He shoved himself past them and past her father, who stood at the door shaking hands. Out on the street he stopped, closed his eyes for a moment, then opened them and started a fast-paced walk that would take him to his new home.

As he walked, he asked himself these questions, "Why did he get involved with Betty? He really wasn't that interested in the literary readings. Did he not mean the words he said to Peggy? Did he need a woman's presence after spending his time aboard ship? These were questions he needed to answer and soon."

Chapter Twenty-Five

To Peggy, teaching was getting easier. A routine had developed for teaching the lower grades, one that involved Becky Schaub. If the teacher had to correct papers, Becky would read with the little ones, and give Jaimie a chance to understand new words. An occasional meeting with a parent was handled after school.

After two weeks she realized a special need—some of the children were coming to school hungry. She started a practice of in-house picnics, done on alternate Fridays. It started with some students being asked to bring an additional sandwich to give the poorest of the class a different taste. There were some poor of her student body whose fathers were in the army or navy, and whose financial situation was bleak. One of the more wealthy mothers came and asked why her two children were being selected to feed others in the school. When Peggy explained the home situation with these kids, the woman agreed and volunteered to talk to some of her friends, to pass the word along as to the reason for the picnic.

On the other hand, there were a few parents who came together and faced Peggy after school on a Thursday. Five women explained their children were being embarrassed with this practice and they asked her if she would no longer continue it. Peggy closed her eyes and prayed a quick, silent prayer for wisdom. After a moment of silence, she said, "Folks, I was never faced with being hungry. My father was, is a highly respected doctor, and we always had food on the table. A child can't learn, cannot concentrate, if that child is hungry."

She saw two of the women react as if they were offended and she said, "I hear stomachs growl as I'm walking up the aisle. I don't mean to offend you, but there are some who have the ability to bring two sandwiches where some cannot. Please, don't take it that I'm feeling sorry for you or pointing out the weakness of some. I'm not. If there was another way of doing this, where the poorer children might have a good lunch or breakfast, I'd do it. In the world in which we live, an education is going to be more and more important. Please let me do this. It's important for the children."

Tears came into the eyes of one woman, Matilda Brown, who said that since her husband went into the army, they had lived on beans and sometimes dandelions and vinegar made into a salad. Another told a different story, but the same result—they were doing their best with little, and didn't want their children to be made butts of jokes.

Peggy said, "If I ever hear of such a thing, I'll have a student meeting and—"

"Oh, no, please, that might make it worse."

Silence hung heavy for a minute as the visitors looked at each other, as if waiting for someone to talk. Finally, Peggy said, "Why don't we leave it as it is for now? On alternate Fridays some will bring an extra sandwich and they'll share. If that doesn't go well, I'll change it."

The outside door opened during that last comment and they all looked up to see a tall, handsome man with a beautiful eight or nine year old girl. He was dressed in a tan business suit and wore a western hat over long blond hair, tied in the back. The two stepped inside the room as he said, "Hello, I was told to see Miss O'Neal. Is she here now?"

Peggy announced, "I am she. And you are?"

"I'm Heinz Becker. This is Tillie, or Matilda. She's eight and in the third grade. She can read to fourth grade level and knows her multiplication tables through six." He paused, and continued, "Was I interrupting something? We can wait if you're talking business."

Peggy looked at the other ladies, "Are you all right with what we decided?" A muttering of affirmatives was their response. "Fine, then, we'll leave it the way it is for a while and see what happens. Perhaps we'll need to change something, but not for a couple weeks."

When the other ladies had gone, Peggy asked, "How did you hear about this school, Mr. Becker?"

He quickly sized up the woman in front of him and gave her his best smile. "We just moved to town. I wanted to get Tillie into a good school to continue her education and happened to meet a man, Albert Schaffer, who told me about this one."

"Yes, Mr. Schaffer is on the school board for the elementary grades in the city. Did he say you had to live within a certain area to be registered here?"

Heinz Becker smiled and said, "He mentioned that was the practice, but the board could allow Tillie to come here under the circumstances.'

'Under the circumstances,' she thought. That either means he has lots of money or is a plant to disrupt my teaching. After their last confrontation, why would Albert Schaffer suggest this school? She smiled as she thought of the rule for children's teachers that a married teacher would have to resign and she snickered a little.

He frowned, "Did I say something funny?"

"No, Mr. Becker, I just had a wild thought out of nowhere. Now, did Mr. Schaffer say anything more about this school or my teaching methods?"

"Well, he only said the reports the school board have received are that you are doing a good job with the various classes and things seem to be going very well."

She raised her eyebrows and quickly tipped her head to the side. That was something she hadn't heard and really didn't expect to hear from Albert Schaffer. But, she was leery of the compliment. She decided to find a chair for the little girl.

There were no individual desks, but some chairs and long tables and Peggy explained the seating to Tillie. A child sat in the chairs when they were reading, but if they had some work to do, they were allowed to go to the table. Paper and pencils were provided, but, with the war on, children were asked to bring their own pencils if possible. They talked a while longer about where the students were in their studies, now that they were a month into the school year, and Heinz expressed every confidence that his Tillie would be able to keep up with the class.

As the father and daughter got ready to leave, Peggy mentioned that the next day was an in-house picnic and those who were financially able were asked to bring an extra sandwich for lunch. He nodded and said, "That's what those ladies were doing here." He looked intently at Peggy, "It must be difficult for you to have such extreme circumstances here, students who come from homes of plenty as well as those who have little. Your bearing indicates you are from one of plenty."

"No, I never went hungry, but my parents separated when I was young, perhaps Tillie's age, so I know of some problems. But, back to the picnic, if you are new to the city, perhaps your moving is incomplete, so I would wave the request for extra sandwiches."

"Oh, that's all right. We've moved in, completely. She'll have a surprise for the others." Without waiting for a reply from the teacher, father and daughter turned and opened the door to leave. In the couple seconds the door was open, she saw a beige saddle horse with a matching Shetland pony tied to the rail out front.

She was right about one part of her thought—he had money.

She had spent Thursday evening grading papers and had them to distribute and explain to the students. Some, whom she thought would be doing better, disappointed her with a poorer showing. She had her papers stacked in grade order and carried them in a valise. Simon had readied her carriage and, after a breakfast of egg, toast and coffee, she was ready to face the students.

Peggy noticed activity at the school property as she approached and, from a block away, saw ant-like scurrying there. There were so many people doing what they were doing she had no place to tie her horse. She noticed men in white hats and aprons surrounding a tub from which smoke rose. Then she saw him, Heinz Becker, with his arms around the shoulders of a man, who appeared to be directing the activity. She drove her buggy up onto the school grounds and as close as she could get to the cooking barrel. She jumped out of the carriage and marched up to it.

She screamed at Becker, "What is the meaning of this. Who are these people and what do you think you are doing here?"

He raised his hand, palm out and said, "Calm down, teacher. You said some of the children come here hungry, so I decided to offer them a good breakfast."

"And who gave you this authority? Who gave you this permission to interrupt the school process this way?"

"I told you I saw Mr. Schaffer and he told me about your school. When I left there yesterday, I saw him again and asked if I could provide a good breakfast for all the students. He asked my plans, I told him and he gave me permission. I told him I'd like to have a bar-b-q for your students."

Peggy stood internally fuming, fisted hands on hips, unable to say a word. She wheeled her back to him, took two steps and stopped, returning to face him. "We do not have a breakfast at the school. We have a lunch period of an hour. <u>One hour</u>! The students are bringing sandwiches, they have no plates nor does the school have equipment. If you want to provide a lunch, you provide plates and flatware. You provide a drink, and it has to be done within the lunch hour with you picking up the mess. Other than those conditions, pack up your stuff and leave."

She stomped her way back to her carriage and as she boarded, he said, "You sure are pretty when you're angry." She jerked the reins and pulled them in an extreme turn. He shouted, "Careful! You'll tip it!" Just in time to see the inside wheels of the turn lift from the ground. Becker rushed to the carriage and put his weight against the tip, straightening it back on all wheels.

She had pulled the horses to a halt when she felt the wheels rise, and she turned to look at him. "Thank you, but what I said still goes. Lunch only, and clean up your mess." With that, she drove closer to the school door where she tied the horse to the hitching rail. Students were gathering, only a few were there now and they wanted to know what was going on in the yard. She said when all the students are here, she'd tell them.

She sat, trying to collect her emotions. "Who does he think he is and why would Mr. Schaffer give him permission to disrupt the school this way? And what do I do with him? If he persists in his. . .why did he say that? I look pretty when I'm angry. Well, I have other things to do." She busied herself with passing out papers, talking to the children as they came in, trying to forget what was going on in the yard.

The clock on the wall announced it was time for classes to start and Peggy rapped on her desk with a ruler to get the attention of the students. "The school board gave someone permission to prepare a bar-b-q in our yard for lunch today. If you can't resist looking out the window, I shall have to pull the shades. Since that is the South window, and the sun shines that way, to keep the sun shining into the room, ignore what is going on out there, at least until your lunch time."

A little girl raised her hand and asked, "What are we going to do with our extra sandwich? My mother said I had to bring two today."

The teacher bowed her head an instant and raised her had to her cheek. "I'm sorry about that. I didn't know this was going to happen, nor do I approve of it now. If you children want to, we can go on with the plan I had at the start. But it does seem a lot of food would go to waste. Why don't we vote on it at lunch time?"

The hours passed as the smell of the cooking wafted through the open window. Even pulling the shades didn't help. The children just couldn't concentrate. So, an hour before their lunch period normally started, Peggy called a halt to the school work and had the oldest run out to see if it was ready. He came back excited and said, "They had food and drinks an' everything!"

Keeping the students in line was a task Peggy hadn't envisioned. She lined the little ones up first with Becky Schaub walking with them. The oldest two girls walked with the middle children and she with the older students. She reminded them they had to keep their line straight and not drop the food, but to find someplace to sit. "But don't start eating until everyone gets food."

The boy who ran out said, "They got tables an' chairs."

As the last of the older students cleared the school door, she saw that handsome man guiding the little ones to the plates and up to the serving line. She wanted to run back inside, but her stubbornness refused to let her be cowed by the man, so she kept walking. One by one the children were fed and went to the tables set up for them. When it came her turn to pick up her plate of food, she refused and walked past to a table without it.

The teacher stood and in a clear voice, said, "Now, we will thank God for our food," and she prayed a prayer of thanks. Heinz Becker stood off to the side and hid a smile behind an empty plate.

The rest of the day was almost total loss. Children of the first three grades could hardly keep their eyes open, but there was no place, except the dusty floor, for them to lie down. By two o'clock it was apparent to Peggy she had to accommodate them somehow, so she told Becky Schaub to get the children of those grades to lie on the floor. She wanted the others who were older to stay awake for their lessons, but saw that was going to be difficult. With the little children sleeping, the older ones began to yawn too. Peggy chose to create theater—she told a story from her high school life, of a play they gave, with actions and different voices for the participants. She told of the beating her mother gave her father as she marched back and forth, voicing both parents in angry tones with different voices. The children seemed to love it. The school day was wasted but she kept the attention of those who were awake, including some of the third graders who woke from her play acting.

At the end of the school day with the children gone, she and Becky stood at the door and Peggy expressed her gratitude for the help Becky gave her. She had never inquired about her assistant's financial status, and she felt she needed to apologize for that, so she asked, "Becky, I don't know what I would have done without you here to help me. You have been a God-send and I wonder how are things for you, financially? I was told when they hired me that the pay was for one teacher for one school year. But, if you weren't here, I don't know what I would have done. So, how are you fixed financially?"

Becky was slow in answering. She carefully chose her words as she said, "I asked myself if you really cared whether I was here or not. You—"

With emotion, the teacher answered, "Oh, Heavens Becky, do I care if you were here or not? I just told you how much I am thankful for your help. Look, Becky, I'm sorry if I caused you to feel that way. This is my first job, ever. Perhaps some of my people skills need to be better developed, and I acknowledge that, but please, don't think I don't appreciate what you have done. I do, from my heart."

A very quiet "Thank you," was her response.

"Now," Peggy hastily continued, "what about your financial situation?"

Becky looked at the floor and quietly answered, "You never asked me about my husband. I'm a single mother, and I don't need to go any farther than that. When Jaimie was born and he appeared to be. . .uh, he seemed to have a problem. I tried to teach him, but I didn't have an education myself. The day we heard this school was going to have a young woman teacher, I thought that, perhaps, she might understand. Then, for a while I wondered if you did. Then you prayed for him and now he's learning like all the rest. For that I can never thank you enough. But, to answer your question, I, we're living with my parents. My father is a business owner so we're doing all right."

"Becky, thank you for trusting me with that. I need you so much I was going to ask the district to pay you for your work, even if they had to take it from my salary."

"That isn't necessary. We're all right. But, can I talk to you about something else Monday? I have to get him home now."

"Of course. What's the topic?"

"I want you to teach me about life. I want to be like you." As she walked out the door, she met that tall man who looked in and saw Peggy alone at her desk.

He stepped into the doorway. "Miss O'Neal, may I talk to you for a minute?" She motioned for him to come in and he continued,

"Miss O'Neal, why do you dislike me? If you would let yourself like me, you might find I'm a nice guy."

"Mr. Becker," she said, with a sharpness in her voice, "I'm not interested in quote, letting myself like you. I'm having a problem with the so called coincidental meeting between you and Mr. Schaffer. Is he related to you, Mr. Becker? How did you come to meet him the first time? How did you know where he lived to go and get approval for this morning? No, Mr. Becker, I have no interest in getting to know you better."

She paused to take a breath and continued with more passion than before. "As far as future plans, Mr. Becker, as far as what Mr. Schaffer wants this to develop into, that will never happen. I am sold completely for life, to a sailor in the United States Navy who is now somewhere, fighting the Rebels. When this war is over, or when the first opportunity arrives, he and I will be married. So, Mr. Becker, I am not interested in knowing you, or in what Mr. Schaffer might have planned by your incidental meeting."

He smiled his most charming smile, "You don't trust people very much, do you?"

"I trust those people I know, and I don't know you, nor do I want to. More, with the confrontation I had with Mr. Schaffer, and the coincidence of this meeting, I don't trust him. So, if you have completed your inquiry, you may leave while I gather my personal items."

He didn't move, but continued to smile. "You know, Miss O'Neal, you are very pretty. Wouldn't you like to know the man who could make you the most happy and wealthy woman in all of Cincinnati?" He took one step toward her.

"I told you my feelings, Mr. Becker, now, unless you want trouble from the police, you should leave. Now!"

His smile widened. "I don't see any policeman, Miss O'Neal, just the two of us. And who's going to believe you when the rumors of former dalliances are made known?"

As Becker reached out for Peggy, the door opened and Becky stood there. "Miss O'Neal, I forgot—". She saw the picture of

Becker's arm reaching for the teacher, while she tried to move behind the desk for protection."

Peggy screamed, "Becky go find a policeman! Help!"

Ignoring her friend's appeal, Becky stepped into the room and headed straight for the aggressor. "Sir, leave her alone. Leave her alone, now." As she walked she reached up to her wide-brimmed hat and pulled an eight inch hatpin, letting the hat fall to the floor. "I told you to leave her alone." She was within a good thrust length and she held the hatpin in her right hand.

Becker was standing with his right arm straightened out toward Peggy and in one swift motion, swung his arm in a wide arc, aimed at Becky's head. She ducked and with one quick reaction, jabbed the hatpin, up to her fingers, into his side, just under his ribs. She left the pin in his side and stepped back.

He looked at her and down at the blood seeping from the wound and tried to reach for the pin with his right hand, but was not able to get control of it. He tried with his left hand and couldn't reach it. He begged, "Take it out. Please take it out. I'll leave."

Becky didn't trust the man but Peggy came around the desk to extract the hatpin. She stood there, holding the long, bloody pin in her right hand and, with her left, pointed to the door and ordered, "Get out, now! If you come back, I'll tell the police my story with Miss Schaub's backup. Get out!"

Becker glared from one woman to the other and didn't move for a couple seconds, as if he was thinking of more mayhem. Blood was starting to stain his shirt and seep down to his trousers, and he finally headed for the door.

Chapter Twenty-Six

Margaret O'Neal was a busy woman. As a teacher who was involved with other activities, she set aside a block of time each evening to correct her student's papers. But what happened at the school that afternoon had robbed her of her emotions. She spent the whole evening pacing, praying and talking to Evelyn. Evelyn's suggestion was to go to the police and explain what happened, but, Peggy wanted to forget the whole incident. Perhaps, Heinz Becker would just disappear.

Wednesday of the week past, she received a visit from the pastor, Gary Carpenter, who asked if they could start using the big room for church this coming Sunday. Evelyn had to be asked, and Simon alerted to get the chairs cleaned and dusted for use. By Saturday, he had been in that process for two days and was now about finished with setting up the new worship center.

Then, there was another request. Gary Carpenter, the working pastor, had just been informed his group had to go on a seven day work week and would either have to close down the church or find someone else to preach. Just what she wanted to hear. He asked her to preach the coming Sunday and see how it worked out. If it wasn't possible considering her teaching and preparation, they would have to forget the church. She said she'd try.

Her Saturday Bible study with Becky and Carolyn brought two new ladies into her group. She was studying the Gospel of

John, explaining his relations to Jesus and reading the verses that indicate their closeness. The two new ladies, about thirty years of age, Martha McCowan and Winifred Morgan, had a Sunday school understanding of the Bible. As children in the New York area, they went to a Sunday Bible Study, but when their families moved west, they got busy making a life in Cincinnati and forgot about their religious needs.

Becky had said she was bringing two new ladies and Peggy was hardly ready for the two who came. She expected someone in the same general financial level of her friend, but the two who came were of high fashion. The clothes they wore reminded her of some she and Evelyn saw when they looked for her clothes. These were Paris fashions. Wide brimmed, feathered hats decorated their heads. One had a gold broach pinned to her shoulder. Their hair was perfectly positioned, as if they had used the custom of sugared water to "glue" it in place.

When the hour was over, Peggy asked if they had any questions and Martha McCowan asked, "How is it that you, a woman, are going against the Apostle Paul's instructions about a woman speaking in the church?"

The question took Peggy completely by surprise, because of their backgrounds. Neither said they had much more than basic Sunday school and that question showed some specific training. She stammered as she tried to answer. After some seconds of trying to recover and answer, she said, "That question shows more understanding of some theology than you indicated when you first came in here. Was that a family belief?"

Martha McCowan answered, "Perhaps we were unfair in that regard. Yes, it was a family belief. Winifred's and my families attended the same congregation and that was preached by the pastor."

With that understanding of their question, Peggy asked, "Is that a problem? Which is better, to find a woman who will teach the truth of salvation or an Ordained Elder in some church whose religious philosophy is 'Be good and don't hurt anyone.' You have to remember Paul was talking to people who knew the Mosaic Law where women had no voice. In fact, many women couldn't read or write and relied upon their husbands totally. This is a new era, and women have the same freedom a man has in the Gospel. In fact, in Paul's letters he mentions five or six ladies who helped in his ministry."

She invited the ladies to their worship service which began at ten o'clock Sunday morning, and they left. Becky remained, the two left in their own carriage. When they were alone, Peggy asked, "How did you know what to do? I would never have thought of the hatpin. How did you know?"

In a quiet voice, almost apologetic, Becky said, "I grew up with scum like him. It's a long story, and I don't like to repeat it, but God saved my life when I got in the family way. It was someone like him, big smile, fast talker, and I fell for it. I carry a hatpin any time I'm away from my house or school."

"At school Friday, when you came back in, I heard you say 'I forgot'. What did you forget?"

"I was going to say I forgot to tell you I was bringing two new friends."

Becky and Carolyn bid Peggy good bye and she was alone. Since the pastor asked her to preach the coming Sunday, Peggy's mind was a total blank. She searched the Bible for a topic and could put no words to anything she found, until Martha McCowan asked the question about women being silent in church. When Mr. Carpenter asked her to preach, he brought her several books and a complete two volume commentary. She found the scripture verses in question in First Timothy, chapter two and decided to talk about women in public, especially the ministry.

She prayed for half an hour before she opened a book. It was a matter of the blind in search of light, and she was hoping for a single flicker of light from somewhere to trigger her thoughts and her search. It was to be a sleepless night.

Pastor Carpenter had done a good job of instructing people to invite others to church. The previous Sunday he had no knowledge of the new work schedule. When the new people came to the service, they were surprised to find the minister missing, and a woman in his place at the lectern. Susan Carpenter, the minister's wife, stood to announce the pastor's work obligation and to introduce the teacher who would be speaking that morning.

A man passed out some song pamphlets with the promise there would be more the next week and led the congregation in a pair of instrument-less hymns. The offering was taken with the instruction that if they didn't come prepared to give, not to worry about it. But, they were receiving money for a new church building, so if they were able, gifts would be accepted with gratitude.

It came time for the sermon and Margaret O'Neal walked to the pedestal. She laid her Bible on the top and opened it to reveal sheaves of papers stuffed there. She began, "Let us pray," and she prayed a simple prayer for God's help and guidance in the message that day. When the prayer was finished, she continued, "The Scripture is found in First Timothy, chapter two, and is only two verses. Verse eleven, 'Let all the women learn silence with all subjection,' and verse twelve, 'But I suffer not a woman to teach or usurp authority over a man, but to be in silence.'"

She closed her Bible and looked at her papers. "We have a Bible study on Saturday and one of the ladies asked how it was that I, a woman, was going against the Apostle Paul's instructions about a woman teaching. I did some studying and thought I would try to answer the question in case some of the rest of you have the same question."

She stepped around the lectern and said, "I am not a minister. I am a school teacher. This is not my normal class, but Brother Carpenter asked if I would bring the message this morning with the hope of a more capable person next Sunday. Now, what did Paul mean when he wrote that to his student, Timothy? Was he against women helping him? Was he against women in any authority? If you turn to Romans sixteen, you will find some names listed there, including six women—Phoebe, Priscilla, Mary, Tryphema and Tryphosa, who may have been twins, and Persis. Did he mean that these women, who were important in the church at Rome, should give up their status and not speak? I don't think so. What did he mean?

"I have a commentary from the Evangel Seminary which said some women rarely left their homes, their duties consisted in running the household. That was then. This is now. Times have changed. One day, and it may not be too long, women will get the right to vote. There is already a movement in one Western territory to accomplish that. The tradition says that Jewish husbands had a duty to teach their wives if the women spent all their time in the house. Now, I ask you women, do you always agree with your husband in all things?" There were some snickers and a lot of smiles at that.

"So, why did Paul give Timothy those instructions? We will never know, but only suppose. Paul was what one might call 'Old School Jew,' he persecuted the church until his conversion. Sometimes, when God changes a person's life, not all the ideas are changed. Some are retained. In writing to Timothy, Paul was writing to a young man who was beginning his ministry and, where Timothy was ministering, Paul knew there would be a lot of Old Testament Jewish men, who would take him to task over things as important to the Jews, as women in the church.

"In Rome, it was a different matter. The church in Rome was made up of a mixture of people, including servants and slaves, who had no previous exposure to the old Jewish laws. The church in Rome sprang up out of grass roots. People who had been converted, we can only guess where, happen to congregate and believe the little bit they had been taught. That's the reason for the letter. It was a doctrinal yardstick for new Christians, for those unlearned in Jewish religious practices."

She paused in her teaching for several seconds before continuing. "If there is a problem with any of you, seeing me here in the pulpit, talk to me after the service and, if it is a problem, we'll try to deal with it somehow. With that out of the way, I feel I need to give a short lesson on what Jesus came to earth for. Turn with me to the third chapter of John's gospel and I will read through the eighteenth verse."

The sound of pages turning followed, with Peggy reading. She then launched into an explanation of God's plan for our lives, ending with an invitation for any who wanted to pray, to follow the minister's wife into one of the smaller rooms. As previously agreed, Evelyn went with the six men and women who chose to pray. Chairs had been set in a circle for the instruction purpose and directions given.

Peggy stood at the door with the song leader shaking hands as the people left the building. Most women complemented her but the men were less willing. One man stood, holding Peggy's hand. He tried to explain his position about permitting women in authority, but said he'd pray about it and come back the following Sunday.

As he left, a carriage pulled up in front of the house and an army general got out.

He was wearing his uniform, but the sleeve of left arm had been folded below the elbow and pinned to the upper part of his jacket. There were still five or six people in the yard and he looked at them and then at the two still standing in the doorway. Peggy whispered, "The general. Go get Evelyn, quickly."

Angrily so he wouldn't be misunderstood, and loud enough for everyone to hear him, General Courtney Clay Patterson said, "What is going on here and who are these people?" He pointed at Peggy, "What have you done to my home? Where is my wife?"

Evelyn appeared at the door and when she stepped through and saw her husband, she brought her hands to her mouth and uttered, "Oh, Clay. Oh my poor dear." She walked down the two steps to the ground and put her hands on his shoulder, "Oh, Clay, I'm so sorry. How did it happen?"

"Forget this. Who are these people and what are they doing here? And what did <u>she</u> have to do with it?" He glared at Peggy.

"We had church here this morning, Clay. We had thirty people in the room and if you mean Miss O'Neal, she preached."

He exploded, "She what! I want that woman out of the house, now!" Having been brought up with the attitude, mostly by the parishioners in his father's church, that women were not to have anything to say in church, he again said, "She what? She preached? She's a woman!"

"Yes, she's a woman, a very smart woman. She teaches school during the week and now, has been asked to preach on Sundays."

He growled at his wife, "You know what I think of church. You know what I think of her. Why did you let her come into my, our home and use it like that? I will not have it! I will not permit my home to be used by a bunch of radical phonies. I will not!"

Evelyn stood with her hands holding her husband's shoulders and quietly answered him. "Clay, is there no one in your life who is not a radical phony, as you call them. Is there no one to whom you can look, if you wanted to say, here is an honest Christian, an honest Church goer? Thinking back, was there no one you remember in all of your contacts, whom you might say was a man of God? Not one?"

He glared at his wife. They had been through a lot together and she had never, <u>ever</u> gone against him in any of his beliefs. <u>Never</u>. What made her do it now? From Florida to California, from Texas to here and now in Cincinnati, his wife had never contradicted him, never opposed him in anything. Why was she doing it now? "You've become one of them."

He said it in disbelief, which sounded like a whine. "How could you do this to me? You know how I feel about those people. How could you join them and go against me and my stand?"

Evelyn held her tongue and didn't say anything for several seconds. Finally, she looked him in the eye and said, "Clay, Margaret O'Neal is not like what you must have faced as a child. And the people of this church are honest and true believers. I can't imagine them, and I've been with them for a month now, but I can't imagine them saying or doing what those people did to you and Orville. I just can't." She turned and pressed her hand against his shoulder, "Come, let's go inside. We can talk in there. Come."

Peggy stood in the doorway and watched as Evelyn led her husband to the house entrance and through it. Simon was out cleaning up the manure from the horses to haul it away in a wagon. She escaped to her room and shut the door and fell down at her bedside to pray. And cry. She cried out loud. This was not a time of weeping but of serious shedding of tears, with the concern of what might happen to Evelyn's new faith and what might happen to her if the general decided to forbid Margaret from further use of her room. She had nowhere to go. So her prayer was, in a sense, a selfish prayer, and intense. After a half an hour, she was washed out, emotionally. The effort of preaching, as well as this, had drained her. Now, she rose and sat on the edge of her bed. She could only wait for his decision. Her head ached and she needed something in her stomach.

There was a light rap on her bedroom door and she opened it to Evelyn and a policeman. He spoke, "Miss O'Neal, I am John Briggs, Homicide Lieutenant and I have a few questions to ask you. Could we do it here or would you prefer coming down to the police station?"

Stunned, Peggy stammered, "Police? Questions? Why, what happened that you want to talk to me?"

Officer Briggs had a pencil and some papers folded to a small pad. He wrote as he asked, "Do you know Herman Goble?"

"No, I don't think so. Why?"

"He died this morning from an infection caused by a hatpin that punctured his lung. Before he died, he said you attacked him and stuck him with a hatpin, a long one."

"Me! I don't even know Herman Goble."

'Tall man, perhaps thirty, blond hair that he tied in a knot behind his head. Are you sure you don't know him?"

"That describes Heinz Becker. He's the one who set up the cookout for the students Friday. And, as he was attacking me, my aide stuck him with the hatpin, but that was purely self defense. He had me backed into a corner when she came to my rescue."

"Your aide? I understood you were the only teacher. You aren't shown on the records as having an aide. What is her name, please?"

"Becky Schaub. She's an unpaid volunteer. She has a special needs child and she brings him to school and helps out with the younger children as I do other things, you know, teach the upper classes."

Officer Briggs unfolded the paper he was writing on and refolded it to a clear space. He paused in his writing. "Do you know where she lives?"

"No, I never asked her."

He looked up, "Isn't that a bit unusual, that you hire someone without knowing more than her name? Did you get approval from the school board?"

Peggy was getting annoyed, "I just told you she was an unpaid volunteer. And no, I didn't get approval from the district. It didn't seem necessary as long as she taught what I approved."

Briggs unfolded the paper and read his notes. "You say you didn't know Mr. Goble, that you knew him as Heinz Becker. When did you first see him?"

"He came to the school Thursday afternoon with his daughter to—"

"Mr. Goble was unmarried."

Peggy exploded. "As I said, he came to school Thursday and introduced himself as Heinz Becker. He introduced an eight year old girl as his daughter and enrolled her in school. He overheard us trying to provide sandwiches for the poorer among the students and he came Friday morning with cooks to prepare a bar-b-q. During the day, he made suggestive comments to me and later, at the end of the day, made very unwelcome advances. I had backed into a corner between my desk and a book shelf when Miss Schaub came in and stuck him with her hairpin. You know the rest of the story. I would suggest you contact Mr. Albert Schaffer. Mr. Becker came to school because of him."

He wrote some more and turned with, "We'll be in contact," and walked away. Her peripheral vision caught movement to her left and she turned to face a glaring general.

The general coming home was a little upsetting, and add to it there may be a murder charge was too much. She hadn't eaten anything since her coffee, toast and fruit earlier that morning. She wouldn't go to Evelyn's kitchen as she usually did, but look for some canned fruit and salted fish from a package in her eating area.

Chapter Twenty-Seven

The Hannibal was in the last two weeks of the shake-out cruise and things had not gone well. Four of five boilers had blown up at some point along their trip and they had to steam under limited power back to St. Louis for repairs. The last time they came back, the fifth boiler was changed as well, making it a clean sweep of the power sources. The gun Jake and his crew were on, the aft forty-two pounder blew up severely injuring the main gunner. An opening was created at that position when one other gunner injured his foot. The gun he was on wasn't fully secured and the recoil forced it off the track. A pair of new thirty pounders was put in aft gun mounts and Jake was given lead position at that post.

Jake saw his former ship, the Great Expectations, and the captain, Captain Thomas, and managed to get the general's home address and wrote to Peggy, telling her of some of the frustrations, but leaving out details. He wrote:

> My dear Peggy:
>
> We have been in St. Louis now for most of the month and have yet to do the important stuff of checking out this ship. I guess that's what happens when a new one is launched. I think about you all the time and hope you have time to think of me once in a while. I can't tell you where I am going, but it will obviously be on a river somewhere, since I am in the Navy. I don't know how much or how often

I will be able to write, but I will when I can. Peggy, do you believe in fate? But, you said Christians can't consider fate for that is not believing in God's ability to take care of us. Anyhow, I consider it the luckiest day in my life when I was asked to walk with you around that boat.

You probably don't believe in luck either.

I miss our talks. I miss holding you and I miss the smell of you. I don't know what it was that smelled so sweet, but I miss it. None of the guys here have that wonderful smell.

Sorry I can't say more, but you know my heart and it's in your hands.

Please take care of yourself. I don't know if there's such a thing as leave for this crew. Probably not, but if there is, I'll see you then.

Thinking always of you,

Jake.

PS: I got the address from the captain of the old ship we met on and he asked about you.

He reread the letter, then added:

PPS: I guess you ought to look at this as confidential. Don't tell anyone.

Jake took his letter to the leading Petty Officer, who found an envelope for him. With the address in place, Jake let the P.O. mail it for him and went back to his bunk.

He hadn't been able to get to church during these week ends. He didn't want to go to that English church and meet Betty again and didn't know of another church he would feel comfortable in. He did read his Bible, spending a lot of time in the Psalms. David seemed to have a lot of problems, and Jake felt he did too, considering the way the boilers and the guns were acting. Maybe he needed to pray more for God's will in the future. And read more about faith.

Jake accepted his new duties as if he was trained for them. Some of the men couldn't get over the fact that he was still under five years in service and had reached the level of Chief Gunner. Of course, it took a couple accidents to make it happen, but he was at that position. Most of the lead gunners had been in the Navy around ten to fifteen years. But promotions in the old Navy before the war started were really slow, because there were too many men for the number of ships available. Now that the government was building a mass of gunboats, both for the river war and out in the ocean, there were more needs for men, and more opportunities for promotion.

Meals were served in shifts. The food was pretty good, but two hundred fifty-one men required either a larger room available or eating in three shifts. Sometimes the mess eating order was A through Z, and sometime it was reversed with the men with Z names eating first. Prosser was generally in the middle and most of the time ate during the second eating shift.

His rank gave him choice of bunk. He thought selecting the lowest bed was better, but soon found out that everyone who climbed to the top bunk stepped on his bunk and sometimes, on him. He tried the second bunk and the same condition existed, so Jake chose the top bunk. Since the river was mostly free of waves, he didn't fear being thrown out onto the floor. The storm they had on the Great Expectations on the trip north was the worst he saw and nothing like that happened on this ship.

The repairs all made, they left St. Louis and headed north, past the Missouri River and on farther north. They had been told to test the ship on narrower and shallower streams, so they came past the Illinois River to the Wisconsin River and entered those waters. The Bo's'n had two men sounding the depths of the stream to insure no damage to the bottom of the vessel. When they had gone to a place where the river narrowed and the stream was only a little deeper than the ship's draft, they reversed and got back to the big river.

The order the captain was given was to find out if and how the guns worked. He looked for a place along the river that was uninhabited, where the river walls were steep and they found it. Jake remembered the cliffs at Prairie du Chien, north of their river test, and told the captain, Ephraim Czerny.

They steamed up the river, blasting the rock walls, steaming back south to test the guns on the other side of the ship. They found that their guns were set and the elevation was restricted. They could not hit higher than halfway up the side of the cliffs. For most of the

Rebel forts, that would not be a problem, but a few, Fort Danielson for one, were on high hills above the rivers. The guns on this ship would not reach that high. Probably, the guns on other ships of this class would have the same restriction. Something had to be done to counter the advantage of the Rebel's guns on high places. Jake told the captain about the Gatling gun and how it ended a battle with rebel Indians. The gun and fifty cartridge sticks were in storage on the ship.

The captain called the chief gunner's mate and Jake explained how the gun's nest was situated on the Great Expectations, he called the Chief Carpenter and explained the problem to him. The construction workers were called and soon the workers had a nest built, as Jake described it to them. The gun was brought up with some ammunition sticks. The next trip up the river, Jake aimed the Gatling gun just below the crest of the bluffs along the river and fired, showing the captain how effective it could be in some difficult situations.

Their tests complete, they stopped at fort Two Rivers to replenish their coal need and, while that was being done, the captain called a ship's meeting. He said, "We have had some success against the Rebels. But first, and more important, on 5 September, Captain Andrew Foote was promoted to Commander in Chief of Western Naval Operations. His charter is to work with the new commander of land operations, General U. S. Grant.

"On 6 September, the gunboats Lexington and Tyler spearheaded the capture of Paducah and Smithland, Kentucky. That effort secures the mouths of the Cumberland and the Tennessee Rivers. On 10 September, gunboats Conestoga and Lexington covered advancing troops by silencing Rebel guns in Missouri. So, Gentlemen, things are happening to our advantage. We are about to get involved." The men gathered there shouted a roar of approval at the news. The morale of the crew was definitely higher as they ship headed downstream to join Captain Foote's forces.

Chapter Twenty-Eight

Peggy prepared for school Monday with an almost dread of what might happen. She had not seen or heard from the general since the policeman left. She almost expected, at any moment, that he would come bursting into her room and tell her to leave. Then, of course, there was the cop and what he had to say about the man she knew as Heinz Becker. Who was he? Why did he come to school and try to get her involved with him? What part in this play did Albert Schaffer have and how well did those two know each other?

And then there were the students. What would the more affluent parents say about their sandwiches being wasted? What will the children say about the bar-b-q—will they expect one every Friday? What about Becky? Whatever she did, it was to protect me from him. How can I help her?

She was distraught so that she tried three times to leave, each time remembering something else she needed to take. Finally, she dumped what she was carrying onto the floor, sat in her chair, buried her face in her hands and cried. "Oh, God, what is the matter with me? Why am I so disconcerted? I have given my life to you and whatever you permit is for some reason. I will remember Romans 8:28 and go in the strength of that verse. And thank You for the confidence you have given me to trust You."

She went to the sink to wash her face. She gathered her stuff together again and, straightening, up and headed for the door.

Simon had gotten into the schedule of her need and so her carriage was ready and waiting. This morning, however, it was not hers, but another of the general's possessions as the clouds indicated rain. This one was a two seater that had a top and isinglass roll down curtains. She put her school material in the foot and greeted him, "Good morning, Simon, I hope you have a wonderful day."

He responded as he helped her into the carriage, "Yes, Ma'am, and with a smile like that, how can I be dark and gloomy?"

It was the same route she had driven for more than a month. A few sprinkles were starting as she approached the schoolyard and she noticed there were few children outside. She clicked the horse into a trot and was soon at the hitching rail where she flipped the reins over and around for a quick tie, grabbed her material and headed for the door. More wind and heavier rain came together and she thought of the children who had to walk to school. And Becky. There were only three children in school and all were young. Someone had left an extra coat at school at some time and hadn't come to retrieve it, so she threw the coat over her head and stood at the door for a minute, hoping the rain would slacken, but it did not.

She called to the children that she would be back and bolted out the door to her buggy. The horse had stepped on the reins and it took extra time to get them freed, but she made it and was soon on her rescue mission. She rode around the block and up and down the streets picking up students. She met some parents who had picked up others in addition to their own.

When she arrived back at school with her twelve soaking wet passengers, she found twenty-five others and four sets of parents waiting for her. One of the parents had started a fire in the old wood stove that sat in the middle of the room and it was warm and toasty for those who were wet.

She thanked those parents and asked them to stay for a while to see how the school was run, but they all had other things to do. Soon, it was just teacher and students, with several missing. Becky was the last one to come, having her father bring her. Class proceeded as usual.

An inside recess and lunch was the order of the day. Peggy remembered some of the games she read about before classes began and tried to get the students to participate in controlled activity, but was unsuccessful. They preferred running around the room screaming and laughing. In the middle of this chaos, the door opened and three men entered—Lieutenant Briggs, Albert Schaffer and a man Peggy had never seen before. When the children saw Lt. Briggs wearing a uniform, and some remembering Schaffer from earlier in the year, they quieted immediately and returned to their seats.

Schaffer spoke, "Miss O'Neal, this is Donald Yarborough, your replacement. We just cannot have our teachers being the subject of police investigations. You are relieved of your duties as of this very moment. Please hand over your keys to this building."

Peggy stood straight and said, in no uncertain terms, "I will not. I have a contract and a question. The man who called himself Becker came here after talking to you. We find out his name is Herman Goble, that he was unmarried and yet had a child to register in this school. My questions, Mr. Schaffer, are what was your association with Mr. Goble, why did you tell him to change his name and to come here with a. . .a. . .kind of rent-a-child? Tell us, Mr. Schaffer, how did you know this man?"

Huffily, the school board president answered, "I don't have to answer your questions. I don't have to tell you a thing. I'm not the one on trial here. You are. And you are being replaced today by Mr. Yarborough. Get your things and leave, now."

Peggy ignored Schaffer and directed her question to the policeman. "Officer Briggs, why did you come here? Did he ask you to come to enforce his removal demands, or was there another reason?"

He smiled and said, "That's a fair question, Miss. The answer is I wanted to get you, Miss Schaub and Mr. Schaffer together in one room without arresting anyone. An arrest seems to shut the mouths of the ones in question and I wanted a good discussion." He turned to Becky and said, "Miss Schaub, tell me where Miss O'Neal and Mr. Goble were when you came back into the room."

Becky walked to the desk and said, "He was here, reaching for her. Miss O'Neal was backed into that corner behind the desk," and she pointed to a space next to a large book shelf. "I saw him reaching for her and I took the hatpin out of my hair and walked over to him. He swung at me, I ducked and stuck him with the pin. He begged us to take it out, for it was in a position where he couldn't reach it. Miss O'Neal pulled it and he left."

Briggs looked at Schaffer and said, "Now, Mr. Schaffer, Miss O'Neal brings up an interesting question, in fact, two or three. Number one, what was your association with Mr. Goble? Number two, why did you suggest he change his name and three, what was the purpose in sending him here with, as Miss O'Neal described, a rent-a-child?"

Albert Schaffer became beet red in his face as anger showed itself. He shouted, "I am not the subject of this visit." He pointed at the teacher, "She is responsible for his death, she and her. . .her ignorant puppet. I will not suffer any more humiliation. I'm leaving," and he jammed his hat on his head and turning, stormed toward the door.

Officer Briggs called after him. "Mr. Schaffer, don't leave. If you do I will arrest you. I am conducting an investigation into what appears to be a murder. The ladies acted, as far as I can tell, in self defense. The questions of your involvement still remain to be answered. Now, will you answer them here or should we go downtown to the station?"

Schaffer roared, "I will not lower myself to having her in the room with me. If you must, take me downtown," and he stormed out of the room into the diminishing wind and rain.

Briggs took two steps toward where Schaffer disappeared and stopped. He looked at the other man in the room and said, "Well, Mr. Yarborough, I guess you're on your own." With the men gone, the room was quiet.

Peggy walked to her desk and stood behind it. She addressed them all, "Students, look at me." They all obeyed the request. "I'm sure this day is ruined as far as school work is concerned. I have to ask you a question, and with the turmoil we have had these last two weeks, I'm fearful of the answer, but do you want me to return to be your teacher tomorrow? Take time to think—"

Before she was done with her request, a loud, unanimous shout of "Yes," filled the room.

"I'm going to let you go home now. The rain seems to have stopped, or at least, diminished. Be careful walking to avoid the puddles. If you need a ride, I can give some of you a lift, but not everyone. You older students who know these young ones, can you kind of shepherd them?"

It was agreed and as the last pupil walked out of the room, Miss O'Neal went to her desk, sat in the chair and cradled her head in her hands. "Father, God, is this what You want me to do? Is this where You want me? Am I able to present as good an image of a Christian as You want me to? I pray for open door or closed doors, so that there will be no question in my mind. Please help me."

The trip home was a mixture of enjoying the cool refreshing breeze and a reminder of the general and his attitude about Christians in general and her in particular. She uttered, "Lord, how can I face him knowing how much he hates me? Is there anything I can do to change it? And help Evelyn. She's caught in the middle here. She recently announced her faith and yet, she is his wife. Thirty years they have been together. Give her strength and guidance."

The distance passed quickly with her praying and before she realized it, she was home. She saw another carriage in the drive and moved hers around it, and stopped. She told Simon to wait on caring for the horse until she talked to Mrs. Patterson, as she needed to go somewhere. As she and Simon stood there, the general and Evelyn came out of the door.

Evelyn exclaimed, "Peggy! You're home early. Is everything all right?"

Peggy answered, "It was wild today. That policeman and Mr. Schaffer came to school I guess to either arrest me or to throw me out. As it turned out, Mr. Schaffer was taken to the police station for questioning. I need to see Mayor Hatch and talk to him."

Evelyn expressed sorrow, "I'm sorry, dear, but Clay has to see a doctor. The, uh, the stump is seeping blood and is painful. I don't know when we'll be back, but we must go now." They stepped down off the porch and Evelyn stopped. "Why don't you just go ahead and see him. He knows you now so it shouldn't be stressful. Go ahead, and oh, the key. Simon will have to drive us, so the back door is unlocked."

With that, Simon helped his bosses into their carriage and climbed into the driver's seat. The matching bay horses were eager to run as he snapped the reins, leaving Peggy wondering what to do. She wanted to see Mayor Hatch, so, to the mayor's office she would go.

What would she say to him? Thoughts crossed her mind as she drove as to how to present her concern. She prayed as she drove, asking for words and thoughts that right now she couldn't express. "And what do I do if he's busy?" What options did she have? She had to get this problem with Albert Schaffer resolved. He seemed to want her out of that teaching position. When they first talked, he was sociable and kind. Since she prayed. . .she prayed with Jaimie at school that day, and their relationship changed. "He's angry at me being a Christian!" Then she remembered Schaffer coming to the house when Jake was there, and his attitude about them kissing on the street. "He's been against me from the first day!"

She arrived at the building that served as the city hall and found a long line of buggies at the hitching rail in front. She drove the length of the building, turned around and came back. Someone was in the process of backing his rig away from the rail, so she waited. "He's backing it. Oh, dear, how do I do that?" She watched and listened.

Inside, the wait wasn't as long as it appeared, as there were several other offices in the building. She waited her turn and, when granted entrance, found the mayor expecting her. He greeted her and pointed to a chair. She sat.

"I expected you'd be here," he said. The surprised look on her face prompted him to add, "You're surprised? I have some very good and thorough people reporting to me and I knew what was going to happen before they arrived. The <u>only</u> reason Lt. Briggs went was to get you all together so he could get answers to those questions."

He smiled and continued, "Now, outside of a peaceful job situation, what do you want?"

She sat with her mouth open for several seconds, surprised at his statement. That was all she wanted. She didn't want to have to face Albert Schaffer every week of the school year. Finally, able to speak, she said, "That's it. That's all I want." Before he could say anything she continued, "That day when you came to support me at the school, I thought that would be the end of it. But instead, he has constantly picked at me. I don't think he like the fact that I'm a Christian."

"I've known Albert a long time. We don't agree on much, but, until now, he's been an honest adversary. We'll talk it out. I don't know if we can fire him or if we have to vacate the whole board election. We have other schools they are responsible for. We'll have to discuss it."

"Has he ever gone against a teacher he hired, or am I the first one?"

"He's done this before. I've called a meeting of the city council for tomorrow morning."

She sat quiet for the moment. The reason for her coming had been resolved. She no longer had to fear going to school, wondering what that man would do or want. She was ready to leave and asked, "Did you know General Patterson?"

"Only at some social functions that involved military and public activity. I understand he was wounded."

"He lost the lower part of his left arm and hand. It started seeping blood and they are at the doctor's office now."

"That's too bad. From what I understand it was some clumsy kid in his own outfit that shot him. When you see them, give them my regards."

She rose and said, "I will Sir, and thank you for everything." Outside, she remembered what she saw and heard of the other driver backing his team out of the spot. She'd try it. She could only hope.

She sat in her own little corner on her own little chair and pondered the day's events. She heard the rush of galloping horses and someone shouting, "Miss Peggy, Miss Peggy, come! They need you! Miss Peggy, come!"

She went through the big room to the door and saw Simon sitting in the carriage the Pattersons had left in, shouting for her. She opened the door and before she could say anything, he once again repeated the need for her to come with him. She quickly went back and picked up her purse, her Bible and her bonnet. As she was doing that, Simon had turned the carriage around, ready to hit the street. Simon whipped the horses into a gallop and they tore out of their drive, onto the street. Simon was a good driver, but Peggy feared for her life until they stopped at the city hospital.

Simon jumped down from his driver's perch and helped Peggy to the street. "They're upstairs on second floor," he breathlessly stated, getting back in the carriage. Peggy turned toward the hospital door and made her way up to the second floor. There was a small waiting room at the top of the stairs and Evelyn was there. There were chairs and tables spread around the room and a group of men and women, presumably doctors and nurses, comforting an almost hysterical woman.

When she saw Peggy, she pushed the others aside and rushed to grab the younger woman, almost pushing them down the stairs. Peggy managed to grab the railing and hold on while Evelyn, crying, in frenzy, sobbed out her story—the arm has an infection and they may have to amputate up above the elbow. "Please," she begged, "pray for him and the arm to be healed." In the instant of hearing, Margaret O'Neal's mind went back over sixteen years to a mother she never had and, with all Evelyn had done for her, Peggy felt a family relationship.

She whispered, "Where is he?"

Still sobbing, Evelyn managed to explain he was in his room and they were preparing for the operation. "They may not let me in," Peggy explained. "We might have to pray right here."

"No! They will let me in and you will come with me. Please."

At the general's room, a staff of medical people hovered around the bed, talking in code Peggy didn't understand, but looking at the man on the bed, she realized how much pain he was in and how much his wife was pleading with the Lord for healing. With no hesitation, Peggy walked over to the bed, read the twenty-third Psalm, gently placed her finger tips on the infected arm and began praying. The people in the room were slow to react and it varied from "Miss, you can't be in here," to "Hush, she's praying for him."

It took less than a minute for her to ask God to intervene, to blot out past hurts, to prove His glory and power to the man and to the hospital staff. As she ended, she leaned over and whispered, "I love you, General Patterson and your wonderful wife. I will continue to pray for your healing." She turned and led Evelyn from the room.

Chapter Twenty-Nine

General Courtney Clay Patterson came home the following Thursday about noon and when Peggy came home, he had Evelyn call her to their parlor for a talk. She came, a little apprehensive, wondering, almost anticipating, that he would insist she move out. Her week had been busy trying to settle students down after Monday's visit by the police and the other two men. When the students carried the news home to their families, several parents came to school to voice their support for her.

Class procedure had settled down so that even on days when it rained, students honored the teacher's request for control. Tuesday was much like Monday, weather wise and the older students helped the younger ones at play during the recess and lunch periods.

Wednesday, Becky came to her with a request—please help her to become a teacher. After a time of prayer and deliberation, Peggy decided to help by adding an hour to the prayer and Bible study on Saturday. She would teach Becky the art of teaching, with emphasis on learning facts and information that she might have learned as a senior high school student. At the start, Peggy thought it was a novelty that Becky would give up in a couple weeks, but that didn't happen. Peggy gave her student a lot of homework to get the information required and every day Becky would mention something she had found that followed the homework requested.

So Thursday, as Peggy approached the parlor, she had the fear that General Patterson would ask her to leave. She stopped as she entered the kitchen and prayed for God's presence and His control and then walked down the hallway to the little room.

He greeted her with, "Why did you do that?"

Stunned, her mind raced over what she might have done. Slowly, she responded, "What. . .did I do?"

"When you prayed for me, you leaned over me and said, 'I love you and your wonderful wife.' Why did you say that?"

Still a little confused, Peggy answered, "Well, I do. I mean, your wife has given me a home and helped me get a job. This is your home, so in a sense, you are responsible for my being here. I just wanted you to know that, as a Christian, I believe everyone is worthy of God's love and I was just trying to convey that to you."

She stood there, hands clasped at her waist, melting under his look. It wasn't anger, it wasn't even a glaring look, he just sat there, quietly looking at her. After a while, he said, "You have destroyed my anger, did you know that? All these years I carried a hatred against Christians and church people, because of the way they treated my parents. When Evelyn said you were different, I didn't believe her. When you came and prayed for me, I told myself it was part of the game you people play, that you didn't really mean it. Then you said you loved me. Why? Are you so different from the others? Would everyone who is a Christian say that?"

"I don't know, General, it—"

"No, I'm not a general anymore. Call me Clay, that's Evelyn's name. I guess you are part of the family that is if you want to be. I've called our family together to apologize to them for my stand on being a Christian. They'll be here for next weekend."

Peggy twisted her hands in discomfort. She concentrated on the floor for several seconds. "Sir,Gen. . .Clay, Mr. Patterson, I—" She realized the order of her approach and said, "There, I guess I've covered them all. If it's all right with you, I'll call you Mr. Patterson, at least for a while. When we are more comfortable together, perhaps I'll use Clay."

He smiled, "And yet you didn't hesitate to use my wife's first name."

Flustered, Peggy's face tinted pink and she stammered an answer. "I. . .I'm sorry, I—"

The general quickly came to her aid, "I'm sorry, I didn't mean to embarrass you. Mr. Patterson is all right until, as you say, we get better acquainted. Now, there's another matter. Do you know what cauterizing is?"

Evelyn interrupted, "Let the dear girl sit down, Clay. You've kept her standing all this time. She just had a day of teaching the children. Peggy, please sit. You can talk just as well from a sitting position. I've seen you." Before Peggy could move, Evelyn continued, "Oh, I forgot. With this, uh, meeting, I got a letter delivered to you today. It's from a sailor somewhere on a river. It's on the table behind you."

Peggy wheeled around, saw an envelope and grabbed it. Verifying it was to her, she tore it open and read. It wasn't very long, less than a page. But she devoured it and, after reading it at least twice, crushed it as she brought it to her lips and tears formed on her cheeks.

He said, "Is that the young man with the gun? Perhaps you would like to take some time to read it and prepare a reply?"

"No, that's all right. I'll do it later. Why did you ask about cauterizing? It has something to do with burning, doesn't it?"

"Yes. When you came into the room, the medical staff was split between cauterizing the arm and cutting more off, up above my elbow. They said the infection had gone that far. They were worried. Those who suggested the cauterizing felt it would correct the infection. Anyhow, after you prayed and left the room, I felt a burning in my arm and I yelled with the pain of it. They took off the bandage and the skin was hot, but clean. No infection. I know my father used to preach about God's healing, but he never saw it happen. Until now, I didn't think it was possible."

"I don't know what to say. Of course I praise God for the healing, and give Him the glory. It was His touch, not mine that healed your infection."

Later in her room, she read the letter and read it again. She went out to the other part of the house to ask the general if there was some way she could send a letter to Jake and the former general suggested sending it to the Center for Naval Operations at the fort here in Cincinnati. She thanked him and returned to her room. She took paper and pen and began to write.

My dearest Jacob.

I received your letter today and thank you for thinking of me. I am living with the Pattersons. The general is home, having lost his hand above the left wrist.

He says he is no longer in the army.

I understand that you cannot tell me where you are. I'm thankful you are all right and are thinking of me. Now as to your questions about fate and luck, you are right, I don't believe in either. I believe in God's will and in His plan for our lives. Jacob, read Psalms 37 and then Psalms 91. Read them again and if you get discouraged, read them again. And remember, I love you. I will always love you. Bury that in your heart and hold on to it.

Silly, no man would be caught dead with female scents (we don't call them smells, they're scents.). I miss your touch, your kindness and your determination to do the right thing. I miss our talks and the times we spent holding hands on the fantail of that ship.

Oh, I hate this war. I want it to end so we can be together. Remember, I love you. You are dear to me. Please take care of yourself.

All my love, Peg.

She got an envelope and addressed it. She walked out to where the Pattersons were to ask how to deliver the letter and was told that they had mail to go, and that Simon would take it in the morning.

In her room again, her spirits were lifted by those few words of love. She had some papers to correct and some assignments to make for the weekend. She had a sermon to prepare for Sunday and a Bible study and school assignment for Becky. With the lift from the letter, those things would be no problem.

She spent some time early Saturday morning in the library of the Evangel Seminary, reading up on First Corinthians, thirteen. She signed out one of their commentaries and, even though a woman, was given permissions to take it with her. She told the librarian she was preparing a sermon for Sunday and was rewarded with a smile and the nod of her head. She spent an hour making notes before hurrying back to the Bible study with Becky and any women she would bring. After that, she agreed to spend an hour with Becky to teach her the basic high school education. Peggy felt that Becky has shown a temperament for teaching and decided she would do what she could to give her that opportunity.

At lunch time, Evelyn invited Peggy for a salad. Her husband, Clay, was there in the kitchen and Evelyn served salad and coffee. The conversation was limited at the start and Peggy began to feel uncomfortable. With a nervousness that showed itself in her dropping food and utensils, she moved the chair back and said, "General, forgive me, but I have to call you that as an honor of your rank. I don't feel comfortable with your first name, and as close as we are here, Mr. Patterson isn't good enough, so, it will be General. Is that all right?"

He nodded and she continued. "Now, Evelyn has told me some of your problems with people called Christians, and I don't want to aggravate that, but I'm going to preach again tomorrow. The topic is 'God's Love,' and if you are unhappy with me, or uncomfortable about my being here, I can move out."

Evelyn cried, "What! Of course not! Clay, tell her she's alright to stay here and preach on Sundays."

General Clay Patterson held the coffee cup in his hand, with the left stub next to it, while looking at the table. He spoke quietly and slowly. "Until Monday afternoon, I would have been unhappy to have you here. You came and prayed for my hand and said that about loving me, and that has given me pause. I don't understand you, Miss O'Neal. I don't understand how you can show that kind of concern for me, having seen and heard me in St. Louis and having heard what Evelyn has said about me. Do you, as Evelyn has suggested, live the question—what would Jesus do?"

"I try, Mr. Patterson, I really try. I'm not perfect and I have the problem of all humans in some of the decisions I make turn out wrong, but I do try."

"You don't have to move. It may take a while but, I'll try to get to one of the sermons before too long." He smiled and looked at is wife, "Imagine that, me with the attitude I've had for thirty years, committing to go to a church service, with a woman preacher. Mother would have been pleased."

Whether someone at the hospital told someone outside about the prayer for the general or whether one of the military visitors the general had told somebody, no one knew. All they knew was there were nearly seventy people at the service on Sunday, and most of them were talking about the woman who prayed for the general's arm.

Simon had a problem finding chairs so several had to stand along the walls. Becky was there and when Peggy and Mrs. Carpenter saw how many children there were, Peggy entreated the other two women to take the children into another of the small side rooms to teach them there. They agreed that after the song service and announcements, they'd leave with the kids.

There were not nearly enough song books for the crowd so after a quick conference, they decided to sing Amazing Grace, Fairest Lord Jesus and Rock of Ages, with the second being the most recently published. They figured that those who came this morning would have had some contact with churches in another city, and would most likely be familiar with those songs.

The preliminaries done and the children out of the service, Peggy stood and said, "The sermon this morning is from First Corinthians thirteen. I beg your permission to change a word. That word is Charity. Charity has taken on a different meaning from the original Vulgate writing and doesn't now convey the real meaning. With your permission, I will use the word Love, in place of Charity. This is not my own decision. In the commentaries I read yesterday, there were four translations, including John Wesley's that use the word Love."

She started at verse one and substituted Love in place of Charity and ended with the first phrase of verse eight, "Love never faileth." She closed her Bible and stepped back from the lectern. "We are now engaged in a Civil War. We hear minimal reports from the front as to who is winning, but there are two losers in this conflict already, and they are truth and reason. That is always the case in armed conflict."

She read, "'Though I speak with the tongues of men and of angels and have not love. . .' We hear politicians saying things, making threats against people of our own country. Yes, they were the aggressors, or so we hear, but they are still our friends and family. In this case, we can expect brother to be shooting at brother, friend against friend, and for what purpose? Could not men have gathered in prayer and tried to gain a meeting of the minds? This will go on for years. It will last forever.

"'Though I speak with the tongues of men and angels. . .' Politicians make speeches and threats. There is no love, only anger, hatred and even fear, fear of what may happen if the other side wins. This wasn't written for a Civil War situation. It was written because of problems in a church and perhaps Paul was afraid the conditions would deteriorate into physical battles."

She continued with the verses, applying them to the conditions of the time and to the potential deterioration of relations between families, friends and southern relatives. "There might be a time when giving all our goods to feed the poor will be a need rather than an act of charity, the proper use of the word. What will happen to the poor after the war? What will be their situation when the war ends? What part will we have in the reconstruction of the South after the war? Remember, they are, or were, part of us. We know some of them. They are family. Will we act in love when this is all over?"

There were no "Amens" or applause when she ended. People sat, or stood quietly, as Peggy walked off the small platform and stood at the door to greet the people. No one praised her. Not too many commented on her sermon, but one comment indicated disappointment that she didn't have a healing service. Alone, she sat in a chair and wondered what the future would hold. She wanted to teach, but had been thrown into a position as preacher in this body of worshippers. Right now, she didn't feel she could quit and turn the preaching over to someone else. She felt the need of more prayer.

Chapter Thirty

Margaret O'Neal's schedule was full, too full. But she had agreed to the things she was involved in and didn't know how to withdraw from any. Becky was developing both in her Bible study and in her private instruction times and her insatiable hunger for learning seemed to grow every day. Gary Carpenter felt he had to resign the formal position as pastor because of his work schedule. His wife helped in the ministry by taking the children and teaching them, with Becky's help. But as a teacher, instructor and minister, Peggy was running dry, spiritually and emotionally. Things irritated her and she didn't seem to be able to control them. And she cried more often.

Evelyn noticed it and she mentioned it to her husband. He didn't want to get involved, but, with his wife's insistence, he agreed to talk to Peggy. When Peggy came home that afternoon from school, Evelyn invited her into the kitchen for tea and crumpets, a habit from her English ancestors. At first, Peggy refused stating she was exhausted. Evelyn persisted and, finally, the teacher followed, anticipating a lecture.

Clay Patterson was there, sitting at one end of a rectangular table. He appeared to be concentrating on the cup in his hand and only looked up after the ladies sat down. He didn't wait for a lead-in by his wife, but started immediately. "In the army, we were taught to never get ahead of our supply lines, and to never split our forces in the face of a persistent enemy. We were taught to concentrate our strength on the most vulnerable positions along the enemy line and to hammer at that position with all our strength."

He stopped talking but continued to look at her. She was silent for a minute and finally said, "I gather you are trying to tell me something. Is it that I'm spreading myself too thin?"

Without changing his expression, he said, "Yes."

After another period of stillness, she quietly said, "Splitting our forces and a persistent enemy I understand, but what is the enemy's vulnerable position?"

He smiled, "Come now, Miss O'Neal. You are a Christian who prayed, and continues to pray, for your interests. Do you not understand the source of your power? Your strength? I'm sure you understand who the enemy is."

Peggy bowed her head and tears came to her eyes. She took her napkin, wiped her eyes and looking up, trying to smile. "But what can I do? Brother Carpenter is working and can't be available for church. I have a job teaching that pays my salary. There's the Bible study and the instruction for Becky, and correcting papers and planning for the next school day. I am just exhausted at the end of the day and yet know the next day will be the same."

"In the army, planning is imperative. Not everything works out the way it's planned, there is always the opponent, but at least, there is the plan. Adjustments may have to be made, but that, again, is based on a plan." He looked at her and spoke as tenderly as he could. "Now, what do you consider your first priority, teaching, preaching or instruction?"

"But," in a tone of apology, "if I don't—"

"That's not what I asked. What do you consider your first priority?"

She clasped her hands on the table and rubbed one against the other. She didn't speak for several seconds. Finally, with tears in her eyes, she answered, "I understand what you're getting at, Gen. . .Clay. I'm not the focus here. The focus should be on God and His plan. Whom does <u>He</u> want to do these things? But if I don't. . ." A long pause followed. "General, I do thank you for your concern.

I must admit a bit of surprise that you are the one to remind me, but I thank you and promise to spend some time in prayer for guidance."

He smiled and nodded his head. "I must admit to a bit of a surprise that I'm the one to bring this to your attention. We like you, Miss O'Neal. Evelyn has adopted you as one of her own. I saw my parents destroyed by trying to do too much, trying to appease and placate when it was not accepted. We don't want to see that happen to you."

Peggy felt she had to get away from them quickly or would break down in front of them. She excused herself and rushed out of the kitchen to her own room, where she fell down on her knees at her bed and broke down. She sobbed and apologized to God for taking on more than she should. After a while, she stopped crying and, still on her knees, fell asleep.

Meanwhile, in the kitchen, the wife looked at the husband with her eyebrows raised and a slight smile on her face. "'Never split our forces, and never get ahead of our supply lines?' Clay, you like her don't you?" She reached for his hand. "Honey, that's all right. I like her too. And I am concerned that she's trying to do too much. But you didn't have to say anything. I don't think she expected that of you, but I'm glad you did. I think that you will face up to your decision before too much longer." She lifted his hand and kissed it.

The family members came late that Friday. Clay the youngest, a lieutenant in the army, was first since he was stationed there outside of Cincinnati. The daughters, Esther, the oldest child, Phyllis and Grace, the youngest and unmarried, came with their families, to meet their newest "sibling."

Grace came smiling, holding out her arms to Peggy. "So you're the one who's disrupted our family by bringing religion home? Good for you."

The father and mother stood shocked at her comment. How had she found out about bringing religion into the home? They looked at her and she said, "What? She did, didn't she? At least that's what Uncle Orville says."

He father stepped up to her and exclaimed, "Orville! When did you hear from him?"

"We all have," she defended. "He's been in touch with us all. He's in town here somewhere, and he knows about your hand and her praying for you. He has enough money to pay spies. He told us that she's ruined your life, but that's his opinion. He thought you were going to order Mother to turn her out, but you didn't. We all agree that it might be the best thing to happen to you."

Clay Junior added to her explanation. "Father, we all have some contact with a church. We remember your feeling against them, and when we first heard from Uncle Orville, we all thanked God for this newest member of our family. Orville doesn't see it that way, but, don't be surprised if he comes around too. We're praying."

Esther, the oldest, added, "Daddy, we didn't want to offend you or make you feel bad. But, one thing led to another in Fred and my lives, and we saw that without something strong to anchor to, especially in these times, we'd have problems and maybe separate, so we looked for a church, the kind that your father preached in."

"How did you know the kind my father preached in? I never mentioned it."

Phyllis, the middle girl, joined the conversation. "Well, you did and you didn't. You never told us the church, but you told us the town and we all did some writing, asking the town fathers about the churches in that area, and came up with a name. Then we looked for one in our towns and found out that not everyone was like the people who hurt you so much. Perhaps, just perhaps, this young woman moving in here is the result of answered prayer." Evelyn smiled, remembering the path that brought Peggy to them.

They spent the evening talking and making Peggy a part of the family. She reminded them she had to preach Sunday, and begged their permission to leave, which was granted.

She went to the Evangel Seminary early Saturday morning to talk to an administrator about some substitute ministers, and met three men. Peggy told them about the church situation and asked if any of them could preach, once a month, for the next three months, or until Christmas. They all agreed. She asked them to come so she could introduce them to the congregation that Sunday and they all agreed. Now, she had to prepare her own sermon, so she went and waited for Becky for the Bible study and everything else that followed.

She prayed quite a while before deciding on a topic. The commentaries she got at the seminary helped her in her studying. Her sermon was to be built on two words found in the book of Acts—"Brother Saul," found in chapter 9, verse 17. She stood before the full church of about seventy people, including the Patterson's families, and after the preliminaries, read the last part of the verse: "Brother Saul, the Lord, even Jesus that appeared unto thee in the way as thou camest, hath sent me that thou mightest receive thy sight."

She carried her Bible and the commentary to the lectern. After reading the scripture, she set her Bible aside and opened the commentary. Not trained in the ministry techniques, she drew a faint pencil line around some parts of the commentary and read verbatim about Saul, who became Paul. She read abut his background, his education and his anger at those of "The Way." She emphasized that Ananias knew who Saul was, and yet called him Brother. She read from the book about Saul's position and his acceptance by his elders, and how they turned against him when he was changed.

"I am told," she said, "that every sermon should have three main points. If that is true, and I have to state the three points of this sermon, they would be, one, the change required in man, two the journey man, and I mean the generic man, including women, the journey man has to take and three, the acceptance by man."

She expounded forty minutes about the Brotherhood of Christians. She reminded people that there are forces allayed against the Christian that only God can combat, and we, as God's people, must join together to resist the evil in the world, even though there are times when we disagree on an item. When she finished, she introduced the three men who were to help in the ministry, at least until December: John King, Albert Weinmeister and Joseph

McGruder. They stood and she invited them to stand with her at the door to greet people on the way out.

When everyone was gone except Evelyn, Clay and his children had gone back into the house, the four stood at the door and McGruder grasped her hand and said, "You have given us an almost impossible task to follow you. That was one fabulous sermon. May I have your sermon notes?" She laughed. It started out as a little giggle, an embarrassing kind of apology for no notes, and built from there. The tension of the week, plus the pressure of the preparation, caused her to laugh uncontrollably for several minutes until Evelyn realized something was terribly wrong. She screamed for Clay and went to grab hold of Peggy. Peggy was still shaking when Clay got there and, recognizing the problem, slapped Peggy on the side of her face.

Peggy slumped in Evelyn's arms and McGruder, who was still standing there, helped Peggy into a chair. Clay came to the chair and knelt in front of the girl. He patted her cheek, calling her name, until she woke up with a start, grabbing for Evelyn.

Clay explained to the three men what Evelyn had told him, that Peggy felt responsible for the church because of Carpenter having to work and there was no one else willing to preach. He told them of her week's activities and they began to see the amount of pressure Peggy had taken on herself. Daughter Grace came out, curious of her mother's delay, and she and her mother led Peggy into her room and put her in bed.

The three men had gotten together and when Evelyn and Grace came back, they met the ladies. Albert Weinmeister said, "We agree to share the ministry, at least until after Christmas. I'll take next Sunday, John the following week and Joseph the third Sunday. That will give Miss O'Neal time to think about her next sermon. It would be a great mistake, based on what we heard today, if she decided to give up the preaching ministry. We might be able to rotate every three Sundays or, perhaps find someone else to fill one time."

Grace Patterson was impressed with the three men, primarily Albert Weinmeister. As the three left and the family retreated to the house, she watched the men. He was the tallest of the three, with deep blue eyes set in a narrow face, and straw colored hair tied in a bun behind his head. When he spoke, his bass voice carried authority, like what she thought a minister should sound.

Her mother had to remind her to come into the house for dinner.

Chapter Thirty-One

Three months went by almost overnight. The Patterson children and their families went to their various homes the week following meeting Margaret O'Neal. They accepted her almost immediately as one of their own and spent the available time in family discussions. In the first get together Sunday afternoon, the others were laughing and talking and Peggy became suddenly quiet. When asked the reason, she said, "This is the first time I ever felt like being part of a family," and tears came to her eyes. Grace, sitting next to her, turned and threw her arms around their "new sister," expressing their joy at her being there.

They soon had to disperse. Fred and Esther left Tuesday afternoon for Columbus, to his job at the State. Phyllis and her husband, George, left Wednesday after a tearful goodbye with Peggy, thanking her for her example and steady life. Monday morning, Grace had sent a letter to her employer in Pittsburg that she was resigning for personal reasons, and moving back to Cincinnati. It came as a surprise to her parents when she announced she would be moving into her old room. The move required her to return to Pittsburg to go through the exit process. She was back in Cincinnati within a week

Peggy's school moved along with classes and tests after the first six weeks. She set up time for the slowest students at recess and after the regular school hours. It added to her teaching time, but with the three men taking the responsibility of the preaching ministry, she didn't have that extra pressure.

October was rainy and cool, with some days of clear skies. Because of rain storms developing rapidly, Evelyn insisted Peggy use their reverse landaulet, a small carriage Clay had built with the ability to enclose both driver's seat and rear seat separately. The small rear luggage box was uncovered. The normal landau had an open driver's seat and enclosed back for passengers. Simon greeted Peggy each morning with a smile, whether the day was clear or potentially rainy. He had a large umbrella, but warned her not to use it if there was much wind.

The school day had become routine with Becky's helping the younger children. Peggy was amazed at how Becky had developed in her class control and teaching. Each day, they spent fifteen or twenty minutes at the end of the day for Becky to ask questions and get answers while a problem was still fresh in her mind. One day her parents came to watch the process and were impressed and expressed their thanks for what Peggy had done to help their daughter.

Becky had confided to Peggy that her parents were older, having married late. When Becky was born, she was handed over to volunteer child care people as her folks were trying to get a business started. When Becky got in the family way at seventeen, they ignored her completely, letting her raise her son however she could. She admitted making many mistakes. She felt that some of these mistakes had resulted in Jaimie's limited learning ability. It wasn't until she started helping at the school that her parents began to think of her as part of the family, and Jaimie as their grandson.

A bar-b-q once a month was the reward for pupils doing their work. With the student's help, she remembered the name of the crew that set up the last one, and she contacted them to provide one the last Friday of the month. Some parents thought their children were doing so well at school, they agreed with the reward policy and collected funds for the event. All parents were invited, so that some of the poorer were fed as well. Tables were set up by the food provider and children and their parents sat and ate together. During those meetings Peggy made herself available for parental questions.

Peggy had to settle one fight between one sixth grade boy and a girl who came to the church she attended. The boy objected to the many references Peggy made to God and His love, saying those arguments should be left at church. The girl declared God is everywhere and in everything, and that it's only right to thank Him for all He has done. The argument became explosive and soon involved most of the students. It took several minutes to calm the kids down and get school back in swing.

Grace had moved back into her parent's house and most every night, she and Peggy shared the events of the day. With Grace, opinions about a certain ministerial student who shared preaching duties at their church were part of their discussion. Peggy reflected on how she had fallen for Jake after a short time and smiled as Grace told of her feelings for Albert Weinmeister. Her father's only comment was "Why didn't she fall in love with someone named Jones?"

Albert was the best preacher of the four, the seminary administration having assigned one more student preacher to the rotation. They asked a few people to evaluate the sermons each week and discovered the people were very careful in their critique. The seminary sent word to Peggy and the Carpenters that on a Sunday when John King was scheduled to preach, they needed to have a graduate substitute to see how he would do in a real pulpit. He was a student who had perpetually gotten high marks for classroom sermons, and the administration needed to determine if he could fill a pulpit in a small church. The arrangement was made.

The student came, the sermon was preached and the crowd, those who had been asked to appraise his work, filled out their notes for delivery the next day. The general feeling was he would be an excellent pastor, but that German preacher was the best. That gave Grace an exultant feeling. She had already made that determination. Her talks with Peggy centered on how she should act when she obviously cared so much for the man. Peggy's fist suggestion, "Find out if he has a wife at home, or if there is an 'intended' someplace. If not, make your presence known as often as you can."

Peggy watched with interest as the plan became fact. Grace asked her parents for help. Clay laughed, but didn't hold back his suggestions. Evelyn was horrified that a daughter of hers would be so aggressive in affairs of the heart and not let nature take its course. Grace said, in defense of her actions, "Mother, I'm twenty-five. Most girls I know have two or three children by that age. I thought I would wait until I found the right man, and now, I think he's here."

They found out that Weinmeister grew up near Cincinnati in a German settlement, that his parents were followers of the Dutchman, Jacobus Arminius, in his belief that God's Love was stronger and more apparent of divinity than His judgments. Originally a Calvinist, his followers developed a theology that was the basis for John Wesley's Methodism.

Albert's next preaching assignment was two Sundays away, so Grace sent an invitation to the school, inviting Albert to dinner after church that Sunday. He wrote back, accepting the offer and thanking them for their kindness. Thus began a series of menu proposals and rejections, primarily because of their lack of information about his food preferences. Evelyn found a recipe for stuffed bass, baked in a sauce of butter and herbs, and she decided on that for their meal. Fortunately, there was a fish market at the end of a street past their house, next to the big river.

The fish didn't come from the river but from a small lake north of the city. The fish were filleted from fish weighing three or four pounds, giving each person a substantial portion. Both Evelyn and Grace worried over the menu until time for church. The service was great, as someone at the seminary donated an older harpsichord to the church. It was received with great joy and dedicated to God during the church service. Only one person, a woman and mother from Philadelphia, had played that kind of instrument and she volunteered to play it. The leading members, including Mrs. Carpenter and Peggy, met to order music for the congregation.

There was no lack of conversation at dinner that day, to Grace's distress. She wanted to control the topics, but Albert was so happy about the musical instrument that Grace didn't have a chance. She finally kept quiet, letting other carry the conversation. As soon as dinner was done and, after a short time of conversation, Albert left. When the door closed behind him, Grace ran to her room and buried her face in her bed cover and cried. Wednesday, a thank you card with a hand drawn picture arrived at the Patterson home, thanking Grace for her invitation. She floated around the house all day.

The end of October brought a Halloween party. The students were excited about dressing as demons or werewolves or something, so Peggy decided to explain where the day's celebration came from. She gathered information from Catholic Churches and a World Book type encyclopedia. She explained that about the year 835 AD, the Roman Catholic Church set November first as a day to honor God and all His Saints, known or unknown. They called it All Saint's Day.

It so happened that a religion called The Druids celebrated the day before that, October 31, as a day of contacting the dead. It was thought that the Church started their practice as a counter to the other activity. People watched all night as, they believed, their Saman, their worship leader and the Lord of the Dead, called forth hosts of evil spirits. They believed these spirits revisited their earthly homes on that evening, so fires were lit to ward them off. Soon, a modification of their beliefs spread and was accepted more than the original All Saint's Day. Today, it is called Hallowe'en. She wrote it on a large slate, the night to celebrate the dead.

When she finished, the students all sat quiet, seeming afraid to move, afraid to ask questions. Slowly, they began to loosen up and talk and Peggy took her Bible to read first from Exodus, 22:18 (Thou shalt not suffer a witch to live), and then from First Samuel about King Saul looking for a medium, or witch, to give him an answer for his troubles. "God did not want people trying to get information from witches or other mediums like palm readers or some kind of card reader. Do you know why?"

The children looked at each other, not wanting to venture a guess, until a sixth grade girl said, "He wants us to trust Him."

"That's right," Peggy exclaimed, "He wants us to believe Him and trust Him." She continued, "So should we dress up in evil costumes now and go around scaring people?"

A chorus of "No" was the response, and she thought that had settled the question.

A student held up her hand and asked, "If we want to dress up, what can we do if not some Satan kind of image?"

The teacher left it open for suggestions and someone offered, "How about famous people? We can dress up like famous people." That was discussed and approved. The older students then began learning about people who were famous before their time and a number of musicians were mentioned, along with political leaders and doctors. The party went off with a great amount of fun and learning. When the teacher saw how it was going, she asked each fourth grader on up to explain about the costume they wore.

About the middle of November, the students started asking Peggy if they could put on a Christmas play, something for their parents to see. She wrote to school supply houses for any information regarding a play for young children and received several synopses. She sorted through those and, after praying about which to present, selected one. Every pupil was to be involved and they were to use their recess time and thirty minutes after school to practice. The excitement was high. The problems were: would the school building hold everyone who wanted to come, and the weather probably would not permit outside presentation.

That evening at supper Peggy mentioned the need and discussion followed. Clay sat quietly eating, watching as the ladies carried the conversation. Finally, he interrupted with, "Miss O'Neal, that's pretty slick. You come here with a problem of space, knowing that we have the space and chairs and side rooms in which to dress. You presented a problem waiting for us to offer you our room. I must say I'm disappointed. I thought you were different. In fact, I almost was ready to believe you were authentic in your beliefs. Too bad. You had me fooled."

Grace reacted, "Dad! How can you say such a thing?"

Before he could answer, Peggy started to rise. "I'm sorry you got that impression, Mr. Patterson. I was not begging for your building. This house is two miles from the school and some of the people live farther out than that. It's winter time and some of the people don't have buggies. With the possibility of storms, or if the streets are slush from a previous storm, it would be too far for some to walk. I came with a problem. I did not come begging. I simply wanted to get some suggestions. I'm sorry." She moved her chair and stood, preparing to leave.

Courtney Clay Patterson had not been in this situation often, if ever, where he had to apologize to someone. They usually came begging to him and he was slow to respond. His wife and daughter glared at him with an unspoken demand for him to say something. He cleared his throat and began, haltingly. "Miss O'Neal, Peggy, I'm sorry. My anger at some who are Christians is so deeply ingrained that I guess I look for an excuse to label all in that manner. I'm sorry. I apologize. I was wrong and I'm sorry. Please sit down and we'll try to solve your problem."

Peggy sat and clasped her hands in her lap. "Mr. Patterson, knowing your background, I would never say or do anything to reflect poorly on my Christian standards. I'm sorry I presented my problem in such a way as to give you pause. I'll try to be more careful in my presentations from now on."

"We could carry this apology on ad infinitum, and would never come to a decision. I accept your explanation. Now, let's talk about your building. How does it compare with our room? How many people do you think will be there?"

"It's going to be full. We have forty-five students currently on the rolls. Some have moved away and some have been added. So, if two people come from each family, we will have nearly a hundred people there." She paused a moment. "As far as the room, it's not quite as large." She stopped again to think, and added, "And we have the desks and chairs. The small chairs couldn't be used for adults to sit on, and the desks might be inconvenient if the person is, uh, well, unevenly proportioned."

The others laughed. Grace howled and said, "You mean fat?"

Peggy limited herself to a smile. "Well, I didn't know how to put it." She put on her sober face, and continued, "Well, yes. The sixth grade desks are large enough for two normal chairs, so it would be best if we could move them out."

Evelyn had been silent until now. She asked Clay, "Why couldn't we use our chairs. If they take their desks out, we could put our chairs in for a hundred people." Peggy opened her mind to object, but Evelyn said, "Don't say anything. I believe you and we are here to help. So, if you can move the chairs and desks out, we will supply our chairs. If that isn't enough, some of the men will have to stand along the walls. Now that the decision has been made, we have food waiting to be eaten."

The children worked hard to memorize their parts. The program was scheduled for the last Friday before Christmas. This year, Christmas is on Tuesday, with holiday time on Monday, Tuesday and Wednesday. By Thursday and Friday, the students were to be back in school. The following week, Monday and Tuesday were holiday time with the second semester beginning on Wednesday, January second.

Two dress performances were given Wednesday and Thursday before the scheduled presentation on Friday. Grace was there both days, and gave her critique. Peggy, Becky and Grace huddled with the students to compliment them on their effort and promised a party after the production.

Peggy had anticipated perhaps two parents for each student, or ninety people coming. When people filled all the chairs and started lining the walls, she became nervous and started worrying that the room would be too full to have a good program. She had planned for ice cream and cake afterwards, but it began to look like there would not be enough. Grace saw her father and begged him to order more ice cream and cake.

The production was a great success. The smallest first grader, a girl, played the Baby Jesus. Two sixth graders became Mary and Joseph. Wires had been hung and sheets had been purchased to create rooms. The Inn-keeper, the shepherds and the choir of angels, even the "Three Wise Men" played their parts to perfection and all received loud applause at the end.

Clay missed some of the program when he went to get more food, but with a cold wind outside, the inside was the place to be. The party carried on for an hour until people came by to congratulate Peggy and Becky. After another half hour, the two teachers and their friend Grace were by themselves, exhausted, flopped across two chairs, recounting their success, and that of the students. To make sure Becky got home all right, Peggy and Grace took her first, and then slowly plodded on to the Patterson's home, thankful for a couple days off.

Chapter Thirty-Two

Jake knew something big was up, and it would be soon. All ships of the River Fleet were at anchor south of St. Louis while each captain and all chief Lieutenants were meeting at Jefferson Barracks. The meeting was a planning session with the army and their new commanding general, U. S. Grant and his host of subordinates. It was the last day of January, 1862, and the attitude of the group approached a passion—something had to be done and ASAP.

The Rebels were drawing strength from the West and it had to stop. There were some naval engagements the South had won, the most prominent was that of October 12, at Head of Passes on the Mississippi River. A Confederate force led by the Ram ship Manassas, took on a Union force of steam sloop Richmond, Vincennes and others. It rammed the Richmond and forced it and the Vincennes aground under heavy firing. The General was not happy and demanded that be the last time for a Rebel victory. The Union was getting victories in the east and General Grant demanded the same results in the west.

Flag Officer Andrew Foote reported at the meeting that the gunboat Conestoga led an expedition up the Tennessee and Cumberland Rivers to get vital information about the areas around Forts Henry and Donelson. He found out that the Tennessee River had just flooded and put the guns of Fort Henry underwater. Removing silt and debris is not an easy task and could be dangerous to anyone using the guns afterward. The danger of a weapon exploding in these circumstances is always present. Ten days later, the gunship Lexington joined the other ships to gather further intelligence. In every group of sailors Jake was in, the topic was the next battles, and the prediction was the forts on the two rivers just mentioned. Adding to Jake's curiosity, a Gatling gun was installed on two of the ships of the squadron.

Jake met Captain Thomas, captain of the Great Expectations, and Phineas O'Rourke, the Marine Lieutenant he had met earlier. Captain Thomas was transporting marines and soldiers to the battle area. He wouldn't comment on his orders, saying the men would find out soon enough.

February 6, the combined army and navy forces sailed up the Tennessee River toward Fort Henry. It was the first time a naval squadron with the power such as this had been put together. The gun ships were all St. Louis class, built by James Eads, leading transports, including Great Expectations and Captain Thomas, with seventeen thousand men. The gun ships sailed past the fort, back and forth for more than an hour, laying down a heavy barrage, so heavy that the commander of the fort raised the white flag. The seventeen thousand men of the Union Army didn't get into the fray because their ships were delayed. During that hour, the three thousand defenders managed to get away to Fort Donelson, twelve miles away.

The victory at Fort Henry was so complete that the overall Naval Commander, Andrew Foote, received a commendation from the government. Fort Henry was also renamed Fort Foote. President Lincoln notified General Grant and the award was given a day or two after the fort was secured. The men Grant brought with him were bivouacked at the fort while the next steps were being planned.

Though it was only twelve miles from Fort Henry to Donelson, the attack on Fort Donelson required the navy to go back out to the Ohio River and enter the Cumberland. The terrain was completely different between Donelson and Henry. Fort Henry was on a peninsula at river level. As the gun ships sailed past the fort and bombed it, there was no defense against them. Donelson, on the other hand, was on a high bluff that looked down on the river below. Big guns, mounted on the cliffs above, looked down on the river and gave approaching ships a formidable foe.

The Flag Ship, the ship Commander Foote was on, was to the left of the Hannibal, Jake's ship. The guns from the ships were aimed at the top of their arc, but it was not high enough to hit the top of the cliffs where their heaviest weapons were stationed. Captain Czerny came to Jake in his gunnery location and ordered him out, that he had to man the Gatling gun and aim at the top of the cliffs. Since these fifty caliber bullets would carry two miles, hitting those targets would be no problem.

The Hannibal was moved to give Jake a chance to sweep the bluffs with his gun and he did. Two powder monkeys were assigned to help him with his cartridge stacks, as firing the weapon took both hands of the operator. One monkey had to pull the spent stick, while the other inserted the new one and let the gunner keep shooting with as little interruption as possible.

The flotilla sailed past the fort's position with a thunderous explosion echoing through that river cut like eternal thunder. Seven ships with thirty-five guns, exploding at least three times each, making it a total of one hundred five shells blasting the bluffs the fort's guns stood on. Jake was able to silence some guns, or cause them to reposition the weapons, with his sweeping the bluffs. As the fleet turned around for another attack on the fort's guns, Jake's ship was in the lead position. Shelling from off the bluffs was extremely heavy, and Jake's ship, being in the front position, was hit several times, the last one, the shell went down the stack into the furnace, creating a fireball. Jake's position in his turret was just in front of the smoke stack and the explosion tossed him and his powder monkey into the air. As he landed among falling debris, a burning timber fell across his left arm, breaking it, hitting his face, setting the left side of his beard on fire. It burned up the left side of his face into his hair before someone saw it or heard him scream and threw a cover over it.

Other ships were hit, Commander Foote's ship being one, and he was injured prompting a retreat from the front position. The firing was so severe that the iron case that covered wooden timbers was split open, causing the men to have to fight fires and quit their attack. With that, the whole battle line of gun ships fell back to a defensive line away from the defenders power, so they could check the wounded. Commander Foote and several others were gathered together and loaded on the Great Expectation, to be taken to a medical facility. The facility at Jefferson Barracks was suggested, being the closest, but they had received other wounded men from battles in the west and had no room.

The ship Jake was on sank and another was towed to Cairo in inoperable condition. Generally, the iron-clads built by James Eads withstood most of the heavy shelling from the cliffs. That optimistic report was given to President Lincoln.

When Jake was carried onto the rescue ship, Captain Thomas recognized him and, once determining his injuries, had a handful of butter slathered across Jake's face and into his hair. He then tried to set Jake's left arm. There was a medical team aboard the Great Expectations—a doctor and a male orderly, whose main function was to hold patients so the doctor could perform some operation on them. He wiped away the residue of the butter and bound the burned area of the face and head with a light fabric, coated with a medical ointment. Another heavier cloth was wrapped over the other, with more ointment, to keep the first wrapping from drying out.

Some of the less seriously wounded men, like Commander Foote, were taken to Jefferson Barracks, as they did not expect to be hospitalized. But Jake was so seriously burned, his injuries were expected to require months of care. The government was building a new hospital on the grounds of the army base at Cincinnati. It was not done yet, but some men were being admitted to empty barracks, since some of the medical staff was already on hand. The trip took four days and when Jake was unloaded and taken to his barracks room, he met Rebecca Shiley, the woman to whom he was married for a short time.

At first, as she cared for her patient, she didn't recognize him with the burn blisters on his face and head. She had seven patients to care for and he was just one. Even after she read his name, it didn't fully register with her that this was her former husband. She knew the Prosser family had several boys and it wasn't until he spoke to her that she became aware of whom this man was.

Her first reaction, which she didn't hide very well, was shock. That response enforced the sense of rejection which he had built up in his mind—that no one would want to have anything to do with him now that he looked this way. He hadn't seen himself in a mirror, but had seen burn victims, and could imagine how he looked.

She explained that the doctor she had worked for joined the army, leaving her without a job. She read of Clara Barton and Hannah Ropes, who ministered to the wounded in the eastern battles, so she volunteered to work in the new Cincinnati Army Hospital. She had married again and her husband was stationed on the base there. Her married name was Barber. As she walked away, she said she would see him several times a day to change the bandage on his burn. His acknowledgement was a slight shrug of his shoulders as he turned back onto his side.

Chapter Thirty-Three

The burn area didn't affect Jake's eyes. He could still see, but his forehead was scarred up into his hairline, and down along the left side of his cheek to his chin. The right side of his face was unaffected. Jake refused to look into a mirror. He imagined what he looked like and that was the way it was fixed in his mind. No matter how hard the medical staff tried to get him to see himself, he refused. He imagined what he looked like, and that was the way it was going to be. He had seen pictures of burn-scarred men and they scared him. Nurse Shiley tried to get a doctor to talk to Jake but the patient refused.

Jake's left arm was bent slightly where the break occurred. It had been poorly set and healed in that position. He would still be able to use it, but it would always have that bend, unless some doctor broke it again and operated on it to set it right. Jake refused any thought of that. He'd live with it the way it was. He told some male orderly to change the location of his bed so he could lie on his left side with his face close to the wall. He didn't want to see anyone, nor did he want anyone to see him.

Evelyn had easy access to the new hospital for her ministrations, since her husband was a general who had been stationed there. She was one of the regulars. She had some special patients she saw each visit. Each time she arrived the nurses told her of new patients, as they did this time. She heard the name and was surprised. It just couldn't be, not Peggy's Jake Prosser. The nurse told her the patient had gotten burned severely over the side of his face and scalp and wanted to die.

The nurse took her to a barracks that was forty feet long, with beds on both sides of a central aisle. Some kind of a temporary partition had been installed to separate beds and give each patient some thought of privacy. There was no attempt at an alphabetic ordering of patients. They were moved in as they came. Patient Zachary might be next to patient Abbott. Jake's bed was near the door on the left side of the main aisle. When Evelyn saw the patient, she went into unspeakable shock. She stood with her hand to her mouth and looked. She spoke his name, quietly, "Jacob. Jacob, it's Evelyn." There was no response, so she tried again. "Jacob, please look at me." He didn't move. "Jacob, please, Peggy will want to know you're here. She'll want to come and see you. Please, look at me."

Finally, he said, "Go away. Don't tell her I'm here. I don't want to see her. I don't want her to see me. Just go away."

Evelyn was so distressed she left the care center and had Simon take her home. When she got there, she found her husband and told him the story. As he listened, he thought of the multitude of men he had seen in just the short time he was in hospital care, and how so many of them were wounded, losing arms and legs and worse, the ability to see. He decided to go see Jake the next morning.

The people at the barracks that was made into a medical facility knew General Clay Patterson. He had been there for several years before the war. He came back there after his hand was shot off. So they knew him and were happy to see him. He talked to several of the nurses and doctors and found out that Jakes burns were third degree across his face and into his hair line. His eyes weren't affected, but the skin around the left eye was withered and scarred. The general decided to go talk to him, hoping that somehow he might be able to give some words of encouragement.

Courtney Clay Patterson, a Major general in the army of the United States, had seen pain and he had encountered despair. For thirty years, from Florida when fighting the Seminoles to Texas and the Mexican War, as he worked his way up the grade ladder, he saw pain and injury. He had never had one affect him as this one did for what it did to his wife, and more, what it would do to Peggy. He was dressed in his uniform and when he came to the bed, saw it was close to the partition as it could get. Clay called for the male orderly to help him move it. The orderly hesitated because the patient had requested that position, so the general, with his one good hand, started pulling on the bed, pulling it away from that partition. The orderly reluctantly helped

Clay then ordered a chair. He was intent on getting Jake to speak to him, so he took the chair and moved it into the space just created between the bed and the partition, near the patient's head, and sat down. He sat that way for several minutes. He crossed his left leg over his right knee and sat there, quietly, without a word. Jake had pulled the covers over his head when Clay moved in and sat down, but after several minutes, the air under the cover became stale, and Jake had to have some fresher air. He pulled back the cover and looked at the general.

Clay spoke softly, hoping to keep the conversation private in a full hospital barracks. "Jake, I remember you from St. Louis. I remember a man who was given a critical job to do, who didn't turn it down because it was different from what he was trained to do. He just did it. I remember how this man taught men in the army how to use a gun that will change the way war is fought, just because he was asked to. Now, you have been given a harder challenge. One that is personal. And that is where the difficulty lies." Clay changed positions and moved his chair closer to the bed.

The general continued, "Jake, that woman who loves you has changed the lives of my wife and me. You should have seen her when that first letter arrived." Clay spoke passionately, "It stirred her deeply, Jake, to her very soul. You had taken time to write her and nothing could have made her happier. She didn't care where you were or what you wrote. She cared <u>that</u> you wrote. Now, are you going to disappoint her? Evelyn said you refused to talk to her. We wonder if you'll treat Peggy that way." His voice was less passionate, more questioning. "The nurse told Evelyn you wanted to die. Is that the way you want to be remembered by that young woman who loves you so much? You, who took on the job of teaching men, going against men with Navy experience, is that your answer? You want out?"

Clay stood to leave. He moved the chair from its position so the bed could be put back where Jake wanted it. He spoke, "Jake, you may not want to hear this, but if you think your looks will make a difference to the woman who loves you, you aren't worthy of her. You don't deserve her." With that, Clay Patterson walked away from the patient and out the door.

He and Evelyn spent the evening isolated from Peggy. He didn't want a chance for misspoken words to affect her thoughts about Jake, at least not while there could be a chance for him to change. After supper, they ordered their carriage and made some excuse about having something to do, leaving Peggy alone.

The next day, after the teacher had left for school, the former general found a friend, a Psychiatrist, and asked him some questions about how to deal with Jake's despair. They met in a small room dedicated for counseling near the room where the beds were placed. After Clay explained the circumstances, the doctor, Albert Moegle, said, "Would you believe the medicine for this kind of depression has been around since the time of Christ? In fact, some think it might have been named in favor John the Baptist. His birthday is traditionally set in May and that is the time of year this plant blooms. It's called St. John's Wort, and the founder of medicines, Hippocrates, is known to have prescribed it for such illnesses as dysentery, tuberculosis, colds and insomnia. It grows everywhere as a weed."

Clay was silent for a moment while he processed what the doctor had told him, and then he answered, "Now, Doctor, you aren't known as a man who plays games with the mind. I trust you that what you say is fact. I haven't known you long, but long enough to have an opinion about you. You don't play games. But a weed? This is going to help this young man?"

"Of course I'll have to talk to him, but in his present state of mind, he wouldn't listen to me for a minute. We'll give him some tea, laced with honey and a second helping will calm him so I can talk to him."

"Amazing," was all the general could utter.

Dr. Moegle called for and received Jake Prosser's file and wrote a prescription for St. John's Wort Tea, to be given twice an hour apart. After the second cup of Wort's Tea, Dr. Moegle came in to talk to Jake. Jake's bed had been moved back to where he faced the partition and had to be moved. The doctor ordered it moved so he could get between Jake and the wall.

"Mr. Prosser, I'm Dr. Moegle. I'm here to talk to you about your injury and your outlook." He lifted a corner of the facial dressing and looked at it for several seconds before laying it back down. He addressed Jake again. "Mr. Prosser, look up at me." Jake reluctantly complied. "Close your right eye." Again, Jake complied. "Now your left eye." For the third time Jake obeyed. The doctor moved his hand across in front of Jake's face, stopping and holding up some fingers. "How many fingers do you see?" Jake replied.

"Mr. Prosser, I'm going to say something that will make you unhappy, perhaps, angry, but you came out of that scrape without any real problems. Your eyes are not impaired. Your hearing wasn't affected. Your arm was mishandled and you will have to learn how to use it, but you have a functional hand that is still attached to your shoulder. Mr. Prosser, thank God your injuries are cosmetic. Don't internalize them. Stop thinking about them as if they are you. That is true only if you let it be, only if you <u>want</u> it to be."

Jake glared at the man. He wanted to shout at him but couldn't think of anything to say, so he just glared. Finally, he angrily said, "Look at me. I'm going to have to spend the rest of my life looking like this. And you say don't internalize it. What does that mean, don't let it affect me personally? Psychologically? And what does that mean? You can say that, 'cause your face isn't burned half off."

Dr. Moegle showed his German heritage by his face getting beet red. He was about fifty years of age and his hair was thinning, so the blush ran all through his hairline. He didn't respond immediately, but waited until he cooled down. After a long minute, he said, "Mr. Prosser, I was just transferred here from the front in Virginia, where

I saw a whole lot worse than your problem. There is going to be war out here like this area has never seen before and when it happens, you might very well be asked to give up your bed for the seriously injured. I saw men beg to be shot when they learned that both their legs had been amputated. I had to console a Rebel father whose son died in his arms, shot accidently, by his own men."

He paused a few seconds before asking, "Mr. Prosser, have you ever thought to give thanks to God for this, knowing that He has a plan for your life that you don't know about?"

"I should thank God for making me look like an ogre?"

"If that is the way you want to think of yourself, then there is nothing I can do for you. You will go through life as a miserable, angry man, and will probably end up taking your own life before you're thirty." Dr. Moegle stood silent for a few seconds, shook his head and started to walk away.

"Wait! What you just said, do you think that could happen?"

The doctor returned to where he was standing and said, "What do you have to live for? If you let this ruin your relationship with that young woman, what do you have to live for?"

Jake started weeping, quietly, slowly, crying. "Doctor, can you help me? Help me to change my attitude. I don't want to hurt Peggy, but what will she think if she sees me like this? Or when they take off the bandages?"

"What do you think she will say? How will she react when she sees you?"

Jake was quiet for a while before saying, "She'll pro'bly cry that I got hurt, and then kiss me and tell me how much she loves me."

Dr. Moegle replied extra loud, "Good grief, man, I know men who'd give their soul for that response from their wife, and you want to ruin it? Grow up!" and the doctor turned on his heels and walked away.

Jake spent the rest of the day thinking about the doctor and his parting shot. Was he being childish in his trying to protect Peggy or was his protection aimed for himself? Could he stand people looking at him, wondering? Was that his problem? He knew he would see Evelyn or Clay, or maybe both, in twenty-four hours. He was somewhat unprepared when all three, the general, his wife, and the one who lived in their home, came to see him. His bed was still facing the partition and, as hard as it was for him, emotionally, he turned to lie on his back. Clay and Evelyn moved aside to let Peggy have full view. She gasped and put her hands to her mouth. Then, emotionally, cried, "Jacob, oh, my darling Jacob." She moved to his bed, carefully wrapped her left hand under his right cheek, bent over and kissed him. She held that contact a few seconds as her tears dripped onto his face. Slowly, she straightened.

She reached for his hand. "Jacob, why didn't you write? Why didn't you tell me you had been wounded?"

Jake hesitated, "I. . .I didn't think. . .I'll never get. . .I'll have this forever."

She stood upright and somewhat angrily asked, "And do you think that will make any difference? Jacob, I love you." In an attempt to explain, she added, "I've given myself to you forever. Do you think I'm so fickle to believe that isn't you inside there, regardless of the outward appearance?"

Jake was quiet for what seemed to be several seconds. When he spoke, he didn't look at her, but at his hands now lying atop his covers. "I'm sorry, Peggy. I didn't want to hurt you. I didn't want you to feel sympathy for me. I didn't know how I felt."

Evelyn interrupted them with, "Well, now you know how she feels, and, I hope, we know how you feel. Now, when they release you, you will come to live in our house until you feel comfortable going out in public. At that time—"

Evelyn glared at Clay as he jabbed her in the ribs. "Let's get him over this, and then we can figure what's next."

Chapter Thirty-Four

Peggy had been to see Jake each Friday. She restricted her visits to Friday because of school requirements. She was unprepared the last Friday when she came into the barracks and found the bandages had been removed. She was just inside the door when she saw him and gasped, her hand flew to her mouth, with "Oh, my!" she uttered. She stopped her walk and stood looking at him, but for only a moment. In that moment her mind raced down the track of what he would say or do if he saw her hesitation.

Her smile was honest as she approached his bed. She was happy to see him and didn't want to show any different emotion from the other times she was there. He was reading a paper when she walked up to his bed and it took a second for him to be aware of her being there. His smile and greeting was a little slow in coming, and she asked, "Aren't you happy to see me?"

His response was quick and perhaps too loud for the surroundings. "Of course!" He then quieted somewhat and said, "Someone gave me a paper and there's an ad in here for ranch hands on a ranch in Idaho and Montana. It covers a million acres and the owner is calling for hands to come up and work for him. He limits the hands to those men who have gotten injured or wounded in the war, North or South."

"Idaho? Montana? Why would you go there? What about us? What about Me?"

"I know." His facial features, as well as his words, exhibited indecision. "Peggy, you have given me hope. I have nothing without you. The doctor predicted I would commit suicide by the time I'm thirty." She gasped and opened her mouth to speak. He held up his hand and she waited. "Peggy, I don't know what to say. I never thought of anything else but being a sailor when I was young, so there is nothing I can do now. I can't go back into the navy 'cause every time we would be in a battle, I'd be afraid of getting hit again, or worse. I don't know what to do."

"But. . .Jacob, what about me? What will I do? Will I sit around waiting for you to come back? I don't think so." He didn't answer immediately and she continued, "You said you don't know what you would do." She pled with him, "I'm a teacher. I have a job here. Do you want me to pack up and leave with you? I don't think I can do that."

Jake was sitting up in bed with pillows behind him. His elbows rested on the ends of the pillows and his hands were clasped at his chest. His chin dropped to his chest and he sat quietly for several seconds.

Impatiently, Peggy said, "Jacob, look up at me. Don't do this to me. We have to talk about this. Now! Not later. Do you know anything about cattle and horses? What would you do if you fell off a horse and were injured? Would there be someone out there working with you?"

Unable to explain, and frustrated at her arguments, Jake let his chin fall again. He shook his head, finally begging, "Peggy, look at me. Just look at me. Is this the face you want to look at the rest of your life? The doctor said the blisters will eventually dry up, but the scars will be there forever. What can I do? I can't live off your teaching the rest of my life."

Peggy stood at the foot of his bed, hands clasped at her waist, tears coursing down her cheeks. "Jacob, stop! There must be something you can do here."

"I have an uncle who owns a farm north of town a ways, but he already has a houseful. I have no money to buy a farm, or anything else. If we got married—"

"What do you mean, 'If we got married?' Are you telling me you don't want to get married? Is that what this is about? Jacob, I love you. I thought you felt the same about me."

In desperation, he answered, "I do. But look at me. Where could I get a job here? I couldn't get a job meeting people. I might get a job on the river on some barge, but. . ."

"So, are you telling me this is the end? There is nothing more?" Peggy started sobbing openly. "You're determined to go to wherever and I'm expected to follow you? I have to think about that, Jacob. I won't be back until I make my choice. Then I'll tell you. Goodbye."

As she walked away the men in the surrounding beds all started hammering Jake about how stupid he was, and what his life could have been with that woman. After several minutes, he screamed, "Shut up. Just shut up. I don't want to hear any more. I'm stupid, I know that, but. . .forget it. Just shut up about it!"

Simon had driven Peggy to the army base since it was outside Cincinnati city limits and when she came stumbling out the door, he rushed to help her. She threw her arms around his neck and cried, deep, raking sobs. Simon looked uncomfortably in this situation, not wanting to have anyone think ill of the woman, so he coaxed her into the carriage. In seconds, he was in the driver's seat, snapping the whip at the horses to get them away from any comments.

At the Patterson house, Peggy ran through the side door and into her room without a word to others. As Simon parked the carriage and tended the horse, Clay emerged from the house to ask him what happened. Simon explained what he knew of the incident and Clay stood there without a word, hand to his chin, looking off at the distance. He instructed Simon to saddle his riding horse.

Inside the house, Clay changed his clothes to a riding outfit, riding pants, knee-high boots and a hip length jacket. He stopped in the parlor to tell his wife and daughter he would be gone for a while, and strode to the barn to his waiting horse. Had the army base been a block from their house, Clay would have burst into the barracks and shouted at Jake about his stupidity in his attitude toward Peggy.

Her actions indicated a break-up. Clay couldn't believe anyone could be that dumb.

The ride to the army base was about five miles and as they neared the facility, the speed of the horse slowed to a stop. They were half a mile from the gate and Clay sat with his hands on the front of the military saddle, looking at the gate. He had impulsively left his house, intending, he didn't rightly know what. Jake was hurting. If they had met at the start of Clay's ride, he might have done more harm than good. As he sat there, he considered the influence Peggy had made in their lives and his thoughts flashed back to one time he asked his father for some advice. The answer was prayer.

It must have been thirty-five years since the last time he thought of praying about something and he couldn't believe that prayer was something he considered now. But the longer he sat there, the stronger the impulse became. He couldn't pray on his horse. He just couldn't! Not with his childhood instruction for talking to God. He looked around for some secluded cover where he could dismount and get on his knees.

There was a place slightly ahead of where he was at that moment, and he urged his horse that way. He dismounted and tied the horse reins to a sapling. He had seen his father pray once while standing, in an emergency, so he took that as appropriate for this time. It took him a while to get into the mood, since it had been so long since the last time, and he stumbled in his request. He finally got his mind and heart in tune and started praying for Jake and Peggy and their situation.

He remembered, to his amazement, the first verse of Hebrews, chapter eleven, "Now faith is the substance of things hoped for. . ." That was his mother's favorite portion of Scripture. But, with his background of the last thirty-five years, how could he ask God for anything and expect Him to answer? His job, he realized, was to present his case. And he did, urgently.

When he started repeating the same words of his prayer, he figured God had heard him so Clay ended his supplications and remounted his horse with a new feeling. His purpose, now was to encourage Jake, telling him of others who had been wounded and were making a life in the current situation.

He approached the barracks and tied the horse to the hitching rail. He entered the building and immediately saw Jake with the bandage removed. The left side was scarred but the right side looked fine. He controlled his emotions and walked to Jake's bed.

Clay stood at the foot of the bed, but Jake ignored him, not looking up. Clay said nothing, but stood quietly, arms crossed at his chest, head tilted slightly to the right. The men in the other beds, remembering the emotion of the past visitor, started calling Jake to acknowledge his visitor. Finally, Jake looked up at the visitor and said, "Well, what did she say?"

Clay frowned, "She? Oh, if you mean Peggy, I didn't talk to her. No, Jake, I wanted to tell you that I stopped on the way out here and prayed. It was good that I did, because I wouldn't have given you a chance to explain, to state your cause." He stopped to look around and asked, "Have you been up today? You need to get up and walk around so when you are released, you'll be able to move into some home without any problem." He saw an orderly down the aisle and motioned for the man to come to where he was.

He asked the orderly, "Have you had this man up today?" The response was negative, so Clay said, "Why don't you get him ready for a walk and I'll take him outside for some fresh air." All Clay's outerwear had his insignia and rank attached and when the orderly saw the general's insignia, he agreed to the proposal. Jake objected, but the orderly made it known that he was outranked and was going to get up for a walk.

Jake shuffled down the aisle to the outside door with the general following. He pushed on the door and was greeted by bright setting sun and a cool blast of air. The orderly was standing back holding a blanket, which he hurried to bring to Jake. Now wrapped, Jake and his escort proceeded to an area where there were four tables with a complement of chairs. Clay motioned for him to sit.

The general asked, "What are your plans, Jake? What are you going to do after you are released?"

"I don't know."

"You must have some idea. You probably aren't fit for active duty now, so you'll have to leave this facility sometime soon. If army procedure carries to the Navy, you'll have to be discharged. After that, you're free. You must have some idea of your life after this place. Do you know when you're going to be released?"

Jake shrugged his shoulders. "Couple of weeks, I guess."

"What about your parents, Jake? Will you go there?"

After a pause, Jake slowly shook his head. He asked, "What's that to you? Why do you care what I do?"

"It's simple, Jake. We have accepted Peggy as one of our own. She has become a part of our family and, more, a part of the fellowship that meets in our home. What you do affects how she feels. If you make her unhappy, that indirectly interests us. We can't do anything about it, but pray, and we can do that. We just don't want her hurt."

"You talk to her?"

"I told you no." He paused, then continued, "She ran to her room without talking to anyone. That was not like her. I came to see what went wrong. What happened between you two?"

Defensively, Jake answered, "That's not your business." An angry glare came back to his eyes. He opened his mouth to say something, but paused.

"That is true, Jake, but like I said, we're very concerned. Now, Simon said she cried all the way home. That indicates a. . .well, maybe not a fight, but certainly a difference of opinions. What did you tell her of your plans?"

Barely inaudible, Jake muttered, "Goin' to Idaho to work on a ranch."

"Idaho? How did you find out about it?"

"There's an ad in the paper today." Clay made a mental note to look for the ad.

They sat and talked until the night had closed in around them. The orderly came to escort Jake back to his bed and Clay stood to leave. He said, "Jake, Peggy has made a tremendous difference in our lives. I don't know if you are aware of my history, but I prayed for the first time in thirty plus years on the way over here, Jake, and I will continue to pray for God to help you make the right decisions. Remember, Jake, she loves you very much. She talked about nothing but your lives together. Don't destroy her."

It was a good thing Clay had ridden his horse to the fort several times before, because Clay rode home with his eyes closed, praying, trusting the horse to know the way back home.

Chapter Thirty-Five

Jake was permitted to move around and to care for himself for the remaining two weeks of his recovery. He had to be available for his medications and dressing changes four times a day, but, other than that, he was free to roam the compound. He was given new clothes, a set of Navy dress blues and a set of work clothes. He passed a window after it was dark outside and he saw himself for the first time since the explosion. At first, it repulsed him, wrinkled and misshapen with a purple hue, but it drew him back and he stared at the image for some time. Slowly, it registered that he was wounded, but he was not dead. He still had his legs, which so many were now missing. He still had his mind, the injury didn't hamper his thinking ability. Except for the side of his face, he was whole. Well, he did have that crooked arm, but he could live with that. His life had changed, but it had not ended. He had to see Peggy.

The ad in the paper gave instructions on how to contact the Idaho ranch and Jake sent a cable to the owner, Reginald Dowdy. In it, he explained his job aboard ship. He explained how he was injured, and that the injury did not affect his eyes or hearing. Two days later, he received instructions on how to get his ticket for the boat ride up the Missouri to the ranch. But he had to see Peggy. She was the key. If she would not go, he wouldn't either.

The battle of Fort Donelson was the topic of conversation when he was called in to see the Chief Medical Officer. Jake was given orders to report to Jefferson Barracks for an extended period to report on the gun he used and to train more men. The assignment was not to exceed six weeks, and would start the following Monday. He was given that Friday and Saturday morning, a thirty-six hour leaves, but had to be on board his transportation by two PM Saturday. This was all he hoped for, but how could he get in touch with the family?

The medical officer suggested sending a wire from the barracks to the police station, and ask that it be delivered to the person's home. Jake rushed to the teletype room and sent a simple message to Peggy—Please, I need to see you (stop) I'll get there as soon as I can (stop) I love you. Jake.

When the officer heard where the cable was going, he volunteered the base courier service for Jake and, after signing his name to the order, Jake was on his way. He smiled at the thought of seeing her, perhaps even before the wire arrived.

His pull of the door chime string was answered by a young woman he had never seen before. Slightly shorter than Peggy, she would have been much prettier without the scowl. "You must be Jake. If I had my way I'd boil you in oil, forever. What do you want?"

"Tell me where you got your happy pills and I'll know never to use them. I would like—"

"She doesn't want to see you."

"And how do you know that?"

"Because she's been crying around here for two weeks or more, ever since you told her it was over between you." Grace was angry before, now she became real mad. She shouted. She stuck her finger in his face. "You've got a lot of gall coming here after what you did. I wish there was some way my father could—"

A voice from behind her whispered, "Jacob?"

Jake pushed himself past the obstruction in the doorway and came inside, reaching for Peggy's hands. "Peggy, I'm sorry. Can you forgive me? I saw myself in the window the other night and the thing I feared was the fear of how I looked. Can you understand that? I need to talk to you and the folks. Are they around?"

Peggy, still subdued, turned to ask Grace to get her parents while she and Jake moved into the parlor. She sat on one of the benches while he stood beside her. In a couple minutes, Grace and her parents were there.

Evelyn greeted him pleasantly, "Good evening, Jacob."

He responded with a smile and "Good evening Ma'am."

Clay extended a hand which Jake took and smiled at the general.

The room opened off the entrance with a wide archway. Grace stood at the corner closest to the door, leaning against the wall, with her arms crossed, still scowling. Clay and Evelyn sat on a love seat across from Peggy while Jake was to their left, Peggy's right. They waited for Jake to say something.

He dropped to his knees and began, "Peggy, I don't know what I was thinking the other day. I love you and don't want to live without you. Now, I'm being discharged in six weeks, but I have to go to St. Louis for that time. The doctor in charge out there today told me they want me to evaluate that gun and train more men in using it. When I come back we'll get married, if you want to. If you don't, I'll tippy toe out of your life and be gone. But, I hope you'll think about it before turning me down. When I come back if you want to wait to get married, I'll get a job and we can stay here in Cincinnati."

Grace, still standing, leaning against the opening with her right shoulder, let out a grunt, "Hmmph. Where do you think you're going to find a job looking like that? Maybe to scare little kids."

Jake slouched down onto his heels while Clay and Evelyn gasped and shouted, "Grace!" Evelyn continued with, "How could you be so unkind as to say something like that?" Either because of their comment or because Grace realized what she said and how it sounded to Jake, she turned and ran up the stairs to her room.

Jake stayed in his slouch, head down, and chin on his chest. Peggy slipped off the chair onto the floor and sat next to him. "Jacob, I'm so terribly sorry. I. . .she. . .look up at me, please." She put her hand on the side of his face affected by the burn and said, "When will your time end? You say you have six weeks? Then what?"

He didn't respond for several seconds. He shook his head and said, "I don't know. I. . .you wanted to stay here so I thought I could get a job, any job, to keep you close to your family. But she's right." He frowned, "Who is she?"

Evelyn answered, "She's our youngest daughter and, I imagine, she's upstairs crying her eyes out. She and Peggy have gotten very close, much like sisters. She looked at you as the one who made her sister cry and she retaliated. Now, she's sorry and will soon come downstairs to apologize. Don't think ill of her, Jacob. She didn't mean what she said."

Jake nod was only a mere tip of his head, almost imperceptible. His eyes were on Peggy as she knelt beside him on the floor. She put her hand atop his and said, "Jacob, I love you. When you mentioned going to Idaho the other day it was a shock. I thought I had a family here and could live here, I don't mean in this house, but in this community. Now I don't know. You might eventually get used to people's stares and their reactions to the way you look, but is that right? Do you have to go through that every day for the rest of your life?"

"Peggy. . ."

"Don't, Jacob. Have you ever read the story of Ruth in the Bible?" Jake shook his head and Peggy continued, "Her mother-in-law, Naomi, moved her family from Judah to Moab because of a famine. After her two sons married Moabite women, her husband and the two sons all died, leaving the women alone. Naomi decided to go back to Judah and Ruth, one of the son's wives, said she would go with her. When Naomi tried to dissuade her, Ruth said, 'Intreat me not to leave thee or to return from following after thee: wither thou goest I will go; and where thou lodgest I will lodge: thy people shall be my people and thy God my God.'"

Jake had lowered his head and now Peggy lifted her hand to his chin and that raised his head. "Jacob, I spent several days fighting against what I realized was God's plan. We met, expressed our love and the war separated us. Now, we are together. It is the Biblical plan for a man and woman to separate themselves to build their own home. Grace's reaction was a shock to me and enlightenment. I will go with you to Idaho."

"Peggy. . .I. . .are you sure? I—"

Strongly, she said, "Jacob, don't ever question your wife's decision once she has stated it." She smiled. "I said I will go with you, but as your wife. We will be married when they discharge you from the Navy."

The six weeks were the slowest, and yet the fastest, Jake ever lived. As he looked forward to the time when he would report to the Navy for the last time, it seemed that each hour was a day's length. He spent time studying the weapon, seeing if there was a non-scientific suggestion he could make. His only thought was to have dual stacks feeding the firing mechanism. That way the helper could keep the stacks going and the operator continue to fire. A second thought was to have a trigger rather than the crank.

On that last day, as he said goodbye to his last class, a message came to him that he was expected at a meeting. He was to be in his dress blues. That surprised him. He changed clothes in his room and left for the meeting. He was led to a parade ground surrounded by rows of barracks, where every captain he had served under during his time in the Navy was here. He was positioned by himself in front of the Captains Thomas, Czerny and White, with Captain Foote and other officers in front of him.

Captain Foot read from a plaque. "To Mr. Jake Prosser, Gunner's Mate Two, for meritorious service above and beyond the call of duty. You accepted a call to duty when only a seaman, that resulted in instructions on a new weapon and men proclaiming how well it was done. You took dual responsibility aboard ship as a gunner on a forty-two Naval Rifle and the operator of the Gatling gun. The reports of your action indicate two of their cannons, mounted at the high cliff, were disabled by your firing when their crews were either killed or chased away from their guns."

He looked up from the plaque. "Gunner's Mate Prosser, it is my great privilege to honor you with this symbol of our thanks and to wish you well in your new life." The men behind him clasped his hand and patted him on his shoulders, expressing their thanks. Captain Foote shook his hand as he handed Jake the plaque. A picture was taken.

Jake's mind flashed to what ship he could get to take him to Cincinnati in a hurry. It so happened that the Great Expectations, with Captain Thomas, was going that way and he offered Jake a free ride. Two days later Jake was at the landing in Cincinnati, heading for the Patterson's home.

He found Grace at their front door sweeping the porch and he greeted her. She looked at him, not knowing whether to run, to fight him again, or wait. She waited for his first comment. It surprised her. "I understand you are Grace. Can we be friends, or at least not fight? I've had all the fighting I need for a lifetime. How about it?" She simply nodded without saying a word. "I accept that. Now, is Peggy home?"

"Not yet. It'll be another hour." Jake stepped past Grace and went into the church. As he looked around, he realized it had been weeks since he had really spent time praying. The platform directly in front of him was raised about a foot above the floor. There was a kneeling pad at the base of the platform and Jake made his way there. He couldn't remember ever kneeling at the front of the platform before and was only sure of one thing—that he needed to get all his doubts, fears and questions out in the open.

He dropped to his knees and started to pray. It was a confused prayer as he groped for words, having had little instruction except from Peggy on that boat from New Orleans. But he laid all his questions about what now, or is going to Idaho the right thing to do? He dedicated his future into the hand of God, without reservation.

He knelt there for some time and didn't hear the door open nor quiet steps across the hardwood floor. He only became aware of another when he felt someone drop to the pad next to him and a soft hand clasped his. He pulled that hand up to his lips and kissed it.

When Jake left for St. Louis and Jefferson Barracks, Peggy and Grace started their wedding planning. The six weeks Jake was to be gone equaled to the time left on Peggy's contract and she increased her study time with Becky. A new school board had been appointed and Peggy had already informed them of her decision to resign and hoped they would accept Becky as her replacement. They agreed.

She refused a wedding gown, saying the one she had for her other wedding was still good enough for her. Flowers and gifts came in from school parents as well as church members and the date was set for a Saturday, two weeks from that weekend. Albert Weinmeister was asked to perform the ceremony. Grace would stand up with Peggy and Clay, after he and Evelyn walked with Peggy to the altar, would step across to be Jake's best man.

Friday, the day before the wedding, the door string was pulled and Grace answered. She walked into the dining room ahead of a delivery man carrying a wedding gown that made the three women oh and ah at its beauty. Evelyn looked at Clay, who frowned and shook his head. The delivery man handed Peggy a small envelope, which she opened. It contained a note of seven words—"I wish you a life of happiness." She handed it to Evelyn.

Evelyn looked at the note. Her mouth dropped open, her eyes darted from the paper to her husband, and she handed the paper to him. "Orville," came as a whisper, but an angry one. "What's he trying to do now?"

There was a short period of silence where Grace started to speak, then stopped. She tried a second time and stopped. Her mother noticed that and asked, "What do you know about this?"

"He's trying to rejoin the family, Mom. We've all talked to him, all of us, and he's trying to change. But he realized you hate him so much he doesn't feel comfortable trying to talk to you two."

"So he's going around us through you and your brother and sisters, to worm his way back into our good graces." Her mother was quite angry.

Peggy had been looking at the gown while the others talked and when she heard the name, Orville, she looked up. When there was a break in the conversation, she said, "I won't wear it."

Jake asked, "Is this the St. Louis guy?" Peggy nodded.

Clay had been silent, listening and when Evelyn looked at him to get his opinion, he said, "I know Orville as well as anyone, but I don't know him. He operates under a different set of rules and I haven't been able to figure out what rules apply at any given time." He thought a second before adding, "Except the rule of self preservation. That's number one."

Evelyn quickly added, "And rule number two is to destroy the life of any Christian girl he sees. Grace, I don't trust him and I'd be careful if I were you. He's like a snake. Don't let him get close to you."

"Mom! He's trying to get back into the family. Ask Clay Junior what he thinks. He's had dinner with him. Ask him what he thinks."

"Your brother has had him in his house?"

"No, they met at a restaurant. But they met, and they talked. Clay thought we ought to try to make peace with Uncle Orville."

The former general had been studying his daughter since she started talking and now he entered the conversation. "Tell him I want to see him. I'll talk to him and find out what his game is—"

Disgustedly, she answered, "There you go again, Dad. What if it isn't a game? What if he's serious? Can't a man change when he sees he's on a losing side?" Grace turned to her friend and asked, "Peggy, you believe in redemption don't you? Of course you do. You believe in prayer, too. I know you do. Would you consider praying about the dress tonight? I'm not asking that you do anything against what you believe God approves, but, would you pray about it?"

"I will, but I want you to seriously pray about it too. He might be using you and you want to help blood family, so you're anxious. Will you pray with me tonight, I don't mean with me, but agree with me for tonight?"

It was agreed. The wedding was set for two o'clock in the afternoon. Jake had already been told he was not to see his bride before she entered the church, so he had to find something else to do and somewhere else to go.

Chapter Thirty-Six

Peggy prayed long into the night about wearing the gown Clay's brother Orville had sent. It was a beautiful gown, Ivory in color, with gold thread highlighting stitches. Delicate hand-beaded lace covered the entire gown. It had a lace bodice that covered the arms down to the wrists, with small pearls outlining the shallow "V" neck. Both front and back featured a beaded dropped waistline with covered buttons. A short train and a veil completed the outfit.

The veil was fine white linen thread worked as Brussels bobbin lace and Point de Gaz needle lace, thirty-eight inches wide and one hundred-nineteen inches long. The mid point had a flowered designation, which fit above the forehead down over the face, while the lengths dropped over her shoulders, down her front below her waist. It was entirely hand worked, even the background net on the Point de Gaz, three dimensional lace roses. These roses were cleverly worked into the floral bobbin lace bouquets. This was the kind of veil women would pass down to their descendants. A three-strand necklace of real pearls completed her attire.

Peggy was afraid Grace had blind-sided her parents with the idea of forcing a family reunion. She didn't want to be used in a situation where both parents had reservations, remembering Orville's past history.

Grace was perhaps three inches shorter than Peggy. The gown was fitted to Peggy as if she had modeled it. That was a concern, for someone, probably Grace, had given Orville Peggy's measurements. That was infringing on Peggy's privacy and she wasn't sure how to handle it. She prayed for guidance and wisdom, not knowing how either would make itself known. She decided to agree to wear the gown, but have Grace promise to have it done over so she could wear it in her wedding, provided Albert would ask Grace to marry him.

Jake had slept in one of the upstairs bedrooms and was awakened early to have breakfast and then leave the house. He caused enough noise with his false objections that Peggy woke. She wanted to see him, but Evelyn had absolutely forbidden that. So, Jake talked Simon into letting him have a horse and a shay to do some running about town. Clay had the foresight to rent a room in a hotel for Jake to dress for the wedding and for their wedding night. He went there after finishing some errands.

The hotel covered a whole block and was across the street from a major bank and other businesses. The canopied driveway up to the entrance paralleled the street for a whole block. The hotel had been rebuilt three years earlier and, because of the traffic into the area, city officials asked if their carriage entrance could be longer than the short drive they had before, so the builder made it a block long. Many evenings the line waiting to get into the hotel lobby covered that whole block.

He stepped into the lobby and stopped. Golden chandeliers hung from the ceiling, tables of marble and ivory decorated the room. People lounged on damask covered chairs and sofas as they waited to check in or out, or conversed with friends. Silk wall hangings covered side walls and thick Persian rugs covered the floor. It was almost as if the hotel and its patrons would be upset if they heard a sound.

Jake walked to the counter and waited as the clerk dealt with another visitor. The clerk was to Jake's right, so Jake's injury was away from his immediate line of vision. He turned to stand in front of Jake with a smile. His eyes widened, his mouth flew open and he made some sound that sounded like "scz me," as he turned and ran toward another man, talking to a large man in a pair of striped pants and a cigar in his hand. As the clerk explained his problem, all three turned to look at Jake.

Jake stood there, getting self-conscious, and he turned to look away from the three. The clerk made a motion with his hand, drawing a circle, and he and the second man walked slowly back to the counter. Jake stood without a hat, which showed the burn area up into his hair. The skin on the left side of his face was shriveled and blotchy red, drawing his mouth into a grotesque smile. There was no smoothness, as he had on the right side. As the pair came close to him, Jake recognized the second man as someone who was ahead of him in high school.

He greeted the pair, "Hello Barney. What seems to be the problem?"

Barney frowned, "Jake? Is that you?" He looked full in Jake's face and uttered, "Oh. Uh, war injury?"

Jake answered, "Yes, why? What's the problem?"

"I. . .we. . .Jake, it's nothing against you, but if you met someone in the hallway after dark, you might. . .well—"

"I might frighten little kids. Is that your problem?"

"Well, uh, Jake, could you try another hotel?"

Jake stood silent and smiled. He spoke, "I am getting married today. General Courtney Clay Patterson reserved a room for my bride and me. I'll let him talk to you and you can explain your stand to him." With that, Jake turned and walked out of the lobby. When he got back to the Patterson residence he drove back to the barn. He found Simon and asked him to get the general. When Clay came, Jake exploded, describing the situation in the hotel.

Clay listened without comment, getting more and more agitated. When Jake explained that he left the hotel, Clay turned and stormed toward the house. He stopped and called to Simon to get his saddle horse ready, and continued inside. Jake watched as Clay, dressed in his riding pants, returned, mounted his horse and galloped out of the yard without saying another word. Jake had been warned against seeing Peggy on this day before the wedding, so he stayed in the barn with Simon.

At one o'clock that afternoon, people started arriving for the ceremony. Jake had been led up the back stairs to get dressed. Peggy was hidden from him to keep the superstition alive. Clay had returned, smiling, and happy. He answered no questions, but said he had talked to the hotel people.

Jake was to wear his dress blues. It would be the last time he wore that uniform and he wanted to wear it in the "last act of his former life." At one forty-five PM Clay came for Jake and escorted him back down the way he had come up. The church and the hallway inside the house were filled and Clay had to almost force his way into the place of worship. Jake knew none of these people, and he was thankful that none of his former shipmates were there.

As Jake passed the people on his way to the platform area, he heard gasp after whispered gasp as people saw his face. It was almost all he could do to not respond, but he told himself, "One more hour, just one more hour."

At two o'clock, the pianist started the wedding march. Grace stepped into the room and drew the usual buzz of appreciation from those assembled. When Peggy stood in the doorway on Clay's arm, the noise was almost a roar of approval. The Ohs and Ahs were expected, but not the volume that came.

When Jake saw his soon-to-be-bride, his knees buckled for an instant as he inhaled. He uttered, "Oh, my, oh, my." Albert Weinmeister smiled as he stood there enrobed, holding his book of all occurrences. Slowly, Clay and the young woman on his arm made their way to the platform. Those on the periphery stood up, the smaller ones standing on chairs, to view this spectacular event.

The pair reached the front and Clay handed Peggy's hand to Jake, then stepped over behind him. The minister began, "Dearly beloved, we are gathered here today—"

The ceremony was rather short. In it Albert explained about Jake's facial injury. When the minister said, "I now would like to introduce Mr. and Mrs. Jake Prosser to you." The roar of greeting exceeded anything Peggy had ever heard. These were her friends—parents of her school kids and friends of hers from her time living in the neighborhood. Jake was satisfied to let her have this moment as he thought of the next few days, perhaps two weeks, when they would be traveling upriver to the end of the Missouri in Montana.

Because of the crowd, people were asked to stay in their seats while cake and punch were brought to them. For those who had to leave, the wedding party stood at the entrance to greet them and thank them for coming. Grace and Evelyn called on their friends to form the service crew and the food was distributed as quickly as possible.

Presents had been stacked in one of the side rooms and, again, people were asked to remain seated while the gifts were brought in. As Peggy opened each one, Grace recorded the giver for future contact. The big boxes were first, then the smaller ones, and finally the envelopes. As Peggy opened the envelopes, she gasped, her hand went to her mouth and she uttered, "Oh, Dear Lord, why did he do this?"

Evelyn and Clay rushed to her side. Jake had been standing there, and he looked at what brought on this reaction. Peggy held a check in her hand for ten thousand dollars, given by Orville Patterson, Clay's brother. Evelyn helped her to a chair and Clay looked over the crowd to see if his brother was amongst those in attendance, but he was not. Both parents looked at Grace to see what she knew about the gift, but she said nothing.

Peggy looked up at Jake who waited for her next action. She tore off the bottom right corner, defacing the signature and said, "I will not be obligated by a man who tried to buy me. This is his second attempt and I'll not be a part of it." She looked up at Grace who stood with her mouth open as if ready to scream.

"What did you do? Why did you do that? All he wanted to do was to give you a wedding present."

Calmly, quietly so most of the people in the room wouldn't hear, Peggy answered, "No, Grace, it was more to have a say in my life after his attempt to buy me for his bride fell through, thanks to your mother. No, it wasn't just a wedding present, but you won't understand that. So, if you know where he is, you can return it to him."

Grace came back loud enough for most people in the room to hear, "I don't understand you. Certainly you can use ten thousand dollars. He offered it as a gift."

"And I rejected it, which is my option. I could accept it, and be obligated, or reject it and be free of him. I have but one man in my life. I don't need someone who holds his money over my head, that no matter where I go, he'll always be a shadow. I won't have it." Those nearby applauded, which made Peggy blush slightly.

Clay came to her aid by taking the check. "I'll see he gets it back."

Evelyn brought a few more envelopes, which Peggy opened, finding a smattering of money. With all the gifts now opened, some of the people started to leave, stopping by the chair where Peggy sat to offer the new couple their best wishes. Becky was among the last to leave and she grasped both Peggy's hands to tearfully thank her for teaching and caring about her. Because of Peggy, Becky had a future.

With everyone gone but the family, there was an embarrassing moment when no one knew what to say. Clay spoke with a general's authority. "All right now. Since the hotel refused to let Jake stay there, I talked to them, and <u>we'll</u> stay in that room. It's large enough. It has an extra room, or alcove, where they promised to set up a bed. So, we'll take that and leave the house to you kids. Simon has the buggy ready, so, take care of the house. We'll see you tomorrow." Before Jake or Peggy could object, the three Pattersons were gone.

The couple stood looking at each other, not knowing what to say, until Jake reached out for her hands. "Peggy, are you sure you can handle the way I look for the rest of your life?"

"What did I just do? I promised to love you through sickness and health, in riches or poverty. Now, kiss me, Jacob. I will tilt my head to the left and you do the same, our eyes will be closed. When I open mine, I'll see your good side. I promise to see your good side the rest of my life."

Chapter Thirty-Seven

The trip was heavenly! It was unusual! It was amazing! Two young lovers rode a paddle-wheel, shallow draft ship from St. Louis to Fort Benton Montana. After leaving Cincinnati, they had to stop in St. Louis to get their tickets and travel money. Every evening at dusk found the two, arm in arm, looking toward the west and the beautiful sunsets. Jake had been told he would be a cowboy, and work around the ranch to learn his job, and then spend a month in a line shack out on the range. They also learned the owner, Reginald Dowdy, wanted to start a school in his new town, Elaine, named in honor of his mother.

The trip was twenty-two hundred miles long, with difficult and treacherous river currents slowing their progress. It cost three hundred dollars apiece for a cabin and an extra twelve cents a pound for freight. Since they brought everything they owned, and then bought more winter clothes in Omaha, they had a wagon load of possessions to care for.

They arrived at Fort Benton at mid-morning and now stood on the dock in the midst of roaring activity as gold seekers, army personnel and a few Indians in their tribal headgear, tried to move through the throng. Men shouted and cursed those who were slow to move and Peggy looked wide-eyed at the mob, having never seen anything like that. There were women in the crowd, the likes of which Peggy had only heard of. She squeezed Jake's arm as she watched them walk past, making their presence known to any man interested. They received some coarse comments from some of the military, which made Peggy gasp.

The boat traffic on the Missouri River was limited to a few weeks after the snow melted in late spring and there were times three boats a day docked at that port. The river had so many hidden sand bars that it took an experienced captain to navigate the waters safely. Burned out hulls of other ships that found those obstacles gave evidence of the difficulty in sailing the river. There were nearly four hundred people on this trip with other stern-wheelers to come in later that day.

Jake and Peggy found a somewhat quiet corner and stood out of the clamor and shoving before them. As Jake looked over the crowd, he saw a sign with his name on it and pointed it to Peggy. A cowboy on a horse was waving his rifle with a piece of white cardboard with Jake's name on it. Jake shouted and waved his arms. Soon, a squad of armed cowboys burst through the mob and showed the pair the way to their wagon.

Boxes of wedding presents and personal clothes had to be located and loaded. As the cowboys finished that task, Peggy had the thrill and surprise of being picked up bodily and placed in the wagon bed. Then Jake clambered aboard with instructions to climb up to the high seat next to the driver.

The caravan of seven riders and two wagons, eleven people in all, left Fort Benton, following the Mullan Road toward Coeur d' Alene, Idaho. The riders were all images of what Jake thought of as a cowboy—some short, some tall, but all sat a saddle like they were born on it. Their driver, Dusty, an old man, told Jake and Peggy, "We ain't goin' ta Idaho. Boss built hisself a new house here in Montana two days out. Still on his propity, but ain't that far ta go."

Jake watched as some riders rode ahead, then came back and pointed a slight change in their direction. Three of the riders were always with the wagons, but the other four kept changing their routes. Finally, Jake asked the reason. Dusty simply said, "Injuns."

After four hours, a rider came back to the wagon and pointed to a grove of trees. Dusty explained, "Time fer dinner." It was a cold meal, except for the coffee. That was hot and almost undrinkable, it was so strong. The first sip made both Peggy and Jake shake their head and Dusty laughed. He handed the pair some jerky and said, "Coffee'll help digest the meat. We'll have deer tonight."

Peggy asked, "How much further do we have to go?"

"Without no trouble, we'll git home t'morra 'bout supper."

Jake asked, "Does that mean we have to sleep out here in the wagon tonight?"

"Wal, ya, it kinda does, less ya wanta share the ground with a snake," and he giggled. It wasn't really a laugh, but a high pitched giggle, a kind of cackle.

Jake watched the man for a few seconds before he said, "You're enjoying this aren't you. You have two rubes and you're feeding them a line, and you're enjoying it. Did you have to bid on this job or were you really picked by Mr. Dowdy?"

Dusty looked at Jake with surprise, then anger. "Ain't gonna say 'nuther word. Drink yore coffee."

Peggy whispered to Jake and he nodded his head. Jake said, "Dusty, could we get down for a few minutes? It's been four hours and. . .we, we both have—"

"Wondered when that was gonna happen. Help yore lady down an' walk behind them bushes. Men ain't gonna watch ya."

Peggy looked at Jake, then at Dusty. "Bushes? I. . .I can't. . .bushes? I guess, since I don't see any buildings. Help me down, Jacob." The pair walked away to a place where they were confident no one could see them and they proceeded with their needs.

As they walked back to where the wagons were, everybody was gone! Peggy started getting panicky, but Jake said, "They're playing with us. We'll follow the wagon tracks. It might be hard for you in those shoes, but we'll make it. They aren't going to leave us, not with the money Mr. Dowdy paid to get us here."

They followed the wagon tracks out of the trees and came to a river. The men and the wagons were on the other side. Jake looked at the wagons and the horses and saw that the dampness was less than hub deep, so he led Peggy to where the wagons crossed, scooped her up in his arms, and started across. She clung to him and prayed, while he walked through knee-deep water to the other side. The cowboys were laughing when he set Peggy down.

They were all dressed the same—canvas pants, chaps and boots, a blue long-sleeve cotton shirt, open at the neck and a western hat. Each man had a gun belt with a holstered gun. One man who looked much the same as the others, perhaps mid thirties, came up to the pair, laughing, and said, "I want to introduce myself. I'm Reginald Dowdy. I own the spread. The boys wanted to test you to see what you were like. You passed. If you had gotten frantic in the trees when you saw we were gone, you probably would have been taken back to town and shipped back down river. So, congratulations, folks, I believe we're going to have a good relationship."

They slept in the wagon that night and then spent another nine hours riding the bumpy wagon over rocky terrain. They listened as Dusty explained the history of the area. "Got Chippewa an' Cree Injuns," he explained, "mostly peaceful. Land's mostly prairie. Great fer cattle. It's one of the six original counties drawed up. Covers lots o' ground. Still ain't got no name. Word is they's gonna name it fer the trapper who started Fort Benton, some guy named Chouteau. They say he was a Canook who got in good with the Injuns."

A small town was laid out on a hillside to the left. Jake pointed it out to Peggy and Dusty explained, "Town's called Elaine fer 'is Mom. 'Ts where people live who run the herd. They's gonna be more. Boss got big ideas." The town had about two dozen buildings with more started and stacks of lumber covered against any rain that might come. "We haul our supplies from Fort Benton."

Late in the afternoon, they topped a rise to see the most elegant and glorious structure imaginable, there in the wilds of Montana, away from other buildings and people. A three story, wooden structure, painted white, with windows facing both sides that they saw, and a long porch across the front of the house. From their perspective, they could see the porch down the north side of the house too. It was a huge building with three chimneys, indicating three sources of heating.

Other buildings looked to be related to cattle raising. Jake had spent some time at his uncle's farm and had seen farm buildings, but these were different than what Jake's uncle had. There was a large corral, holding maybe a hundred horses next to a roughly built building with several buggies outside the fence. A smaller building, built in much the same way, sat next to it, with an open door, with cowboys carrying harness in and out.

Dusty stopped the wagon at the brow of a rise a hundred yards from the house for effect, giving the passengers a chance to see the whole property. After Peggy finished her exclamations and pointing at different things for Jake to see, Dusty clucked the horses into action again and they rolled up to the porch, where the other men had gathered. A woman came out the front door. She was attractive, with her blond hair tied up in a bun. She had a pretty smile as she greeted the new members of their extended family.

She saw Peggy and came down the steps to the side of the wagon where she was. "Help your wife down so I can get her a bath and make her feel like a lady again." Jake helped Peggy down the side of the wagon where she was grabbed by the woman, "I'm Emmy Lou, and I'm thrilled to have another woman around. You'll have to tell me everything about styles and what's going on out there. Come with me." They started up the steps and Emmy Lou turned to the crew and spoke like she was used to giving orders, "Boys, help her mister get their stuff to their room. He'll want to change too."

Before anyone moved, Reginald Dowdy approached Jake and said, "I suppose it's a little late for this, but you'll have to work with men who fought against you. Can you do that? You met Dusty, now you will meet the rest of the crew who are not in the field." He called the men together. All men had some kind of disability. Jake hadn't noticed that on the trail, but here, at the house, he saw there were men with burns like he had, two with an arm amputated and one who walked with a limp from a minie ball in the leg.

"All the men who work here have had some injury in the war, even as short as the fighting has been. You are the last one, at least for a while, to be brought out. There may be more later. I don't know yet. Now, let's get your stuff upstairs and we'll all need to clean up for supper. Wife's particular about eating on time."

The house had a "washing closet" with each bedroom suite. When their possessions were delivered to their room, Jake looked for Peggy but couldn't find her. Water had been provided for his bath, so he slipped out of his clothes and immersed himself in a porcelain tub of hot water. It was the first hot bath he had since leaving Cincinnati, and he almost fell asleep relaxing in it. He heard a call, "Supper in fifteen minutes," and he hurried to get out of the tub, dry himself and get dressed.

Everyone was at the table when Jake got there except Emmy Lou and Peggy. There were two other women, wives of two other men, but they were mid forties or older. The door to the dining room opened and Emmy Lou entered, then stopped. She waved her hand to get the attention of all within the room, and then motioned for Peggy to enter. There might be words to describe the vision they saw, but at that moment, Jake could not think of one. He had seen Peggy on the trip north aboard the Great Expectations. Even in her wedding gown there was a beauty created, to some extent, by the gown itself. But even then, as beautiful as she looked, she didn't match the way she looked dressed up for this moment. She was awesome. Incredibly beautiful. Everyone in the room sat, with mouth open, staring in disbelief.

Jake had never seen her in this dress. It was a blue satin gown, with lace at the sleeve end just above the elbows. The bodice was fitted and the jacket defined by white lace along the bottom. The skirt was gathered with pleats around the whole gown. The bottom had ruffles six inches above the floor so that the skirt just brushed the carpet. A gold necklace, with a large bright blue Sapphire stone, hung around her neck. The others looked between Jake and his wife, wondering what Jake would say or do. He sat there, unable to move, until Dowdy stepped forward and said, "Jake, shall we greet our wives?"

Emmy Lou Dowdy was dressed in an aqua-colored gown with long sleeves and white ruffles around the bottom. There was white lace below the waist and above the white ruffle at the bottom. She wore a broach of what she called an Indian jewel, a turquoise colored stone.

Clumsily, Jake pushed his chair back and stumbled over one leg as he moved toward Peggy. He sprawled on the floor and as quickly as he could, amid the laughter of the others in the room, got up and went to greet Peggy. Dowdy gave his hand to Emmy Lou and he tucked her hand under his right arm. Jake tried to follow suit, but was nervous. He whispered, "I've never seen you this pretty. When did you get the dress, and the necklace? Your hair, what do they call that?"

She put her hand under his arm and as they walked back to their chairs, she whispered, "It's something called a French Weave. The dress and necklace are hers. She just let me use them tonight. Do you like?"

"Not only me but every other man in the room."

The dining room was a large room with a huge mahogany table in the middle, surrounded by eighteen mahogany arm chairs. Dowdy sat at one end with his wife around the corner to his right. Peggy sat across from Emmy Lou with Jake to her left. The others were seated down the table from them. The table was set with white bone china, with matching cup and saucer at each plate. Gold flatware was placed at each place and gold rimmed goblets completed the place setting.

Venison steaks were the menu with new peas from the ladies garden and potatoes from the cool cave dug behind the house. Conversation was brisk with questions from everyone while Peggy answered. She would look at Jake from time to time, in a way to tell him he could, or should, answer that question. But most of the fashion questions came from Emmy Lou, which Peggy answered.

There were questions about how the men were wounded, and Jake answered when the question came his way, but he never told about the special gun he operated. Slowly, conversation drained down and when the grandfather clock struck eleven, there was a general agreement to go to bed. In their room, Jake and Peggy stood facing each other and Jake reached for her hands. "Peggy, you are the most beautiful woman I've ever seen. I'm afraid I'm going to have to fight someone over you."

Shocked, Peggy looked at her husband, "Jacob! Why would you say such a thing?"

"That old guy at the end of the table, on the other side, couldn't take his eyes off you. He's gonna be trouble."

"Are you saying you don't trust me around where he might be?"

"Oh, no, no, no Peggy. I'm saying that he's got his eyes out for you and he's the one who will cause trouble. I can feel it. If you can help it, don't ever be alone in the house with him."

Chapter Thirty-Eight

Montana has a short summer and the time was used by Dowdy and his experienced members to teach the new men about horses and cattle. Had they thought of the difficulty of teaching handicapped men how to saddle a horse and harness a team for a wagon, they might not have started their endeavor. But they had men there now, including Jake, who were inexperienced, to say the least, and they had to spend extra time in their teaching effort. To Jake's advantage, he had tried as a youngster to help on his uncle's farm near Cincinnati.

Jake had one thing going for him. His injury was not to his hands or legs. He was not limited in that way so, with the dedication he extended in learning the Gatling gun, he pushed himself to learn his assigned tasks. He spent extra time harnessing a team of horses, then undressing the horses and hanging the harness back on its proper pegs.

Emmy Lou had set a rule for the evening meal—it was set at six-thirty and everyone not out in a line shack had to be at the table. There were a few times when Jake just made the schedule and was chastised by a severe look from the hostess.

Peggy was frustrated. She had been busy teaching, instructing Becky and, until the preaching ministry was turned over to the students from the Seminary, preaching. Now, she sat in her room wondering if they had made a mistake. The first month of their time here she had talked to Emmy Lou, volunteering for some job, any job, but none was given. The mistress was organized and the people hired to do the house work knew their jobs and did them well. After a while, Peggy stopped offering to do something and just sat and prayed. And cried.

She read her Bible hungrily. Psalms 37 and 91 were her favorites. "Delight thyself also in the Lord; and He will give thee the desires of thine heart." But what were the desires of her heart? Other than having a happy home and seeing her husband happy, she had none. Perhaps it was time to start praying for God's leading in her life. When Jake was released from the hospital and came to church, the reaction of some of the people, in addition to Grace's comment, drove their decision to come west. It wasn't something she wanted to do, but she accepted it for Jake. Now, she wondered, did she do the right thing?

She had to have a ministry somewhere, doing something. Sundays were just another day on the ranch, with little or no religious recognition. What could she do to change that? She had to think and pray about that specific thing.

Jake had listened to the other cowboys talk about herding the cattle, and thought he could do that. Jake was taught about the use of his hand gun. The fast draw was not included, and Dowdy insisted that no one ever practice that "art." He was taught to be selective in firing that weapon, because firing it in a herd might cause a stampede. It was to be used against wolves and coyotes. His Navy experience gave him an appreciation for what a gun could do in the right hands.

In his other instructions, Jake had graduated to the lariat and it was giving him fits. Dusty kept telling him it was a matter of the twist of the wrist, and it would flow out smoothly. But no matter how hard he tried, it didn't work. After a series of futile throws, Dusty called Jake off his horse and sat with him, leaning against the corral fence. "Yore tryin' too hard, Jake. Ya gotta let it flow as an extension of yore arm. Yore doin' the right things but yore hand is tight. Loosen it up."

Jake stood and gripped the rope one more time and Dusty interrupted him. "Jake, ain't ya a Christian?" Jake answered he was. "Well, have ya prayed about this? I mean, ain't God s'posed ta help ya in everythin'?"

Jake was shocked. First, he never thought of God helping him learn how to throw the lasso. Second, he was shocked that Dusty would be the one to remind him. He stood, arm extended with the rope across the palm of his hand, and froze in that position. Slowly, he bowed his head and closed his eyes, praying a short prayer for calmness in his effort to learn his job. He walked toward the post, which was the object of his throw and began to twirl his rope. He reminded himself to stay calm and relaxed his hand as he threw. It hit its target!

He quickly retrieved the loop, rewound the rope and threw it again. Another success. Excited, he dropped the rope and ran for a horse tied to the fence. He led it back to the rope, rewound the rope and mounted the horse. Dusty told him to ride past at a trot, and try his throw. He did, and where it did fall across the post, it wasn't clean. Jake wanted to try it again, but Dusty mentioned the time was approaching supper time so they called a halt to their working.

Inside, Jake rushed into their room to find Peggy wiping tears and he gathered into his arms and held her. "Oh, Jacob," she cried, "I'm so lonely. I miss Evelyn and Becky and even Clay. I miss you. You're gone all day and when you are here, you're so tired." She wept against his shoulder. Jake led his wife to a corner of the room, which she called her 'quiet place,' decorated in heavy damask wall hanging and a flowered love seat. He took her hand and sat.

She hesitated, not knowing if she was going to be chastised for not being able to feel comfortable among the others. He pulled her down to the seat with him and cradled her head against his shoulder and kissed her cheek. "I'm sorry. I didn't know it would be like this. When I saw other women here I thought you'd have some fellowship. I'm sorry. We can't go back. We don't have the money to repay him for what he's spent on getting us here."

She sobbed, "I know." Then she brightened. "Jacob, I said 'Whither thou goest,' and meant it. We'll make it. I love you and all I ask is that you love me. Talk to me once in a while. Now, get washed and changed for supper."

At the table, the seating assignments were changed and Jake and Peggy were moved to the other end so another couple could sit next to the boss and his wife. That put Peggy next to the book keeper, a middle aged man name Fred Knox. He was amicable, but in the back of her mind was Jake's warning about never being alone in the house with him. As they talked, she pushed those warnings back, thinking, surely he can't be as bad as Jake thought.

The practice for a Friday was that when a comfortable time after dinner had passed, everyone would withdraw to the library, a fabulous collection of the works of masters. Dowdy had laughed when Jake and Peggy first saw it, saying, "I'm an Englishman, with ties to Mother and Old London. I used to sit up at night and read the Bard of Avon until mother came to blow out the candle. So, I appreciate good literature." Peggy was enthralled at the possibility and spent a good amount of time here. But, she also had a husband whom she wanted to spend time with.

As they settled down for their weekly discussion of how things were going, a man stood in the entrance and Dusty left. He came in and handed Dowdy a note. Frowning, he said, "We have a problem. Rob Hayes was supposed to spell the man at the west line shack. This note says he left without word. Al Hindman has been there a week and was to be replaced by Rob." He turned to Jake. "Jake, you're the only one who hasn't been there. There's not much to it. Just ride around and check the cattle, see if any wolves got to them. Try to keep them within a mile of the cabin. Would you be interested in filling in for me?"

Peggy bit her lip and bowed her head. Jake answered, "I owe you that much. After what you've done for me, us, yes, I'll go."

Saturday morning, early, Dusty had a wagon loaded with provisions ready to go. He had to make the four hour trip and still have enough light to see on his return. Jake held Peggy close and whispered, "It'll only be a week, but I owe it to him. Try to talk to the other women."

"They don't like me. I think they're jealous."

He looked at her but didn't say anything. He kissed her hard and said, "I love you. Gotta go," and he turned away, walking out the door.

Jake rode in the wagon to have some conversation with Dusty and found out Dusty had been with Dowdy four years, ever since the ranch was established. The old man talked like he was wound up, telling Jake that Dowdy was indeed an Englishman, but had family in this country since before the Revolutionary War. They were rich, and the old line here, who were Tories at the inception, have since used their knowledge and power to become dominant in this country. Dowdy's family knew the right people and when the Civil War looked imminent, Reginald's father "bought" him a million acres in Montana and Idaho. Staffing it with men who were wounded was Reginald's idea.

The "line shack" was a beautiful cabin, twenty feet square, with a covered porch and windows on all sides. Inside, there were curtains on the windows, a wooden floor to walk on and a sink with a hand pump at the west window. A double bed, not a frame with a straw and leaf mattress, was in the corner to the right of the door. The heating stove was across the room in the other corner with two stacks of cut wood next to it. Dusty explained the pine was to start the fire and oak and shaggy juniper was for heat after it got started. A coffee pot sat on top with a skillet and long-handled knife and fork.

Dusty loaded Al Hindeman and his belongings and turned his team homeward. He looked back over his shoulder and predicted, "Yore gonna get a frog choaker. If it comes, stay in the shed. Cows'll be awright, and the horse has feed. Check the herd once in the morning and again before nightfall. I'll be back in a week."

Jake decided to ride around the area and see about the cattle. He found a large herd, feeding on grass next to a creek with high banks. He could not find the source of the creek after he'd followed it for several minutes, but could see a higher elevation north of there and figured that was the source of the stream. He turned back and followed the stream back toward his cabin.

He stripped the saddle and bridle, put on the halter and tied the horse snugly in the lean to. After standing outside a few minutes to watch the clouds, he went in to eat. The cabin was warm with the fire already going when the storm hit. The rains came, blasting the cabin with the fury of a hurricane. The storm came from the northwest so the door and the lean to for the horse were dry. The force of the wind blew the rain far out from the house and Jake went to check on the horse and found it pulling at the halter. He talked calmly to the animal and that seemed to quiet it. With night coming, Jake was concerned that the horse might break loose, leaving him without transportation. And sometime during the night, that is what happened.

Late in the morning the storm abated somewhat, leaving the ground with rivulets in the sandy and rocky soil. The creek was wild, dashing against the banks with a fury Jake had never seen before. His poncho kept him dry against the drizzle that fell, as he watched the stream. He mused what would it be like to be caught in that flow and realized he would have no ability to withstand the pressure. The creek bit into the bank at the curve and Jake watched as he judged that perhaps ten feet of the bank had eroded. With no horse, he would have to wait for Dusty to come back for him. At least he had food.

Chapter Thirty-Nine

Sunday, Peggy did not feel well and spent most of the morning in bed, reading her Bible and praying. It was her worship day and she spent the day worshipping as well as she could, being interrupted by sick calls. When she got up Monday, she determined she was going to move around the house, get out of her room, and try to participate in the family life. She walked to the kitchen and met the cook. After talking to her a while, Peggy moved to the library, thinking to find a book of one of the masters and lose herself in it. She did and had to be reminded that supper was near at hand. The meal was quiet, as her thoughts were on Jake.

Tuesday, she decided to repeat the pattern of Monday. After greeting the cook, Peggy went to the library, closed the door and found a Shakespeare novel, "As You Like It." She had read it before but that was a long time ago. She read for hours. Once, during that time, she thought she heard the door open and close again, but when she looked up, no one was there.

She was almost finished with the book when the door opened and closed again. She looked up to see Fred Knox standing there, smiling, leering. Her immediate thought was the warning Jake had given her earlier about not being alone in the house with him, but now, how should she react. She smiled and greeted him, "Hello, Mr. Knox. Have you read Shakespeare? This one is called a Christian play." Nervously, she twisted in her chair and started speaking rapidly,

"Would you believe it that Shakespeare would write something we would call a Christian play? And do you know why? Because it shows tolerance for other points of view, and emphasizes brotherly love."

"Don't be nervous, Missy. We are all alone here. I saw to it that for the moment, no one else is around. It took some talking to get that nosey cook out of the house, but now we are all alone. But I would ask you one question. How did a scar face with minimal intelligence manage to win someone like you as his wife? You're bright, fabulously beautiful, and so very desirable. In fact, I desire you right now," and he started walking toward her.

She rose from her chair and stood behind it. Angrily, she announced, "Mr. Knox, that scar face as you call him was wounded in the battle for Fort Donelson. He was in the war. What were you doing? I remind you that I am a married woman and my husband will deal with you when he returns."

Knox smiled. "He's gone for the next four days and when he returns, we'll be gone too."

Frightened, but demanding more of herself than she ever required, she stared at him and pointed her finger at him. "Mr. Knox, stop right there. I will fight you to my last breath. I will scratch. I will bite. It will not be an easy conquest."

Knox laughed at her, reached out and grabbed her arm with his left hand and slapped her across the face with his right hand. She screamed, "Help!" and he dragged her across the room. He got to the door and opened it to see an angry old cowboy. The other men on Dowdy's staff joked about him being kids with Methuselah.

"You scum," Dusty snarled, and his fist lashed out, hitting Knox full on the chin, knocking him off his feet. Knox started to get up and Dusty said, "You move one more muscle and I'll kill ya. Yore gonna stay right there 'till Mr. Dowdy gets in." He looked at Peggy, "I'm sorry, Ma'am. We'll take care of this skunk and go get yore husbun'. His horse returned without him. The halter strap was broken so it must've gotten scared during the storm. I didn't know if y'all had heard so I come lookin' fer ya. I found the cook and she said you was in here."

Peggy had regained some of her composure as she leaned against the door jam. She reached out and touched his shoulder. "Thank you, Dusty. Thank you." Then she became more concerned, "Do you think Jacob is all right?"

"Yes, Ma'am. I tol' 'im ta stay in the house, so that's where he is now. It's too late today, but I'll be up at sunup in the mornin'. Now, why don't you go tell the cook to ring the dinner bell? That'll get people 'round perty quick." He glared down at the body of Fred Knox and it seemed to Peggy the old man was hoping for Knox to do something.

Tuesday morning Jake walked outside the cabin. There was no mud. The sandy, rocky soil drained the rain so quickly that where he walked left only his boot print. He walked to the edge of the calm stream, meandering quietly along its controlled path. Something shiny caught his eye and he stooped to pick it up. It was about the size of a walnut and it was yellow. YELLOW? GOLD! He started looking for more along the water's edge. The stream was still muddy from the dirt of the bank, but the high water must have thrown these pieces up onto the bank as the water raged.

After finding more, some pea size and some between that and the walnut, he ran into the cabin. When Dusty packed Jake's supplies, he used some burlap and some canvas bags. Jake grabbed a canvas bag, dumped its contents out on the floor, and threw his handful of yellow stones into it. He went back out to the creek and started picking up more gold pebbles. He walked back toward the bend of the stream, where the force of the water flow had eaten into the bank, picking up golden pebbles along the way, some as large as his thumb. At that curve of the stream, he found fistfuls of the metal. Soon, the bag was almost too heavy to carry.

He lugged it back into the cabin, set it on the floor and sat in the chair. He looked at the bag, his mind racing. His first thought was how to keep it hidden from the boss. That was quickly rejected. Jake was a Christian with higher principles. It belonged to the ranch. <u>But he has so much already, he doesn't need this too</u>. Regardless, it is his gold. Jake got down on his knees and prayed. "Father, I don't understand why all this happened, the injury, the reaction by the people. But one verse Peggy seems to repeat often is Romans 8:28. She believes it. I don't understand how You work, but this is not my gold. It belongs to Mr. Dowdy. I don't understand why I was the one to find it, but You have a reason for it. So, help me to keep my mind clear and not be tempted by what appears to be riches. Amen"

Dusty left the ranch Wednesday morning while it was still dark, with just a glimmer of light in the east. He took saddle horses, the wagon would have been too slow. This way the trip would be completed in the time it took the wagon to get there. He rode at a steady gallop, stopping once to rest the animals. He arrived at the cabin as Jake was drinking his second cup of coffee.

Dusty greeted him, "You awright? Yore horse come back. Figgered y'all'd like some conveyance. Ya gotta come back. Somethin's happened."

Jake set the cup down and grabbed the canvas bag. "First I have to show you something." He reached inside the bag and showed Dusty a fistful of the yellow stuff.

Dusty looked at Jake and, after several seconds of just looking, said, "I knowed men who'd'a shot me outa the saddle and took the horses an' run. Why didn't ya?"

"First of all, Dusty, I'm a Christian. I gave my life to God and He directs my life. This belongs to the ranch. And I have a wife waiting for me back there."

Dusty didn't respond any further, but said, "Let's go home."

Conversation was limited to when they stopped to rest the horses and Jake. He had ridden some around the ranch but never for an extended time, and after a while, he was saddle sore. They stopped twice and Jake walked around for a few minutes, got back into the saddle and rode on. At the ranch, it seemed that everyone was outside waiting for them, even the cook. Jake raised his eyebrows and looked at Dusty, but said nothing. As he dismounted, Peggy broke from Emmy Lou and ran to him, throwing herself into his arms.

"Oh, Jacob, I'm so thankful you're home. I—"

"What's wrong? What happened?"

Peggy explained how Dusty had rescued her from Fred Knox, and that Mr. Dowdy had banished him, never to return to that part of Montana. Jake stiffened as she talked, every muscle in his body taut. She held him close and whispered, "No, Jacob, it's all right. He's gone. Dusty kept me from harm. I was only concerned to what he would do to the. . ." She stopped.

"To the what?" Then it hit him. "You are?"

She smiled and buried her head into his shoulder. "I was so sick the morning after you left, and again the next day. I ate eggs and threw them all up as soon as I got to the room. Yes, Jacob, it appears you are going to be a father."

Dowdy had been waiting until they had talked, and he stepped forward now. "I need to talk to you. Come into the office," and he strode away. Jake followed after grabbing the bag off the saddle horn. The boss led him through the kitchen to a room next to the library, pointed to a chair and said, "Sit."

Before any words were spoken, Jake dropped the bag on the floor at his boss's feet. Some of the nuggets spilled out on the floor. Dowdy was speechless for several seconds, looking in amazement from Jake to the bag and back again. "Where? How?" He collected his thoughts and said, "There must be a story. What is it?"

Jake explained about the storm and how the force of the water ate into the creek bank at the curve. When the horse broke loose, he had nothing to do but walk around the land and spotted the gold. "There's a whole lot more than this."

"This presents us with a problem. If this gets out, we'll have every rock hound in the west on our land. If we keep it quiet, we might as well bury this. So, what is your suggestion?"

Shocked, Jake asked, "Mine? This is yours. It was on your ranch."

Reginald looked at the bag intently for several seconds. "Well, that's a decision for later. I suppose Peggy told you that Knox is gone. That leaves me without a book keeper. How good are you with numbers?"

"I had six weeks of accounting with my last math class in high school. I know what a ledger book is and the three columns on the sheet. I can add, subtract and the rest of the process."

Dowdy smiled. "Wonderful," he exclaimed. "How would you like to move into the office here and be my book keeper, my accountant? It'll increase your pay and you'll be able to spend more time with your wife."

Jake thought several seconds before answering. "I owe you for this job. When I got in a crowd back home, people stared and commented on the freaky guy. The daughter of the family where Peggy stayed even said something about scaring kids. So, I'm yours to serve. Whatever you have for me to do, I'll do my best."

Dowdy said nothing but continued to look between Jake and the bag of gold. "Jake, your honesty is something not seen in the west. I've heard of a man killing his partners over something like this. Yet, you didn't try to hide it and go back later to get it. Why?"

"I told Dusty. I gave my life to God and live by a different code now."

Dowdy looked intently at the bag of gold and muttered, "Interesting."

Later, after all the decisions had been made about the job and the gold, Jake and Peggy were in their room. They stood quietly embracing. Jake heard her sob and lifted her face to see tears coursing down her cheeks. He kissed her lips and asked, "Are you unhappy? What's wrong?"

"Oh, Jacob, I'm the happiest woman in the world. I'm with you, you have a good job, and we will be parents. What more could a girl ask for?"

He pushed her back away from him a little and looked at her. "But, is there anything you would change if you could?" He waited before continuing, "I mean, with all you have done and now you are basically inactive. What would you like to do?"

"Don't laugh, but I want to start a church."

Chapter Forty

Jake did his accounting job for a month, finding questions about Knox's record keeping almost every day. He kept asking his boss about specific accounts and came to the conclusion that Fred Knox had been siphoning money from Dowdy's finances for a long time. It was easy to do for him since he had total, unquestioned control of the financial obligations. It appeared there was a bank account in Fort Benton with over a hundred thousand dollars in it with Fred Knox's name on it. Jake found the account number and told Mr. Dowdy, who was drinking a cup of coffee. When Jake showed him the papers and the numbers stolen, Dowdy threw the cup across the room into the fireplace.

He had Jake get Dusty and two other men who had been with the ranch a while. Shorty Bragg from Texas, and Art Curtis from the Carolinas. Shorty walked with a limp, caused by a bullet in his hip. Curtis ran away from the battle of Shiloh when he saw the way Northern General U S Grant kept charging against Rebel lines. He wasn't wounded except in his emotions.

They rode as Mexican sheep herders with colorful serapes, sombreros on mules borrowed from a community along the Teton River south of the ranch house. Dowdy had allowed them the range along the river because it was abundant in tall grass and would replenish itself. Sheep historically ruined cattle pasture, eating down to the grass roots, and the sheep men appreciated the owner's gesture.

The group caused quite a stir when they walked into the bank in Fort Benton and asked for the money in the account they presented. Dowdy took off his sombrero and his serape and showed the teller the account number.

"You aren't Mr. Knox. You have no right to that account."

"I am the real owner of that account. Mr. Knox stole the money from me. If I have no right to it, how did I get this account number?"

The teller motioned to another man standing apart from the counter. He came over and smiled at Reginald, asking what was the problem Mr. Dowdy answered, "I own the R/O/D. ranch. Mr. Knox worked for me and stole the money he put in this account. My current accountant has records of these transactions if you want to see them."

At the time the teller signaled for help, no one paid any attention to a small boy that ran out the door. As the banker and the men from the ranch moved to a corner to look at the papers Jake brought, the boy and Fred Knox entered the bank. Dusty and Curtis, still wearing their disguises, saw Knox and moved slowly toward the door. Knox was more interested in Reginald Dowdy and the man with him, who had the scarred face. He took two steps into the bank, stopped and tried to turn around but Dusty and Curtis were there to restrain him. The boy tried to kick Dusty but Dusty's growl made him run.

Fred Knox shouted and squealed like wounded pig. He screamed that whatever Dowdy said was a lie, that the money in that account was his. Dusty put his hand over Fred's mouth and whispered, "I still owe ya fer yore actions in the library with Mrs., uh, Jake's wife. Stop yore squealin' or I'll stop it fer ya."

There was a balance of eighty thousand dollars, Mr. Knox not being too good at the poker or black jack tables. Dowdy peeled off three hundred dollars, the price of a ticket down the Missouri River, and handed it to Knox. "Don't show yourself here again. It won't be healthy for you."

As the crew went back out to their mounts, the borrowed mules, Dusty sidled up to his boss and said, "Boss, what does the 'O' stand for? I seen it on the brands an' never thought about it."

His boss smiled and said, "You really don't want to know." Dusty nodded a couple times and backed away.

For two weeks Reginald Dowdy kept to himself. One of the crew was missing one day with his return the following day. Later, another man was gone. Jake wondered what was going on, but he had his job to do and what happened out in the yard now no longer interested him. Then, Dowdy was gone for three days. Dusty refused to talk to Jake about his boss's absence, and no one else knew. After dark on the third day, there was the noise of a returning caravan, which woke Jake and Peggy. Jake went to the window and looked out. The only one he could identify was his boss. After watching a few minutes, Jake went back to bed.

The next morning as Jake went to his office, Dowdy was there, waiting. He said, "Jake, Emmy Lou and I would like to invite you and your wife to a formal dinner this evening. I have some ideas that I want to discuss with you. I'll be busy all day today, but we will eat at the regular time, six thirty, just the four of us in the private dining room. Remember, six thirty." Jake went back to his room to inform Peggy of the dinner and then back to his office to work.

Jake knew nothing of the cattle business. He knew they had a large herd of some kind of red cow—Reginald called them Herefords. They came from England by way of Canada and were showing up in several places in the United States. He knew that Dusty had men take some on cattle drives to the growing village of Great Falls. He didn't know how they were sold, just that he received cash vouchers for a certain number of beeves. His job was to find the net in all their operations.

He closed his office at five o'clock and went to his room to get ready. Peggy was already dressed and as soon as he closed the door, she peppered him with one question after another. Finally, he held her by her shoulders and spoke slowly, "My wonderful wife. I know nothing. I have no clue. He invited us to a formal dinner, just the four of us. I know nothing more than that. So, please, hold your questions for him tonight."

"Oh, you take all the fun out of guessing. Does he want to make you his partner? Is he going to reward you by giving you the money you saved from what Knox took? I'm curious, Jacob, it's got me in a lather."

As Jake turned toward the washing closet, he replied, "Well don't drip suds on the carpet."

She called after him, "Not that kind of lather, silly," but realized she spoke to a closed door.

They met at six thirty at the door of their private dining room. It was fifteen feet square and had a small oak table and four chairs. There was a small hutch in one corner and a serving cart next to it. The table was set with the same white bone china they had seen before with the same gold flatware at each seating. For this special occasion, Peggy wore the same light blue gown she wore at the first dinner, since her collection of special dresses was limited.

Dowdy and Emmy Lou were quite jovial, giving Jake and Peggy some curiosity. As they sat down to eat, Peggy looked across the table at Emmy Lou and asked, "I get the feeling this is a special evening. May I pray for God to give us wisdom and guidance?"

Surprised, both Dowdys mumbled an answer, so Peggy bowed her head and began, "Heavenly Father, this is a special day in our lives and I thank you for this opportunity to dedicate this evening to you. Guide our thoughts and decisions I pray. Amen."

When Peggy was finished, Reginald and Emmy Lou looked at each other and Emmy Lou asked, "Are you. . .do you, uh, do you pray for every decision?"

"I try to." She smiled and continued, "There are times I don't know the full particulars of something, so I depend on God to give me, Jacob and I, the wisdom we need."

Reginald asked, "And what do you do if you make a mistake? Do you blame God?"

"Oh, never! As far as making a mistake is concerned, I continue to trust the Lord that He'll work out what went wrong."

The boss sat quiet for a minute or two and looked at Jake. "Do you think the events of you finding the gold was God's doing? And you're finding the money that Fred was stealing from us, was that God too?"

Jake nodded quickly. "I like to think so."

"And what about your, uh, your injury. Did God allow that?"

"I accept it as that." Jake bowed his head and sat for a few seconds before lifting his head before adding, "Without it I'd still be in the Navy." He paused and then added, "I have to admit I was pretty devastated when I heard the doctors describe the burn. But while I was in the hospital, I saw your ad, and while I'd never ridden a horse very much, it was the chance I needed to get away from the people who knew me." He paused a moment, letting the owners think about what he told them. "I, we, believe that everything that has happened is what God permitted, even Peggy's friend who said I could be used to scare kids."

Emmy Lou exploded, "How awful!"

Jake continued, "But, because Peggy loved me so much, that statement led her to agree to come with me out here."

There was a pause in the conversation and Reginald excitedly said, "The food! We're here for a meal." He rang a little bell and two doors opened, one from the kitchen with a waiter pushing a small wooden server cart with appetizer and drinks. Another door opened with a waitress bringing salads. The food was served and before anyone picked up a utensil, Emmy Lou asked Peggy, "I noticed at our dinner times you bow your head. Were you asking the Blessing?"

Peggy nodded and Emmy Lou asked her, "Why don't you go ahead and ask the blessing for this meal. I'm impressed with your stories and I want to know how you two met and—" Jake interrupted her by laughing. Peggy was smiling. Emmy Lou looked at her husband and added, "This looks like an interesting story. I can't wait to hear it."

He husband said, "That has to wait. We have other matters here tonight. Jake, you saved us eighty thousand dollars so we want to build you your own house." Peggy grabbed Jake's hand and squeezed.

"You can say where you want it, you can describe what you want in it and you can say how you want it furnished. Two things. It can't be bigger than this house and you have to stay under eighty thousand dollars," and with that he smiled.

Peggy still held Jake's hand and she squeezed it to get his attention. He looked at her and nodded. She asked, "The town, how big will it be? Will there be children?"

"Children? Yes. But how big it will be is hard to say. If my plans go as I want, we'll have about two, maybe three hundred people, with a couple stores and banks. Again, I expect there will be kids. You see, Jake, the railroads are coming to this area. The Northern Pacific is making plans and the Union Pacific is too. In addition to that, we're still talking and thinking about that gold find. What are we going to do with that?"

Remembering the house she lived in in Cincinnati, Peggy smiled. "Would you consider building a large room as an addition on our house? I would like very much to start a school and I would ask for a separate building, but don't want to run up the cost. That's why I asked about children. Also, I want to start a church. I will be willing to preach until we can hire a regular pastor."

Emmy Lou frowned, "But you're a. . .a woman and you. . .you have a baby coming. How can you preach? What would people say?"

Jake assured them, "She taught school back home and preached, and people came. I imagine they would here too."

Reginald leaned back in his chair. "Well, this is certainly different than what I expected. Let's eat. We had lobster shipped in live from Maine, and I haven't had a good lobster for, how long has it been, Honey?"

"Almost five years," his wife answered. As they ate they agreed that, since it was nearing October, winter would be coming soon and building would stop. It would start again in the spring and workers would start on the house, having it ready about the time for Peggy's baby to be delivered.

They talked of other things too. Dowdy mentioned he would be gone. "Jake, you are the most honest man I ever met. We're going to be gone for a couple months, maybe more, business and vacation. You will run the inside and Dusty will handle the yard. Meet with him at the start of each day to get your signals coordinated. You know how to order supplies and pay for them."

Jake was overwhelmed and said so, but Dowdy just laughed it off. "You can handle it. Just continue to do what you've been doing."

The place was a madhouse the next three days as the Dowdys prepared for their trip and Dusty instructed the ranch hands. The morning of the fourth day Jake and Peggy stood, holding hands as luggage was loaded onto a wagon and the boss and his wife got into a carriage, heading to Fort Benton to start their trip.

When the yard was clear, the wagon and carriage gone and the ranch hands busy with their jobs, Peggy turned to face her husband. She kissed his cheek. "Jacob, I'm thinking of a Bible verse. Can you tell me which one?"

He looked at her smug smile and said, "Probably, Romans 8:28, 'And we know all things work together for good to them who love God, to them who are the called according to His purpose.'"

"Would you have thought this possible?" as she swung her hand across the horizon.

"I still have trouble believing what I see and know."

She was quiet a moment before looking up at him. "Do you remember what you told me a lifetime ago?"

"You mean, that verse?"

"Yes, tell me again."

He smiled and said,

"Who's that smiling all the while, that's Peggy O'Neal,
With her hair done up in style, that's Peggy O'Neal.
If she talks with a cute Irish brogue,
If she acts like a sweet little rogue,
Sweet personality, full of rascality, that's Peggy O'Neal."

She corrected him, "That's Peggy O'Neal Prosser and don't you forget it."